After a career in finance Tom Williams was encouraged to write, a challenge he accepted having been interested in words from an early age. A love of research unearthed this compelling story, his second book and first novel.

He lives with his wife in East Anglia and has two grown-up sons.

Ma Petite Rosette

Dedicated to Rose, to the memory of her family and to the memory of Abbé Stock

Tom Williams

Ma Petite Rosette

To
Vivienne

With best wishes
Tom Williams

Oct 2013

Austin Macauley
Publishers Ltd.

A CIP catalogue record for this title is available from the British Library.

ISBN 978 184963 404 5

www.austinmacauley.com

First Published (2013)
Austin Macauley Publishers Ltd.
25 Canada Square
Canary Wharf
London
E14 5LB

Printed and Bound in Great Britain

Ma Petite Rosette

Chapter 1

"Maman, Papa, I'm home!" called Rose excitedly as she hurried over the dusty yard to the farmhouse leaving her brother, Fernand, to deal with the horse and cart. The long summer holidays were here at last. There had been the ritual packing of her trunk, the goodbyes to all her friends at school, the train journey and now finally she was home. As she crossed the yard she quickly looked around to see if anything had changed but, as expected, nothing had. The rural farmhouse was little more than a weather-beaten stone cottage that from the outside had seen better days. The front door gave out directly onto the lane and was rarely used. Everyone came through the side gate, across the yard to the kitchen door which was nearly always left open. At one side of the house was a large rickety barn with some stabling. As far back as Rose could remember nothing around the farm ever seemed to change. So it was comforting that on her return everything appeared just the same.

At sixteen Rose was already as tall as her mother, though not quite as slim. She wore her dark, wavy hair down to her shoulders, pushed away from her face as was the fashion, and her face was rounded, more like her father's face than her mother's. But by far the most striking of her features were her eyes; definitely her mother's eyes, dark, penetrating, intelligent and bright. With her beguiling smile and open nature, Rose might appear the epitome of a pretty country girl, but she had growing ambitions of a life removed from her farming background. It was only through a scholarship to the High School at the nearest large town that she was able to continue her education; however the town was too far away for her to travel daily and so she had to board there. It was these new, exciting experiences that fed her dreams.

First to notice her arrival were the two farm dogs who scampered over, wildly wagging their tails in recognition. Then her father appeared at the opening to the barn loft, a big welcoming smile beaming across his well-tanned face. He waved briefly before suddenly disappearing, only to reappear moments later coming round the side of the barn his arms outstretched. Just taller than Rose he was strongly built with nut-brown, powerful forearms showing below his rolled up sleeves. Over his collarless shirt were faded blue dungarees, on his feet were his customary summer espadrilles and rarely was he seen out of the house without his favourite cap on. His eyes too were dark and often twinkled with a light-hearted mischief, like now at seeing his daughter. Respectfully Rose gave her father the customary greeting, two kisses on each cheek, before they hugged each other, the embrace almost overwhelming Rose emotionally as she held tightly to her beloved Papa. In her father's arms a warm glow flooded through her as she realised how much she had missed him and that deep sense of being loved and protected that he gave her, a sensation she had always felt since their earliest cuddles on his knee. They held their embrace, both needing that extra moment to seal the end of her absence in such uncertain times.

"My little Rosette," she heard him say as he held her close, said seemingly more to himself than to her. Hearing her pet name Rose nestled a little more into his arms. It was his special name for her which he used almost unconsciously. At that moment those three words carried all his feelings, seeing her home safe and sound. He pushed her gently back saying, "Now go and find your mother. She'll be in the kitchen," inclining his head towards the house.

Adjusting her eyes to the relative darkness of the low-ceilinged kitchen Rose found her mother at the range taking some freshly baked bread from the oven. "Maman, I'm home," she called startling her mother.

"Rose, Rose. Come, let me see you. I hadn't expected you so early," cried her mother, quickly putting down the piping hot loaves and wiping her flour-covered hands on her pale print pinafore. The traditional greeting was followed by a long, lingering embrace. "How are you? You look well. Have they been looking after you all right? How has school been?" The questions came tumbling out as her mother held her at arm's length to look at her, so delighted and relieved to see her home. Not normally given to showing her emotions, her expression nevertheless also displayed the pride she felt that her clever daughter had completed her first year at High School.

"I'm fine, Maman, I'm fine. Just so glad to be home, to see you and everyone. I've so much to tell you and I've brought some of my work home for you to see. I've even brought home a school photograph. I saved up for it. I'll be able to show you who everyone is. My teachers say I've done well this term; you can read their report."

"Sit down first and have something to eat," her mother said, "you must be hungry."

"I'm famished," said Rose; it was early afternoon and she had not eaten since breakfast. "And oh, that smell of new bread!" she added, lifting her head back to take in the wonderful aroma. "Now I know I'm home. We never have fresh bread at school. Sometimes it's almost stale."

Her mother continued with her questions as she laid a place at the table. "How was the journey and was Fernand there to meet you at the station? Have you remembered to bring everything home? I hope you've brought your ration card and all your soap; soap is so difficult to get."

Rose looked around as she was peppered with her mother's questions and, just as outside in the yard, nothing in the kitchen had changed. Her mother baked bread in one of the ovens of the large range that was always alight and set into an alcove. An array of pots and pans hung on the wall beside the chimney. The family ate at the huge kitchen table which could seat a dozen people and there was an easy chair in the corner by the range where her father sat to warm himself in winter after coming in from the fields. The kitchen, the hub of the house, was her mother's domain. The front room was seldom used and kept for 'best'.

"Of course I have Maman. And yes, Fernand was there on time to meet me. Just as well as I couldn't manage that trunk on my own. The train was very crowded but I had a seat. But I'm home now and everything is fine and I have all the long holidays to look forward to. I want to go and see my friends; I've missed them so much. And I want to go out cycling, round the lanes and down to the sea. There's so much I want to do. I have got to do some homework before I go back but there's plenty of time for that. But of course I'll help as usual. You know how I love harvest time. Oh Maman, it is so lovely to be back home," she sighed, happy that everything was just as it always was.

Rose continued to talk while her mother busied herself putting food on the well-scrubbed table. Her father had come in and sat down at his usual place. Not really listening to the conversation he smiled to himself at seeing Rose so animated, thinking she had really grown up a lot this term. Observing her, though, he could not escape the thought that she was no longer his little girl; that she had become a spirited young lady.

Shortly Rose's brother appeared in the doorway having unhitched and tethered the horse. He stood silhouetted against the bright sunshine outside, one hand resting on Rose's trunk, the other hand leaning against the door post in a pose that was meant to indicate the great effort of getting the case so far. "If you want this upstairs I shall need a hand," he said purposely breathing heavily.

"I'll help you," said Rose getting up, still eating a mouthful. Between them they shunted the large case up the stairs and into Rose's bedroom where it filled nearly all the spare floor space in the cramped room. After the effort, Rose dropped onto her bed which creaked as usual. The little bedroom was sparse, even more so than normal as most of Rose's few belongings were in her trunk, and she felt strangely odd for a moment suddenly realising how long she had been away. But the sensation was only fleeting as her eyes caught familiar bits and pieces like the mirror on the wall with the small crucifix above it and the drab curtain covering the opening to her clothes cupboard which did not a match the curtains at the small window.

"I was glad you were at the station to meet me," she said as she began to open the case. "I couldn't have got my case out of the guard's van on my own, let alone get it home." Looking up at him she continued meaningfully, "It's good you're still at home. Lots of the girls have older brothers who went away to fight and even now some don't know if they're alive or not."

“I know, it’s bad,” he said. “My friend Olivier told me the other day the Renouxs at Le Vigneau still haven’t heard from their son after they were told he was a prisoner of war in Germany.” After a brief pause he added as if to close the conversation, “Anyway, I should get back to work now.”

Her brother resembled her father to look at but they were very different in character; young Fernand being somewhat reserved and in his father’s shadow. Work was his forte, not conversation. But on the way home he had been unusually quiet and uncharacteristically he had made a very pointed remark about their father that made her think perhaps they had had an argument. She had sensed something was not right between them; there was some sort of tension, but Fernand would not be drawn.

“Wait,” she said thinking she had something that would cheer him up. In a lowered, conspiratorial voice she went on, “I’ve got a present for you. A small piece of chocolate. I swapped for it. Here.” She felt into a corner of the trunk and brought out a small package which she gave to him. “I could only get a few cigarettes, they’re for Papa, but you may be able to exchange the chocolate for some.”

“Thank you,” said Fernand already working out how he could trade it for cigarettes. “I don’t expect anything, you know. You don’t have to bring presents.”

“I like to,” replied Rose happily as they made their way downstairs. “It’s only little.”

Over supper Rose wanted to know everything that had happened while she had been away, all the news of everyone and about the farm. But soon the main topic was the Occupation and how much worse conditions had become. Her father particularly showed unusual bitterness about the worsening state of affairs. Rose could see that his complaints about the shortages and restrictions they had to suffer were far more cutting than his typical grumbles about the weather or the potato yield, and it worried her to see him so uncharacteristically pessimistic. At one point she asked anxiously, “What’s going to happen to us?”

Her mother was quick to reassure her that the family would be all right; they would get by and Rose would be able to continue with her studies. It was comforting to hear her mother’s words of reassurance but Rose was old enough and sensitive enough to understand that while people were carrying on with their ordinary lives, like her parents and teachers, not far beneath the surface there were deep anxieties, even fear, about the future.

Although not exactly peasant farmers, Rose's family was like countless thousands of other French smallholders who had to work hard just to make a modest living. Her father, Fernand Neau and her mother Renée both came from local farming families. Rose and her older brother Fernand were their only children and young Fernand, who was not as academic as his sister, had joined his father on the farm as soon as he could leave school. They were tenants of their smallholding on the edge of St. Michel-en-l'Herm, a rural village near the Vendée coast, and they also rented a few extra fields in the area of rich soil towards the bay. They grew a variety of cereal and root crops, had some cows, chickens, rabbits and pigs, and tended a few vines to make wine for themselves. They would also help out other farmers in exchange for a sack or two of something or just as a favour to be returned sometime. Living like this, despite being poor, meant there was always food on the table which was more than could be said for many French families in the summer of 1941. There were chronic shortages of everything and life for everyone under the German Occupation was a struggle just to get by. Being poor did not matter so much when there was little or nothing to buy. Farming as they did was actually an advantage as they could produce much of the food they needed and any surplus could readily be exchanged or bartered for other food and supplies.

Officially a proportion of the farm's output should be taken to the market where prices were regulated. But the attitude of Rose's father towards officialdom was typical of rural farmers who in normal times viewed any interference with disdain and no more so than under the Occupation. Their priority, like everyone else's under the regime, was family first and foremost. Farming friends and neighbours would be helped if needed, whilst satisfying officialdom was a much begrudged chore to be avoided if at all possible. Whilst it was forbidden to sell rationed goods above the set price even with a coupon, let alone without the right coupon, necessity drove both buyers and sellers to deal illegally.

Without a hint of conscience, Rose's father regularly sold to friends and local people at more than official prices like everyone else. "It's normal," he would say with a Gallic shrug. Local committees were set up to control and monitor local food supplies to meet both local needs and the orders of the requisitioning authorities. However, in rural St. Michel-en-l'Herm controls tended to be lax, the officials being either locals sympathetic to the farmers or outsiders ignorant of farming ways, which meant that as long as Rose's father regularly took a little produce to the market the authorities were satisfied.

Renée had charge of the household ration books like women all over France who had the main responsibility for putting food on the table. For them queuing had become a daily occurrence, more so in towns and cities than in St. Michel-en-l'Herm but nevertheless Rose's mother now found herself spending more and more time in the village queuing with the other wives.

"It's ridiculous," Renée bemoaned as they finished supper. "There is so much to do but we have to spend all this time and fuss just getting some basic items. Now that shopkeepers have become more used to the system, some at least are prepared to be a bit more helpful. The baker, for instance, will sometimes give me bread in exchange for some flour which saves me fuel as I have to get the oven to the right temperature to bake. That way I can keep some fuel back for the winter when they say it will be even more difficult to get. But today I baked as a treat as you were coming home, Rose." Renée paused to change the subject. "Enough of our concerns," she said turning to Rose. "Tell us more about school."

Pleased to be asked Rose said confidently, "I've worked really hard and my teachers say I'm doing well. I've good marks for the end of year exams. I'll show you later." Rose was proud of her achievements and she knew her parents would be pleased, particularly her mother.

Indeed Renée listened closely because Rose's academic progress was of great interest to her. She had made every effort to get Rose into the High School at Luçon which offered the opportunity to pass the baccalaureate giving entry into the civil service and other professions. Fernand had given his blessing to her further education – anything that made his darling daughter happy – but it would not have happened without his wife's efforts. The junior school teachers had said Rose certainly had the ability to go on; but securing a High School place for a girl with a poor agricultural upbringing was difficult. There were many forms to complete and endorsements to obtain. Because the High School was at Luçon some ten miles away it was not possible for Rose to travel daily and it was necessary to apply for a grant to cover boarding fees, a cost the family could not possibly afford. It meant sacrifices but Renée was prepared to accept these because her motivation was simple. In Rose she saw so much of herself and she had determined Rose would have the education and opportunities she never had. She had high hopes that one day Rose would have a salaried position at the town hall or suchlike and marry a professional young man, maybe even a doctor or a solicitor. Seeing Rose progress she sometimes reflected wistfully on what she herself might have achieved had times been different when she was young. Not that she was ever unhappy but she had always wanted better for her daughter. Mainly she kept her dreams and ambitions for Rose to herself, careful not to place Rose under the pressure of her expectations. Her belief that Rose would have the confidence and self-motivation to cope at the High School away from home seemed to have been confirmed. She put that down to the independent spirit Rose undoubtedly had inherited from her father. All Rose needed from her now was her support and encouragement. Young Fernand on the other hand had shown no inclination other than to work on the farm with his father; an occupation which had kept him out of the army, much to Renée's relief, and an occupation which the new Vichy Government now encouraged and extolled.

Rose continued, "I really like English with Monsieur Silvestre. He has even taught in England and he uses lots of his experiences in his lessons. He said if times were different he would take a group to London. London sounds wonderful. I would love to go there – one day I will. And history I like. We've been studying Joan of Arc. Did you know she was made a Saint only 20 years ago, after 500 years? One girl in our class said according to her father there has been a lot about Joan of Arc in the newspapers in Paris, calling her a patriotic heroine and a symbol of inspiration for France now. But Madame Garrique, who we had for history this term, said we couldn't discuss that in class. Madame Garrique still hasn't had word of her husband who was in the army. It's hard for her but at least she has a job. Text books are still scarce and we have to share. We have to write with pencils now as there's no ink and we have to be careful to use every scrap of paper. I asked to bring home some text books but I was allowed only one, for English, so that's all right. You can test me and learn some English too."

The conversation continued as the meal was cleared away. When Rose's father and brother went out to do some more work before the sun went down Renée took the opportunity to ask about Rose's health – a year earlier she had been diagnosed with a mild kidney disease and had been placed on a low protein diet. Rose said she had been fine this term, not fatigued at all, adding with a smile that rationing was actually helping her keep to the diet. And, yes, she had brought her medicine home but she had not needed it.

Later Rose went upstairs to her room to unpack and when she finally went to bed that night she was tired and content, the contentment of being at home and in her very own bed.

The following morning, Saturday, Rose happily slotted into her usual routine of helping around the house. One task she always enjoyed was collecting eggs from the chickens. Somehow for her, ever since she was a small child, collecting eggs was a special delight; the eggs still warm and in need of gentle handling, were like an amazing free gift for which she always said, 'Thank you,' to the hens. Rose was used to hard work and although she helped her mother mainly she loved being outside, especially this time of year working alongside her father and brother with the harvest. As she walked back to the house with her basket of eggs her brother brought Hector, the farm workhorse, out from his stable in the barn to start another day's labour in the fields. Rose thought Hector was a good name as he was certainly a handsome horse, shiny chestnut, young and powerful. It was young Fernand's role to look after Hector, and while in the past their father had done all the ploughing and carting, when Fernand was competent in handling a horse and cart they had bought another horse. That way they could do more and had been able to rent more land. But recently conditions had driven them to exchange the older horse for a pig. Rose's mother had explained in one of her letters sent to Rose at school, 'We can no longer afford two horses. We can eat the pig, and if we had two horses, one could be requisitioned and they would have taken the younger, stronger one. Having just the one horse, they will leave us with that.'

Taking the eggs from Rose, Renée said, "Would you like to go into the village? There are a few things we need," knowing Rose would be only too glad to have the opportunity of meeting with some of her friends. She told Rose what she wanted but before handing over the necessary ration coupons she hesitated. "Sit down a moment," she said with a seriousness that sent Rose's heart beating a little faster knowing it meant something unpleasant was about to unfold.

Chapter 2

Rose sat down as her mother had instructed. There was a brief, awkward pause before her mother began, her tone still serious.

"There is something you should know before you go into the village. We haven't told you this before because you didn't need to know." She paused again as if searching for the right words. "It's about your father. The other week he had to go to the court at Fontenay-le-Compte over the matter of some stolen goods. Although he hadn't stolen the goods he was convicted of the theft."

"What!" Rose exclaimed, shocked and completely taken aback at what her mother had said.

"I'll explain," her mother went on, "but you should know about it now as people in the village will know and may say something. We are saying it is all a misunderstanding; that's all we are saying to anyone. So what I am about to tell you must go no further." Renée fixed her eyes on Rose for emphasis. "A sack of stolen beans was found in our loft. A friend of your brother's had been harvesting beans for Alphonse Gouraud and, according to Fernand, thought he was not being paid enough so took a sack for himself. He asked Fernand to hide it for a day or two. Foolishly he agreed and hid the sack in our loft where it was found by the police."

"Fernand did that!" said Rose incredulously. "Why?"

"Something about a favour owed, apparently. But he knew it was wrong and he knows he should never have become involved," said her mother, her stern tone continuing.

"But I don't understand," said Rose, all upset. "Why was Papa had up, not Fernand? Everyone knows Papa would never steal anything."

"I know," said Renée, "but your father decided he did not want Fernand to have a conviction against him as he is not yet twenty-one. So your father did not say Fernand was involved – he felt he had no option – so it was your father who was accused of the theft as the beans were found in our loft. The other lad is from a prominent family and had denied anything to do with it. Your father went to see Alphonse Gouraud who understood and wanted the case dropped; but the police said it had gone too far and were under strict orders to pursue every case as the authorities feared widespread theft and anarchy under the Occupation. Gendarme Avril said on the quiet that in the past he would just have had strong words with both lads, made them hand the sack of beans back to Alphonse Gouraud and that would have been the end of it."

"But it's not right that Papa should have this conviction," said Rose, beginning to feel angry at the injustice. "What happened?"

"It was agreed the lawyer would not call Fernand as a witness so the court believed the other boy and we couldn't do anything more about it. Your father received a fine and a suspended sentence. It wasn't right but your father says it is over now and we shouldn't talk about it any more, especially for Fernand's sake. He has learnt his lesson and is trying hard to make amends. People think the Gouraud and Neau families must be on bad terms but that's not the case." Renée continued, her voice more moderate now, "Alphonse Gouraud understands and after the trial came over to your father to shake his hand and asked to embrace me. We just say to anyone it was all a misunderstanding."

"But it's not right the real thief gets off free," said Rose riled at the iniquity of it all. "Oh Maman, it's just not fair!"

"Go on your errands and say no more," commanded her mother softly.

"But Maman, how could Fernand let Papa take the blame?"

"I've told you. Your father thought it was for the best to keep Fernand out of it but the court didn't accept your father's alibi. Now, that's all there is to be said about it."

"But Maman, …"

"Off you go now," interjected her mother making it plain that was the end of the conversation.

Rose, still unsatisfied with her mother's explanation and with a head full of questions, nevertheless got up to leave giving her mother a look of somewhat petulant resignation. Outside the farm gate Rose turned down the rue de la Fontaine for the short walk to the village shops, her mood now introspective, changed completely by the revelations of the last few minutes.

It was a glorious day, warm with a huge blue sky. The village of St. Michel-en-l'Herm sat like a small jewel in a land flat as far as the eye could see. In all directions the horizon was low and the sky vast. Four miles or so to the south was the shallow water of La Baie de l'Aiguillon which stretched away round to the south to the port of La Rochelle. To the west was the small fishing village of l'Aiguillon-sur-Mer. There had been a monastery in St. Michel-en-l'Herm since early times and in recent centuries the enterprising monks had built a remarkable system of dykes and channels, pushing back the sea from the village and draining the land which was rich and highly productive. Some monastery ruins still remained but religion in the village now centred on the sizable and striking Neo-Gothic church built at the turn of the last century to replace the old church building which had fallen into disrepair. The tall tower of the new church with its spire atop was a beacon from every compass point and rose high above the modest, mostly white-painted village houses with coloured shutters and orange pantile roofs.

Rose had so looked forward to her first trip into the village, bursting with all the news she wanted to share with her friends, there was so much to catch up on. Instead now she was pensive, hardly noticing her surroundings, her thoughts still spinning with the gravity of her mother's revelation. Now it was obvious why Fernand was so withdrawn, the reason for the tension between him and their father – it was the matter of the stolen beans.

Along the rue des Moulins Rose knocked on the door of the house of her best friend, Adélina, her spirits rising somewhat in anticipation of seeing her friend, only to be told she was away visiting her aunt for the day. Disappointed Rose continued on towards the village square. As she turned the corner into the square she looked up and stopped as if frozen to the spot at the sight in front of her. A dozen or so German soldiers stood chatting outside the bar/café of the small hotel on the other side of the square. Further along was a large German military car with the black and white iron cross symbol on the side. Until now Rose had not seen German soldiers anywhere near St. Michel-en-l'Herm. She had got used to seeing them in Luçon as they had taken over the local barracks there. But now suddenly, unexpectedly, seeing so many casually and arrogantly standing around in her village with their rifles and helmets glinting in the sun, she was shocked and upset. A noise to her side startled her even more. Two more soldiers she had not seen were in the shadows, standing only a few yards away, their rifles on their shoulders. Their sudden appearance, their size and the menace of their guns frightened and alarmed her. For a brief moment one of them looked down at her with a friendly smile but Rose was already in flight, setting off across the square, her heart racing. She headed for the butcher's shop on the other side, one of her ports of call. There she composed herself as best she could and joined the short queue, looking anxiously out of the doorway. Preoccupied with the scene outside Rose did not take much notice of the other women in the queue who were nattering amongst themselves.

Eventually Monsieur Latapie, the butcher said cordially, "Hello Rose. Are you home for the holidays?"

Rose answered politely and gave her order, still distracted and looking outside. She spotted a friend of hers, Gabrielle, as Monsieur Latapie wrapped her order of pâté and salami. She went out of the shop and called over to her. She had not seen Gabrielle for some time and as soon as the customary greeting was done they began in animated conversation to catch up with each other's news. In the circumstances Rose was glad not to be on her own and the two went over to sit in the shade on the bench on the island in the middle of the square. Rose asked Gabrielle why there were soldiers in the village, saying she had been shocked to see them.

"You get used to them," said Gabrielle. "There are a lot around here now and some people say they are not so bad. The word is some of the latest arrivals are on exercises – it's said in preparation to invade England but others say they will be sent to Russia. Anyway, it's hoped they won't be here long. My mother says the main camp is at l'Aiguillon-sur-Mer but some are billeted here in the village and the officers have requisitioned part of the hotel in the square here. Monsieur Pilnière is not pleased as the locals won't go in his café when the soldiers are there but I bet he's happy to take the money for the rooms."

Feeling a little happier with the knowledge the soldiers might not be there for long Rose changed the subject to ask what Gabrielle was doing now. Gabrielle told her she had left school to look after her sick father and her elderly grandfather while her mother worked as a secretary to Monsieur Bodin, the mayor, at the Town Hall in the square. "My mother hears all the latest at the Town Hall, that's how I know about the soldiers," she added.

"Do you have a boyfriend yet?" enquired Rose somewhat cheekily, genuinely wanting to know but also half hoping she in turn would be asked the same question.

"Not yet. I don't have much time," said Gabrielle looking coy. "I have to look after the house, Papa and Grand-Papa and I take meals to the rich old lady in rue Basse who pays me. But when this is all over I want to marry a chef and we'll have our own little restaurant. My Maman is a wonderful cook and she is teaching me. What about you?"

"There is a boy at school," said Rose with equal coyness yet pleased to have been asked. "His name is François. He's really quite handsome and has the most beautiful grey eyes. He's not exactly a boyfriend, not yet anyway, but I think he likes me. He stood in front of me at the school photo. I'll bring it to show you. Next term I'll try to get to know him better, but it's difficult at school as it's strictly forbidden." They giggled at the thought of a secret romance.

"I really must go now," said Gabrielle getting up. "I can't stay any longer as Grand-Papa tends to wander off if left alone for too long." She stepped out into the sunshine and called back cheerily, "Come round and see me, and bring the photo."

Rose sat for a little while. She felt calmer now and seeing Gabrielle had cheered her up. After finishing her other errands she too set off for home, taking a backward glance at the soldiers still gathered at the bar/café. She was rather cross at her mother for not telling her the soldiers might be there, but she decided not to say anything. As she walked she thought about all that had happened since she got back and her mood became subdued again. As she neared home she felt she wanted a little more time to herself so she walked on past the farmhouse and yard, round the corner and strolled into the rough pasture where they kept their cows, still pensive. Everything she could see was very familiar. She loved the sense of the wide open landscape and the sounds of the countryside. She could hear a skylark, one of her favourite birds, happily singing away somewhere way up high but try as she might she could not spot him against the intense blue of a cloudless sky. She wanted to sit down for a while on the warm grass, put her head back and soak up the sun and the peace and beauty of the moment, but she had the shopping so turned back towards the farmhouse. Coming closer she could see that Hector was back and tethered outside the barn, his face half covered with his nosebag of feed. He loved attention and when she went up to him and patted his neck he shook his mane in welcome. Rose had taken to Hector more than the other horses they had had; she thought him noble.

"Oh Hector, what do you make of all this?" she asked rhetorically. "This horrible war. France defeated and occupied, even German soldiers in the village. And now Papa convicted of theft of all things. Everything is in a mess. Why has it all gone wrong, Hector? Why can't we just be normal again?"

Pausing, she looked into the horse's large dark, deep eyes to see what he was thinking but he gave nothing away. "What will become of us, Hector? I know there are people suffering far more than us with their lives and homes ruined. At least we are together and we have enough to eat. Maybe I shouldn't complain but I do hate it all so. I know there are people worse off, much worse off, getting by as best they can, having to put a brave face on things." Pondering on this last thought for a moment she came to a conclusion, announcing in a firm voice, "In that case Hector, then so must I. I must put on a brave face. Be brave … like Joan of Arc … then things will get better." She patted his neck again and Hector whinnied rocking his head up and down as if in agreement but his eyes still told Rose nothing. She smiled at him. "I wish I could be like you, Hector. Nothing seems to worry you." With that she turned and started towards the house with a new resolve.

Later on when Rose's father and brother were out in the fields she brought her school report down from her room to show her mother, together with a letter from the school addressed to her parents. She had read the report several times on the way home. It made good reading as she had expected and she knew her mother would be proud of her achievements; indeed some of the teachers' comments were quite complimentary. Showing the report to her mother would be fine. The letter, on the other hand, in its sealed envelope was another matter altogether. Rose did not know what it contained; she liked to think it might be a special letter of commendation but was unsure and therefore uneasy about it.

"Here's the report," she said to her mother, "and the school said I have to give you this letter." Her mother looked at Rose quizzically as she took the envelope, opened it first and read the short letter expressionlessly; then, looking up held out the letter to Rose indicating she too should read it. Rose had been watching her mother's face intently hoping to glean some clue about the letter's content. She quickly sensed from her mother's manner it was not good news and nervously drew back very slightly as she tentatively took the piece of paper. Her apprehension was not misplaced.

Rose read:

> *'We are pleased to tell you that your daughter has progressed well academically this term, particularly in history and English and we are sure she will make similar progress next term. However there is one aspect of her behaviour that we are obliged to bring to your attention.'*

That sentence immediately dispelled any hopes of praise Rose had had and her heart sank. She read on:

> *'There has been more than one occasion when Rose has shown a reluctance to accept the authority of her teacher and of the school and has voiced her objections inappropriately. At times she*

has become involved in matters that do not concern her. She has been advised of our concerns and we expect her behaviour in this respect to improve on her return and as such we do not at this stage propose any further action. In all other respects Rose is a capable and well-liked pupil who should do well.'

The letter was signed by the headmaster.

"What is this all about?" questioned her mother with obvious concern.

Straight away Rose recognised what was behind the letter and was upset the school had written about an issue she thought closed.

"It's nothing really," she said adopting a defensive mode. But with her frustration mounting, out poured a torrent of words with hardly a pause for breath, tears beginning to well in her eyes as she feared the admonishment that was surely to come.

"Sometimes I think the teachers have been unfair and haven't listened to me and I get annoyed and I tell them and they still don't listen. Once another girl was unfairly picked on and I said it was unfair but they told me I shouldn't interfere but what they were doing wasn't right. It's one teacher in particular, who I think doesn't like me, but that doesn't mean she should be unfair. I'm sorry Maman but it's not right that she should be so horrid and now she's complaining about me when it's her that's in the wrong and she should listen."

Holding up her hand to halt Rose's rush of words, her mother said, "You know you shouldn't talk back to your teachers, don't you?" her eyes telling Rose now was not the time to argue.

"I know Maman." Rose wanted to continue her defence but for once thought better of it.

In her mind Renée was weighing up how to tackle this issue which was not entirely unexpected given Rose's rather impetuous character, evident from when she was very young and more recently manifest in some teenage histrionics. At times Renée became exasperated with Rose who all too often would argue her point to the nth degree. She is like a dog with a bone, her grandmother used to observe. Renée did not want to spoil the homecoming but at the same time she also needed this matter dealt with as another embarrassing complaint from the school could place Rose's future there at risk, in turn jeopardising too her hopes for her daughter's future. Normally she would take the primary role in all matters concerning Rose's education and her instinct was to give Rose some further sharp words. But she relented and decided to take a softer approach.

"We'll speak no more about it now but your father will have something to say on this," were her final words on the subject.

Immediately Rose felt the storm had passed. Underneath she was still seething at the school for raising the matter with her parents when she had thought it over and done with after she had been spoken to by the headmaster. But she decided to hold herself in check as she was not too concerned at the threat of her father. She reckoned he would not be anywhere near as strict as her mother over such an issue especially as it was he who had always taught her to stand up for herself. He would no doubt reprimand her but she would say demurely, 'I'll try harder Papa,' and that would probably be the end of it.

"I'm sorry Maman," Rose said again as her mother moved to open the report. They began to look through it together discussing briefly a few points here and there but the mood had been spoilt for both of them and their hearts were not in it. Eventually with some approving words from her mother she took the report back up to her room intending to show it to her father later.

Rose sat on her bed, upset, thinking about her first day at home. She had had such high hopes for the holidays, yet it had gone so horribly wrong – first Papa, then the soldiers and now school. Why is all this happening to me now, she thought, right at the start of the holiday? She closed her eyes and wished it would all go away, that she could wake up in the morning and everything would be all right again, everything back to normal, everyone happy. Then, annoyed with herself for forgetting her earlier promise to Hector, she opened her eyes, drew a breath and renewed her vow, "I must be strong!"

Chapter 3

The last of the four great engines spluttered and the huge yellow-tipped propeller juddered to a halt. All of a sudden the air was full of a blissful silence. The ground crew hurried to jam chocks against the aircraft's wheels, wheels so large they nearly came up to the shoulders of the men themselves. After a few moments the hatchway door on the side of the fuselage swung upwards and was propped open. A set of steps was pushed up to the hatch and one by one the seven aircrew gradually emerged still in full flying gear despite the beautiful summer's day. Even standing silent the enormous aircraft, painted black with guns bristling fore and aft, had an aura of power and menace, dwarfing the ground crew who busied themselves under its belly. This was one of the Royal Air Force's newest heavy bombers. Still unknown to the general public, only two squadrons had received initial deliveries of this Halifax aircraft. Teething troubles had delayed its introduction but now both squadrons were fully operational.

The morning at RAF Middleton St. George in the north of England had been busy as usual but now the last of the Halifaxes was parked up on its dispersal pad the station was quiet except for the odd rumble of a lorry ferrying aircrew back to the station headquarters. Flight Lieutenant Norman McLeod sat on the grass beside his aircraft with some of the other crew waiting for the crew lorry to pick them up, taking in the stillness after the training exercise they had just completed. It had been very hot in his gun turret at the rear of the aircraft and he loosened his clothing. He smiled to himself at the contrast to his usual efforts to keep himself warm during operations which were invariably at night and at altitude where temperatures were bitterly cold. By contrast this morning's exercise had been low level formation flying over the North Sea under a cloudless summer sky.

For Norman, those first few moments out of the aircraft with his feet on the ground were always sweet with relief even after a short test flight or exercise; but after a bombing operation over enemy territory with all its dangers that sweetness was longer lasting and euphoric. Norman's flight engineer, Willie Finlayson, a Scot from Inverness, slumped down next to him. Although Norman was an officer and Willie a sergeant, while they were crewing together rank was forgotten, and the two relaxed in the sunshine. Sharing a Scottish heritage they had an affinity over and above the unique closeness of being members of the same crew. They were, however, very different characters. Willie was well known for his no nonsense and forthright approach to everything. He said it as he saw it, at least whenever possible, and sometimes when he would have been wiser to have held his counsel. He was a somewhat dour Scot, yet partial to a fine wine and classical music. Norman on the other hand was almost the opposite. He was a quieter, thoughtful character, more amiable with an open smiling face and a ready sense of humour. Deep down though, was a grittily determined spirit which could be caught occasionally in his quickly darting eyes. Of Scottish parents he was brought up in Northumberland. He was the oldest of the crew at thirty, balding on top, and in the Royal Air Force went by the nickname of 'Mac'.

Willie broke the silence first, his broad Invernessian accent soft and lilting. "You must know wha'all this formation stuff is about, Mac," he said. "It's obvious by now su'heen's up and all this gunnery practice organised by your Number One has obviously su'heen to do wi'it; aye you must know what it's aw abou'!"

"Willie," said Norman with a hint of a sigh, "you know if I knew and could tell you, I would. If I knew and couldn't tell you, I wouldn't. But I don't know, so I can't tell you. No doubt the Squadron Gunnery Officer is getting us to practice this for some purpose, but he hasn't confided in me; I guess perhaps because he can't. They teach these gunnery techniques at the Central Gunnery School. I know he went there when the School first opened and the techniques were still being taught when I went there last year. Maybe they want to go back to daylight operations thinking these new Halifaxes can defend themselves with their extra firepower. Maybe they want to experiment and we're just guinea pigs. Or maybe there is a special operation in the offing. All will be revealed in due course, no doubt."

Just as Norman was finishing the sentence Flight Lieutenant Austin Lewin, their first pilot and captain, dropped to the ground by them. He was a young Australian, only twenty-four years old yet experienced enough to be selected a captain. Next out of the hatchway was his second pilot Sergeant Gourley, also an Australian.

Directing his remarks at Norman, Flight Lieutenant Lewin said, "You know how difficult it is to keep this beast in close formation for any length of time? Look at me. I'm sweating buckets; and it's all your Number One's doing! What's he up to? Why are we all being kept in the dark about what's going on? Nobody trust us?"

Norman was used to the jibes by now. "If you can't cope, Austin, get your Number Two to fly the thing," he retorted.

"Oh, he'll only fly it into the Wing Commander's tailplane!" was the pilot's reply while winking at Sergeant Gourley. They all laughed and with a dismissive wave of the arm Flight Lieutenant Lewin set off with Sergeant Gourley on a visual inspection round the aircraft.

Norman and Willie gave a chuckle at their captain's sense of humour. But they fell quiet for a moment as they both knew, although it went unsaid, that something serious was afoot. Night-time operations were dangerous enough. Experience of daylight raids at the beginning of the war had proved they were much more perilous, to the degree they had been almost totally abandoned. Neither Norman nor Willie had been involved in a daylight operation and neither of them wanted to dwell on the thought for too long. The crew lorry braking in front of them broke their thoughts and with the rest of the crew they jumped aboard for the short ride back to the main station buildings.

After some lunch Norman had been in a meeting with his Number One, the Squadron Gunnery Officer, discussing the morning's exercise when the Squadron Gunnery Officer had been called away urgently. "Don't go far," he said to Norman as he left the office, so Norman had strolled only as far as the officer's mess. He sat in a sunny alcove taking advantage of a rare quiet moment. He picked up the newspaper on the table and read the coverage of the latest German attacks on Russia then idly flicked through some inside pages. But when he glanced out of the window across the wide expanse of the airfield he could not help thinking of the crash a few days ago when five of his squadron were killed when their aircraft came down on the airfield itself. He had lost many friends and colleagues over the past year, most reported 'missing', yet he tended not to dwell on such events instead trying to concentrate on the present – it was his way of coping. But that crash the other day, a training accident the aftermath of which was witnessed by everyone on the station, was proving more stubborn to move from the front of his mind. But suddenly his thoughts were interrupted when a head popped round the door to the officer's mess. "Briefing Room, 16.00 hours prompt. All crews to attend," announced an orderly loudly before disappearing.

There were several other officers in the mess room, mostly aircrew, and the room fell silent at the sudden announcement. Norman realised this must be why the Squadron Gunnery Officer had been called away. A slight shiver ran through him; doubtless they were about to find the reason for those recent exercises. Norman looked over at a colleague who had caught his eye, gave a somewhat tense smile but said nothing.

At four o'clock the eight crews, nearly sixty men, were assembled in the briefing room, chatting quietly amongst themselves. The noise drained away almost immediately the station's Group Captain entered the room. He was followed closely by the squadron's Wing Commander. Both men stepped onto the small dais at the front and put down various papers on the small table to the side. The Group Captain took a step towards the centre of the dais and looked across at the expectant faces. There was a palpable atmosphere of anticipation and tension.

"The purpose of your recent exercises in formation flying and gunnery tactics is about to become clear," the Group Captain said. His delivery was straightforward but there was clearly an edge to his voice. "Early tomorrow morning you will be given a full briefing on a most important mission. I can't tell you the target now as this operation has the highest level of secrecy placed upon it. What I can say, however, is that this Squadron has been specially selected to carry out a high precision, daylight operation in close formation against a major target. By its very nature it will be a stern test." He looked around the room at the still figures, their faces set. "The operation will be led by Wing Commander Jarman. Wing Commander Jarman will have aboard his leading aircraft the Squadron Gunnery Officer who will direct the fire of air gunners in defence of the formation as necessary – hence your recent exercises." He paused for a further moment to let his words sink in.

"I've called you together now, as shortly you will fly to a forward base and as I can't come with you I wanted you to know how proud I am that we have been selected for this special trip. It is no understatement that success tomorrow will have a profound effect on the enemy's capability. Because of its special nature particularly careful planning has gone into this operation; however, you may expect to encounter some opposition in which case the expertise, courage and organisation of gunnery defences will prove critical. I know you are up to the task and have no doubt your skill and determination will bring success. I wish you all the best of luck." Stepping back he looked over to the Wing Commander to continue the briefing.

Wing Commander Jarman moved forward. He was a hard-nosed New Zealander, not universally liked, especially among the more junior crew members because of his brusque manner and often harsh tongue. It was, however, obvious to Norman why the Wing Commander had been chosen to lead what was evidently going to be a difficult and critical mission for he was absolutely resolute and was renowned for his courage and airmanship. His crews respected him, not necessarily because they liked him as a person, but because he led by example and because he was an intrepid and skilled bomber pilot. Norman himself felt he got on well enough with the Wing Commander possibly, he thought, because he was one of the older, more experienced officer aircrew.

"Tomorrow's operation is going to be very different," were the Wing Commander's opening words. "But for once we will actually be able to see the target!" A small murmur went round the room at his attempt to lighten the mood a little. "You will hear all about it in the morning, but for the moment I will address the arrangements to fly down to our forward base at RAF Stanton Harcourt in Oxfordshire. We will have to take our ground crews because no one there will know our aircraft. Ground crews are being briefed as we speak. Having to move lock, stock and barrel to a forward base this evening is not ideal preparation but it is necessary and we just have to get on with it. All eight aircraft will move. Captains, you must ensure your aircraft are prepared as far as possible before moving to the forward base and that your crew take all they need. For those of you who don't know, RAF Stanton Harcourt is a satellite of RAF Abingdon. As it has sparse accommodation, arrangements are in hand for us to be put up at RAF Abingdon for the night. Captains will be granted permission to take off as soon as they are ready. The trip to RAF Stanton Harcourt is about 200 miles and there will be a navigators' briefing after this meeting."

Wing Commander Jarman looked around the room to sense the mood. It was serious and studied as each of the men was deliberating what this unexpected turn of events meant for them personally. It was always a pain to move to a forward base since anything that interrupted routine preparations only added to the tension. Norman whispered out of the side of his mouth to the colleague by his side, "Well that's my plans for this evening blown out of the water!" He had arranged to meet a civilian worker on the station who lived near his home town in Northumberland in the hope of cadging a lift at the weekend to see his parents as he was due a 48 hour pass. He was then going to write to his parents as he usually did on a Wednesday.

"I can't emphasise enough the importance of this operation," continued the Wing Commander. "And our success will depend as never before on our ability to fly and defend ourselves as a unit. We will be just as dependent for our safety upon the aircraft next to us in formation as we will be on ourselves. Therefore keeping station in your formation is paramount and communication between aircraft is vital but only within the strict protocols you will be given. We have trained for this operation and we have the skill and determination to deal a serious blow against the enemy. I don't want to keep you here any longer as there is much to do. I will see you all at the briefing in the morning; meanwhile give careful thought to your preparations. Thank you, gentlemen."

With that the two senior officers left the room and a hubbub of chatter began. Norman looked over at the Squadron Gunnery Officer who gestured him to come over. "Get all our air gunners to stay behind for a few moments," he said.

The room emptied quickly leaving the group of air gunners gathered around Norman and their Number One. "In these few moments I just want to say that tomorrow we will have a unique opportunity to show what we air gunners can do. A major tactic in the planning of this operation is the element of surprise; nevertheless as we have just heard we may expect to encounter some resistance over the target. Even so the enemy will not be expecting our defensive formation and formidable firepower. That may be enough to dent the resolve of some of their less experienced fighter pilots who could well think twice before pressing home their attacks. As I have emphasised these last few days, defending as a unit requires discipline, nerve and fighting spirit. We have all of that, which gives me every confidence we will put on a good show." He paused, and smiling said, "Oh yes, also remember please, I will be in the astrodome unable to shoot back, so don't let their bloody fighters have any free pot shots at me!" Pausing again, he turned to Norman and said, "Anything to add?"

"Just to make sure the armourers give you maximum ammunition at all gun positions," said Norman. "Any problems come straight to me."

"Right," said the Squadron Gunnery Officer addressing the whole group, "get a good night's sleep if you can, it will be an early start in the morning and a long day."

Alone for a few moments after leaving the briefing Norman thought of his sweetheart, Cherry. She would want to know of these developments. Cherry was a WAAF on the station who he had been seeing lately and had become quite attached to. Her warm character and slightly more mature outlook than some of the other young WAAFs appealed to him. He would tease her that she would be much better off chasing after the young, good looking pilots: she in turn said she was attracted to bald men. She was at her parents in Darlington on leave and would not be back until tomorrow so secrecy meant he should not contact her. He thought for a moment but concluded there was nothing he could do now. She would learn of events tomorrow morning and understand why he had not been in touch before he flew out. And she would be there to count the aircraft back when they eventually returned.

The evening was clear and calm. It was nearly eight o'clock when Flight Lieutenant Lewin brought his aircraft into land. Even on internal flights the aircraft's defences were fully manned in case a rogue enemy raider was trying his luck so Norman had been in his rear turret fully alert as usual. The trip had, however, been uneventful and he began to relax as the plane approached the runway just skimming the thatched cottages and church tower of the pretty village of Stanton Harcourt at the edge of the airfield. Earlier in the circuit awaiting permission to land, he had seen a dozen Halifaxes already on the ground which meant the other Halifax squadron, 35 Squadron, would also be taking part. 'This is going to be some operation,' he had mused to himself.

Moments later the bump and juddering announced they had landed and eventually the aircraft taxied to a halt. Habitually Norman would have simply put the safety catches on the four machine guns in his turret and locked the turret mechanism. Then he would unstrap his lap belt, turn to squeeze through the small hatchway at the back of the turret into the fuselage before alighting from the main hatchway in the side of the aircraft. This time though, with his mind on the following day, he stayed to check around his turret yet again; he had already been through the routine checks twice that day. He told himself he ought to check just once more as there would be little time in the morning but he also recognised this was nervous activity. He fiddled around – gun sight still set to daytime firing; all the correct tools in their clips; ammunition stowed properly. When he could think of nothing else, he left his turret and checked over the two machine guns mounted at portholes on each side of the fuselage making sure their ammunition boxes were full. With that he was satisfied and joined the others waiting to be ferried to RAF Abingdon for the night.

The accommodation officer at RAF Abingdon struggled to find room for the sudden influx of so many airmen and ground staff. Fortunately Norman was allocated a bed for the night; not everyone was so lucky and some found themselves on mattresses on the chapel floor. And there were the remains of a hot meal in the mess which was welcome, but some of the crews who arrived much later had to make do with some hastily made sandwiches. It was half past ten by the time the last of crews had arrived and Norman felt able to retire to his room. On the way he bumped into one of his old colleagues now with 35 Squadron.

"See you are joining the fun," said his friend cheerily. "Early start tomorrow. Better get our heads down. See you in the morning."

In the hurried preparations to fly down to RAF Stanton Harcourt there had been no time to write his usual weekly letter to his parents and he knew they would worry if a letter did not arrive by the weekend. And he thought maybe it was time he told them about Cherry and possibly bringing her up to meet them. Maybe there would be time to write when he got back tomorrow. Better still if he could get up to see them – he'd try. Tired, he soon drifted off to sleep.

Chapter 4

On Sunday, Rose dutifully joined her mother and grandparents at Mass. All the family had been brought up staunchly Catholic and as she grew up Rose wanted to emulate her mother who always appeared serenely and effortlessly committed to her faith. For Rose though, adolescence had brought disturbing questions. Did she really believe in God; could she ever truly believe?

Over the last year or so, the more she questioned her faith the more doubts crept in – her search for a simple faith like her mother's was proving ever more elusive. Her studies of Joan of Arc whose belief, she learned, was totally sincere at the age of thirteen, only added to her anxieties. Latterly these growing doubts were compounded by misgivings she had about the Catholic Church's attitude to the Occupation.

When she first went to Luçon her mother had, not unexpectedly, insisted she regularly attend Mass at the cathedral knowing the school had arrangements for a teacher to take a party of boarders there on Sundays and important Saints' days. Because there was no religious instruction at the state school, nor any compulsion for boarders to attend Mass, the seeds of doubt she left home with had room to grow. Occasionally after school or at weekends a group of boarders would talk about their beliefs. Rose found it refreshing to be able to express her thoughts freely and it was a comfort to find a number of her friends had ideas sympathetic to her own. She readily took part in the discussions although some of the group, she sensed, were reticent to talk openly; some would not even hear of any criticism of the Church which Rose thought somewhat blinkered. It was not that her own views were influenced one way or the other by the discussions; rather the debates tended to bolster her formative views. One or two of those who had dropped out of attending Mass altogether encouraged Rose to do the same. Although attracted at first she refused but as she became more disillusioned she had joined them, though she still felt very uncomfortable at letting her mother down.

What particularly grated with her was the emphasis on what she had done wrong, repeatedly being told to repent her sins. Yet in her eyes all the good things she had done were being ignored which was not right, not balanced. She knew she should strive to be a better Catholic and in her own way she did, but her efforts never seemed to be acknowledged or recognised. It was all on the negative side. And Germany's invasion prompted wider thoughts – she began to question why the Church was not condemning the war and France's brutal occupiers. Her own sins were constantly censured but what about all the other things that were happening? How could the Church stand aside and not rail against all the cruelty and killing going on? Why did it not stand foursquare with Catholic France? Such questions ricocheted around in her head. She wanted to discuss all these growing issues with her mother but a suitable opportunity never seemed to present itself. In any case she thought her mother would be upset at her apparent lack of conviction, at her criticisms of the Church and thought she would be defensive and not really listen. But who could she ask? She lacked the confidence to approach anyone else, let alone the local priest.

Her first Mass at Luçon's Cathedral Notre-Dame-de-l'Assomption gave her hope that such doubts as she had would be dispelled in this awe-inspiring house of God. She had visited the cathedral with her parents on rare trips to Luçon and whilst the church at St. Michel-en-l'Herm was beautiful, with its central stained glass window depicting Saint Michael before Joan of Arc, there was no comparison with the magnificence of Luçon's cathedral – the outside with its quiet cloisters and soaring spire, and the inside with its huge pillars reaching up to the high vaulted ceiling, and light streaming in through the vast, ornate window above the altar. To her consternation though, her experience of the cathedral, rather than an inspiration, turned out to be the opposite. The building could not fail to impress, but for her the character of the place, its ambience, felt increasingly cold and impersonal. Just when she needed someone to talk to she found the cathedral priests patronising and distant. She was at that questioning age; she had important and urgent questions yet felt there was no one there she could approach openly without fear of being belittled and put down. The priests all appeared old, fusty, remote and unapproachable. It was frustrating that both at home and at the cathedral there appeared no avenue open to her to address all these concerns she had. She felt isolated and so remained silent.

For once her father and brother did not accompany them to Mass on that first Sunday she was home; it was a busy time and they had already left the house to work in the fields. Rose was tempted to ask if she could join them but thought better of it. At least she would be able to see some of her friends after the service. The service itself did nothing to change her views – it only served to highlight one of the main contradictions as she saw it, that she should seek forgiveness for her own small sins yet no mention was made of the horrendous sins committed under the Occupation.

Afterwards outside as the adults gathered and chatted socially Rose looked around and quickly spotted her friend Adélina. She hurried over to her and excitedly they arranged to meet up in the next few days to catch up on all the news.

Wednesday was market day and Frédéric Jullien sat with Jules Chopeau at a small rickety table by the open-air bar, set up for the day by Albin Pilnière the proprietor of the hotel in the square; a service he provided because his farming customers tended to avoid his bar/café since the Germans had taken over part of his hotel. He took great pains to tell his customers that he laid on the outdoor bar at great cost to himself and for no profit whatsoever – yet most of the men at the market would avail themselves of an aperitif or two before setting off on the journey home. Both Frédéric and Jules were local farmers who had come into the village as usual for the weekly market and, their trading done, each had a glass of pastis in front of them, the pastis diluted to a milky, soft, yellow colour. Market days were not only for buying and selling, they were a chance to catch up with the serious business of news and gossip.

The two friends had been moaning how set prices for selling food meant they could barely make a profit. That coupled with shortages of just about everything meant times were just getting harder and harder. They were typical of the local farmers, rarely content with their lot, but these days they had every reason to grumble along with everyone else.

"Look at this! Damned official notices, demanding we do this or warning us not to do that – that's all we get these days," grumbled Frédéric, passing over a folded page of the local newspaper. "Last week's Vendée Despatch," he said pointing to a section headed 'Official Notice'. Jules read: '*By order of the Occupying Authorities, the attention of the public is drawn to the orders dated 10 October 1940 (relative to the protection against acts of sabotage). Punishable by death anyone hiding or sheltering evading prisoners.*' The notice went on to warn the same sanction would be brought against anyone helping enemy parachutists or the crews of enemy aircraft forced to land.

"Ah, that explains what my wife told me she heard from the butcher the other day," said Jules. "She said the butcher said the Mayor made an official announcement last week from the steps of his office, all official like to a roll on the drum. It was something about not helping escaped prisoners, she said. A waste of time if you ask me – not many escaped prisoners in St. Michel-en-l'Herm. Not many British airmen either – nothing to bomb around here, thank goodness."

Frédéric continued the conversation, "You hear about innocent people being deported just for being a relative of someone who has attacked a German soldier, or even for living in the same village where an escaper was hidden," he said. "It's terrible; they make everyone afraid, everyone suspicious of their neighbour, trampling us underfoot. Bloody Nazis!" he ended lowering his voice.

Just then Fernand Neau approached the pair. They had all been born and brought up in St. Michel-en-l'Herm, and had been close friends since childhood and now they all farmed in the area.

"Look who's here!" said Jules seeing Fernand and waving him over. "Come and join us, Fernand. Haven't seen you for a while. How are you?"

"Hello Jules, Frédéric. I'm fine, and you?"

Leaning back in his chair Jules called over to Albin Pilnière, "Pastis for Monsieur Neau, if you please, Patron."

Fernand sat down on the vacant chair and a pastis was placed in front of him to which he added an inch or so of water from the jug. For a while the three chewed over important farming matters; cattle prices, the state of the harvest, the poor wine yields this year, what land was changing hands. Then the conversation turned to the war and the Occupation.

"Never any good news," complained Frédéric. "What do you make of it all?" he said, directing his question at Fernand. "You were in the army, weren't you Fernand?"

"I'm still a reservist," Fernand said. "In a way I wished they had let me fight. I wanted to but they said I was in a reserved occupation and too old anyway. At least I could have done something. Maybe if the fighting had gone on I would have been called up. As it is we suffer here, working hard and things go from bad to worse."

"France is just a big mess," lamented Jules. "How on earth have we ended up in this miserable state of affairs?"

Although it was a rhetorical question, Fernand nevertheless picked up on it and launched into an oft stated opinion. "All the old government and the generals. Useless idiots! All of them!" he declared. "They lied to us. Damn lies about how strong our army was, how the Maginot Line would protect us. They sat back and didn't protect us. They saw Germany preparing for war but were smug and did nothing. And now look at us. Defeated, occupied, and told what to do, where to go, even what prices we should charge for our crops. That's what I think."

"But when will it end?" asked Frédéric.

"Who knows? I don't," replied Fernand with a shrug. "The bad news just goes on and on. Mind you, how it will end is more important than when," he said tapping the table with his finger to indicate the seriousness of his point. "We might all end up a part of Germany and have to speak German. God forbid."

"Don't you think Britain should do more," said Frédéric, "set up a counter offensive to drive the Germans back? All they seem to do at the moment is send over planes to bomb factories and railways here and there. And they're not very good at that!"

"At least they are holding out," said Fernand becoming somewhat animated. "They're doing all they can for now. They lost a lot of men and equipment – remember Dunkerque – and it will take time for them to mount any sort of campaign. We're just going to have to hold tight for the time being and do the best we can. Not much else we can do. What gets me most was the defeat of our army, humiliating that was; that and the loss of our freedom. Last year was the worst. After a while you get used to some things. But no freedom …? I can't accept that. Liberty is in our blood. Without it, what's left? Hopefully the British will return and we will fight for it again before too long."

"Maybe before that the Germans will end up being defeated by the Russians now they're in the war," said Jules.

"That might be even worse!" retorted Fernand.

"Anyway, enough of the war. What's the latest with you, Fernand?" asked Frédéric. "Been in any good courts recently?" he added jokingly. Fernand ignored his friend's jibe. A few of his close friends knew the truth about the stolen beans and sympathised with him, even admired him for protecting his son.

"Binding twine," said Fernand with a grin, his mood swinging back to the usual market-day banter. "I'd none left for the harvest. I've been looking for months now but no one had any. Was going to pinch the wife's knicker elastic! Then I heard the ironmonger would have some today so I came in early. And, hey, I now have some. Cost me a small sack of potatoes, mind, but at least I've enough for this year's harvest and Renée's drawers won't fall down. Stupid, isn't it, being pleased about a few balls of twine! Such is this war."

His companions chuckled – Fernand was usually good company.

"Well the harvest shouldn't be bad if this weather holds," said Jules. "Hopefully we won't starve this winter, unlike some poor wretches."

"Didn't I see that son of yours earlier?" said Frédéric to Fernand changing the subject again.

"He's about somewhere. He's meeting with Monsieur Millet who's in charge of the working party to repair some of the dykes. They start work tomorrow and I said my boy could go. It will do him good to get out from under my feet for a few days and he will earn a few francs for himself. It's not the best time for me but Rose is home now and she will be a help. Really they should have done the work much earlier in the year but I guess it's been difficult with everything else."

"I hear there is quite a bit to do this year. How many men are they taking?" asked Jules.

"There's most of the men from the mayor's civil works office," said Fernand, "under their foreman, Monsieur Millet, and about a dozen lads from around; about forty in all I think. Last year's storms did quite a bit of damage to the dykes and the work needs to be done before the Atlantic storms this autumn. My boy will enjoy it. He's a good worker; and very strong. He's getting his instructions this morning. He's a good lad really; learned his lesson, hopefully. He's twenty now and I can leave him to get on with most things. He's even started arguing with me about what we should do on the farm! Thinks he knows better. But he is very good with the horse."

"You're lucky still to have him. He could have been called up, and could have been either dead or a prisoner of war by now," said Jules.

"Or he could be sent to Germany. There's rumours young men may be ordered to work in factories there," said Frédéric.

"I'd rather he'd fought," was Fernand's response. "But so far he's been let off all that because he works on the land with me. Maybe he won't be spared. Who knows? Everything is so uncertain."

At home Rose looked around the yard for signs of her father. Not finding him she went back into the house to ask her mother.

"He and Fernand went into market early. Your father desperately wanted some binding twine and the ironmonger was supposed to be having some in today and your father didn't want to miss out as no one else has any to spare. I hope he gets some otherwise I don't know what we'll do. What did you want him for?" her mother asked.

"I wondered if I could have the bike this afternoon if no one else wants it and if I finish all my jobs. It's such a nice day maybe Adélina can come on a bike ride with me."

Her mother looked up from what she was doing and smiled. "I'm sure that will be fine," she said. "Go and see if Adélina is free. Why don't we pack up a lunch for both of you and you could have a picnic."

"Really," said Rose excitedly. "Are you sure?"

"I'm sure," said her mother. "Tomorrow your father will need you to help him because Fernand is away working on the dykes. He will need the bike all day. Go and see if Adélina can come."

Adélina was the same age as Rose and they had grown up together. Her father was the local pharmacist, an important man in the village. He knew everybody and all their aches and pains. Adélina went to school in the large town of Fontenay-le-Compte about twenty miles inland from St. Michel-en-l'Herm. It had been much easier for her parents to get her a place at the much favoured High School there than it had been for Rose's mother to secure a place for Rose at Luçon. Despite their different backgrounds Rose was always welcome at Adélina's house. Adélina herself was quite a quiet girl, academically brighter than Rose and from a more cultured background. Nevertheless they had been firm friends since childhood having been in the same class all through junior school.

Rose scooted off to ask her friend and came back shortly to tell her mother Adélina was able to come. She then busied herself with her chores, working hard to ensure everything was done early.

A little later Rose and her mother were together in the kitchen seeing what they could prepare for the picnic. There was some bread, pâté, a little cheese, a couple of slices of salami and some home-made elderflower cordial. All the food was carefully wrapped in some napkins and placed in a wicker basket with the bottle of cordial. "Where will you go?" enquired her mother. She had no concerns at the children having the freedom to roam around the many lanes and tracks that criss-crossed the flat landscape. They knew the area like the back of their hands and were sensible.

“We might go to Eperon Plage. If the tide is in we can go for a swim, it will be a hot afternoon,” said Rose. “There’ll be families there so it will be safe. We won’t go out of our depth,” she said anticipating her mother’s usual caution.

Renée waved Rose off. “Have a lovely time,” she called as Rose pedalled across the yard and out onto the lane towards Adélina’s house, the picnic basket swinging on the handlebars.

To both Rose and Adélina this was blissful – setting off on their adventure, the sun shining down from an intense blue sky, the breeze soft on their faces. Joyfully they embraced the carefree freedom that they had always enjoyed together. They chatted excitedly as they cycled along the rue des Moulins towards the western end of the village. They rode side by side as there was hardly anyone about and pedalling was effortless on the flat road. Near the edge of the village they turned south and picked up the main road to l’Aiguillon-sur-Mer but when that road turned to the west they carried on southwards on one of the many access tracks to the patchwork of fields that characterised the region around St. Michel-en-l'Herm. There were hundreds of small fields divided by raised tracks or just a low bank, and so with no hedges and only the odd diminutive tree the whole area felt like one vast open space. They talked mostly about their schools, their friends there, the teachers and the teachers’ foibles, comparing facilities or complaining at the lack of them. Rose just had to tell Adélina about the letter from school she had been obliged to give to her parents and how cross she was over it. It was no surprise to Adélina that Rose got into a spot of trouble at school; she had always considered Rose headstrong and rather envied her for it, for she saw herself as rather shy. It was not long too before Rose mentioned her crush on François and the hopes she had for getting to know him better. François was frequently on her mind yet she dare not mention him at home. But with Adélina, however, she had someone she could share news of this secret love.

They took a short cut around the edges of a couple of fields before picking up the track again and heading for the piece of raised ground known as La Dive on which there was a small settlement. Centuries ago this limestone outcrop had been an island before the sea was pushed back by the series of dykes. The girls skirted La Dive and soon met up with the road which ran along the edge of the estuary from the fishing village of l'Aiguillon-sur-Mer to La Pointe de l'Aiguillon, the south-westernmost tip of La Baie de l'Aiguillon.

The two started to go faster and faster as their excitement rose at the sight and smell of the sea. The little sandy beach, Eperon Plage, was only a mile further along the road towards La Pointe and they reached it in no time. When they had found a spot to have their picnic they pushed their bikes off the road and on to the warm, soft white sand. Rose was right; there were quite a few families on the beach, mostly mothers with young children. They laid their bikes down, got out their towels and plonked themselves down.

"Let's eat, I'm starving," said Rose opening the wicker basket.

"Look what I've brought," said Adélina, producing some strawberries from her copious canvas bag. "They are from my aunt's garden."

"Wow! What a picnic!" said Rose enjoying every moment.

The two talked idly in the sun as they ate. After a while they ambled along to the small jetty at the end of the beach to see the small fishing boats anchored in the shallow water. They paddled and swam in the warm calm water, then dried off in the sun.

They lay there chatting about what had been happening in their lives since they had last seen one another. In time the conversation came around to their hopes for the future.

"What do you want to do when you leave school, Adélina?" Rose asked.

"I might follow my father and be a pharmacist if I can make the grades. I help him now in the pharmacy. I like it," she said. "How about you?"

"A civil servant, or even a lawyer, perhaps," said Rose. "I don't want just to marry a farmer and spend all my life here. Not that there is anything wrong with that, but I want to earn my own money, live in a big town or city. I could go to Paris or even London. I know I could do it."

"My brother says it isn't worth studying to get any qualifications because no one knows what is going to happen. I think he says this because he's lazy," said Adélina.

"He can't be right. Take your father. People will always need pharmacists; it's an important job," said Rose.

"It upsets me though," said Adélina, "when people say Papa shouldn't supply the Germans with medicines. Papa says he has to. If they are sick he must treat them the same as anyone else. But some people say that because medicines are in short supply they should be for us. Papa says he makes up a lot of medicines himself now because supplies are so short and only gives the Germans the minimum. He says if he didn't supply them they would close him down and then no one would get anything. What do you think Rose?"

Rose thought for a moment. Sympathetic to the idea of not giving precious treatments to the Germans, she nevertheless realised the difficult position Adélina's father was in. "I suppose he must but it can't be easy for him. Especially when you see how the Germans treat everyone else. Have you seen some of the newsreels at the cinema showing those poor prisoners of war? It's so horrible. I cried when I saw that. How can they treat people like that? They are so cruel. Those poor men, they looked frightened, starved and wretched. I feel so sorry for them and there is nothing we can do. And all those from the north who had to flee the invasion, forced to leave their homes and beg for food and petrol. I know a lot have gone back but lots of families are still split up. One of our teachers doesn't know where her husband is even now. Why does there have to be this war?"

"It's just so awful," agreed Adélina.

"Why do they have to do it, war I mean? Why all this hate? I don't understand. It wasn't that long ago since the last war. Papa said millions were killed then. Why don't they learn? People are almost starving. I feel so sad when I think about it."

"Me too," said Adélina. "Now they are persecuting Jews and communists, Papa says."

"I worried about Papa last summer. When France fell he was so distraught," said Rose. "It took him ages to come to terms with it. He's mostly all right now but he is still angry underneath I know. We all have to be brave, I suppose. It's been a year since the Occupation and yet no one can see an end to it all. Oh how I wish it would all go away," lamented Rose, "and we could be normal again."

"My Maman says we must pray and hope," said Adélina. "In the meantime, she says, we must make the best of what we have. We're not so badly off here, compared to some. Anyway," she said after a pause, "we should be leaving soon, let's have another swim before we go back?"

"Race you into the sea," Rose challenged, getting up and rushing into the water. Adélina followed, squealing and shrieking as Rose playfully splashed her.

On the way home Rose was reminded of something she had been looking forward to, the village dance to celebrate the harvest. Rose was always entranced by the music, the dancing, the lights and the whole atmosphere. The entire village turned out and everyone was determined to enjoy themselves thoroughly. She asked Adélina if she knew whether the dance had been organised yet. Adélina said she had not heard. "I'll ask Fernand, he'll know. It will be such fun," said Rose.

Later, the Neau family sat around the kitchen table eating their evening meal catching up on each other's news of the day.

"You know you can't have the bike tomorrow," young Fernand said to his sister. "I shall need it to go with the working party."

"I know. I'll be helping Papa tomorrow," said Rose defensively sensing her brother was having a dig at her for her outing that afternoon, and at the same time reasserting his superior proprietorial rights over the family's only bicycle. Rose quickly changed the subject. "Fernand, is there a harvest dance this year?"

"I heard dances had been forbidden by the Germans," said Rose's mother.

Young Fernand said, "It's true, they have."

Rose, indignant, raised her voice, "That's not fair!"

"Even the Vichy government has banned them in the south," said Rose's father. "We shouldn't be enjoying ourselves when there are still French prisoners of war, they say. But I don't see anything wrong with people enjoying themselves once in a while."

Young Fernand leaned forward and lowering his voice as if to divulge a confidence said, "There's talk of one being organised, unofficial like, out of town, away from prying eyes."

"Oh, find out!" said Rose excitedly. "Ask tomorrow if anyone knows about it. We could have such a good time."

Early the following morning, Rose's brother was preparing to leave. For his lunch his mother had cut some chunks of bread and some generous slices of ham which she wrapped in a large white napkin. The bread and meat together with a bottle of red wine were carefully placed in a strong canvas bag which had a long leather shoulder strap. Because he would be riding the bike he wore the strap bandolier style. Across the other shoulder he carried a large shovel with a length of binding twine tied to the handle and to the bottom of the shaft making a loop for his head and arm to go through. He wore his usual working clothes; a collarless beige shirt of heavy cotton and faded, blue denim, rather baggy, trousers. In view of the likely heavy work he wore his only leather boots rather than the espadrilles he habitually wore this time of year. The day was going to be hot so he could do without his jerkin and unlike his father he never bothered to wear a cap.

Young Fernand got on the bike. "Now don't go breaking my best shovel on municipal work!" said his father half joking, half serious. "And bring all that twine back."

"Don't worry," assured young Fernand.

"And show them the Neau family are strong and not afraid. Work hard and truly earn your money," his father encouraged as the young man pedalled off into the village. He was to meet up with the working party in the square. He knew what his father's words meant about being strong and not afraid. After the case of the stolen beans there had been murmurings about his father among certain people in the district and young Fernand had been on the receiving end of some of their snide remarks, which he had reported to his father. 'Stand up to them,' had been his father's advice. 'Don't let them get the better of you.' Young Fernand felt acutely his parents' obvious disapproval over the affair, particularly his father's. His father loved him no less for his foolishness and held no bitterness over the outcome of the trial but young Fernand felt sure his father must be resentful underneath. He interpreted his father's efforts to ensure he learnt a lesson from the beans' affair as a growing disaffection. His father was only concerned his son understood the implications of his wrongdoing and wanted to steer him away from those who might influence him down the wrong path but young Fernand misread his father's mood and felt alienated. As such he was keen to make amends, to regain his father's esteem, to restore some of his father's affection. To make amends young Fernand would often work longer hours than his father and undertake the heavier work on the farm. Volunteering for this working party was another way he hoped to gain approval. It had taken him a while to understand the family name had taken a knock over the fallout from the stolen beans but he recognised now that he must play a part in restoring their name. There was one thing he was good at and that was hard work. Today was an opportunity for him to be noticed, to be seen doing something essential, for repairing the dykes was certainly vital in protecting the community.

As he turned into the square young Fernand saw the group of labourers milling around the only municipal lorry still operating. The Germans had wanted to requisition it but the mayor had successfully argued that unless the roads and bridges could be maintained their troops could not move around. But lack of spares meant it was always breaking down. Luckily Monsieur Bon, the local garage proprietor, could coax most engines into life and Fernand recognised Monsieur Bon's rear end poking out from beneath the lorry's bonnet.

"Try again now," he heard from under the bonnet. The engine laboured, then suddenly fired up belching clouds of black exhaust fumes, scattering nearby onlookers. "There you are!" said Monsieur Bon triumphantly withdrawing from under the bonnet. "Good as new."

Above the noise Monsieur Millet started a roll call. Fernand stood at the back of the group propped against his bike. Two people had apparently not yet turned up to the obvious disgust of

Monsieur Millet. With the lorry engine now turning over, Monsieur Millet was keen to get going and told those who had no bike to climb on the lorry which was already heavily laden with material for the dykes. The train of workers set off, many with tools of various kinds which they had been encouraged to bring in view of the shortage of tools in the municipal stores. Everyone had their lunch with them, carried in a variety of containers. Young Fernand fell in alongside a friend, Olivier, and they pedalled near the back of the group of cyclists following the lorry which still belched unhealthy amounts of smoke. As the strange assemblage headed along the rue de l'Abbaye out of the village it drew some ribald calls from a few early risers. Taking the Route de la Mer, which was no more than a wide track across the open fields, the small army made their way to the eastern end of the dyke called the Digue du Maroc, about four miles away. Monsieur Millet had explained at the roll call that the main breach was at this eastern end and that was where most of the party would be needed. Small groups would also work on other more minor collapses along the length of the dyke. That day had been chosen for the repair work because high tide was late afternoon so work could be carried out at the base of the wall for most of the day without interruption.

The Digue du Maroc was the main sea wall along the western section of the Baie de l'Aiguillon. It stretched for nearly two miles from La Pointe at the western tip of the bay to one of the large drainage channels controlled by a series of locks. It had been built about thirty years earlier, pushing back the sea from the previous sea wall built in the middle of the nineteenth century, allowing more land to be cultivated. The dyke was built about ten feet high mainly from limestone rocks quarried from La Dive and covered with sand, earth and mud; all readily available materials but not the strongest. Six miles out to sea was the Ile de Ré which sheltered the bay from the worst of the Atlantic storms but a combination of spring high tides and westerly gales could funnel large seas into the bay which could rise nearly halfway up the dyke.

Fernand was very familiar with the area and loved the peace and tranquillity it offered. As a boy he would spend many hours birdwatching on the dykes, especially in the autumn when vast flocks of migratory birds made a stopover in the bay where it was safe for them and rich in food. He often went fishing with his Uncle Bernard who kept a small boat near La Pointe; a special flat-bottomed boat adapted for the shallow waters of the bay. To those unfamiliar with the bay, though, it could be a very dangerous place. The tide went out a long way; so far that at low tide it was not possible to discern where the mud flats ended and the sea began. Because the bay was so flat the tide would rush in almost as fast as a man could walk, but only the many estuary birds would venture onto the flats as the mud was deep, thick and very sticky. Fernand thought it a magical place on cloudless, moonless nights when everywhere was pitch-black. In the distance to the west could be seen the rhythmic flashing of the lighthouse on the Ile de Ré and the twinkling lights of the houses on the island, and to the south were the brighter lights of La Pallice, the deep water harbour of the town of La Rochelle. But the breathtaking sight was the sky above – a wonderful canopy of a million stars.

To young Fernand's disappointment he was not allocated to the main breach but was detailed to go to the far end of the dyke near La Pointe where there was a partial collapse in need of repair. He was to go with two municipal workers whose names he learned were Claude and Marcel. He had imagined the work on the main breach would be more interesting and more fun in a big group and he was not enamoured at the thought of being stuck with these two older men all day. But he said nothing.

The three of them set off along the top of the dyke carrying assorted tools. Marcel appeared to be the senior of the two municipal workers and he set a suitably municipal pace. Fernand brought up the rear pushing his bike laden with yet more tools, including two metal buckets hanging from the handlebars which clanged regularly against the metal frame as they made their way over the rough track. Eventually they reached the spot where the sea had certainly gouged a wide but not deep indentation in the wall. Much scratching of heads and debate followed as to the best way to tackle the problem. Scattered at the foot of the wall were the rocks and material gouged out by the sea and it was decided to collect and use the larger rocks first. Fernand volunteered to do the heavy lifting. It was soon clear that Claude and Marcel were first-rate at their work, taking care in placing the rocks that he handed up. Progress was good and after a while Marcel declared a period of rest. It certainly was warm work on yet another cloudless day. As they chatted and sampled their lunch baskets, Fernand decided his two companions were all right. They were in their forties, local men who talked of their families. Shortly they resumed their work, quickly breaking into a sweat as the heat of the day was by now firmly established.

When the sun was high in the sky Marcel said, "We'll stop for our lunch when we've finished this bit." The announcement brought ready agreement from the other two. The three of them lay on the bank, chatting and eating. They wondered how the other gangs were getting on and what time they might expect an inspection.

"Monsieur Gaudin, the inspector, is very strict – our work had better be good," said Claude looking at Fernand.

"Our work is excellent! The Inspector can come any time!" said Marcel indignantly with a dismissive wave of his hand.

Young Fernand certainly had an appetite and always enjoyed his food. Although his mother had put plenty of bread and ham in the canvas bag for his midday meal he readily accepted some titbits generously offered by Marcel and Claude from their own lunch packs. It gave them pleasure to see him eat well. Replete and his thirst quenched, there was still a little food and some wine left over in young Fernand's sack; something for a well-earned snack later on, he thought.

They were about to resume their work when Claude said sharply, "What's that?"

He was the first to speak when they heard a series of distant booms coming from somewhere to the south. "Look, over there!" he exclaimed, pointing out over the bay. Fernand turned round and could see puffs of black smoke in the sky over La Pallice. Then the unmistakeable drone of aircraft could be heard. Quickly the booms became a continuous barrage of noise and the puffs of smoke became a dark pall.

"It must be an air raid!" said Marcel incredulously. They could scarcely believe what was happening in front of their eyes for the area had not been a target for bombers before.

Fernand stood transfixed at the scene. He had not witnessed first-hand any sort of military action before and he found it both compelling and unnerving. To begin with he was intrigued by the puffs of smoke silently appearing in the sky with the boom, boom, boom of exploding anti-aircraft shells reaching him several seconds later. But his curiosity rapidly turned to apprehension. The intensity of the battle unfolding before him increased. Aircraft were wheeling. The pall of smoke in the skies rapidly darkened and thickened with the barrage of bursting anti-aircraft gunfire, the sound of which grew to a continuous loud rumble. Heavy explosions shook the ground and smoke rose from the port area across the bay. The ferocity of it all frightened him and when he began to realise there were men in the thick of it both on the ground and in the air, his blood ran cold.

Chapter 5

A sharp rap on the door woke Norman McLeod.

A head appeared round the door. “It’s half past five, sir,” said the orderly. “Breakfast is available in the Officers’ Mess and briefing is in Room 10 at 0700 hours, sir.”

Norman had slept surprisingly well and he was already starting to get out of bed before the door closed. As usual when he had to be up early he was quickly able to shake off any sleepiness and address the business of the day. This morning though, he needed an extra moment or two to acquaint himself with both the unfamiliar surroundings and the reason for being there. He paused a second as he sat on the edge of the bed. Unconsciously he took in a long slow breath, the thought running through his mind that today would be far from normal. During his time in the RAF there had been many early starts, occasionally for a flying exercise but none for an operation. Because all his previous bombing operations had been at night he was used to starting his routine preparations in the afternoon. But today, although wide awake, he recognised he needed to shake himself up a little mentally and adjust to a very different situation. Much was out of the ordinary; the time, the room, the airfield and most significantly, the day itself.

He moved over to the window. The room was quite light already as the curtains were somewhat inadequate but when he pulled them back he was shocked to see a dense blanket of fog. Immediately his spirits dropped as it seemed inevitable the fog would frustrate the day’s plans.

The briefing had been called for seven o’clock so Norman decided to get going in order to give himself as much time as possible to prepare even though there could well be delays. He shaved, washed and dressed, occasionally looking out of the window to see if there was any change in the visibility. The mist appeared just as dense as he walked along the corridor to the

Officers' Mess. There he spotted his captain, Flight Lieutenant Lewin, already tucking in to his breakfast. Norman went over.

"May I join you?" he asked politely.

"Of course, Mac, grab yourself some grub. It's jolly good."

Not knowing when he would next have a decent meal, Norman asked for a generous helping of the fare on offer and took it over to where Flight Lieutenant Lewin was seated, nodding a 'good morning' on the way to some familiar faces.

"Bit of a surprise," said Flight Lieutenant Lewin indicating the weather outside. "I'm told by the locals it's not unusual even at this time of year and it should soon lift. Hope so. Shame to have gone to all this kerfuffle for nothing. Sleep all right?"

"Fine," answered Norman. "Any idea yet what this is all about?"

"Not yet. But we'll soon find out. Wouldn't be surprised if we're not in for a tough one though. Bloody hard work keeping in formation for any length of time. But at least we'll be able to see where we're going, fog permitting. And I expect more than ever I will need you to look after my rear end!"

After finishing the food on his plate Flight Lieutenant Lewin got up immediately. "See you in Room 10, 0700 hours," he said as he moved to leave. Sensing the Flight Lieutenant wanted to be on his own for a while Norman did not try to continue the conversation.

Each airman had his own routine to prepare for an operation, his own way of coping with nerves. Some wanted to be quiet; some even to be alone, yet at the other end of the scale some masked their anxiety by loud bonhomie and busy activity. Some, it was said, had no nerves at all. Norman had not flown on an operation with Flight Lieutenant Lewin before, only exercises and air tests, and judged from their encounter over breakfast that his captain needed some space. He was a very personable young chap, not the stereotypical brash Australian, and Norman liked him as an individual. As a pilot and captain, Norman put him in the 'he's a natural' category. He had flown with many pilots, not all of whom exhibited the confidence and competence Austin Lewin displayed and he had no concerns at being on the young Australian's crew. It never ceased to amaze Norman how good these young pilots were, and having been selected to fly the new four-engine Halifax he rightly supposed Flight Lieutenant Lewin was among the best in Bomber Command. Being the oldest aircrew on the Squadron and one of the most experienced, Norman adopted a paternal role at times often mingling among the crews before an operation aiming to calm the nerves of less experienced flyers.

During breakfast one or two others from his own squadron and from 35 Squadron came up to him and commented on the weather, adding a joke or two before making their way to their rooms to prepare. On his way back to his own room, Norman noticed the visibility outside had improved a little; the locals are usually right, he thought.

He tidied his room and put his few things in his over-night bag. He had purposely left his flying gear in the aircraft so nothing would be lost. Should he write to his parents while he had a moment, he wondered? He knew they worried, especially his mother. But he could not reveal where he was or why, so on reflection he decided against starting a letter. Perhaps he would get the chance to go home when this was over. That would be the best, he thought, and resolved to make a big effort to travel home to see them.

Unaccustomed as Norman was to such apprehension so early in the morning these spare moments prior to the briefing felt very strange to him. The period between standby and the briefing for an operation was an anxious time but normally the anxiety was tempered by familiar surroundings and friendly faces. Some airmen sought out their lucky charms; others had a set routine or laid their room out in a certain fashion. Norman did not have any superstitions per se or mascot, except lately he carried a photo of Cherry in his wallet; but he was a stickler for the right time and always took great care to wind his RAF issue Longine watch fully last thing at night. He decided to kill a little time now and left his room to find out where Room 10 was and to get a time check. The mist was definitely lifting, albeit slowly; in all probability they would be flying. But would he be flying, he wondered. The squadron had brought all eight aircraft, but not all would be risked on one operation; undoubtedly some would be held as backup. He felt sure, however, his crew would be on the operation because Flight Lieutenant Lewin was one of the Squadron's more experienced pilots, despite being only twenty-four years old. Plus, of course, he was second in command of the squadron's air gunnery section. 'Yes', he said to himself, 'you'll be on for this one.'

As seven o'clock neared, Norman made his way to the briefing room. Small groups of men emerged from various buildings heading in the same general direction. Norman joined a group from his squadron; all the talk was speculation about the target now that visibility was improving. As they entered Room 10 the conversation tailed off as each airman sought out his own crew. Norman saw Flight Lieutenant Lewin and the rest of the crew and he also saw the Squadron Gunnery Officer towards the front of the room. Norman went over to him.

"Morning, Mac," said the Squadron Gunnery Officer. "Everything all right?"

"No problems as far as I know at the moment, apart from the weather," replied Norman.

Ignoring his comment about the fog the Squadron Gunnery Officer continued. "There'll be sandwiches and coffee in here at nine o'clock before we go out to Stanton Harcourt. I'd like to gather our air gunners together for a few words then. Can you set that up?" Before Norman could respond he continued, lowering his voice, "You had better join the others; we're about to start."

Norman acknowledged the order and moved over to join the other six members of his crew. The room was filling up, nearly 150 men in all. The normal briefing room was too small for the numbers involved and Room 10 had been modified for the purpose. At the front was a temporary dais on which were three large covered easels with an orderly standing guard. There was a low hubbub of tense anticipation.

A small party entered and made its way onto the dais, led by the station's Group Captain who walked with a pronounced limp and a walking stick. He tapped his stick on the stage and the room fell silent.

"Good morning and welcome, gentlemen. I can see a few familiar faces among you, but for those who don't know me I am

Group Captain Massey, Officer Commanding, RAF Abingdon. Your sudden arrival last night meant we were not able to accommodate you all as we would have liked, however I trust you have all been suitably fed and watered this morning."

After a short pause he continued. "Today's target is the German battleship Scharnhorst. You will all know the Scharnhorst together with the German capital ships Gneisenau and Prinz Eugen have been at Brest for a while undergoing maintenance and improvements. Concerned that these German surface raiders will again take to the Atlantic to ravage our vital supply convoys, Prime Minister Churchill specifically charged Bomber Command to remove the threat these ships pose whilst they are vulnerable at Brest. So far the success of our many night operations against them has been disproportionate to the effort involved. The Gneisenau has been superficially damaged requiring repairs; the Prinz Eugen has received only minor damage. The Scharnhorst, however, remains undamaged and recent intelligence reports indicated the maintenance work on her is nearing completion. The matter was becoming urgent. In response Bomber Command drew up plans for a major raid in daylight which would significantly improve our chances of success by allowing bomb aiming to be much more accurate. The original plan called for a force of 120 bombers including a force of Halifaxes to be deployed in waves escorted by long-range fighters. A diversionary operation against Cherbourg would be timed to draw away some of the enemy's defences. On Sunday orders were issued for this operation to take place at the earliest opportunity commencing from today, Thursday 24th July.

"However," he said pausing to convey the importance of his next words, "reconnaissance on Tuesday morning revealed the Scharnhorst had slipped out of Brest under cover of darkness. For a while her whereabouts was unknown. However, yesterday morning reconnaissance found her at the jetty at La Pallice, the deepwater port of La Rochelle some 250 miles south of Brest. In view of this development, stopping her before she can resume her Atlantic forays is now an imperative. It was therefore decided to withdraw the heavy bombers from the Brest force and as a matter of urgency direct them against the Scharnhorst at La Pallice. Late yesterday evening a small force of Stirlings and during the night a larger force of Whitleys attacked the ship. Reports indicate she has not been hit; therefore the planned third phase will go ahead. This phase calls for a force of fifteen Halifaxes to attack early this afternoon, possibly our last and best opportunity. Gentlemen, that force will be made up of six aircraft from 76 Squadron and nine from 35 Squadron."

The Group Captain looked around the room allowing a moment or two for the significance of his announcement to sink in.

"You will now understand the need for all those last minute changes. The operation will be led by Wing Commander Jarman of 76 Squadron, here on my right. Squadron Leader Bradley, on my left, will lead the 35 Squadron contingents. Take off will be at 1030 hours. The attack on Brest will go ahead largely as planned as will the attack on Cherbourg which is timed to draw Luftwaffe units away from Brest. Similarly the attack on La Pallice is timed so Luftwaffe units there will have been draw away to defend Brest.

"I don't need to emphasise the importance, or the risks, of this operation any further. But before I hand you over to Wing Commander Jarman I would just like to say that I know you have the skill and determination to succeed and I wish you luck. I look forward to seeing you all back here safely later on this afternoon."

Norman stood still, looking ahead, his mind working on the implications of the plan. He would never have guessed the much awaited special operation would turn out to be this. And by the silence in the room, no one else had anticipated it either.

The Wing Commander began by announcing the fifteen captains who would take part. The lead aircraft would be piloted by himself, he confirmed, and in his echelon of three would be Flight Lieutenant Lewin and Sergeant Drummond.

Once Norman knew he was on the trip he was only half listening as the rest of the list was read out. No one likes to be left out and in that sense Norman was pleased he was going. He also felt a touch of pride that his crew had been placed in the vanguard. Other than that he was unsure how he felt; attacking a heavily defended target in daylight had not been attempted for some time now due to the level of losses sustained.

The list completed, Wing Commander Jarman pulled back the cover on one of the easels to reveal a map of the west coast of France and pointed to La Rochelle about half way down towards Spain, a distance everyone quickly realised was way beyond any fighter escort. It was no surprise when the Wing Commander confirmed the force would be unescorted. He went on to describe the route, leaving the English coast at Lizard Point, near Land's End, heading low out to sea giving a wide berth to the French coast before turning in for the attack. Adopting this tactic, he explained, meant they would remain undetected and would give them the element of surprise since the Germans would not be expecting a third raid, let alone in the middle of the day. The return route would follow the route out, total distance 1,228 miles. Further detailed briefings would follow, he stated, then introduced the Squadron Intelligence Officer, Flight Lieutenant Mitchell.

The Flight Lieutenant pulled back the cover on the second easel revealing a detailed map of the La Rochelle area. He began by indicating where the Scharnhorst was moored and ran through the expected defences. Apart from the Scharnhorst's own defensive armament of 50 anti-aircraft guns, there was a flotilla of destroyers and ground defences that no doubt had been fortified prior to the arrival of the battleship. He also pointed to the small airfield immediately to the north of La Pallice where, he anticipated, there would be a strengthened Luftwaffe fighter unit. The timing of the arrival at La Pallice had been carefully planned, the expectation being that some of the enemy's fighters at La Pallice would be sent urgently to defend Brest at the commencement of the main raid there. Even so, he said, he expected stiff opposition which was why the element of surprise was so important and why holding formation was vital for their protection.

Flight Lieutenant Mitchell went on to explain the need for armour piercing bombs to penetrate the Scharnhorst's heavy deck plating and that the bombs should ideally be dropped from 19,000 feet. He then pulled back the cover of the third easel. This time there was a blown up reconnaissance photograph clearly showing the Scharnhorst lying alongside a lengthy jetty which stuck out from the land like a crooked finger.

"This is your target!" he said, pointing to the shape in the photograph. "In clear daylight it is unmistakeable."

Finally, he said the weather would not be a problem; the mist was clearing and the forecast was for a cloudless day here and across France.

"Any questions?" said Wing Commander Jarman stepping forward and looking round the gathering.

"What if an aircraft becomes detached from the main formation?" came a voice from the back.

"Priority will be to regain formation. Otherwise it will be the captain's decision whether to press on or not."

He paused. "No more questions? … Right, thank you, gentlemen; let's get on."

The forecasters and the locals were right. By the time Norman reached his aircraft the mist had been burned off by the heat of the sun and the sky was a clear summer blue. The fuselage of the black-painted aircraft felt warm to Norman's touch as he leaned against it chatting to the rest of the crew. At the end of the briefing Wing Commander Jarman had given a few stirring words of encouragement and, with the mist lifting and the mission clearly understood, the usual group spirit was evident, at least on the surface. Even Norman's spirits had lifted, although not entirely.

The Squadron Gunnery Officer had a similar message at their gathering after coffee, emphasising again the important role he expected the air gunners would play that day. He himself would be in the lead aircraft directing the gunnery defence from the astrodome as they had practiced. Still, Norman detected a slight underlying unease among the group at the predicted strength of the German defences at La Pallice – a disquiet he shared. The cloak of the night, their friend when in trouble, had been taken away from them. Daylight would allow them to see their target and undoubtedly improve hugely their chances of success but the enemy would be able to see them clearly in the battlefield of the wide open skies.

Norman had already made his initial checks inside the aircraft; ammunition trays full, parachute stowed on the ledge just inside the fuselage from his turret. What to wear was a conundrum. At 20,000 feet it could be minus 20°C but at low level his turret would be hot in the summer sun. Since most of the trip was planned at low level he decided to wear just the inner part of his flying suit over his battledress tunic and to have his gloves stowed nearby in case.

"I've got my sunglasses and sun hat for this trip," joked Flight Lieutenant Lewin.

"And I've got my swimming trunks too in case you put us in the drink!" was Sergeant Gourley's response.

Norman tapped his breast pocket checking his sunglasses were there along with the emergency supply of French francs he had signed for. He looked at his watch; it was a quarter past ten.

"Let's get aboard," said Flight Lieutenant Lewin climbing into the side hatch. The others followed, with Willie Finlayson and Norman the last two.

"Keep those engines turning, Willie," quipped Norman.

"I watch my dials and gauges like a hawk, don't you wurry," said Willie with a wink.

Norman climbed in last, secured the hatch and made his way aft. He clambered into his turret, fastened his lap strap and settled himself. His turret was almost like a second home to him, except there were no comforts. Everything was functional; throughout the entire warplane everything was purely functional.

Once Norman had completed his checks, including a satisfactory short burst of his machine guns into the ground, he looked outside at the line of fifteen aircraft, armed to the teeth and manned by skilled and determined airmen. This was the first time such a large force of the new four-engine Halifax aircraft had been assembled and as the sixty Rolls Royce engines started up Norman could not help feel a huge surge of pride. It was a magnificent sight and just at that moment he felt invincible.

As his aircraft lifted in turn into the air Norman looked at his watch; it was thirty-four minutes past ten. The navigator had said the round trip was just over seven hours, so back in time for tea, Norman thought. He always felt wonderfully exhilarated when first airborne and even today was no different despite his heightened apprehension.

They climbed into the airfield circuit to join the lead aircraft taking up their 'Red Number Two' starboard position and to await the others to form up before heading off. The plan was for the six aircraft from 76 Squadron to form up and set course, to be joined over Exeter by the formation from 35 Squadron.

"Captain to all crew," Norman heard over his earphones. "Squadron Leader Williams is held up with a jammed turret. Also engine problems mean one of his formation has to change aircraft. They are now due to join us over Swindon."

Norman saw the airfield below rapidly recede into the distance. To his left he could see the tail of Sergeant Drummond's aircraft gently bobbing alongside only twenty or so yards away and he could see clearly Flight Sergeant Begbie in the rear turret. But quickly Norman returned to scouring the skies for any threat, possible even though they were over English soil. Swindon slid below and behind them without any sight of their colleagues. As they held station over Exeter Norman saw formations approaching, soon identified as 35 Squadron aircraft.

"Captain to all crew. Leader says we will not wait for Squadron Leader Williams. Setting course for Lizard Point." The formations of 35 Squadron aircraft manoeuvred into position line astern and Norman could see Squadron Leader Bradley and his second pilot busy at the controls of the lead plane.

The main force, now four echelons of three aircraft each, was flying low, skirting just north of Dartmoor heading south-west. Norman could make out the villages and hamlets nestling in the folds of the moors, the bare rocky tors and the sliver threads of the streams glinting in the sun. As they crossed the coast near Looe he could see families on the beach waving energetically in support as the large force roared low over their heads.

"Captain to all crew. Setting course for Position 'A'."

As the Flight Lieutenant's voice came over the intercom, Norman saw below him the shape of Lizard Point disappear aft. He looked again at his watch; it was midday. The aircraft swung almost due south and dropped even lower skimming a sea of intense blue-green under a cloudless sky. The aircraft of 35

Squadron turned to line up on the new course, gently bobbing as the pilots worked to hold station, their shadows swiftly sliding over the shimmering surface of the sea.

The aircraft was quiet save for the rhythmical drumming of the four great engines. There was no chatter over the intercom. Everyone had settled down to concentrate on their role. It would be an hour's run to Position 'A' which was about fifty miles out to sea south-west of the island of Ushant at the north-western tip of France. The leg passed without incident.

"Captain to all crew. Position 'A'. Setting course for target. Climbing to bombing height. Estimated time over target 1429 hours."

Norman checked his watch. The time was four minutes to one o'clock. Moments later he heard and felt the surge of the engines as Flight Lieutenant Lewin started the long climb. His neighbour Sergeant Drummond's aircraft was still beside him and his 35 Squadron colleagues still held station to the rear. It was an odd sensation for Norman to have such company in contrast to his usual lonely vigil at night and he rather relished it.

Flight Lieutenant Lewin's voice came over the intercom. "Captain to rear gunner. Fishing vessels spotted below. Report anything suspicious." Norman acknowledged the order as he looked down. There were six small craft and two much larger vessels briefly in his sight and in the few seconds he had to scan them he could not make out anything suspicious. He reported as such. But were all the boats innocent or had their cover been blown, he asked himself? He hoped not; there was still 250 miles to go to the target.

Shortly, Norman's intercom clicked again. "Captain to all crew. Action stations!" For Norman this instruction meant he was to take his firing instructions from the Squadron Gunnery Officer in the lead aircraft. It also meant the beam guns were to be manned by the wireless operator and by flight engineer Willie if necessary. The formation had been climbing steadily but Norman sensed the rate of climb was a bit slow; he could tell the engines were not at maximum power. He thought this was possibly because the leader needed to keep the formation tight and was using less than full boost in case an aircraft fell behind and needed to catch up. He estimated they would be lucky to reach 15,000 feet let alone the intended 19,000 feet and as such they would be much more vulnerable to flak.

Norman looked at his watch once more. He reckoned there was about twenty-five minutes to go before they reached the target. Just then his intercom clicked again.

"Captain to all crew. Enemy destroyer below. Expect flak. Do not engage." Despite the heat inside his turret Norman felt a cold shiver pass through him. 'Bloody hell! That's torn it!' he said under his breath, realising their cover was almost definitely blown now. Surely, he thought, it must be all too obvious to the destroyer where we are heading.

All of a sudden there were explosions all around them and Norman felt the aircraft being buffeted about. Closer explosions sent small pieces of shrapnel rattling against the fuselage. Now he could see the ship far below and the flak hosing up at them. It was fairly accurate but the incident was over in a matter of seconds as they were quickly out of range of the ship's guns and all the aircraft pushed on apparently undamaged. When the immediate danger was passed Norman's concern turned to the probable consequences of this brief encounter for almost certainly the element of surprise was lost. He had to hope that most of the enemy's fighters at La Pallice had already gone north to Brest.

Not long afterwards, below to his port side Norman could see the outline of the Ile d'Yeu and beyond that the coast of France. They were just fifteen minutes away from the target.

A few moments later the intercom came on again. "Captain to all crew. Commencing bombing run. Intercom will stay fully on to receive instructions from leader. Heavy flak ahead surrounding target. Looks like a bumpy ride."

'This is it!' thought Norman tensing a further notch.

The next voice Norman heard was the Squadron Gunnery Officer in the lead aircraft just ahead of them. "Twenty plus fighters above ahead. More taking off from airfield. Await evasive action and firing instructions."

'So we have a reception party,' said Norman under his breath. Steeling himself to the task, he scoured the sky above for sight of the first enemy fighter.

"Fighter port quarter above astern preparing to attack. Pilots prepare for Rate One turn to port. … Wait. … Wait. Turn now! Rear and port gunners open fire at 300 yards." Norman picked up the fighter in his sights and followed it in closer and closer, and then pressed his trigger button when the fighter was at 300 yards distance. Ignoring the deafening noise of his four machine guns and the juddering of his turret, Norman kept the fighter in his sights and watched as almost immediately after he opened up his guns, the fighter pulled out and disappeared upwards without firing. So far so good, thought Norman, our fire power and evasion tactics are working.

Just then there were two almighty flak explosions which violently rocked the aircraft, peppering it with shrapnel, large chunks of which smashed into Norman's turret. It all happened in a flash; the Perspex bubble windscreen shattered and Norman put his arms up to protect himself. He suffered a heavy blow to his left thigh and felt a sharp pain in the ankle of his other leg. The wind was howling in and when he looked out of what remained of the Perspex windscreen he could see some debris spinning away and vapour trails streaming past him.

"Christ Almighty!" he said aloud. "Rear Gunner to Captain. Turret damaged. Testing." Still shaken by the severity of the blast he manoeuvred the turret and fired a short burst. All seemed to work. He was about to report as such when he heard Flight Lieutenant Lewin calling urgently, "Captain to Flight Engineer, check engines, I'm losing power. Rear Gunner, can you operate?"

"Turret operating," reported Norman.

"Number One engine out, Number two lose'een oil pressure," came Willie Finlayson's voice, his manner remarkably matter of fact.

Before Flight Lieutenant Lewin could respond, the Squadron Gunnery Officer's calm voice came on again. "Fighter starboard above astern attacking. Rate One turn starboard, now. Rear and starboard gunners open fire at 300 yards." Then more urgently he ordered, "Red Number Two close up, you're falling behind." He called again, more urgently still, "Red Number Two close up!"

"Losing power …" came the Flight Lieutenant's voice but his words were cut short. The fighter began firing its cannon at 400 yards and as Norman was about to pull his own trigger he heard loud explosions and terrible crashing coming from the front of the aircraft which juddered and jolted severely. Norman fired but the fighter was already pulling away fast. Vapour trails from both sides of the aircraft streamed past him now.

"Rear Gunner to Captain. Reporting vapour from both wings." There was no reply.

A moment later Willie Finlayson came on the intercom his voice now highly charged. "Captain and second pilot badly injured. Three engines out."

That sinking feeling of sheer terror came over Norman. 'Jesus!' he said under his breath. He had been frightened many times, but none like this. With their captain and co-pilot possibly incapacitated, as the senior officer he had to take charge of the situation. His training took over despite his own painful injury.

"Come in Captain, second pilot. Are you in control?" Norman called. Again there was no response.

"Rear gunner to all crew. I've taken command. Stand by!" he said using the phrase for use in a bail out situation. "Flight Engineer, any hope of pilots gaining control?"

"No, they're both in a bad way and the cockpit's been badly shot up," was the swift and grim reply.

"Rear gunner to all crew. Bail out! Bail out!"

As he gave the order he tried to centre his turret. But there was no power. He quickly leaned down for the manual lever and yanked it hard several times till the turret was central and he could open the small doors at the back to reach for his parachute. He grabbed the parachute and pulled it through, but to his horror he saw the front of the pack was in tatters. He looked out. Black smoke now streamed from the burning engines and from their trails Norman could see the aircraft was arcing down in a slow spiral. You've no choice, you have to get out, he said to himself and he clipped the parachute pack on, undid his lap strap and pumped the manual handle furiously until he had turned the turret through 90 degrees. He dragged off his flying helmet and was immediately aware of the roar from the rushing wind. Gritting his teeth, he pushed on the turret with both arms and tumbled backwards out of the turret into the open sky.

One, two, three, he counted and then gave the ripcord a firm pull. He knew that if the parachute did not deploy or hold together, death was only moments away. Instantly a white flash passed his face as the pilot chute was released; then a huge flurry of white seemed to smother him. In a second that disappeared and he felt a violent jerk between his legs as the main parachute opened.

All of a sudden everything went quiet. He muttered thanks to God that his parachute had held and for a brief moment he had the weird sensation he was actually floating upwards until gradually he became orientated. Although seconds earlier he had thought death imminent, this strange floating sensation produced a sort of euphoria in him. He raised his arms to grab the harness above his head and as he did so he looked up. His parachute had hundreds of holes in it; spots of light shone in the shadow of the canopy like stars in the night. Alarm replaced euphoria in an instant. That blast of shrapnel had turned his parachute into a colander. Is it going to hold, was Norman's first concern, scanning the canopy for signs for any tearing? Reassuringly it had not ripped apart when it deployed so maybe, he thought, just maybe it will hold together long enough.

Norman looked down and the scene immediately took his thoughts away from his own plight. To his horror he saw his plane crash into the sea just off the coast. There was a tremendous crash and a huge explosion of spray. His heart sank – it was obvious no one could survive that. Fearfully he cast around. There was one parachutist not far away, higher up. By the lanky shape beneath it that could be Willie Finlayson, he thought. Looking over his other shoulder he could see one more parachute in the distance, much lower and way out to sea. That made only three parachutists out of a crew of seven. Overcome with emotion that four of his friends had just died, tears filled his eyes.

He shook his head briefly in an effort to clear his mind, realising he could not dwell on the fate of his colleagues and he began to assess his own situation. He was out over the sea, gently heading for the land which fringed a huge, wide open bay so he willed the wind to carry him to the land as he certainly did not fancy ditching in the sea. Satisfied he was all right for the moment he searched around again. Over his shoulder in the distance there was still a savage barrage going on and a thick pall of dark smoke lay heavily over the La Pallice area to the south. There were still many fighters in the air; one sounded close overhead but he could not see it and he hoped the pilot would not fire at a defenceless parachutist. He glanced the other way and thought he saw a couple of bombers heading away north. Despite his own perilous state he called after them somewhat weakly, "Good luck chaps! Make it back!"

By now his hands were nearly numb with cold and from gripping his harness so tightly, and he realised he was shaking like a leaf. Everything had happened so quickly and he was still very frightened. Only a few moments ago the earth seemed a long way down but all of a sudden it was rapidly coming up towards him. A new fear hit him. The holes in his canopy were allowing his descent to be much faster than normal. Better to fall into the sea and make a swim for it, he now thought, but having no control, in trepidation, all he could do was hang below the canopy. Helpless, he looked down and judged that he would land some hundred yards or more from the shore. He braced himself for the fast approaching impact, unsure how deep the muddy-looking water would be. But before he could think any more he hit the water with a huge jolt that twisted him half around causing excruciating pain in his injured ankle. The water splashed all over him, so much so he thought he had gone right under. But when it all settled he found himself up to his armpits, not in water but in deep mud. Just an inch of water lapped at his chest. He had landed spear-like in the thick, slimy mud of the bay.

He put out his arms thinking this would stop him sinking in any further. He tried to lift himself, gently at first, then he pushed harder but his hands felt no resistance and just sank into the mud. He panicked when he could not immediately pull his arms back out; they seemed to be held by the clinging mud. Only by leaning this way and that could he extricate his arms. He tried lifting his good leg, but it was firmly held. A sense of desperation flooded over him. Surely he had not survived so far only to sink beyond trace into the mud or to be drowned by the tide. He cleared his head. He needed help. He cast around and saw Willie who had landed quite close by.

"Willie, Willie, is that you? It's Mac. Are you all right? Help me, I'm stuck fast!" he shouted at the top of his voice in the direction of the figure he could see also in the mud about fifty yards away but much nearer the shoreline.

"I'm awright, Mac. I'm shap'een to get out but I can't," Willie called back.

"Try harder," shouted Norman.

"It's no good. I'm stuck!"

"Call for help, then. We need help!"

They both started yelling at the tops of their voices with what strength they had left. Meanwhile, almost imperceptibly yet inexorably, the water about them rose with the flat calm incoming tide. Then Norman saw what he thought were some people on the shore, in the distance on the top of the bank. They were too far away to make out but they were definitely people. His elation that rescue was at hand was almost instantly quashed by the chilling thought they might be soldiers; but their situation was too desperate to worry about capture – rescue was the imperative.

"Over there, Willie," Norman shouted frantically, pointing in the direction of the figures. Willie too saw the small group and started shouting and waving his arms. Norman tried to do likewise but he could not raise much energy now; he knew he was weakening fast.

Chapter 6

Motionless, young Fernand and his two companions stared at the aerial battle. The pall of smoke over La Pallice grew heavier and the noise reached a frightening crescendo. They could make out the fighter aircraft wheeling high up in the blue, their trails making it look as if the sky was being brutally scratched by some disturbed vandal. None of them spoke – just stood, awestruck, hands by their sides, watching.

"My God!" said Marcel eventually, pointing. He was the first to speak but they had all seen what he was pointing at. One big aircraft with a twin trail of smoke was in a slow arc downwards, obviously severely damaged.

"Look, a parachutist! Someone's jumped out!" It was Marcel again, his pointing finger jabbing to direct the others urgently to the small dot of white he had seen in the far distance.

"That aircraft's heading this way. It's going down! It's going to crash!" Claude cried out. "My God! It looks as though it's going to crash right near us," he added with alarm. But no one moved; it was as if they were transfixed by the scene, rooted to the spot.

As the aircraft approached they could make out its detail; four engines, one on fire, smoke streaming from both wings. It was as if it was fixed in its trajectory, almost as though it was under control, but it was not levelling out. It just came down and down in a wide arc heading for them with no undercarriage visible, looking doomed.

"Another parachute. And another!" cried Marcel. None of them knew how many crew the aircraft carried but they waited with bated breath for more to bail out. The roar from the aircraft got louder and the pitch higher as it headed directly at the three men who were mesmerised at the sight of the aircraft's impending doom.

Marcel eventually shouted, "Get down!" fearful the plane might crash almost on top of them.

They all dived down the bank for cover, craning their necks as the plane thundered over them so low they could see the RAF markings, the flames from the burning engines and the damage to the undercarriage. It was so close they could even see the rivets on the side of the fuselage. Were those the faces of the pilots he saw, young Fernand wondered as the plane careered over him? It was only a fraction of a second and he could not be sure what he saw; and knowing their imminent fate he was glad he could not be certain. The plane's speed meant it overshot the land to crash into the sea just beyond La Pointe. There was a deafening crash and a huge plume of spray – then it all went quiet. Young Fernand's heart sank. It was almost too much for him to bear that he had most probably witnessed the death of several men. Marcel and Claude were similarly affected and all three stood unmoving in respectful silence. In the background the rumble of the distant battle continued just as ferociously as before.

Young Fernand turned to see what had happened to the parachutists. One was about to land in the shallows several hundred yards away. He was descending much faster than the other one and seconds later hit the water with a splatter rather than a splash. The tattered parachute collapsed and crumpled on the muddy water next to the man. When everything settled, young Fernand could see just a head and shoulders above the water.

"He's in dead trouble – he won't get out of there on his own," said young Fernand immediately recognising the man's plight. Without a second thought he started climbing up the dyke.

"At least he's moving," declared Claude as the airman began to struggle.

"I tell you he won't get out of there on his own and the tide's coming in," said young Fernand forcefully. "We must help him and quick!"

"The other one doesn't look as though he'll make land either," said Marcel. Sure enough, as they watched, the other parachutist landed in mud, nearer to them and nearer to the shore where the tide had not quite reached. He went into the mud up to his middle. Young Fernand looked out to sea where they had seen the first parachutist but could no longer see him.

"Come on. We must help them," urged young Fernand again. "Bring some tools." He set off carrying his spade and the others followed for a short distance until Claude suddenly called out, "Whoa! Stop! Wait a minute." The other two stopped and looked back at him. "We can't get involved. Think about it a minute. If the Germans find we helped these British airmen we'll be in real trouble, there could be reprisals and we could even be shot. There have been warnings. I'm serious. We can't get involved. I have a wife and children. I have to think of them."

Marcel started nodding in agreement. "He's right. There's been official warnings. It's too dangerous. I have a family too."

Young Fernand could not believe what he was hearing. "They need help – urgently! Now!" he retorted.

"We can tell Monsieur Millet. He can inform the authorities; they'll get help. It will be up to them," said Marcel.

"They need help now!" young Fernand shouted at them. "There's no time to get help."

"I'm going back," said Claude although he looked uncomfortable saying so.

"Me too," said Marcel avoiding young Fernand's eyes.

"You can't leave them," he shouted even louder, but the two men turned round and started to walk in the opposite direction. "You can't just go – they'll drown!" he yelled after them but they carried on without responding.

Hesitating, young Fernand considered what to do. His father's words came into his mind about being strong and not afraid. He knew what his father would do. He looked at the two parachutists one of whom was waving frantically and shouting and he knew it was certain they would drown before any other help could be organised. Convinced his father would not turn his back on them, he told himself neither would he. Ignoring Claude's warnings, he ran towards the end of the dyke. He already had a plan in his head. He just hoped the boat that used to be moored at the end of the dyke was still there; without that it was hopeless. He ran hard, waving to the two parachutists to say he had seen them. 'Thank heaven,' he said to himself when he saw the boat was there. He dropped his shovel and ran down the bank. There was just enough water in the channel to launch the boat and he pushed it out, jumping aboard. But he could only find one oar. "Damn it!" he swore out loud. "Where's the other one?" He searched frantically around the bottom of the boat but it was not there. 'I'll just have to punt it,' he decided quickly.

Young Fernand manoeuvred the flat bottomed boat along the narrow channel that led into the bay eventually meeting the incoming tide. He kept looking over to the man who had sunk the deepest, waving at him to indicate he was coming for him first. He punted the boat a little further out into the bay until there was just enough water beneath the boat for him to turn off the channel. By now he was further out than Norman but his plan was to approach the airman from the sea. When the airman was directly between him and the shore he turned the boat again now inching towards Norman who was stuck facing inland. Hoping and praying the boat could get to the airman before it beached on the mud, he edged the boat forward. But ten feet away the prow of the boat rose up having run onto the mud. Sticking the oar in the mud he tried to drag the boat nearer but it was no good. He clambered to the prow and picked up the painter but the short rope was not long enough to act as a life line. Even reaching out with the oar he was several feet short. The water was beginning to lap over Norman's shoulders now and young Fernand thought that even if he waited for the tide to rise another inch or two he still might not get the boat near enough in time.

Norman had been frantically turning round as far as he could to see his rescuer's approach and began to panic when the boat stopped short. By then he had realised the tide was coming in and time was running out for them.

"I'm nearly there – hold on!" young Fernand called. He had an idea. He saw that Norman had gathered his parachute around him, perhaps in hope of some buoyancy. If I can get hold of some of the parachute, he thought, I can drag him out with that.

"Throw me the parachute," shouted young Fernand. Norman turned round looking anxious and perplexed but did nothing as he did not understand.

"Throw me your parachute," repeated young Fernand gesturing with his arms for Norman to throw his parachute over his shoulder. This time Norman caught an English word, parachute, and then understood from the gesture what his rescuer wanted. He grabbed the top of the parachute and summoning all his strength hurled it over his shoulder. Because it was soggy and muddy it landed only a few feet behind him, still six feet short of the boat. Young Fernand called and gestured for Norman to try again. Not comprehending the words but understanding the gesture, Norman tried again but it landed no nearer the boat.

"Wait," called young Fernand and picked up the oar. Leaning out as far as he could he fed out the oar. The blade just about reached the parachute and he was able to catch some of the canopy on the end. Slowly, gently so as not to lose it, he dragged the parachute towards him until he was able to reach out and grab it. He edged back into the boat pulling the parachute canopy with him. He yanked it hand over hand until he was pulling on the suspension lines, eventually feeling resistance. Young Fernand had heard in the past how difficult it was to pull people out of the mud as a vacuum formed holding the person tight and that vacuum had to be broken. Bracing one of his feet against the thwart he leaned back and began to increase the tension. But the boat just slid further onto the mud. He pulled again and felt some resistance as the prow of the boat pushed mud up in front of it. He kept the tension on and gradually increased it, pulling harder and harder.

With water now lapping over his shoulders Norman realised this plan was his only hope – this just had to work.

"Pull, pull!" called Norman who could sense some movement.

Young Fernand too thought he felt some give but was not sure if the airman was moving or the boat was sliding forward. He maintained the pressure but the strain was beginning to tell. He could not keep it up much longer yet he knew if he relaxed all his effort would be wasted. He had to keep going. A bit more, he told himself, a bit more.

All of a sudden with a squelching noise Norman slid out, and young Fernand crashed backwards into the transom and nearly fell out. At the same time Norman gave a loud yell from the sharp pain in his ankle. When the commotion settled young Fernand got up on his knees to see Norman stretched out on the mud with his head just above water near the prow.

"Don't move, don't move!" ordered young Fernand. "I'll bring you round the stern." Norman did not understand but in any case could not move because the pain was so severe. Using the parachute harness young Fernand dragged Norman round to the stern and started to pull him over the transom. Norman tried to help but he was so weak he did little other than hold on to the transom. Norman was a dead weight and young Fernand struggled despite his youthful strength. Eventually with a final heave Norman slithered into the bottom of the boat like a caught eel.

Relief flooded through Norman as he lay in the bottom of the boat, his pain almost forgotten. Exhausted and breathing heavily he looked up at young Fernand to thank him but could utter no more than a breathless and barely audible, "Thank you".

Young Fernand who was seated on the thwart and who was also breathing heavily returned a brief smile. There they stayed for a few moments to catch their breath.

Young Fernand looked over to where the other airman was stuck and seeing the tide had reached him knew they had to get moving. He had already worked out that he would have to take this airman to the shore and come out again because he needed the boat to be as light as possible.

"We must go," he said to Norman, propping him up against the transom and packing the parachute alongside him. He dug the blade of the oar in the mud and pushed the boat backwards. At first it did not budge. Young Fernand pushed and rocked the boat at the same time to lubricate the underside and gradually it slid off the mud until it was floating free. With strong pulls he manoeuvred the boat back into the channel and punted them to the shore. He beached the prow and jumped out, pulling the boat out further.

"Come on, come on!" he urged Norman, but Norman's weak efforts on the slippery floor of the boat meant young Fernand had to clamber back on board to help him. It was a struggle to get Norman over the thwart, over the prow and onto the bank where he eventually slumped, shocked, gasping for breath and utterly exhausted.

"Stay there," young Fernand ordered totally needlessly. "I'll be back."

Even though Norman did not understand the words, young Fernand's gesture was clear and in any case Norman was simply unable to do anything else, struggling to utter again a weak, "Thank you." His ankle was still hurting badly and instinctively he put his hand down to support the damaged leg but he could not see the injury as he was covered in mud.

Young Fernand turned and waved at the second airman to say he was coming to get him now. He pushed the boat off the bank and jumped aboard. Buoyed by his success with Norman and expecting this rescue to be the easier, he felt a second wind as he paddled out along the channel. Following the same procedure as before young Fernand brought the boat in towards Willie from behind. By now the tide was several inches above Willie's waist. This time, however, Willie was ready to assist; he had watched Norman's rescue and had gathered up his parachute in preparation. As before the boat slid onto the mud well short of Willie. Neither spoke, each understood his part. Willie had been getting more and more anxious to be rescued as the water had crept up him but as the boat approached he began to feel confident of rescue. When young Fernand clambered to the prow Willie threw his parachute over his shoulder. Because he was higher out of the water than Norman was he was able to get more leverage and the parachute this time just reached the boat. Young Fernand gathered it in and began his pull, gradually increasing the tension. Willie slid out much more quickly than Norman and moments later he was in the boat.

"Thanks. Thanks," said Willie leaning forward offering a handshake which young Fernand took, smiling. "Luck'ee for us you were around otherwise we were goners!"

Fernand wanted Willie to sit in the bottom at the stern. "Sit! Sit!" he ordered pointing. Willie did not understand the words but understood what he should do and gathered up his parachute. They set off and shortly reached the shore where Norman lay.

Willie was able to stagger off the boat by himself and he sank to his knees by Norman.

"Mac, are you awright?"

"Beginning to get my breath back," said Norman. "Nearly had it there."

"Would be gone if it hadn't been for this chap," said a relieved Willie. "Some bloke – saved our lives without doubt!"

"Some bloke indeed," added Norman looking up at young Fernand who had secured the boat and was coming over to them.

"What can we say? Thanks again – yes, thanks," Willie said to young Fernand, choking with emotion. Norman, who was now trembling in reaction to everything that had happened, just nodded in agreement.

Young Fernand sat down and a strange silence fell over them. The two airmen knew the fate of the rest of the crew and realised what a close shave they had had. Young Fernand felt awkward not being able to talk to the two men and was wondering what to do next. It was Willie who spoke first. He had hesitated expecting Norman, the officer, to take charge but he could see Norman was struggling and in shock.

"We must get out aw here," he said well aware their emergency was far from over. "We must find somewhere to hide tonight and then make our way south towards Spain somehow. The Germans will come look'een for us. We must bury our parachutes. We must be quick and get a head start." Willie stood up, unclipped his harness and leant down saying, "Come on Mac, I'll give you a hand. Unclip your harness. I'll bury the parachutes first. Under the boat will do." He gathered the two soggy, muddied parachutes and dropped them at the side of the boat, and with the oar pushed them into the soft mud under the flat bottom of the boat. Once young Fernand realised what Willie was doing he grabbed his shovel and lent a hand. Then, with Willie's help Norman tried to stand up.

"Aaah!" he cried out with pain as he set down his right foot. He nearly fell but was steadied by Willie and by young Fernand who leapt up to lend a hand.

"It's my ankle," said Norman, pain still showing on his face. "I can't put any weight on it. It may need some strapping."

"We'll see to it la'er. We must get go'een. Lean on me," said Willie.

They tried a few steps but it was obvious to them both they could not get far.

"It's no good," said Norman who paused momentarily then continued, "You go, Willie. I'll hide up and set off later when the ankle's settled down."

"I can't leave you, you'll get caught," said Willie. "We'll both hide for a wee while and decide la'er what to do. Per'aps this chap will help us hide."

Young Fernand had watched as they tried to move off, then listened perplexed at these exchanges as he no idea what they were saying.

"What's the French for 'hide'?" Norman said rhetorically, trying to think back to his schoolboy French lessons.

"Aaw! I didn't learn any French," answered Willie thinking he was expected to know.

"Cacher; I think it's cacher, like a cache of hidden treasure," said Norman. Hesitantly he turned to young Fernand and said in French with the best accent he could summon, "To hide … we to hide."

"You know French!" said Willie.

"No. No." replied Norman. "Only at school; long ago."

Amazingly young Fernand understood. "Hide?" he asked. Remembering a place nearby, he said, "I know somewhere. I'll take you. It's near. Come with me."

But he spoke too quickly for Norman to pick up the words and Norman could only look at him blankly. Gesturing young Fernand said again, "Come, come. Quickly."

With Norman in between the two men they started to scramble up the bank of the dyke, young Fernand carrying his father's precious shovel wedged in his belt. It was a struggle but they made it.

"We walk along the bottom in order that we won't be seen," said young Fernand indicating they should go down the other side of the bank. It was even more difficult going down than up. On reaching the bottom, young Fernand said, "This way," pointing eastwards. Norman and Willie had given up listening to young

Fernand's words and just followed his signals. The trio staggered slowly along at the foot of the dyke towards the section where young Fernand had been working, occasionally stopping to rest.

Shortly they came to a small open-sided hut made of old planks set into the dyke as shelter for farm workers, there being no trees or any other sort of cover from the elements for miles around. It had a rough bench in it and they eased Norman down gently to sit there. The other two stood breathing heavily after their efforts.

"We won't need our suits, Willie. We must hide them," Norman said after catching his breath.

"He has a spade," said Willie pointing to the shovel by young Fernand's side. "Ask 'im."

"To hide," said Norman to young Fernand in French, tugging at his suit and then making a digging motion which young Fernand seemed to understand. Beginning to overcome his shock and starting to think in escape mode, he then addressed Willie.

"We should hide our tunics too. Get the French money, the maps and take off the compass buttons. Empty them of anything we might need."

They struggled out of their wet flying suits and took off their damp uniform jackets and checked all the pockets. Norman had gingerly removed his injured leg from his mud-covered flying suit to reveal a ragged and bloody tear in his boot which made him worry that the injury was more serious than he first thought; but he said nothing. His other leg hurt where he had taken a blow and getting out of his suit he felt a sharp pain in his back which he had twisted on landing. But it was his ankle that worried him most. Willie took his watch from his tunic pocket, saying, "Will need this. Strap broke the other day." He put the watch in his trouser pocket and dropped the jackets by the suits, indicating to young Fernand they should all be buried. Young Fernand nodded in agreement, dragged the soggy suits and damp tunics along the bank a bit and started to dig a shallow hole next to a pile of hay. When the hole was covered over with earth he grabbed some hay from the nearby pile and spread it over the obvious disturbance.

"What do we do now?" said Willie when the two had returned to the hut. "Wait till nightfall? We'll need su'heen to eat to keep our strength up. Maybe this chap could get us some food. What's the French for food?"

Norman thought but could not remember the French noun for food. "Food?" he tried in English, mimicking eating with a knife and fork. Willie rubbed his stomach in emphasis.

"You are hungry? You want food?" asked young Fernand. "Stay here a moment. I'll come back with some food. Wait here." Norman caught enough French to make a guess at what young Fernand had said and nodded. Young Fernand ran off not forgetting his father's shovel. He ran the short distance back to where Marcel and Claude had resumed work on the dyke. When he appeared they stopped work and questioned him.

"What's happened to the airmen?" they wanted to know. "Where are they?" They had seen at a distance their rescue and that young Fernand had taken them over the dyke and out of sight.

Young Fernand stared at them momentarily still angry at their reluctance to help, then grabbed his canvas bag with his food in it and ran off without saying anything. He returned to the two airmen and proffered his bag. Willie took it, opened it and his eyes lit up. "Food!" he exclaimed taking out some of the bread and meat that young Fernand had saved for later. "And wine, too!" Young Fernand smiled with satisfaction on seeing the looks on their faces.

"What now?" repeated Willie between mouthfuls.

"You go," Norman said again knowing his injury would seriously prejudice their escape. "You have the best chance of a home run without me. You get going before the Germans come looking for us. I'll hide and set off when the ankle's a bit better."

Willie was torn between going, which he recognised was his best chance, and staying out of loyalty to his colleague who needed help. He made up his mind to stay, for now at least. On his own and having no language was daunting and it was easier to contemplate staying with his officer who had some French and with a local man who seemed willing to help them.

"We'll talk about that tomorrow," he said to Norman. "We'll hide and recover and maybe your ankle will be better with some stra'peen. Then we'll decide what to do."

Norman thought about pulling rank as he considered splitting up now the better option, but somewhat selfishly agreed to Willie's proposal and said, "All right, we'll decide tomorrow."

Young Fernand started to get anxious as the longer he stayed with the airmen the more dangerous it was. He tried to guess what they were saying but could understand nothing. He could not just leave them having rescued them and one of them unable to make a getaway. His father would know what to do, he thought. If the men stayed here hidden he could bring his father at dusk and work out the best way to help them evade German hands.

"You must hide now," he said. "Hide," he repeated slowly to Norman reckoning he would understand the word. "I'll bring my father this evening."

"Hide, yes," said Norman nodding agreement. He recognised the word 'father' and 'evening' and guessed what was meant.

"Hide, there," young Fernand said pointing to the pile of hay just along from the hut.

Norman nodded again, explaining to Willie what he thought he had understood. "He's suggesting we hide under the hay, Willie," said Norman, "It's as good a place as any. I think he's saying he'll come back this evening with his father." Again Norman nodded at young Fernand and started to get up. Willie helped him hop over to the stack of hay and the pair burrowed in at the bottom while young Fernand made good the outside. Young Fernand leant down and said, "You'll be fine there. Till this evening." Picking up his bag and checking there was no evidence of the airmen's presence about, he took off to resume his work.

"What's happening?" asked Claude urgently when he reached them. "Where are the airmen?"

"They've gone," young Fernand lied, rather brusquely so as to deter further discussion.

"Wonder if they'll escape. At least you saved them from drowning, Fernand" said Claude, a touch of grudging admiration in his voice. "Wouldn't want to be in their shoes, though."

"Nor me," said young Fernand quietly, turning away to clamber down the dyke making it obvious he did not want to talk.

His ploy succeeded; Claude and Marcel looked at each other, a look which said, 'Say no more.' Somewhat sullenly they returned to their work. The last hour of the afternoon continued in almost silence with only the odd, necessary exchange directly to do with the task at hand.

Under the hay, Norman and Willie settled down. The hay was not heavy and they had made narrow tunnels with which to ventilate their hiding place and also made spy-holes which enabled them to look in both directions along the dyke. They made themselves as comfortable as possible; their damp clothes were drying and they were not cold.

"We must listen carefully for any movement outside and talk in whispers only when necessary," said Norman. From then on, as their heads were only inches apart, a whisper was enough.

"But can we trust that chap?" Willie asked. "Should we wait till he's well gone then try to make for another hide'een place? We have a map and a compass."

"He saved our lives, at great risk to himself if he gets caught. We'll stay here till it's dark and if no one has come as he said, then we will move. We need to rest." Moving his wrist up to his face, carefully so as not to make any rustling sound, Norman said, "It's half past three now. It will be a while before it gets dark. Let's rest." They fell silent. But neither slept as their minds raced trying to come to grips with the predicament they now found themselves in. They were also tormented with thoughts of the crew who did not bail out; horrific flashes that kept repeating. Norman had visions of Cherry watching out for his plane to return and his parents being handed the dreaded 'missing in action' telegram.

"Here comes the Inspector," announced Marcel after he had looked up and saw Monsieur Gaudin approaching with Monsieur Millet the foreman. The three workers stopped what they were doing and waited for the officials to arrive. On arrival there were the customary introductions and handshakes all round.

"What an air raid that was!" said Monsieur Millet. "Never seen anything like that in my life. Terrible! And that plane that came down; must have been very near you."

"Crashed into the sea beyond La Pointe," informed Claude. "We thought it was going to crash right on us at one point. Really frightening."

"What happened to those parachutists we saw? Did you see what happened to them?"

Young Fernand butted in almost before Monsieur Millet had finished speaking. "Don't know," he lied again, "They didn't come our way. Perhaps they made for l'Aiguillon." His glance at Marcel and Claude told them to keep quiet.

"Lucky to be alive, them two. The Germans will soon be swarming all over here looking for them, no doubt. There's little chance of them getting away, I reckon; nowhere to hide around here for miles."

"How's the work progressing?" asked Monsieur Gaudin bringing the topic round to the matter of the repairs.

"It's been good," said Claude. "There's enough material here and we should finish today. It needed three of us though. Fernand here has been a real help."

To his relief that remark told young Fernand he was not about to be denounced. He watched as the two officials and the two council workers carefully inspected the repairs. There was a stamping of feet to test the work and there were approving remarks. Another glance by young Fernand at his colleagues this time conveyed his unspoken thanks and the three returned to their work. Satisfied, the officials shook hands all round again and began their long walk back to the main party. Finishing the repairs in good time the three of them collected up their tools and with one last approving look at their work set off back along the dyke. The two older men passed the odd remark but said nothing about the afternoon's events. Young Fernand remained silent, his mind turning over what he would say to his father. He was anxious to be on his way but had to restrain himself; everything must appear normal, he kept telling himself. When they met up with the main party, again all the talk was about the air raid. Young Fernand joined in briefly then said he had to go. Waving goodbye to Claude, Marcel and the others he rode off, pedalling harder when he thought his haste would not be noticed, his heart racing with the exertion and with nervous excitement; this was the most extraordinary news that he had ever brought to his father. How he had kept himself under control all afternoon he would never know.

Young Fernand raced through the village causing several elderly ladies to remark at his reckless and inconsiderate speed. He turned into the farmyard and dropped the bike to the floor outside the kitchen door. He rushed inside calling, "Where's Papa? I must speak to Papa straight away. It's important!"

Rose was sitting at the kitchen table sewing. She was startled by her brother's sudden appearance. "What's the matter? What's happened?" she asked immediately curious at his outburst.

"I must tell Papa. Where is he?"

"He and Maman are with Grandpapa and Grandmaman. They'll be back soon. What is it, though? You look in a right state."

"I've raced all the way home. Go and get him Rose. I need to talk to him now. But I don't want to go over to Grandpapa's."

"I'm busy. I have to finish this," she said not willing to be ordered around by her brother.

"It's urgent, Rose. Take the bike."

Seeing he was out of breath and clearly agitated and with the offer of the bike, she began to relent. "You must tell me something. I have to tell Papa something," she urged getting up.

"Just that something very important happened at the dyke – that's all."

"Is everything all right? Are you all right?" Rose asked anxiously. "Papa told us he thought there was a big air raid over La Rochelle when he was in the fields. We heard something too. And he said he saw one aeroplane very low over the bay. Is it about that?"

"I'm all right. Just go. Quickly!" he said ignoring her question.

Rose took a concerned backward glance at her brother as she went out of the door but he had his back to her so she learned no more. She picked up the bike and hurried off to her grandparent's house on the southern edge of the village. When she arrived she went straight in. Her parents and grandparents were out in the garden which overlooked the flat fields in the direction of the bay. Her father was still talking about the aircraft he had seen earlier which he thought must have crashed.

"Papa! Papa!" called Rose waving briefly to her grandparents. They all looked round to where Rose stood in the doorway. Rose beckoned to her father to come over. "Papa. I have something to tell you."

"What is it," he said as he walked over to her, as always pleased to see his pretty daughter but wondering why she had not come over to greet her grandparents.

"It's Fernand. He wants you to come to the house now. It's urgent, he says; something happened at the dyke. But he wouldn't tell me any more."

Her father looked at her quizzically; not used to being summoned in this way he was somewhat irritated.

"Is he all right?"

"He says so. But he has raced all the way home and he says it is very important." Rose added, "From the look on his face I think it is important."

Her father became worried, wondering if it was to do with the aircraft crashing. "Come on then, we'd better go," he said. Rose's mother had been watching the exchanges but was out of earshot. Seeing they were about to leave she called over, "What's happening?"

"Fernand's back. Something he needs to tell me. Won't be long," Rose's father called back not wanting to worry Renée.

Rose's father peddled with her on the crossbar. On the way he asked again what it was all about but Rose insisted she knew no more. Young Fernand was seated at the kitchen table having a drink when they got back. He got up when he heard them and took a couple of steps towards the door as they came in.

"Papa. You'll never guess …" he started

"What's this all about?" his father butted in; his concern not totally overcoming his irritation.

Without hesitation young Fernand began to tell the story of the afternoon's events. The words spilled out in a rather jumbled fashion and with much animation in his haste to tell his father what he had seen and done.

At one point his father interrupted, "I saw that plane coming down, way in the distance. I thought it must have crashed." Astonished he added rhetorically, "It came right over your heads?"

"I reckon it crashed in the sea near Eperon Plage," young Fernand surmised.

"Oh no!" exclaimed Rose, shocked. "Adélina and I were there yesterday."

Young Fernand carried on without responding, telling how he rescued the two airmen. His father and sister just stood in near disbelief.

"They're hidden under a pile of hay near the shelter," ended young Fernand. "I didn't know what else to do." With wide eyes he looked earnestly at his father waiting, hoping and praying for approval.

Rose too looked at her father for his reaction, her own expression incredulous. Her father was stunned yet appeared at the same time to be quickly turning over in his mind the implications of this startling news.

"Who knows?" was his first question. The question was given quite sharply as though his military training, albeit from many years ago, had begun to take over.

"Claude and Marcel saw me rescue the airmen but I don't think they will tell anyone. I told them and the others the airman had gone."

"Do you think the Germans saw anything?"

"I don't know," answered young Fernand, "Their parachutes may have been seen by one of the fighters. There weren't any soldiers around. We didn't see any all day."

"Will they be able to escape the Germans on their own, do you think?"

"They've got maps on pieces of cloth and I saw some money. But the injured one can hardly walk. The other one might. They are both pretty shaken up though. They need food and drink."

"What are we going to do, Papa?" asked Rose. She could see her father was making up his mind to do something.

"They need help," he said resolutely. "We must help them. No one else knows where they are hidden and no one else must know. Only we can help, so we must. It's down to us. I'll go and see them. Then we can decide what to do. Rose, find us some food to take."

Rose had seen her father in this decisive mode before. He could become steely determined, unwavering, directing and expecting his instructions to be unchallenged. She idolized him in this commanding mood. She envied his strength of character, was reassured by it and in her way tried to emulate it. There were occasions when she did not totally agree with him but her respect for him suppressed any rebellion – Papa has spoken so that is what we are doing.

Swept up with her father's plan Rose offered to help. "I could come with you. I could try to speak with them in English otherwise you won't be able to help them."

Her brother was looking worried, concerned at the warnings Claude and Marcel had sounded about getting involved with the airmen.

"Wait a minute, Papa," he said. "Claude and Marcel wouldn't help me. They said there could be serious trouble for helping British airmen. The Germans will be looking for them. We must be careful, Papa."

"I know. But they need help," was all their father replied. "You had better come with me, Rose. We'll go on the bike; that will arouse less suspicion if we meet any soldiers. First get the food and drink to take. We shouldn't be too long before we go. Fernand, you stay here and tell your mother. You have done enough for today. You did well to rescue the airmen; very well. Now tell me again exactly where you left them hidden. Do you know their names?"

"No, Papa. And I didn't give them mine either. I didn't think of asking names." He went on to tell his father where to find the men. Meanwhile Rose put the food in her brother's canvas bag.

Shortly they set off on the bike, Rose balanced on the crossbar with her father's powerful arms reaching round her to the handlebars, holding her in. Young Fernand stood in the kitchen doorway. He had been elated at hearing his father's words of praise, but now he was concerned seeing them ride off, apprehensive at what might happen.

It was a long ride through the village and across the fields down to the Maroc dyke. The pathway along the top of the dyke was too rough to ride along with two on the bike so they had to walk, Rose's father pushing the bike. They talked briefly about what to say when they reached the airmen. Mostly Rose was deep in thought trying to remember some English words and phrases she might need. She was totally thrilled to be on this mission with her father, and for the moment set aside her brother's warnings. This was grown-up business; her father needed her because she could do something he could not – speak some English. It was a beautiful evening; the warm breeze brushed her hair and they were on their way to an exciting rendezvous – she felt so alive.

They did not meet anyone on the way and saw only a few figures working in the fields in the distance. The omens were good; no German patrols. Rose was not quite sure what her father was going to do when they arrived at the airmen's hideout. Her brother had said one of them had an injured leg and could not possibly escape on foot. What would they be like, these airmen, she wondered? They must be wonderful men to fly those huge planes she had seen pictures of in magazines. Would they be handsome? She had heard that many were young and very dashing.

"Do you think that's where they are?" said Rose pointing to the pile of straw at the bottom of the bank ahead of them.

Through his spy-hole Willie saw them approaching and had nudged Norman to alert him.

"There's a man coming with a girl; not the chap who rescued us. He's older." whispered Willie. Tensely they lay stock-still, watching.

The reality of the situation came home to Rose. Will they still be there? What should she say first? Would they understand her? After all she had only learned her English at school; she had not actually spoken to anyone English.

"What shall I say?" she asked her father, almost whispering, as they approached the hideaway.

"Just say we're here to help and have some food for them," said her father, "We must not frighten them. Hold out Fernand's bag; they might recognise it."

"Hello Englishmen," began Rose haltingly. "Are you there? This is my father. We come to help you. It is safe. No Germans. We have food for you." Rose held out her brother's bag.

"It's the same food bag," whispered Willie. "Could it be a trap though?"

"We've nothing to lose now even if it is a trap," reasoned Norman. "We have to trust them. We can't get away. At least I can't."

There was a rustle and Rose and her father saw a clump of hay lift just enough for them to see two faces peering out, blinking in the evening sunlight. It was such a strange setting that none of them spoke. Eventually Rose broke the ice by holding the bag out further as an offer of food and when Willie nodded in acceptance they clambered down the bank. Willie pushed the hay out of the way and sat up, helping Norman to sit up too. They were still very tense, on guard, half expecting something to happen but as nothing did their tension eased a little. They looked around but saw no threats. Rose handed the bag to Willie.

"Thanks," he said smiling at Rose, taking the bag slowly. Rose's father eyed the two airmen cautiously; they looked frightened, exhausted and dishevelled, and their clothes were still damp. He and Rose took a pace back and watched as the airmen helped themselves to some bread.

"We help you from the grips of the Germans," said Rose.

"You speak English?" Norman asked, surprised.

Rose gained in confidence. "A little," she replied demurely.

"We need to get away from here and hide somewhere tonight," said Norman.

"But he's hurt his leg and can't walk far," put in Willie.

Rose struggled to follow their English but then she noticed Norman's torn and bloodied boot. "Papa. Look!" she exclaimed, reverting to French. "Fernand said one of them was injured." Willie too saw and shot a surprised look at Norman.

"It looks really bad! Why didn't you tell me?"

"It's probably not as bad as it looks," said Norman trying to make light of it.

"We must see how able he is," said Rose's father. "Maybe they will have to hide here for the night if we can't get them somewhere better without attracting attention."

With a series of gestures and Rose's efforts at English, and with the occasional help of Norman's schoolboy French they debated what should be done. They helped Norman up and he tried to walk on his own but it was obvious he could not go far even with support.

Norman had been mulling over their situation while they were hidden. He had come to the conclusion they could not get away on their own, but to stay risked being found by German patrols that would undoubtedly be looking for them. They needed a better hiding place, perhaps a barn or outbuilding, but it could not be far. In a whispered conversation he had explained this to Willie who had agreed.

Norman explained this to Rose as simply as he could. Eventually, after using different words and gestures Rose thought she understood and explained as best she could to her father. But as they considered what to do Willie's eye caught a movement in the distance.

"Someone's come'een," he said quickly through gritted teeth. "Hide!" He dived into the haystack and dragged Norman after him. Rose and her father looked round and could see a horse and cart some way away but approaching on the track the other side of the field. To them it was immediately obvious this was not a German patrol but someone local. Rose and her father stood by the stack unsure how to act. Norman and Willie lay stock still not knowing what was going to happen.

After a moment Rose's father said, "We'll say we have come to see where Fernand was working and have stopped for something to eat."

They waited apprehensively, wondering who it could be. As the horse and the large four-wheeled cart neared, Rose's father said, "I think it's Alphonse Gouraud. If it is, there'll be no problem. He's no friend of the Germans."

"But didn't you get into trouble over his stolen beans?" said Rose anxiously remembering her conversation with her mother.

"He knows the truth. He's all right about it. He said he would never have reported it if it was going to end up like it did. Everyone thinks we are enemies, but we are not." Peering at the man on the cart her father continued, "I'm sure it's Alphonse Gouraud. Yes, it is him."

Alphonse Gouraud pulled up his horse at the end of the track almost opposite them. He had seen them and waved in their direction. They waved back, and to their surprise and alarm Alphonse geed up the horse and steered the cart across the field towards them.

"Fernand, Rose what are you doing here?" he hailed them pulling up the horse and getting down.

"Hello Alphonse." said Rose's father. "We came to see where Fernand has been repairing the dyke today."

Alphonse Gouraud joined them and the two men shook hands. Leaning closer Alphonse Gouraud lowered his voice, "You know there's talk in the village that two airmen came down near the dyke from that aircraft that crashed. You've not seen anything, have you? I hope they get away. Don't expect they'll get much help around here though, most people are too scared of the Germans. Your boy must have seen them."

"He said he saw them come down. It was amazing," Rose's father said being cautious.

"I'd help them though. One way to get back at the Boche," Alphonse said firmly, making it clear he meant what he said.

Alphonse Gouraud was a couple of years younger than Rose's father. He was a big man, thick set with jet black hair smoothed back. He farmed in a large way, much more so than Rose's father, and also ran a transport business owning several horses and carts. He regarded himself as much a businessman as a farmer. His two lorries had been requisitioned by the Germans which had incensed him to the point he never missed an opportunity of making known his antipathy towards the occupying forces, often repeating how they were ruining his business.

Rose's father decided it was safe to take Alphonse partly into his confidence and said he could tell him more but he must swear to keep it to himself. Alphonse, intrigued, said he would. Rose's father told him that young Fernand had actually rescued the two airmen from the bay otherwise they would have drowned. He told how the two other workmen refused to help and how single-handedly his son had rescued the airmen using a boat. Alphonse was all agog.

"Your son has shown great courage. He is a good Frenchman. He will turn out all right," he said, amazed and clearly impressed. Rose's father took pride in the compliment, even though he recognised it was a reference back to the episode about the stolen beans.

Hearing that the other men were unwilling to help he tutted disapprovingly adding he was not surprised. He often voiced his opinion that people complained at the Occupation but when an opportunity came to stand up to the Germans they did nothing. When Rose's father mentioned one of the airmen was injured and could not walk Alphonse showed concern.

"They won't be able to get away then without help," he said and paused, obviously thinking hard. Beginning to grasp what was going on, slowly he said, "You have come to help them, haven't you? … You know where they are!"

While this conversation was going on Willie and Norman stayed absolutely still and they could hear the discussion but could not understand. Yet from the tone of the exchanges this visitor did not appear to be a threat, nevertheless they wished he would go away quickly.

Rose had become uncomfortable, concerned her father was saying too much although he appeared to trust Alphonse. Alphonse had a sharp mind and was no fool. He looked at Rose, looked back to her father and then at their bag which lay against the haystack. His expression slowly changed as the situation dawned on him. He pointed at the haystack and without making any sound mouthed, 'In there?'

Rose's father nodded. "They need help or they'll get captured. I could hide them at my place but we can't get them there. One of them is injured."

Rose grabbed at her father's arm at this surprising and disturbing development, a questioning look on her face. He had not mentioned his intention of taking the airmen home before!

She had thought they would just give them some food and perhaps move them to a better hiding place, but the prospect of having them at the house worried her. But before she could say anything Alphonse spoke.

"We could take them on my cart," he volunteered, his tone resolute. "We could hide them under the load of hay. No one would suspect. What do you think?"

Somewhat taken aback with Alphonse's offer, Rose's father considered the idea. It would certainly be a risk taking the cart through the village where there would probably be soldiers about but it did provide the solution to getting the airmen away from the dyke. Gradually he nodded his agreement. Rose tugged at his arm wanting to tell him her concerns but her father's look did not invite interruption and in deference she kept her counsel.

"Are you sure, though?" said Rose's father. "It would be risky. We could find a better hiding place nearer here for now, come back tomorrow and hope they are not found."

"We would still have the same problem tomorrow," said Alphonse. "It's getting late. If we are to take them to your house we should go now and work out tomorrow what to do with them."

"Rose," said her father, "tell the airmen we will hide them on the cart and take them to our house." Seeing her hesitate, her father insisted, "It'll be all right, they can't stay here. Don't worry. But they must come with us now, immediately."

With her father's mind obviously made up Rose decided she would do as he directed. "Hello Englishmen," she started. "Our friend will take you on his cart to our farm, under the … er … grass. We go now. Come!"

Norman and Willie whispered to each other and decided to see if this plan could work. They edged their way out from under the stack, checking there was no one in sight and peering warily at the man with the cart. Alphonse gazed back, not quite being able to believe his eyes as the two British airmen emerged. They certainly appeared to be in a poor way.

"Where is your house? How far?" asked Norman inspecting both Alphonse and his cart.

Rose understood and worked out her answer. “We live in the village … er … eight kilometres.”

He and Willie briefly discussed the situation. Certainly they could not get out of the area under their own steam and surely the Germans would soon arrive looking for them. There seemed no alternative but to go with these people. Rose tried to follow their discussion but they spoke too fast for her and she managed to pick up a few words only from Norman. She had given up trying to understand Willie; his Scottish accent defeated her.

“We’ll go with you,” declared Norman; then added in French, “Thank you.”

“It’s agreed,” said Rose turning to her father.

“Let’s go then. We must leave no trace of them being here,” he said patting down the haystack to make it look undisturbed.

Alphonse dropped the low backboard to the cart and shifted his sacks of potatoes to one side. The two airmen were helped on to the back and burrowed under the hay until they were completely hidden. Alphonse moved back the sacks of potatoes, and Rose’s father loaded the bike then helped her onto the backboard so she was facing backwards, her legs dangling. The two men then climbed onto the driver’s seat. Alphonse untied the reins, let off the brake and slowly turned the cart to go back the way he had come. All this was done with little said, everyone aboard full of apprehension.

“Stop!” called Rose suddenly. “Fernand’s bag!” She jumped off the cart to retrieve her brother’s bag that had been left on the ground then jumped back on quickly.

She held on as the cart rumbled across the field and onto the rough track, her grip tight, her mood tense. Earlier she was excited to be at her father’s side, thrilled at setting out with him on this improbable escapade. Now absorbed in thought, she was oblivious to the gathering twilight as the sun began to dip beneath the low horizon. On the one hand there was her compassion towards the airmen – after all what would happen to them without their help: on the other hand were the dire warnings of giving that help. With the airmen hidden on the cart only feet away from her, those previously suppressed ideas of danger were brought to the fore. Had they been seen? What if they met someone? Would the men her brother worked with talk? Surely there would be soldiers about? Doubts and fears began to nag.

Chapter 7

Captain Le Berre sat in his office at the police headquarters in Luçon, weary after another long hot day, finishing a last piece of paperwork needed by the ever insistent German occupying authorities, while knowing he would be in trouble yet again from his wife for being late home from work. His wife did not understand, or did not want to understand, that since the occupation he had more to do, her argument being there were all these soldiers to help keep law and order. He had tried to explain many times that there were new orders almost every day and the authorities required this return and that report all of which had to be completed properly and on time. Captain Le Berre was a career policeman who had risen to District Police Commander. He was used to following orders from his superiors, and also from his nagging wife. When the Occupation came he was instructed to cooperate fully with the local German military police, accepting and implementing their orders in relation to maintaining the peace among a potentially hostile populace. As an agency of the occupying powers the local gendarmerie was in the front line against some of this hostility as people saw them no longer on the side of the French. But on the whole there had not been the wholesale anarchy and looting foretold when France came under occupation. Still it was a difficult balancing act at times for Captain Le Berre not only with the general public but also within his own demoralised ranks with many acting truculently at their Occupation role yet not resigning because they needed the job to support their families. Other than resigning himself, which he definitely did not want to do, he saw he had no choice but to carry out his orders like most of the gendarmerie. In his own mind by maintaining a neutral stance, keeping his views to himself and performing the job as instructed, he might do well out of the war whoever won in the end.

Captain Le Berre's internal phone rang. As he answered it he looked at the wall clock; it was nearly six o'clock. He certainly did not want anything to delay his departure further. The duty officer was on the line saying a report had just come through from the officer in charge of the unit at St. Michel-en-l'Herm that an RAF bomber had crashed in the area and there were rumours that two parachutists were seen to land near La Dive, an area near the village. He questioned the officer about the report. Where did these rumours come from? Were they likely to be true? How long ago was this supposed to have happened? Unfortunately all the answers meant it was not possible to avoid his standing orders to report such matters to the local German Military Police Commander and it was too serious a matter to delegate. Frustrated he heaved a sigh and ordered his duty officer to get the German Commander on the phone.

From experience, conversations with his German counterpart took ages largely because of the language barrier but also because there were procedures to be followed, endless questions to be answered. Today's call was no different and at the end of it he was told to stay in his office to await further instructions while the matter was reported to the District Army Commander. Captain Le Berre told his duty officer to inform his wife he must remain in his office; that something had come up. Half an hour later the duty officer came into the office with a message from the German military; a search for the British airmen was being mounted by army units in the area. He was to order his local gendarmes to be on standby to help if needed and he may be called out later to supervise them. Having told his duty officer to inform the St. Michel-en-l'Herm gendarmes accordingly, he announced without further ado he was going home where the duty officer should contact him only if it was really necessary.

After the phone call from the German Military Police Commander the District Army Commander made a series of phone calls himself. He had been made aware of the bombing raid on La Pallice and that a number of British aircraft had been shot down. Indeed he had already been told that several parachutists who had come down over La Rochelle had been swiftly captured. One report told of the crash of an aircraft into the sea south of l'Aiguillon-sur-Mer. It was thought there were no survivors. This information rather contradicted the report from the police at St. Michel-en-l'Herm that two airmen were seen to parachute down in the vicinity of La Dive. He decided to act on the report from the local police; he could not take the chance even if these rumours turned out not to be true. He ordered the officer at the camp at l'Aiguillon-sur-Mer to search the coastline from the village down to La Pointe. He also rang Captain Schulz, the German officer billeted at Albin Pilnière's hotel at St. Michel-en-l'Herm who apparently knew nothing of the parachutists since he and his men had just returned from manoeuvres. Captain Schulz was given his initial orders which were to mount a search of the area around La Dive with which he immediately complied despatching a corporal and about twenty men who set off in two trucks. There were some disgruntled murmurings among the soldiers, out of earshot of the corporal, about being sent out on such a mission after a long, hot day out on manoeuvres. The corporal had similar thoughts but accepted his orders without demur.

With the search party underway Captain Schulz sent for the Mayor, Monsieur Bodin. Félix Bodin was nearly seventy years old, short, portly and bald. He was proud of his achievements over many years as Mayor looking after 'his flock', as he called the local people. But the German Occupation had broken his spirit and his health was now poor. As the locally appointed representative he had been obliged to introduce the many new orders and directives from both the local German military and the Préfet for the Vendée at La Roche-sur-Yon. Félix Bodin struggled with this much-changed role; that of leading and representing his 'flock' while at the same time being the agent for introducing measures under the Occupation which were both draconian and intrusive, and therefore much resented. He had stayed on as Mayor as he felt it his duty to protect the village and to hold it together through these turbulent times. But it was a hard and a mostly thankless task which, coupled with his poor health and disillusionment, had led him to decide not to seek re-election. He was at home sitting in his favourite chair reading a newspaper when the demand came for his presence at the hotel.

Captain Schulz was writing when the Mayor entered the hotel café. The officer looked up and quickly explained what was happening, and asked Mayor Bodin if he knew anything about the parachutists. The Mayor said curtly he knew nothing of them as he had been in his office all day and then had gone straight home. Their relationship was businesslike, polite but nothing more than matter of fact. Both men recognised each other's position and the need for a working liaison where their aims for security and stability coincided. But the officer saw the Mayor's persistent petitioning against his measures as irritatingly uncooperative. After a while each had come to accept the other's situation and they rubbed along, the Mayor negotiating a bit of leverage here and there whenever he could, not succeeding that often but taking each success as a minor victory.

The Captain's current demand was the issue of an official notice to be announced immediately to the village population requiring anyone with information about the parachutists to inform the Mayor's office. It was the wording of the proclamation he had been scripting when the Mayor arrived. He handed the note to the Mayor with his instructions that any information forthcoming must be passed immediately to him without fail. Before dismissing the Mayor the officer eyed him carefully and wanted to know if the most recent notice had been given properly to the population – the one that warned against assisting enemy airmen. It had, confirmed the Mayor abruptly, irritated at yet another interrupted evening. The Mayor was told he was to return home once the proclamation had been made but to be available if necessary. Barely disguising his distinct lack of enthusiasm, Félix Bodin left Captain Schulz's office stating he would make the announcement shortly.

Captain Schulz lifted the phone receiver. He reckoned he was going to need many more soldiers to mount further searches effectively and to set up road blocks, perhaps as many as a hundred in view of the wide area to be covered. He dialled his commanding officer explaining his requirements, which to his surprise were readily accepted. But reinforcements would take an hour or so to arrive he was told as they would have to come from garrisons further afield. The Captain was, however, left in no doubt of his commander's expectations: these airmen must be caught – they must not be allowed to slip through the net. Not that he needed any motivation; he was due for promotion and handling this situation well could seal it.

Not long after leaving the café Félix Bodin was standing on the steps outside his offices in the village square accompanied by his deputy who was beating vigorously on the mayoral drum. It was customary to call the inhabitants of the village to important municipal announcements by several rolls on a drum and that method of official communication was deemed to be notice given to all. This time though because of the latish hour only a few curious residents appeared to hear the Mayor's announcement which he read out twice so he could not be accused of skimping his duties. Afterwards he pinned the proclamation to the public notice board and trudged homewards. As he walked he mulled over what his deputy had told him when organising the announcement. Having heard the reason for the German edict, his deputy had reminded him of the working party that had been at the Maroc dyke during the day. Perhaps that was where the rumour came from, his deputy had speculated. Should he find out more, thought the Mayor, maybe call in on the foreman on his way home? No, better not get involved, he decided, and made his way directly to his house.

While Captain Schulz waited impatiently for his patrol to return he took a call from his commander conveying a report that had come through from the Luftwaffe airfield at La Rochelle. One of their fighter pilots had reported two parachutists coming down near La Pointe de l'Aiguillon.

'Aha,' said Captain Schulz to himself as he put the phone down. 'The hunt is definitely on!'

A little later the sound of trucks entering the square prompted Captain Schulz to stop writing the report he had started and in eager anticipation prepared himself to accept two prisoners of war. He had read up on the relevant instructions in his officer's field manual as this was the first time he had been in charge of capturing any enemy. He remained seated quite relishing the expectation of two British airmen being marched in to his custody and of reporting success to his commanding officer. But his hopes were quickly dashed. There was no bustle outside, voices were subdued; his men would be noisy and animated if they were bringing him the prize. The corporal came in, the expression on his face confirming the Captain's suspicions.

"Nothing," the corporal reported. "No sightings; no evidence found." He went on to say they had searched the raised ground of La Dive and around the foot of it and he reckoned the airmen could have moved away along the many dykes and ditches. It was a very big area to search, he said, and it would need many more men to make a thorough search. Hoping he and his men could be stood down he offered his opinion that as the fugitives could not get far on foot a major search in the morning was the best course of action.

The Captain listened and then disabused him of the notion of calling off the search now. He told the corporal that a number of platoons were on their way, some from Luçon, the rest from Fontenay-le-Compte. The nearest unit at La Tranche-sur-Mer could not support the search here, he explained, as they were mounting their own search in the area around the village of Angles where another British aircraft had come down. Because the corporal and his men knew the area better than any reinforcements he was ordering them to continue the search until darkness, adding that when the reinforcements arrived they would be used to search the village and mount road blocks throughout the night.

He knew his men were expecting to be told they could stand down and that ordering them out yet again would be unpopular, but they had become sloppy and complacent recently, evidenced by their inconsistent performance on manoeuvres that day. But as he expected they would be hungry he had ordered Albin Pilnière to make up some baguettes and drinks for the men to take with them. At the news provisions were being provided his corporal's mood visibly improved. The two of them looked at a map of the area. The corporal was to take his men down to the bay along the Route de la Mer and to search the length of the Maroc dyke patrolling at the foot of the dyke on both sides at the same time. He was to report anything suspicious immediately.

With twilight approaching the two trucks set off again, this time heading south on the Route de la Mer.

Rose bumped uncomfortably on the backboard of the cart as it made its way along the track, her mind still troubled by how risky this mission had become. They were approaching the junction with the Route de la Mer when she heard her father say something. She turned her head and saw him pointing to another horse and cart in the distance which appeared to be heading back to the village. It could only be a villager and probably no threat but she watched it carefully.

"It looks like Alfred Brard," said her father to Alphonse when they were nearer. Everyone knew Monsieur Brard, the dairyman, who was a regular sight around the area in his two-wheeled cart fetching and carrying his milk churns. "What do we do? It looks as though we'll meet up with him."

"We should carry on. It would look suspicious to do anything else," said Alphonse. "Tell him nothing, though. The fewer people who know the better. Try to be natural."

"Did you hear that, Rose?" her father called over his shoulder.

"I understand," Rose replied. Then leaning back she addressed the airmen in English, "A friend comes. Stay …," she paused trying to think of the English word for 'still', but could not and used the French, "… immobile," hoping they would understand.

"It may be less suspicious if he does come along with us," suggested Fernand.

They carried on and reached the junction with the Route de la Mer at the same time as Alfred Brard.

"Good evening, Alfred. What brings you here?" called Alphonse. The dairyman, being younger than both Alphonse and Fernand, respectfully jumped down and came over to shake hands.

"Good evening Alphonse, Fernand. I heard a British bomber came down near here during that big raid on La Rochelle this afternoon and I came down to see if I could see anything. But there's nothing. On my way home now." He lowered his voice and said, "I hear two RAF airmen parachuted down hereabouts. Someone said they got away. Good luck to them, I say." Then resuming his normal voice, he continued, "You finished for the day? I'll call round tomorrow for some of your potatoes, Alphonse, if I may."

"Any time," replied Alphonse. "Following us back or do you want to go on first?"

"You go first, I'm in no hurry. … Hello Rose. Holidays started already?"

"Hello Monsieur Brard. Yes, I'm on holiday. It's wonderful." Then turning to her father Rose said, "Can I ride the bike now please, Papa? It's bumpy on the back."

Her father jumped down and came to the back of the cart, helped her down and lifted down the bike. They all set off, Alphonse's cart first with Rose riding alongside her father and the unwitting Alfred Brard following on. At one point Rose's eyes met her father's; his look emphasised the earlier instruction to keep silent about their secret cargo. As they made their way towards the village Rose needed to pedal only occasionally to keep up with the gentle pace of the horses.

It was a still, summer's evening with a glorious sunset. Although the light was beginning to fade it was possible to see a long way across the flat terrain as there was only the occasional low farm building by the track. Rose listened to the rhythmic clop of the horses' hooves on the hard, dusty track, the only vehicular route back to the village. Evidently all appeared tranquil and normal to Alfred Brard as he had no reason to suspect anything different. But Rose was very tense and she could sense her father was tense also.

Suddenly Rose's attention was caught by something way ahead along the straight track. She peered. Was that a cloud of dust she could see? It was difficult to make out.

"Papa," she said quietly whilst still concentrating on the point in the distance. "Papa, what's that ahead?" A cold sweat came over her as she was now certain it was dust and she could also hear what she thought was the distant sound of an engine. "Papa, it's a lorry," she whispered so as not to alert Alfred Brard. Her father nodded solemnly in acknowledgement and then leaned towards Alphonse to whisper to him. Alphonse stared straight ahead. A German truck was clearly visible now and rapidly approaching. There was a hurried exchange between Alphonse and Rose's father. Her father then leaned over to her and said quietly so that Alfred Brard could not hear, "They'll see us if we do anything. Act naturally. Be brave." He turned round and called to Alfred Brard.

"Looks like a German lorry coming. We'll have to pull over just up ahead so it can pass."

Alfred Brard called back, "I hope they don't hurtle past, my mare is scared of those noisy things."

Rose dropped back to the side of the cart and still looking ahead so Alfred Brard could not see her face whispered a warning to the airmen, "Germans!" as loud as she dare without Alfred Brard overhearing.

A little further up the single track was a hard standing for passing where the two carts pulled in just as the German patrol reached them, only they could now see it was not just one troop-carrier, but two. Rose's father and Alphonse sat stock still with fear; Rose, equally terrified, was frozen to the spot, one foot on the ground the other on a pedal trying to look normal whilst trembling within. She silently prayed the vehicles would rattle straight past them. In contrast Alfred Brard was hoping they would slow down and pass without frightening his mare.

The note of the lorries' engines changed. Rose could see the faces of the soldiers in the cab of the first lorry as it neared them. It was slowing down; then to her horror, the driver hit the brakes sharply and the lorry came to a halt in a cloud of dust.

Under the hay, Norman and Willie lay side by side absolutely rigid barely daring to draw breath. Through the hay they had heard Rose's warning and then the vehicles stopping. Willie looked at Norman whose eyes betrayed his thoughts; the game was about to be over.

A corporal alighted from the cab and several soldiers dropped down from the rear of the lorry and came round to the front, rifles at the ready. Slowly the corporal approached them, eyeing back and forth at the two stationary carts. Then a look of recognition came over his face.

"Ah! Monsieur Gouraud and Monsieur Brard, the dairyman," he said slowly in just about understandable, but heavily accented, French. "What keeps you out at this time?"

Alphonse had recognised the corporal instantly. It was he who had brusquely seized his two lorries when they had been requisitioned. The corporal obviously recognised him, probably because of the fuss he made at losing his most valuable business assets. Alphonse noticed that this evening, however, the corporal and his soldiers seemed somewhat casual and uninterested as if they had other things on their minds.

"We have to work all hours at this time of year. Harvest time, you know," said Alphonse as calmly as he could.

"I understand," said the corporal. "We're searching for two British airmen. Have you seen them?"

Rose kept still, trying as hard as she could to act naturally. She had taken a dislike to the corporal with his superior manner, and she was feeling very uncomfortable at the stares the other soldiers were giving her.

"We've seen nothing. How about you, Alfred?" Alphonse said turning round.

"No. I don't even know where their aircraft crashed," said the dairyman.

"It came down near l'Aiguillon. Two parachutists. Tell your friends do not aid them. Bad penalties," said the corporal as he walked alongside the carts looking into them, only looking. He walked back, waved his soldiers into their lorry, turned and said, "Goodnight, Monsieur Gouraud and Monsieur Brard."

With that he climbed back into the lorry and the two vehicles revved up and moved on past gradually disappearing down the track towards the bay.

"I have seen that corporal around when I deliver milk to the hotel," said Alfred Brard. "Good job he only had a cursory look at us. I have some cheese here I shouldn't have, under a sack!" Alphonse, Fernand and Rose barely heard him as they heaved a collective sigh of relief at their escape.

"That was lucky, then," said Rose's father with half a smile. Turning to Rose, he said with a wink, "You go on ahead and warn us of any more Germans," thinking they may not be so lucky next time.

"Yes, Papa," replied Rose understanding her father's wink. She pedalled off fast, feeling the cooling air on her face, the tension draining away and for the first time since her father agreed to help the airmen she began to feel confident they would succeed. She even thought for a moment it was a shame the airmen were not young and good looking like she had imagined. Dusk was descending. Soon she would be home and safe.

Rose had gone way ahead of the two carts and she could only just make them out in the closing gloom as she approached a low farm building where the track veered to the right just before the first houses of the village. As she turned past the farm building she could see ahead where the Route de la Mer entered the village and to her horror there were several soldiers standing by their vehicle which almost blocked the road. This time the soldiers looked as though they meant business. Panic overtook her. She braked hard and hoping she had not been noticed turned around and pedalled back furiously. She realised the low farm building was shielding the advancing carts from the view of the soldiers and that she must stop her father as quickly as she could. She looked over her shoulder and when out of sight of the soldiers she began waving a warning.

Her father saw her and immediately knew something was wrong. Alphonse too saw her and called to Alfred Brard to stop then pulled up his own horse. Their improving mood evaporated instantly.

"What's the matter?" called Alfred Brard puzzled. Alphonse and Fernand ignored him preparing for action as Rose reached them.

"There's a road block at the entrance to the village with lots of soldiers," she blurted out breathlessly, "Don't go any further, Papa! It's too dangerous."

"We'll hide the airmen here then and come to get them after dark," her father decided quickly, back in military mode. Alphonse agreed. Rose's father then jumped down and ran to the back of the cart.

A bewildered Alfred Brard sat behind them open mouthed.

"Get the airmen out, Rose. We'll hide them in that ditch. There's plenty of cover there. Tell them I'll come for them after dark."

Rose moved to the side of the cart and rustled the hay. "Airmen," she said, "you must get out. Germans again. Quick."

The hay shifted and two faces appeared as Norman and Willie sat up.

"Quick," urged Rose. "Hide. Over there," she added seeing her father pointing to the deep ditch which ran off at right angles to the track. The two men clambered down off the back of the cart as quickly as they could, Norman with the help of Fernand and Willie, and they scrambled into the ditch.

"What's going on? Who …? Are they the airmen?" Alfred Brard was stunned, unable to believe his own eyes.

Alphonse turned to Alfred Brard. "Forget what you have just seen. You know nothing," he said sternly through gritted teeth, fixing a stare at the shocked dairyman who slowly and silently indicated his understanding and agreement.

"Rose, tell them to make their way along the ditch far away from the road. Tell them I'll come back for them after dark," her father instructed. Rose did as she was told as best she could.

"We stay here? Come later for us?" queried Norman seeking confirmation of his understanding. Fear and anxiety showed on everyone's faces, all except Alfred Brard, that is, whose expression was a mixture of bewilderment, alarm and incredulity.

The ditch was deep, dry and dense with vegetation. Rose's father waved them further away from the track and when they settled down at the bottom of the ditch they were invisible.

It was nearly dark by now and the small party set off again, in silence, knowing they would shortly run into the German roadblock.

"Rose," her father said, "you go on home. Tell your mother to get some food ready for the airmen. They'll be tired and hungry."

Rose set off. She reached the roadblock in a few minutes and got off her bike. She was scared as she walked through and looked down to avoid the stares of the soldiers who fortunately made no move to stop her. On the other side, relieved, she mounted her bike again and rode off home as fast as she could. Alphonse and Fernand were stopped by the soldiers at the roadblock and the hay on the cart was prodded and poked. Alfred Brard's small cart was just looked into; it being obvious no one could hide there. All three gave one word answers to a few curt questions and then they were let through. Fernand looked at Alphonse, gave a puff of his cheeks as if to say, 'that was a narrow escape'.

Out of sight of the soldiers Alfred Brard pulled alongside Alphonse who looked him in the eye, put his finger to his lips then as casually as he could said, "Goodnight Alfred."

"Goodnight," added Fernand.

Alfred Brard's response sounded calm, "Goodnight. I'll see you about those potatoes tomorrow, Alphonse." But underneath he was still very frightened, anxious to be away and he geed up his mare for home trying to get his head around the extraordinary events of the last twenty minutes.

Alphonse turned to Fernand and said he should get home as his wife was unwell but he would help tomorrow if needed. Fernand got down from the cart, looked up at Alphonse and winked in acknowledgement of his part. "Thanks," he said with feeling. "I'll go back to the airmen now. I'll get them to my house. We'll manage somehow; it's not far. I'll take them the back way so we won't be seen; it's dark enough. I'll talk to you tomorrow."

"Good night, Fernand and good luck. You are a good Frenchman."

Chapter 8

Rose's mother sat at the kitchen table extremely agitated, becoming more worried and impatient by the minute at not knowing what was happening. Young Fernand had explained the afternoon's events to her and that Papa and Rose had gone to see what help they could give the airmen who were in a poor state after their ordeal. But what Papa actually intended to do he did not know and could not say, despite his mother's urgent and persistent questioning. The questions exhausted, they both sat silently waiting. It was nearly dark outside now. As the waiting went on the tension in the room grew; young Fernand knew his mother was worried sick, made worse by her irritation that his father had gone off on one of his antics without telling her.

He had seen it before; his father's impetuosity leading to domestic tension and argument. His mother's tongue would be sharp; his father would brush it all off as a fuss, and after a while the issue would be forgotten, at least by his father.

Young Fernand sat quietly thinking. His mother had paid due tribute to him for saving the lives of the airmen which he was pleased about and looking back on the rescue he began to realise how pretty amazing it was. He had managed it all by himself, an achievement he was now beginning to see in its true light. He waited with a mixture of excitement and anxiety, keen to know what was happening but concerned at this delay. Was there a problem? Could his father not find the airmen? Surely he should be home by now?

They heard the farm gate rattle as it was opened and both got to their feet at the same time, their eyes set on the kitchen door which was still ajar. Seconds later Rose rushed in out of breath and before she could speak her mother snapped out at her.

"What is going on?" she demanded to know. "Where is your father? What's happening?"

"He's coming," Rose managed to get out. "We've been helping the airmen that Fernand rescued. He says to get some food ready for them. Maman, we brought them on Monsieur Gouraud's cart, hidden under some hay."

"What – they're coming here?" exclaimed her mother.

"Yes, later. We were stopped by a German patrol but they didn't search the cart. It was frightening. But there was a road block at the village so the airmen have hidden in a ditch. Papa will bring them soon after dark. One of them can hardly walk."

Her mother was alarmed; not only at hearing of the narrow escape but also because the airmen were being brought to the house. "What is he thinking of?" she said aghast, throwing her arms up at the thought of the risks he had taken. "We can't hide British airmen here; it's far too dangerous!"

"They are in a poor way, Maman; aren't they Fernand?" panted Rose. "They would have drowned if Fernand hadn't saved them. Papa says we have to help them. He said to get some food ready."

"Fernand go and stop your father. Tell him not to bring the airmen here – it's too dangerous. Persuade him to find somewhere else for these men to go. Go quickly! Rose, we'll prepare something to take to them." Rose told her brother where the airmen were hidden and as young Fernand hurried out her mother looked in the larder for some ham, cheese, tomatoes and bread. "This will have to do" she stated. "Get some wine and some water." As they busied themselves, Rose's mother became curious. "What are they like, these airmen?" she asked.

"One is tall and thin. He's very difficult to understand," chattered Rose who had not yet fully regained her breath. "The other one is smaller, older and has a kind face. He understands a little French. He's the one who is injured. They have had a terrible ordeal, Maman. They look dirty and all in. Maman, you should see the looks in their eyes. They are so frightened of being captured by the Germans. They want to get to the Free Zone then south to Spain. Papa has taken pity on them. So did Monsieur Gouraud who offered to bring them to the village on his cart because the one who is injured could not walk this far. We met the dairyman on the way. He saw the airmen get off the cart and hide in the ditch. Monsieur Gouraud told him to say nothing.

Papa thinks he will keep quiet. I can't believe this is all happening."

Later as they waited patiently there was a noise outside. Rose dashed out and in the darkness there was just enough light from the kitchen doorway for her to make out her father leading the airmen through the gate, obviously trying to be as quiet as possible. Her brother was there too helping the injured one. Rose ran over to them at the same time as the farm dogs scampered over and fussed around the strangers but did not bark as their master was there.

She whispered to her father "Maman has some food ready but said she doesn't want the men in the house."

"I know," her father replied, "but it will be all right, just for now. We'll search them to make sure they have no weapons. Tell them I must search them."

Rose then said to Norman, "My father you search for …" but she did not have the word for gun. She mimicked shooting a pistol with her hand and shook her head to indicate 'not allowed'.

Norman was too exhausted to resist anything. He thought he understood and just held his arms out sideways signalling his willingness to be searched. Neither he nor Willie had any weapons but there was no point in trying to explain. Rose's father briskly frisked both men, finding nothing. He waved them to follow him into the house. The dogs followed, their tails wagging, but they stopped at the door as they knew they were not allowed in the house. There Rose's mother stood staring at the two bedraggled airmen for a moment then shot a black look at her husband as if to say, 'I told you not to bring them here!'

"I had to bring them – one of them needs his leg looked at – he's badly injured."

Although Renée was still fuming at her husband, her steely resolve melted somewhat at seeing the sorry state the men were in and she began to think of what they might need. She gestured them to sit at the table and was soon fussing around, laying a plate, offering food and drink, indicating they should help themselves or have some more. It was all done a little embarrassingly with gestures and expressions. Not that the airmen needed much invitation.

Rose, her father and brother stood back a little watching Norman and Willie tuck in. Fernand and Renée always took great pleasure at seeing guests at their table but soon Renée's fears returned at having the airmen under their roof and on the side she pleaded again that they be found somewhere else to hide away from the house.

"They could hide in the field," she pressed and on seeing her husband beginning to shake his head in rejection of this idea added persistently, "Or in the barn at least. I'm frightened, Fernand, to have them in the house."

"Look at them," said Rose's father. "They have had it. They can't endure any more today. We must give them shelter for tonight. It'll only be for tonight. Tomorrow we'll find a good hiding place, somewhere else; somewhere where they can rest up before setting out for the Free Zone. But tonight we must look after them. We must."

"It's too dangerous to have them here," she insisted.

"Only Alphonse Gouraud knows they are here, no one else. He won't say anything. Tomorrow we'll move them somewhere safer." His wife saw there was no changing his mind. "When they have eaten, have a look at his injured leg, it's been bleeding," he said pointing at Norman. "The sooner that is better the sooner they can get away. They can sleep in our room. Fernand and I will sleep downstairs. You take Fernand's bed just for tonight. Rose can be in her room. Find some blankets for us." Renée glared at him again even more disapprovingly. It was normal on the rare occasions they had guests to stay to offer them their room but this was rather different; however, she decided not to argue in front of everyone.

Rose's father looked back at the two men at his table. He felt excited, proud, adrenaline still pumping. His actions were not borne out of vengeance against the Germans. He had no pretensions of starting a resistance movement like the organisations he had heard were starting up in Paris and in northern France. He was not driven by any political motive; not aiming a tilt at France's conquerors. These men were in desperate need; he did not have his army uniform on these days but they were military allies and in trouble. If the roles were reversed he would hope to receive similar help. But for now it was he who could help and should help. Any plans for tomorrow would be tackled tomorrow. For now, tonight, they needed his roof.

While they ate, Norman and Willie discussed their situation. They both acknowledged their utter fatigue, that they could do nothing else than go along with these rescuers and also that they were in no fit state to make plans for tomorrow. Having eaten, all they wanted to do was to lay down their heads and sleep; anywhere would do just so long as they were relatively safe. Willie wondered whether they should offer the family some money to help further curry their favour, after all they were utterly dependent on these people now and probably would be for a few days before they were strong enough to make their own way south to Spain. Norman was not so sure.

"They've already risked their lives for us," said Willie. "They're hardly going to fleece us now. Offer them a wee something, for the food."

"All right," said Norman reaching to unbutton the pocket on his shirt breast. The franc notes were still a little damp. He peeled off a ten franc note from the small, damp bundle and put the rest back. He turned to Rose.

"For the food," he said holding out the note. Rose looked at her father.

"He wants to pay us for the meal, Papa. Should I accept it?"

"They are our guests," he said somewhat indignantly. "Our guests do not pay for their food!"

Rose shook her head at Norman. "No, thank you." was all she said. Then her mother said to ask the airman if she could look at his injury. "My mother look at your leg?" was the best Rose could manage.

Norman nodded his agreement. They had finished eating and their fatigue was beginning to take its toll on them.

"Take my boot off Willie, carefully. It's still very painful. God knows what it will look like. But I guess it should be looked at." Willie knelt down and lifted Norman's leg on to the bench seat as gently as he could. Norman winced and gritted his teeth, holding back as much as he could. Willie did not want to cut away the boot as that would only hamper their eventual escape.

Tensing himself he very slowly pulled it with both hands while Norman held his leg tightly. As the boot came off Rose's mother quickly stepped over to hold Norman as she feared he was about to faint. The sock was soaked in blood and there was a nasty, deep gash just below the ankle bone.

"Rose, get some bandages and some antiseptic from the cupboard, quickly," ordered her mother. "Fernand, get the scissors. We'll have to cut his sock off." Rose put a small, rather worn cardboard box on the table, the family's first aid kit and medicine chest. "Hold him, Rose, while I take a look." Rose sat next to him and took his hand. She did not like the sight of blood, unlike her parents and brother who were somewhat inured to suffering and gore having looked after animals for years. She felt Norman tense as her mother knelt down by his ankle to inspect the damage. Rose herself looked the other way. When the wound was exposed her mother said, "Tell him it's bad but could be worse. Ask him to wiggle his toes"

Rose could not find any English so just wiggled her fingers and pointed to his toes. Norman found he could just move his toes a little but doing so was very painful.

"I think it is just a flesh wound; bad but nothing broken," said Renée.

"Bad but not to break," Rose advised Norman, a bit flustered at having to translate difficult medical terms.

"It's quite a gash you have there," said Willie peering at the injury, trying to help the situation. "Done by a bit of shrapnel I should think. Luck'ee it didn't get you any deeper. You'll mend," he ended trying to be encouraging.

Hearing earlier that the airmen would soon set out for the Free Zone had given Rose an idea and she took the opportunity to disappear upstairs, to return a few moments later with a small book that she showed to her father.

"Papa, look what I've found." Rose held out a French/ English phrase book. "It has a map at the back," she added. "It will help them escape, don't you think? It's the one Monsieur Bon gave me to help with my English studies." Her father recognised it; it was a guide for touring English motorists and the garage proprietor had given it to Rose, jokingly saying he was unlikely to sell many after the invasion.

"Give it to them," her father readily agreed. "Later we'll show them which way to go."

Offering the book to Norman Rose said in English, "For you," smiling demurely as she did so, pleased to be a real help.

"For me?" said Norman taking the book and smiling back. He quickly looked at it and understood. "Thank you," he said, "it will be very useful." Handing it on to Willie he explained, "A phrase book with a road map." Willie looked at it and passed it back.

"You look after it," he said, acknowledging it was better in Norman's hands. Norman tucked it into his trouser pocket.

The wound was cleaned and bandaged up tightly. A sock was found to put over it. Norman insisted on having the boot put back on, just in case, although it was terribly painful to do so as the couple of aspirins Renée had given him had not yet taken effect.

"We have a bed for you. Up here," said Rose when all was done. Carrying a candle she led Willie to the narrow stairs which led off the kitchen. Renée nipped in front of her, anxious to make sure the room was tidy for her guests.

"Most generous of you," said Willie to Renée realising they were being offered the parents' bed. Rose did not understand but took it the arrangement was acceptable. Norman hopped up the stairs to the bedroom, helped by young Fernand who eased him on to the bed and then Renée made him comfortable.

"What's the time, Willie? I make it a quarter to eleven." asked Norman taking his watch off and beginning to wind it. Willie felt in his trouser pocket for his watch. It was not there. He felt in his other pocket; it was not there either.

"Damn!" he said. "My pocket's torn and my watch has gone. Some loose change too, but guess I won't be need'een any English money for a wee while."

Norman looked up at Renée and said thank you in French, then looked at Fernand and repeated his thanks. Renée smiled and picked up the candle to leave. Young Fernand too smiled, and turned away a little embarrassed.

"What do you reckon, Mac?" asked Willie when they were alone.

"We must sleep now," he said sounding totally shattered. "Maybe tomorrow the ankle will be better and we can get away from here. We shouldn't rely on these folk any longer than necessary. They don't appear to be part of any resistance movement but even so they are at great risk. I'm thinking if we could get to La Rochelle we may be able to stow away on a boat to Spain. Get some sleep now."

"Aye," said Willie. "Bloody luck'ee we've been to get this far. How's the leg?" There was no reply. Norman, despite the pain, had already succumbed to his overwhelming fatigue. In the silent darkness Willie found himself alone with his thoughts which quickly turned to his friends who had undoubtedly perished in the crash a few hours ago. Heavy at heart, he, too, soon drifted into a deep sleep.

In the kitchen Rose listened to her father spell out in military tones what to do now. He wanted young Fernand to get a pitchfork from the barn as a weapon to have by him in case of any trouble. They should all go to bed now but not change out of their day clothes to be ready to act quickly if necessary. In the morning they should carry on just as normal so as to arouse no suspicions. Tomorrow decisions would be made about where to hide the airmen – this remark aimed directly at Renée. Rose must stay in the house as translator. But now they should all try and get some sleep. Everything would be sorted out in the morning. Everything would be fine.

With that, they all retired and the house fell silent.

Rose lay on her bed. Quite suddenly she felt extremely tired after the roller coaster last few hours of excitement, of fear and the mental gymnastics of translating. She was pleased with her attempts at the latter. That was fun especially when she was understood by the airmen. She had not understood them as much as she expected but overall she felt she had really helped both her father and the airmen. On that satisfactory thought sleep overtook her.

At the café Captain Schulz was taking stock of the situation. It was after ten o'clock and dark now outside which meant there was little point in initiating any further searches of open areas until dawn. A short while ago he had received a report from l'Aiguillon-sur-Mer that was not encouraging. The patrols had discovered nothing of any parachutists; there were no reported sightings or evidence on the ground. The report did say that the body of a British airman had been found washed up on the beach but it was not wearing a parachute harness and the presumption was that it had been washed free from the crashed aircraft. It had been taken to l'Aiguillon-sur-Mer for identification and burial. His own men had returned from the search of the sea wall unable to make a thorough search as darkness had fallen before they had reached the other end. They had found nothing and would need to return at daybreak to complete the search.

When the reinforcements from Luçon and Fontenay-le-Compte had arrived he had ordered road blocks at all entrances to the village and for a sweep search of the village. He waited impatiently for reports, becoming more anxious as the time passed, worrying that the parachutists had slipped through the net. His superiors would not be pleased. He decided he was going to need some local help. Local people were the source of the rumour in the first place and he was going to prise out of them the information he needed by threats and reprisals if necessary. Someone somewhere knew something, and he was determined these enemy airmen would be found.

Firstly he phoned the police headquarters in Luçon instructing them to call out Captain le Berre saying he was to make his way immediately to St. Michel-en-l'Herm to supervise personally his local force as they would be needed to aid the search. In particular he wanted Captain le Berre to give him a personal report on the source of the rumours which had originated from the St. Michel-en-l'Herm gendarmes. Then, as a second prong to his move against the local population he ordered the Mayor to be brought in for questioning. He wanted assurance his earlier orders regarding the proclamation had been carried out correctly and whether anyone had come forward with information; he wanted the Mayor to know that harsh measures would be taken against the whole population if cooperation was not forthcoming; and he wanted names, names of those whom the

Mayor suspected might be sympathetic enough towards the airmen to help them.

Félix Bodin arrived first at the café in an extremely grumpy mood having been rudely ordered out of the house just as he was preparing for bed. He had guessed what the palaver was about but given the hour and since he knew nothing he was disinclined to assist Captain Schulz any more than the absolute minimum, as his demeanour rather gave away as he entered the dimly-lit café.

"Ah, Monsieur Bodin," said the Captain whose French was passable. "Please sit down. I need your cooperation in tracking down these airmen. More importantly I need the cooperation of your village. At the moment we have not found them but I am determined we shall – they cannot have got far. My concern is that one or more of your inhabitants are concealing them which can be very dangerous for the whole village. I have no wish to impose severe restrictions but I may be forced to do so if your people are acting against my authority. I hope you understand." Whilst the tone of the Captain's delivery was flat there was no disguising the menace in his words. He went on, "I am sure none of us want that after we have built a good relationship for everyone. Now, firstly have there been any responses to the announcement? You did deliver it to the whole population?"

"It was delivered in the usual manner," said Félix Bodin wearily. "The drum was sounded – you must have heard it – the note read out, twice, and it was pinned to the notice board as per normal. Tomorrow the word will get around, as it usually does. So far I have had no responses." He deliberately ignored the implied threats which he decided were no more than that, at least for the moment.

Captain Schultz was irritated by the Mayor's apparent unconcerned manner which was typical of Monsieur Bodin's initial reaction to any contention. Well, the Captain said to himself, if Monsieur Bodin is not concerned about the matter now he soon will be if I do not have the airmen very soon. He moved on to his next tack.

"I see," he said slowly. "Then I need your assistance in identifying those who are 'in the know' in your village, those who generally have their ear to the ground, who always seem to know what is going on; also those who tend to be uncooperative, shall we say, who perhaps don't understand the benefits of our being here. Every village has such people and I want a list of names. You must know who they are. I shall need to bring them in for questioning. Some may even need to be sent away for further questioning."

The menace in this statement was obvious to Félix Bodin who was only too well aware that under the Occupation some of those sent away for so called questioning ended up in labour camps in Germany.

"I'm not sure I'm the best person for that," said the Mayor deliberately being vague. When he himself wanted 'the word on the street' he turned to his deputy who had his sources on most matters. But he was not about to volunteer his deputy as informer.

"We will come to that in a moment," said the Captain. "What I also want to know is who will have seen this afternoon's events over the bay. Who lives in La Dive area? Who could be eye witnesses? You must know who lives there, who would know something?"

What a silly question, thought the Mayor. "You have not been there, have you?" said Félix Bodin somewhat disdainfully. "No one lives there. The land is unstable, unsuitable for buildings. It's farmland, good farmland. Many farmers rent pieces of the land there to cultivate; some graze cattle on the common pastures. It's possible there may have been one or two people working in the fields this afternoon, but I have no idea who they may be. Not everyone who has a field there would work there every day. As I told you earlier I was in my office all day."

"So you said," said the Captain becoming frustrated by the tepid nature of the Mayor's help. "Is there anyone who may have seen something?" he pressed.

At this the Mayor hesitated, recalling the remark his deputy had made about the working party on the sea wall. It was bound to come out that he knew there were workmen on the Maroc dyke and he could find himself in trouble should he not offer up that information in answer to the officer's direct question.

"I believe there was a working party on the sea wall today, making good some storm damage. Maybe some of them saw something."

"Show me. I have a map here," said the officer picking up on what appeared to be a significant piece of information. He got up and moved over to a nearby table strewn with maps of various scales. "Here, show me where the working party was," he said smoothing out a map of the whole area.

"I'm not exactly sure. This was work organised by the Clerk of Works," said the Mayor slowly getting up from his chair. "It was on the Maroc dyke I think, the eastern end mostly. Thereabouts," he said pointing to where the main breach had been.

"H'm. From there they could see a great deal," said the officer. "Who was on this working party?"

"I don't know. It was organised by the Clerk of Works, Monsieur Richard and the foreman Monsieur Millet."

"Get them here," the Captain ordered abruptly. He called in one of the soldiers from outside and told him in German to accompany the Mayor. "This soldier will go with you."

"What now? It's very late," protested the Mayor.

"Now! If you please," countered the Captain in a manner that left the Mayor no option.

Shortly after the Mayor and the soldier had left Captain le Berre arrived.

"I am glad you are here, Captain le Berre," said the officer. The words were cordial but there was no warmth in their delivery. "I have need of you and your men. Tell me exactly where this rumour came from that two enemy airmen are at large. My patrols have found nothing. I'm scaling down the search till daylight. In the meantime I must pursue other lines of enquiry. What can you tell me?"

"I see you have road blocks in place. It appears I was not expected. Fortunately one of the soldiers recognised me." Captain le Berre could not help having a little dig to ensure his status was not overlooked. "As for the British airmen, I told your Commander all I know."

"You must please tell me again," he said briskly, ignoring the gibe. Captain le Berre repeated the story. The rumours had been overheard from women chatting in the village. No names had been given, but he did not doubt his gendarme's reports, which is why he himself had reported it to the Commander.

"Bring your men in. How many do you have here?" Captain Schultz demanded. Three was the answer. "I will need them here to help with my enquiries. Question them again. Find out what they know and I want names of local troublemakers. The Mayor informs me there was a working party on the sea wall today. They must have seen something. I am getting names. Your gendarmes will accompany my soldiers to bring witnesses in for interrogation. They will know where they live."

The police captain could not fault Captain Schultz's line of enquiry and so acquiesced; he left leaving the German officer satisfied that actions were underway. It was not long before the Mayor returned together with Messieurs Richard and Millet who were introduced to Captain Schultz. The Clerk of Works explained that he was not at the dyke, he merely scheduled the work and authorised the council resources; it was the foreman who organised the day's work. The Inspector of Works, Monsieur Gaudin, was also there at one point to check the work in progress.

Monsieur Millet was tired and bewildered, and the soldier who stood by the door, rifle at hand, unnerved him. Finding himself in this unfamiliar situation, he looked questioningly at the Mayor uncertain of what he should say, or not say. "You should answer the officer's questions," said the Mayor gently.

"Tell me what you saw this afternoon at the dyke," requested Captain Schultz trying a calm voice to start with. "What did you and your men see?"

"We saw the air raid over La Pallice and we saw one large aeroplane shot down. It came our way but veered and must have crashed over near l'Aiguillon, I think."

"How many parachutists did you see?"

"Three, I think. One way out to sea and two who landed out of sight somewhere near where the plane crashed."

"What do you know about the two who came down near you?" said the officer still adopting a restrained approach.

Monsieur Millet glanced at the Mayor, a glance that said I know something but should I say. The Mayor gave the merest nod to say he should go on.

"One of the workmen at that other end of the dyke said the airmen had got away," said Monsieur Millet uneasily.

"Ah," said the officer alighting on this new information, "you had men working at the end of the dyke where the parachutists came down?"

"Yes, there was a minor breach at that end and three men repaired it."

"Their names, please. I need their names," requested the officer his tone hardening despite the politeness.

"I'm not sure … I can't remember. There was a lot going on today. I had about forty men working."

"You must know these men, they work for you," Captain Schultz said with a definite edge to his voice.

"No, no, not all of them. We do these repairs every year and local farmers help because they rely on the sea walls holding. There were several breaches that needed repairs this time, the main one was at the eastern end which I supervised myself."

"But you have a list, surely. I need the names of the three men."

Monsieur Millet again looked at the Mayor as if for permission to answer.

"You must do as the Captain asks," said the Mayor who sensed the officer was not to be diverted from this line of questioning.

"Yes. I have a list. It's in my office."

"Fetch me the list."

"The office is closed. I will have it sent over before lunch."

"You must go now and bring it to me," said the officer, his original gentle tone now abandoned.

Turning to the Mayor, Monsieur Millet asked meekly, "It's been a long day and I'm tired. Is this really necessary? I'm not paid for this. My wife is worried and I should get back to her."

Before the Mayor could respond Captain Schultz interjected, "I have to have the list now! Fetch it immediately." He said something in German to the soldier at the door who went outside.

Captain Schultz resumed, “One of my soldiers will go with you to get the list now.”

“You had better do as the officer says,” said the Mayor reluctantly and with that Monsieur Millet and the soldier departed.

“At last we are getting somewhere,” said Captain Schultz. “Please, sit down over there till they get back.” It was more an instruction than an invitation and wearily the Mayor and Monsieur Richard sat down at a table in the corner. The old clock on the wall showed it was well past midnight.

“By the way, this Monsieur Gaudin, the Inspector, would he have inspected the repairs at that far end of the sea wall?” the officer asked Monsieur Richard after a few moments thought.

“He may have done, although the major repair was at the eastern end,” said Monsieur Richard.

“Please bring this Inspector to me. One of my soldiers will go with you. You may then go home.”

At long last, thought Monsieur Richard as he left with one of the soldiers giving a glance over his shoulder at the Mayor which said, ‘hard luck, it seems you have to stay.’

Soldiers came in and out with reports from the search parties and the road blocks. None seemed to have anything to say that pleased their officer. A little while later Captain le Berre re-appeared. He saw the Mayor seated in the corner.

“Monsieur le Maire,” he greeted him with a polite nod.

Addressing Captain Schultz, he said his gendarmes were outside waiting to assist. Unfortunately, he went on, he had no further information on the parachutists and his men could not offer the names of any troublemakers. This was a quiet, rural area he explained, well policed and well administered. It was no hotbed of anarchists.

“I can report good progress here in your absence,” said Captain Schultz pointedly. “I have discovered there were workmen in the area who saw the parachutists. I have instructed their names be brought to me. When I have the names I will want your men to accompany my soldiers to their houses to bring them in for questioning. Time is of the essence; this cannot wait till the morning. We wait for one of the Mayor's staff to bring me a list of workmen."

They waited. Captain Schultz who, unlike the Mayor, did not appear at all tired busied himself with some paperwork and occasionally a soldier entered for further orders. After a while he became impatient, looked at his watch and then at the old café clock on the wall; it had just ticked past one thirty.

"Where is your foreman? He has had plenty of time." The question was directed at the Mayor who by now was feeling extremely weary.

"He has had to go to his home to collect the keys to his office and then go to the council yard where his office is. Then he has to find the papers you require. It all takes time," said the Mayor defending his foreman.

It was nearly two o'clock when Monsieur Gaudin, escorted by a soldier, appeared at the doorway, blinking in the light of the room. The officer invited him to sit down and began questioning him on his movements that afternoon. Assuming the Mayor's presence gave him the authority to cooperate he answered truthfully, confirming, yes, in the middle of the afternoon he had inspected the work at the far end of the sea wall from where the main breach was. As far as the parachutists were concerned he remembered one of the workmen saying they had got away. He was not sure who the workmen were; one of them may have been Claude Rabillard, he thought. The Mayor was asked if he knew this Claude Rabillard, to be told he did but only as a council worker. Satisfied with the confirmation of the foreman's story and with the name of one of the workmen, Captain Schultz dismissed the Inspector, content to await the return of the foreman.

Monsieur Millet returned eventually with his list of names. The delay was due to his wife, he explained who had made an unholy fuss, stating in no uncertain terms all this nonsense could wait until the morning and insisting he must come to bed. It was only the intervention of the soldier that enabled him to collect his keys and leave for his office.

"Yes, yes," said Captain Schultz testily. "Tell me the names. Your Inspector believes one of them was Claude Rabillard. Is that right?"

"You've spoken to Monsieur Gaudin?" said Monsieur Millet surprised.

Ignoring the question, the officer insisted, "Was Claude Rabillard one of the workmen?"

Monsieur Millet spread out his crumpled and dirty list on the table and ran his finger down the column of names. He stopped and tapped his finger on the name of Monsieur C. Rabillard.

"The list doesn't state who worked where, just who was on that duty. I probably made a note somewhere who was to do the smaller repairs. I think I remember speaking with Claude when I took the Inspector to see the repair work. He could be relied on to work without supervision. In which case the other worker would have been Marcel Taupiez, they always work together. Yes, there's his name."

"Who was the third man?" said the officer as he wrote down the two names.

"I don't know … possibly one of the volunteers," said Monsieur Millet who was getting decidedly flustered. "I'm not sure. … I, I don't remember. The list doesn't say. Oh, wait a minute. I have made a note on the back of the list. Here. Yes, Claude Rabillard, Marcel Taupiez and Fernand Neau did that repair. I don't know Fernand Neau, perhaps he's a farm worker."

"I need all these men brought in for questioning," Captain Schultz said to Captain le Berre. "Please order your men to accompany my soldiers to the houses of these men. Monsieur Millet will give you addresses." He then turned to the guard and rattled off something in German. The guard left and returned a moment later with Second Lieutenant Brandt from the Fontenay-le-Compte contingent. Again in German he ordered the Lieutenant to detail three groups of ten soldiers each to go to the houses of Claude Rabillard, Marcel Taupiez and Fernand Neau and bring them in for questioning. A gendarme would take them to the houses which were to be searched thoroughly.

Monsieur Millet had been trying to say something. "I don't know where they all live, only Claude," he said at last. "I won't have Fernand Neau's address; he doesn't work for the council."

Captain Schultz turned to Captain le Berre. "Ask your gendarmes, they may know these people," he said and the police captain duly went outside to question his three local gendarmes. He returned with Gendarme Avril.

"I know Fernand Neau. I'll fetch him," offered the gendarme thinking it was Rose's father who was the subject in question. "He lives at the end of rue de la Fontaine at the edge of the village. It's about a quarter of a mile from here. I won't need your soldiers."

"My soldiers will go with you," stated Captain Schultz in such a way that the matter was not negotiable. He spoke to the Lieutenant and then turned back to Gendarme Avril. "Go with the Second Lieutenant in the lorry. Bring this Fernand Neau to me." He looked at the café clock; it was now half past four.

Gendarme Avril followed the Lieutenant out to the lorry and climbed with him into the cab alongside the driver; eight more soldiers climbed in the back. The gendarme pointed the way and it was not long before the lorry pulled up near to the Neau farmhouse. There were no lights on; all appeared quiet. Several of the soldiers, some with torches and pistols in hand, others with rifles at the ready, were sent through the farm gate and across the yard to cover the back of the house. The noise brought the two farm dogs racing from the barn barking furiously at the intruders. The Lieutenant, Gendarme Avril and the rest waited in silence at the front of the house giving time for the others to get in place. The officer gave the signal and Gendarme Avril stepped forward to the front door and rapped on it hard while one of the soldiers noisily banged his rifle butt against a window shutter.

The gendarme called out loudly, "Get up Fernand, the Germans want to speak to you."

Chapter 9

Rose awoke with a start at the shouting, the banging and the dogs barking. It was still dark and for a moment she was confused but quickly she realised all this commotion must be to do with the airmen. Petrified, she was afraid to move from her bed. There was shouting in German now in the yard as well as at the front of the house, more banging and rattling of doors.

Young Fernand was the first to react. He had been dozing on and off in the chair by the range. His father who had tried to get some sleep in the front room rushed into the kitchen, pitchfork in hand, but young Fernand was already at the door to the yard shouting angrily, "Go away! Don't you know what time it is? You're waking everyone up. You can't come in, go away!" His father quickly joined him.

"Go away! Go away!" he too shouted.

Suddenly there was a tremendous crash as the door burst open and both young Fernand and his father were sent sprawling as soldiers rushed in, the pitchfork sent skidding harmlessly across the floor. Young Fernand was first up. In the scuffle that ensued a rifle butt brought down on his shoulder sent him reeling to the floor crying out in pain.

In trepidation and with her heart racing Rose tiptoed out of her room to find her mother who was sleeping in young Fernand's bedroom. But her mother was already on the landing.

"Maman, what's happening?" asked Rose anxiously as they held on tightly to each other. It was difficult to make out what was going on with all the shouting and noise. Rose was so frightened she was near to tears. She heard one of the dogs gave a yelp and whine as if it had been kicked and both dogs stopped barking. Tentatively they edged to the top of the stairway and could see torches flashing around the kitchen, lots of them, and heard the sound of heavy boots on the flagstones. There was a glint of torchlight off a helmet and another off a rifle – soldiers were charging into the room shouting loudly in German, sending all sorts of things crashing and clattering to the hard floor.

She heard her father shouting, "Leave him alone! What are you doing? Get out of here, get out of my house!"

In the darkness, punctuated by the stabbing beams of the soldiers' torches Rose could just make out her father being roughly pushed aside and a soldier heading through the kitchen to the front door of the house. Her father tried to stop him but another soldier shouted at him and pushed him out of the way, pinning him hard against a wall with the point of his rifle. The front door was unbolted and more lights appeared accompanied by more shouting adding to the commotion.

"Fernand!" cried out Renée in panic as she started hesitantly down the stairs, her arm held out to keep Rose back. "What's happening? What are they doing?" But her cry was almost drowned in the noise of the general din from downstairs.

"Maman," screamed Rose, "they've hurt Fernand!" A torch had pointed out the prone figure of her brother by the door, a soldier's rifle aimed straight at him. They rushed down the rest of the stairs but when they reached the bottom a soldier quickly moved to bar their way while others barged past them to search the upstairs of the cottage.

Rose and her mother tried to push past the soldier to reach young Fernand but the soldier held firm. Rose called out, "Fernand, are you all right?" Her brother, eyes closed in pain and holding his shoulder, nevertheless gave a brief nod.

Soldiers were everywhere searching the house casting around for possible hiding places, knocking everything out of their way.

All of a sudden a loud, "Hände hoch!" was heard from upstairs and everyone stopped and turned to look at the stairway. All went suddenly quiet and in the silence two trembling figures stumbled down the stairs and shuffled into the middle of the torch-lit kitchen their hands held high and their heads bowed followed by soldiers with rifles pointing at their backs.

At that moment Lieutenant Brandt and Gendarme Avril appeared. The scene that greeted them was as unexpected as it was dramatic. It was like a tableau in a museum, no one moving, silent, the torches still, faces set in the dim light, expressions varying from utter surprise to utter fear, but all eyes were focussed on the two dishevelled, dejected figures in the centre of the room, their arms raised in surrender, rifles and pistols levelled at them. The first to speak was Gendarme Avril quickly taking stock of the startling scene before him.

"The two British airmen!" he said, his exclamation rhetorical. Looking at Rose's father still harshly pinned against the wall he said, "But we only came to bring you in for questioning Fernand, that's all. … For questioning, that's all," he repeated almost apologetically. "What are they doing here? Why are you hiding them here?" he went on pointing at the airmen unable to conceal his disbelief at the turn of events. "Why? Why in your house? Didn't you hear the warnings?"

Fernand Neau stared at him and said resolutely, "They needed help. They were in a bad way and needed our help."

Second Lieutenant Brandt then stepped into the middle of the group, imposing himself and taking charge of the situation. He turned to face the two airmen unable to conceal the satisfaction he felt at his good fortune.

"What have we here?" he said in his broken French.

One of the soldiers said in German that they found the men hiding in one of the upstairs rooms under some blankets.

"Our two missing enemy airmen, I assume," the Lieutenant continued. "Well, well. We did not expect to find you here. Our search is over, I think." He said something in German to one of the soldiers who promptly patted down the two airmen to make sure they had no weapons. During this quick frisk the soldier discovered the phrase book in Norman's pocket but lifted it only enough to see the object was harmless before letting it drop back and resuming his search. When his task was done the soldier nodded in confirmation that all was safe and backed away. The officer moved forward and raised his drawn pistol under Norman McLeod's chin forcing his head up so he was obliged to look the German in the eye.

"English?" the Lieutenant asked coldly, in English this time.

With everything that had happened in the last twenty-four hours, exhausted and now clearly with no hope of escape,

Norman had no resistance left in him and decided it was name and number time.

"Flight Lieutenant Norman McLeod, 43259," he said almost imperceptibly.

"Ah, Offizier," the Lieutenant said to his soldiers, a slight smirk of pleasure on his face. He then turned to Willie Finlayson.

"Warrant Officer William Finlayson, 565372," said Willie in as firm a voice as he could muster.

The Lieutenant issued an order to his men to take the airmen to the truck and as they were being hustled out they looked across at the family, their expressions full of dread and regret. They saw staring back four fearful, bewildered and downcast faces. As Rose watched them go she wondered what would happen to them.

Gendarme Avril interrupted the scene and said to Renée, "Light some candles, Madame, we need to see better."

As Renée began to light some candles on the shelf over the stove the Lieutenant paced around the room. "Who do we have here?" he asked menacingly, looking first at Rose's father.

"Fernand Neau," said the gendarme.

"And here?" pointing to Rose's brother who was now sitting propped against the wall just inside the kitchen door, holding his injured shoulder.

"Fernand Neau, his son."

"Two Fernand Neau. We came for one, now we have two," said the Lieutenant with sarcasm.

He then gave an order to one of the soldiers who dragged Rose's brother to his feet and pushed him to the middle of the room facing the Lieutenant. There he stood shakily, head bowed, still holding his shoulder. Her father was then roughly handled to stand next to him. Resistance was useless and he stood there intimidated into submission, his eyes averting the Lieutenant's. He lifted them to glance reassuringly at Renée but in the dimness he could see only cold fear in her eyes.

The Lieutenant paused a moment then enquired, "And who else have we here?"

"Madame Neau and her daughter Mademoiselle Rose," replied the gendarme.

"For now, our two Fernand Neau will be taken for interrogation," stated the officer. "The Madame and Mademoiselle should stay here. We may need to question them later." He barked out an order in German and two soldiers began shoving Fernand and his son with their rifles towards the front door.

"Leave them alone," shouted Renée stepping forward to try to stop them but another soldier intervened pushing her to the ground and aiming his rifle at her.

"Maman!" cried Rose shocked and trembling at seeing her mother treated so roughly.

Fernand turned and moved to protect his wife shouting, "I'll kill you if you hurt her," but he was set upon by three soldiers who forcibly prevented him and manhandled him towards the door again.

"Let them go! You can't take them," Rose's mother pleaded desperately looking up from the floor, humiliated, with tears in her eyes. "They've not hurt anyone. Leave them be," she persisted as loudly as she could, her tears now flowing. Rose, distressed by it all, started crying too.

But Renée's pleading was to no avail and she knew she was powerless to prevent them being taken away. She looked desperately at her husband as he turned and looked equally forlornly at her and at Rose.

"They needed our help," he called back defiantly, not directly to Renée but generally to everyone in the room as if in justification of his actions.

"Fernand!" Renée cried out in anguish, her arm and hand outstretched towards him as both her husband and her son were forced out of the house.

Meanwhile some of the soldiers who had gone upstairs were rummaging around searching for anything incriminating and other soldiers had gone to the stables and barn. Their searches did not take long and when they came back it was clear they had found nothing of interest to them.

"Try not to worry," advised Gendarme Avril trying to calm the situation. "Stay here and wait for news."

Satisfied there was nothing more to be done at the house the Lieutenant, Gendarme Avril and the other soldiers noisily made their way out to the troop lorry. Rose helped her mother up from the kitchen floor and went with her to the doorway; by now the sky to the east was just beginning to get light. They stood there as the truck passed by heading back into the village, Rose peering into the back hoping to see her father and brother to give them some sign of support; but she could not see them, just two soldiers looking blankly back at her.

"Papa, Fernand!" she cried out, but her voice was lost in the noise and dust as the truck sped off.

Mother and daughter stood there as silence gradually returned, both of them unable to fully comprehend what had happened, how their world had been turned upside down in less than no time and how powerless they had been to stop the German soldiers wreaking havoc in their own house. Distraught at seeing her husband marched away at gunpoint, Renée began to sob uncontrollably, again frightening Rose who thought her mother near to collapse. Although frantic and shaking herself, her mother's near hysteria called for her to do something − try and be strong, she thought.

"Come back inside. Come in and sit down," she said, putting an arm on her mother's shoulder and guiding her into the house. "It may not be as bad as it seems."

It was as if in those brief moments of crisis Rose became even more grown up than before, almost instinctively taking the parental role trying to soothe and reassure in what was a reversal of the normal mother and daughter relationship.

Between sobs her mother poured out her anguish. Why did Rose's father bring the airmen to the house, she deplored? She had told him not to! Now look what's happened! What will they do to them? Where will they take them? When will they be back? Rose had no firm answers. Maybe they will be released later on this morning once they have been questioned, Rose offered hopefully. After all, she said, the Germans had the airmen they had been looking for and nobody had been hurt. For a while her mother was inconsolable. Her shock turned to anger, anger at the Germans, against their brutality in taking away her husband and son without even giving them a chance to defend themselves. Look at the way they barged into our house and the mayhem they caused, she said waving her arm at the mess the kitchen was in. Rose agreed and said she would tidy up when it got light but first of all she would tend the graze on her mother's arm.

Bathing the arm, Rose tried to calm her mother. "We will have to be brave for Papa and Fernand," she said remembering her maxim. "They need us to be strong. I'm sure it won't be long before they are home and this will all be over, over for us at least. Not for those poor airmen though, they are prisoners of war now."

They sat holding hands until gradually Renée calmed down. Rose got her mother a handkerchief so she could blow her nose and dab her eyes which were red from crying. They stayed sitting there, Rose taking her mother's hands, not talking, both immersed in their own thoughts, which for Rose were dominated by her mother's distress – she had never seen her mother in such a state before and it scared her.

After a while her mother said reassuringly, looking at Rose, "Thank you, darling. I'm better now. It's all a shock but I'm sure they'll be home soon." Comforting words but Rose understood full well her father and brother were in great danger.

Outside the café the troop truck drew up and the Lieutenant ordered the driver to go into the café to alert Captain Schulz that he was bringing in the two airmen captured at the Neau house. Captain Schulz was staggered and delighted in equal measures; it had been a long, tiring and frustrating night but now given this news all that was forgotten. Before the driver could say any more he butted in, now animated and fully alert.

"Have you arrested Fernand Neau?" he wanted to know. The driver, unable to suppress a smile, confirmed they had arrested two men at the house. The Captain leant back in his chair thinking this was indeed a much unexpected and most satisfactory outcome to his night's work for which he would receive considerable credit. He would enjoy meeting these two enemy airmen. At the beginning he was doubtful of their existence but now their capture would gain him valuable kudos with his superiors.

The Second Lieutenant strode into the café followed by his downcast prisoners: Willie and the limping Norman guarded by several soldiers, followed by Fernand and his son also under escort. Gendarme Avril brought up the rear. Captain Schulz rose and the Second Lieutenant saluted him briskly. Captain Schulz returned the salute but more slowly as he was already surveying his prizes. He ordered the two groups into opposite corners of the now crowded room and then invited the Second Lieutenant to give his report which he listened to intently nodding his approval every now and again. He asked some short questions which were answered to his obvious satisfaction and at the conclusion he congratulated the Second Lieutenant on his work.

"So," he said in English moving over to where Norman and Willie were standing; Norman determined to stand without assistance. "You are prisoners of war now. You will cooperate fully. If you try to escape you will be shot. Cooperate and I will see you are treated well. Tell me your names." Norman and Willie repeated their names and numbers. "We have an officer I see. I expect you to act as an officer," he said to Norman. He then turned and crossed the room to Fernand and his son. This time he spoke in his broken French.

"Messieurs Neau. You are in very serious trouble. You have violated the official ordinance of 10th October 1940 which strictly forbids the concealing or giving accommodation to the enemy. This ordinance was repeated only two weeks ago here in St. Michel-en-l'Herm. You must cooperate fully otherwise the most severe punishments will follow."

The Mayor, who had been abruptly roused from his drowsiness by the drama, now looked on with growing concern not only for the fate of Fernand Neau and his son which he greatly feared but also for the community. He was well aware from reports of similar episodes elsewhere that the Germans could bring harsh reprisals on the whole of the village. He also felt a degree of compassion for the two dishevelled British prisoners of war whose future was now bleak. He looked on but said nothing. Till then he had just wanted to go home to his bed but he felt he should stay now to see the outcome of these startling developments and to lobby against any threat of reprisals.

Captain Schulz gave orders to move everyone into the restaurant area next door with strict instructions that no one should speak and then proceeded to phone his commander's office with his report which he gave with barely disguised pleasure. He was to await further orders and meanwhile he should obtain what information he could, he was instructed. As he put down the phone Claude and Marcel were brought in. They looked very frightened. They too were marched into the restaurant. Starting with Norman, Captain Schulz interrogated each in turn under an armed guard. His command of both English and French was just sufficient not to require an interpreter.

With Norman he tried the tactic that as officers they should respect each other and he promised medical help when he saw Norman limping badly, offering him a chair which he refused. But Norman would only repeat his name and number to questions about how he came to be found at the Neau house. Captain Schulz tried to encourage him to cooperate by intimating other, later interrogators would be far less tolerant of any lack of cooperation; nevertheless Norman, despite everything, refused to give any further information. Willie likewise refused to say anything other than his name and number but Captain Schulz lost his temper with the sergeant, bawling threats and whacking his baton on the desk.

Next the Captain turned to the two witnesses Claude and Marcel. Here he had more success as his threats of deportation soon produced a corroborated story of what happened at the dyke. Armed with this Captain Schulz called in Rose's brother from the restaurant next door. Young Fernand stood and stared at his interrogator, his expression a mixture of anger and hatred yet underneath he was taut with apprehension. Yet when Captain Schulz started by praising him saying he was a very brave man to have rescued the two airmen in the way he did, young Fernand was slightly wrong-footed. It was obvious this information came from Claude and Marcel and there was no point in denying his involvement at the dyke, at least as far as Claude and Marcel knew. However when questioned further about how the airmen came to be hidden at his house and about his father's part young Fernand played dumb much to the Captain's annoyance, his tone quickly turning nasty. Even though the Captain threatened dire consequences of his non-cooperation young Fernand refused to answer questions about his father's motives or about anyone else who might have been involved.

It was nearing half past seven when the Captain ordered Rose's father to be brought before him. He tried the same ploy, at first flattering him about his son's rescue but Rose's father was wary. The phone rang, however, as the Captain was about to demand answers and Rose's father was returned to the restaurant area.

It was the District Commander on the phone and Captain Schulz gave him an update. He was delighted when the Commander commended him on the successful outcome but slightly less pleased when his orders prevented him carrying on with his questioning. The two prisoners of war were to be taken immediately to the camp at l'Aiguillon-sur-Mer to be examined by the doctor there before being taken on to La Roche-sur-Yon for interrogation and processing. The Neau father and son should be taken to the military barracks at Fontenay-le-Compte for further questioning, the soldiers returned to their barracks and the Mayor and witnesses released. Captain Schulz put down the phone and called again for Rose's father.

"I have a question before you are to be taken away. Who helped you? You must have had help. Who was it? It will be easier for you to tell me now and then I can say you have cooperated which will be better for you. You may even receive just a reprimand. However if you do not cooperate I have to warn you, in accordance with official ordinances which warned against assisting or giving accommodation to the enemy, you could be shot."

Rose's father had had a little time while in the restaurant to think of his predicament. Over the years he had talked himself out of many situations with a cheeky confidence – but this was different. He was only too aware of the Germans' reputation for ruthlessness and brutality both during the invasion and since in occupation, which made him very frightened indeed. But adding to his predicament was the need to conceal the identities of others, particularly Alphonse Gouraud. On top of that was his concern for his son and how his wife would cope with all this. He decided to plead now for his release in the hope this officer was naive enough to fall for it.

"Look, I did not know about these ordinances you talk about, I'm just a local farmer out in the fields all day. My son told me of the terrible ordeal those airmen had been through and I took pity on them as they needed help, just as anyone would have done. There's no harm done, no one hurt and they are your prisoners now. So you can let us go. I know not to do anything like this again. Let me and my son go and they'll be no more trouble I can promise you. Gendarme Avril will vouch for me, he's known me for years and …" The Captain held up his hand.

"Stop," he barked. "I repeat, who helped you?" Undeterred Rose's father ploughed on.

"Let us go, there's no harm done. As I say I have just a small farm and my wife and children depend on me and I did not realise I was doing anything wrong, just helping …" This time the Captain, exasperated, hammered his fist on the table.

"You have one last chance to give me the information," he said slowly with all the menace he could muster.

"Nobody helped. So you can let us go and there'll be no more …"

At that point Captain Schulz turned and ordered the guard to take him back to the restaurant and although he tried to carry on with his plea the guard shoved him with his rifle into the other room.

The Captain sat in his chair and leant back taking a moment to reflect on a good night's work before ordering the removal of his prisoners and the return of the troops to barracks. He stood in the doorway of the café to witness the departures. Firstly young Fernand and his father were bundled into the back of the Second Lieutenant's car, both scared as never before while Norman and Willie waited for the large covered truck to back up to the café door.

It was the face of Rose's father at the rear window of the car which caught Norman's eye. The mournful gaze was so full of despair that Norman's heart became heavy with dread for this brave Frenchman. There could be no handshake, no further word of thanks; all Norman could do was to nod his head briefly in salute and murmur under his breath, 'Good luck'. But as the car sped off Norman feared that despairing look would haunt him for ever.

Moments later Norman and Willie were hauled on to the back of the truck but Norman slipped awkwardly for a second and felt the phrase book fall out of his pocket on to the ground. He feigned a cry of agony to divert attention and prayed it had not been noticed. Almost immediately the truck began to move but one of the soldiers who had not yet sat down shouted, "Halt!" and jumped off as the truck came to a sudden stop. Looking back Norman saw him pick up the book and wave it. The soldier then hurried to hand over the book to the corporal in the cab of the truck explaining what he had seen before climbing back aboard. The truck set off again, heading in the opposite direction to the car, passing the Mayor, Claude and Marcel as they shuffled dejectedly homewards. Norman rued the discovery of the book which, after the soldier had earlier left it in his pocket, he had planned to dispose of secretly as soon as possible, but now he was forced to think of an explanation that would not implicate Rose and her family.

After a while Rose made her mother a cup of ersatz coffee, substitute coffee was all they had now, and began clearing up the mess left behind by the ransacking of their home. In the kitchen the table had been barged into and everything on it had scattered across the flagstones. A chair was on its side, one leg broken and several pots and pans had been knocked off their pegs and dented. The other rooms had been turned upside down. Upstairs there was clothing and furniture strewn across the floor, cupboards left open and bedclothes thrown back. Fortunately it did not take as long to clear up as she had expected given all the racket there had been in the dark.

"It's early yet but I'll lay the table for breakfast. I'll lay it for four; they may be home sooner than we think and hungry," said Rose with a weak smile, trying to be positive.

"Are you all right?" said her mother. "You seem to be doing everything."

"I'm fine," replied Rose as she busied around while at the same time keeping an eye on her mother. A little later her mother stirred.

"Let me finish that. I must do something. You feed the chickens and collect the eggs and check on the stable and barn while you're out there."

When she came back her mother had obviously been thinking.

"We must get your Grandpapa and Grandmaman over here; they must be told what has happened. Maybe Grandpapa can go into the village later to find out what is happening. And we must also tell your Aunt Sophie, Papy and Mamie. They will tell your Uncle Bernard. Do you think you could go over to Grandpapa's and ask them to come? Try not to alarm them too much."

"We'll have something to eat first and then I'll go on the bike," said Rose. "Will you be all right on your own? I'll come straight back."

After some breakfast Rose rode over to her grandparent's house. They were surprised to see her so early. All Rose told them was that when her father had left them yesterday he had gone to help two British parachutists and now he and her brother had been taken in for questioning. She told them her mother wanted them to come up to the farm.

"Maman is very upset," she added to ensure they would leave straight away.

Shaken at the news her grandparents started to ask questions but Rose just said she had told her mother she would go back immediately and that, please, they should follow as soon as they could. When they arrived at the farm a short while later Rose and her mother began recounting at length the events of the previous twenty-four hours, punctuated by incessant questioning from both grandparents incredulous and alarmed at the unfolding story. They were indignant and sympathised at the harsh treatment the family had received from the German soldiers and said they would do all they could to help, of course. A discussion ensued about what should be done. Rose's mother said they had to remain at the house but that they desperately needed to find out what was happening. It was eventually agreed that Rose's grandfather would go into the village towards midday to see what he could learn. He suggested Rose meanwhile help him around the yard to take her mind off things.

"The horse will need feeding and given some exercise," he said getting up. "It doesn't look as if he will be working today. And we need to feed the other animals," he added, at the same time inclining his head towards the door as if to say they should leave his wife and Rose's mother alone together for a little while.

Later, when Grandpapa arrived back from the village Rose was cutting some bread for their midday meal. The look on his face said it all; there was no news. He said he had called at the Mayor's office. The Mayor told him he had been at the café when Fernand Neau and his son and the two airmen were brought in, but not long afterwards the Mayor said he had gone home to bed. All he had been informed that morning was that the airmen had been taken away towards l'Aiguillon-sur-Mer. He didn't know what had happened to Fernand Neau and his son. Maybe the local gendarmes would know, he had said. But none of the gendarmes were in their office and Grandpapa had been advised to return later. He was sorry, but he had no information. They all sat down to some bread and cheese in a rather despondent mood not feeling particularly hungry. A little while afterwards Rose's grandmother announced she would go to church to light candles and to pray for everyone, it was the least she could do to help she said.

As the clock neared half past four Rose's mother announced that she had to go herself to the village despite the warning to stay at home. She could not bear this waiting, she said. Although Rose could see her mother had regained some composure she did not want her to go alone and said she would go with her. Leaving the grandparents at the house, the two set off with purpose heading for the Town Hall before it closed at five o'clock. There they were told the Mayor had gone home unwell and they were seen by Monsieur Caillaud his deputy. He was sympathetic but unable to add anything to what the Mayor had said earlier. Again his advice was to go to the gendarme's office where they may have the latest information. Rose and her mother set off again, trying to be resolute. The gendarme there said he thought the civilian prisoners from last night would have been taken to Luçon or possibly to Fontenay-le-Compte but he could not be sure. They should ask at the café where the German officer there must have the information they seek. Outside in the bright sunlight Rose noticed tears welling up in her mother's eyes and she realised her mother could not cope with any more disappointment or humiliation.

"Let's go home," she said softly taking her mother's arm. "We don't want to go to the café, it might make things worse. Let's just go home and wait. We can try again in the morning." They turned and walked home trying to hide their obvious distress in public.

Since her father and brother had been taken away Rose had been in trepidation the Germans would return to arrest her mother, possibly herself or even both of them but she tried hard to keep a brave face. Now on the way home she worried Germans would be there waiting to arrest them for leaving the house and was relieved to see no sign of soldiers as they neared the farm.

Her mother had similar worries too but tried not to show it for her daughter's sake. On top of everything, though, she knew she could not take much more and had to summon the strength to struggle home.

Rose and her grandfather did some more chores around the farm, both of them feeling it was better to be doing something. Her mother accepted Grandmaman's offer to stay the night; Rose too was pleased to have her grandmother stay. All the time they kept an expectant ear for anyone returning; but no one turned up and in the end they all went to bed early as the day had taken its toll. As Rose lay in the dark on her bed she could not help but think of her distraught mother; of not knowing where her father was and if he was afraid; and of her injured brother who might be locked up somewhere, alone and bewildered. She was also worried for herself in case she was taken for questioning but the more she thought about the others the more her heartache overwhelmed her and she sobbed quietly on her pillow until tiredness sent her to sleep.

In the morning she went downstairs early only to find her mother and grandmother were already busy in the kitchen. She was shocked to see her mother looking so awful, as though she had had no sleep.

"Are you all right, Maman?" Rose enquired. "Did you sleep?"

"Not a lot," said her mother somewhat wearily.

"Oh Maman!" said Rose trying to console her.

"But I've decided to go to Luçon this morning," her mother announced, "to find out where your father and Fernand are. It's not really possible to get to Fontenay-le-Compte but they are bound to know at Luçon."

"I could go with you," said Rose thinking her mother should not go alone.

"Why don't you let Rose go on her own, Renée?" said Grandmaman. "You're too upset. Stay here in case they come home or news comes here. I'll stay with you. Rose knows Luçon. She'll be able to find out."

"I should go," argued Rose's mother but only weakly. She did feel totally washed out; it was her spirit that was telling her it was her duty to go.

"What if they come home and you are not here. What will they think after all they have been through? And you not here to greet them," said Grandmaman making her thoughts on the matter very clear.

"I can do it on my own, Maman," said Rose outwardly confident but nevertheless nervous inside. "I know where to go. Grandmaman is right."

Renée relented. She should go, she told herself, and she would have made the effort but she conceded the argument for staying. She had seen how Rose had grown up this last year, how she was confident and competent and she could be very persistent. In a way she took a little satisfaction in seeing how well her daughter was coping with all this and her willingness to take on the responsibility of going to Luçon.

“Are you sure you can go on your own?” she asked Rose just to be certain.

“Oh, yes,” answered Rose feeling buoyed at the thought of being given this important mission but not wanting to show it.

“You had better hurry,” said Grandmaman now content with the arrangements. “The first train leaves just before eight o’clock and you want to be on that. It will be crowded remember, it is market day at Luçon.”

Rose bought her train ticket to Luçon at the station and walked on to the low platform, tucking her ticket in her school purse which she wore schoolgirl-style with the long strap diagonally across her. Journeys to Luçon had always been a thrill. She recalled her excitement the first time she went there with the family for a day’s treat to the big Saturday market held once a month. She remembered also the time her father took her for her first term at the High School there; and how grown up she felt at being allowed to travel home on her own for the first time at half term. She had become very fond of the little narrow-gauge railway that ran between l’Aiguillon-sur-Mer and Luçon. As a child she had watched the train go by countless times as it trundled along near one of her father’s fields, pulled staunchly by a grimy green saddle-tank engine with a tall funnel which billowed steam and smoke noisily into the air. Back then it was just a fascination, now the train was a symbol of her growing independence taking her away from her family to an outside world which was different and exciting. Today the little train had a special duty to perform for her – it would carry her on a journey to find her father and brother, maybe even bring them home. Usually she loved just watching the fields pass by as the train rattled its way slowly across the flat terrain but today her mind was taken up by planning what she would do when she got to Luçon, practising what she would ask, determined to be positive and stay in control. She decided to call first at the Town Hall; the people there should at least be able to direct her even if they did not have the information she needed. It was going to be another baking hot day and she was glad of the breeze through the open windows. The little train made only 20 mph at the best of times and with a scheduled stop at the next village, Triaize, and occasional unscheduled stops along the way the journey took nearly 50 minutes. Rose's ticket took her to the main station on the north side of Luçon but she worked out if she got off at the Luçon Port station to the south of the town centre she could save about ten minutes in getting to the Town Hall. It was nine o'clock when Rose approached the imposing Town Hall building which she knew well as it was next to the entrance to the beautiful public gardens where she and her school friends walked at weekends during term-time. Rose climbed the steps to the entrance, her heart beating a little faster, rehearsing the questions she wanted to ask. She approached the information kiosk behind which was a large lady reading something on the counter, a pen poised in her hand. She did not look up immediately but when she did she merely peered over the top of her glasses.

"Mademoiselle?" was all she said.

Rose started her prepared piece. "I have come from St. Michel-en-l'Herm to find my father and brother who were arrested yesterday morning. We were told they may have been brought to Luçon. Can you help me please?"

"We won't have any information here." said the large lady. "You need to go to the main police station in rue du Calvaire. Do you know where that is?" Rose not recognising the street name shook her head. "Left out of here and it's not far on your right."

"Thank you," said Rose. In St. Michel-en-l'Herm the Mayor's office would have known what was going on, but the tone of the lady's voice did not invite further query so Rose turned and made her way to rue du Calvaire. Inside the police station the sergeant at the desk was dealing with someone so Rose waited by the door taking in the reception area. It was functional, nothing else. The room was painted in drab colours, there was a board with various notices pinned to it and there were a few chairs set against a wall; that was all. Rose found it depressing. When the sergeant became free Rose approached him.

As she reached the desk the sight of a pretty young face brought a brief smile to the sergeant's face – here was someone who might brighten the start of the day, he thought.

"And what can I do for you, Mademoiselle?" he invited.

"I have come from St. Michel-en-l'Herm to find my father and brother who were arrested yesterday morning. We were told they may have been brought to Luçon. Can you help me please? The lady at the Town Hall said I should come here."

"What are their names?" asked the sergeant.

"My father's name is Monsieur Fernand Neau, N.E.A.U." She spelt it out to avoid confusion. "My brother has the same name."

"Let me look," the sergeant said reaching over for the custody register. Rose held her breath as his finger moved down the last few entries on the sheet.

"Neau, you say. Nothing of that name here. Are you sure they were brought here?"

"They were taken away by soldiers. The gendarme said they might have brought them here or Fontenay-le-Compte. If they are not here can you contact Fontenay-le-Compte to find out if they are there, please?"

"Ah. You say they were arrested by soldiers? In that case they won't be held by the Gendarmerie but by the German military. You need to go to the guardroom at the barracks and ask there. Go back and turn right. The guardroom block is along there by the gates in the tall iron railings." The sergeant could see Rose was disappointed. "It's not far," he said kindly. He wanted to ask this pretty young lady why her father and brother had been detained but he knew it was best to avoid getting involved with military matters if at all possible.

"Thank you," said Rose turning to leave, trying not to let her disappointment show. Outside she tried to pull herself together as she walked to the barracks; she had not expected to be directed to a German military place and the thought unnerved her. She was frightened to go there but she knew she must; she would just have to summon the courage and hold back the bitterness she felt at the treatment her family had suffered.

She walked alongside the tall, black-painted railings until she came to a large two storey block with a set of gates at the side guarded by a soldier. She could see a sign over the door to the building which read 'Corps de Garde' that meant she was at the right place. She went up to the soldier and said she needed to go to the guardroom to ask for her father, pointing at the door. The soldier nodded her through and Rose stepped inside and into a reception room like the one at the police station, only this place was far more frightening as it was manned by a German soldier rather than a gendarme. Bracing herself Rose stepped up to the soldier at the desk in a confident manner, at least she hoped she appeared confident.

"I have come from St. Michel-en-l'Herm to find my father and brother who were arrested yesterday morning. We were told they may have been brought to Luçon. Can you help me please? They both have the same name, Monsieur Fernand Neau."

The soldier did not answer her but in response merely called in German over his shoulder to a colleague who appeared a moment to two later. Rose repeated her question to the new soldier who seemed to struggle to understand. Rose picked up a pen and a piece of paper that were on the desk and wrote her father's name. She turned the piece of paper around and pushed it forward.

"My father and brother," she said. "Arrested; yesterday. Are they here, please?"

The two soldiers spoke briefly in German, then one of them reached for a large register which he opened and checked the piece of paper against the names in the book.

"Nein, nicht hier," said the first soldier.

"No, your father and brother not here," said the second soldier in French although Rose had guessed the answer from the first soldier and her heart was already sinking, tears coming to her eyes. She blinked them away.

"Maybe they're at Fontenay-le-Compte then. Can you find out where they are?" she said, her frustration beginning to show and in her exasperation she spoke more quickly and insistently. The second soldier's understanding of French was poor and he could not follow Rose's appeal.

"Not here," he repeated shrugging his shoulders and becoming clearly uninterested.

"You must help me!" pleaded Rose but all the soldier did was to turn to his colleague and shrug his shoulders again.

"No understand."

Nearing tears again Rose tapped the piece of paper and said more loudly, "My father! You must help me find my father! Please."

Deliberately this time the soldier said firmly, "No understand," and turned away into a corridor and out of sight. The first soldier, who obviously had no French, just looked unfeelingly at her.

"Nicht hier," he said with finality.

She was getting nowhere and her head was spinning with frustration. Someone must know. Why was it so difficult? Why would no one help? Tears began to stream down her face and she turned and ran out. She ran down the road only slowing down when she had passed the last of the barracks' railings. She walked back to the public gardens, past the Town Hall and sat down on a bench where it was quiet. What should she do now, she asked herself? Where else is there to go? The only people who could help were the soldiers and they did not want to know. She could go back and try again but could not face that prospect and accepted she would have to go home with no news. Somehow she could not help thinking she was failing her father. She had imagined travelling back with him on the train and everything would be all right. Now all she felt was despondency, not even knowing where he was and what he and Fernand were going through. And when she reminded herself it was not just her father but her brother too who was locked up somewhere, she held her head in her hands and a tear trickled down her face. When she eventually stopped sobbing she was glad no one had seen her. Gradually she composed herself and planned to go home. She looked at her watch, it was nearly eleven o'clock and she realised she was hungry having had no proper breakfast only the slice of bread she had quickly grabbed as she hurried to catch the early train. The next train home was at ten minutes past twelve so she had a little time to spare. She decided to go to the market fair where she could get something to eat with the little money she had. The monthly fair had always been a fascinating place to wander around even if just looking.

As usual the market was lively, colourful and noisy. Rose bought a baguette and a pastry and found a seat under a shady tree to sit and eat. As it was holiday time and a beautiful day the market was crowded with families, some on a day trip like the day she was brought here as a child. The children were all excited and desperate to spend their few centimes pocket money, perhaps at the sweet stall. Mothers were inspecting the produce, feeling, smelling, selecting, and finally bartering before they purchased. Fathers were more interested in the practical things on sale, things which would help mend and make do at home because there was little money to go around and anything new was in short supply and expensive. But everyone was in a good mood, enjoying a rare day out, forgetting for now the cares of the war. The scene cheered up Rose and she felt better. She wandered round the stalls idly stopping here and there saying 'no thanks' to constant urging by the stallholders to buy their goods. It was all a game, she knew that and usually it was fun, except today the fun was tempered by her worries and the contrast that all was normal for these people but not for her and her family.

After an hour or so she made her way to the main railway station where she sat in the sun watching the passengers gather for the train to l'Aiguillon-sur-Mer, some with their purchases from the market, others on a trip to the seaside. When the little train puffed into the station she climbed aboard the last carriage where she was able to find a seat. Families with bags or luggage and excited children filled the train. As it left Luçon and rumbled along through the countryside Rose hoped her melancholy did not show. On a different occasion she might have exchanged a few words with some of the other passengers whom she might have known in passing but this time she was glad there was nobody she recognised, her thoughts being taken up with the news, or lack of it, she would have to relate when she got home. She tried to cheer herself up with the idea that maybe Papa and Fernand had already been released and would be at home to greet her. It is possible, she tried to tell herself, but she was unconvinced somehow particularly as the day had been full of disappointment so far.

The train began to slow. Rose recognised they were nearing Triaize where many of the passengers would alight. She sat looking out of the open window on the side of the carriage away from the station platform not really taking much notice when she became aware the carriage had fallen silent as the train came to a halt. She looked around and saw the reason for the sudden change of mood among the passengers. To her dismay, on the platform was a detachment of German soldiers. Two of them entered the carriage calling, "Ausweis bitte," which everyone knew by now meant they wanted to see identification papers.

Initially Rose froze as she thought they must looking for her but she soon realised they were merely carrying out a spot check on people's papers. She began to relax a little and felt in her purse for her papers. She found her ticket, but her papers were not there. She searched again in the main part and then in the little pocket at the front; but no papers. Her heart began to race. Had she lost them? She thought hard, then realised she had transferred her papers from her school purse to her every day purse but in her haste she had chosen to take her school purse today because it was smarter for her visit to the big town. How could she have forgotten her papers were in the other one, she thought? She started to panic but just as she looked up a soldier moved right in front of her saying in a monotonous tone, "Ausweis bitte."

"I've left my papers at home," said Rose nervously.

"Ausweis bitte," repeated the soldier holding out his hand, obviously not comprehending.

Rose opened out her hands to demonstrate she did not have any, saying again as she shook her head, "I've left my papers at home." Her heart was pounding and she was glad to be sitting down.

The soldier called over to a colleague and Rose again explained the problem.

"You must come with me," demanded the new soldier taking Rose's arm to usher her off the train. Rose tried to pull her arm away in resistance.

"I only live at St. Michel-en-l'Herm. You can check my ID there," she protested but the soldier was not interested, just tightened his grip on her arm forcing her up and towards the carriage door. In anguish Rose cast around for help among the staring, silent passengers in the carriage, but there was no one she could see whom she knew. Everyone was now following her contretemps with the soldiers but nobody tried to intervene on her behalf. Rose gave up her resistance and found herself being hustled to the stationmaster's office. She was more alarmed than embarrassed at being escorted off in front of a whole trainload of passengers. What sort of trouble would she be in?

In the stationmaster's office Rose was made to stand against a wall while an officer was fetched, and as she waited her heart sank at hearing the little train puff out of the station. Rose looked across the room at the stationmaster for help but he stayed seated behind his desk. He did however acknowledge her presence with a concerned yet kindly glance. Before the officer arrived she tried to think of an excuse for leaving her papers at home but could not think of anything convincing. She decided to tell the truth, at least as far as possible without mentioning the situation at home. An officer entered the room and looked Rose up and down and seeing her youth the hardness in his eyes seemed to soften a touch.

"You have no papers," he stated accusingly in French.

"No, sir," said Rose looking at the floor.

"Why not? You know you must have papers at all times."

"I swapped purses when I came out. My papers are in my other purse at home. I live in the next village, St. Michel-en-l'Herm. I'm sorry, sir, I won't let it happen again."

"What is your name?"

"Rose, Rose Neau. I just went to the market at Luçon. Here, look, here is my ticket," offered Rose hoping this would be sufficient.

The officer took the ticket and handed it to the stationmaster asking if it was valid. The stationmaster confirmed it was valid and then said he would telephone the stationmaster at St. Michel-en-l'Herm as he might know the girl. While he made the call the officer turned back to Rose.

"You have not bought anything at the market?"

"They didn't have what I wanted," replied Rose deliberately not answering his question directly.

The stationmaster put the phone down and told the officer Rose was known to his colleague at St. Michel-en-l'Herm.

"Very well," said the officer. "This time there will be no punishments. Next time ..." he tailed off the sentence leaving the threat in the air.

"Leave her with me," said the stationmaster. "I will see she catches the next train."

With that the officer turned and led his soldiers out to the station forecourt where their vehicles were parked and Rose watched with relief as they drove off.

"Thank you," said Rose to the stationmaster. His kindly face gave her reassurance although she was still shaking from the experience.

"Here, come and sit down. Was it your father who was arrested for helping some English airmen? The stationmaster at St. Michel-en-l'Herm told me about it."

"Yes," nodded Rose sitting down on the chair in front of the desk. "You didn't tell the Germans though, did you?" The stationmaster just shook his head slowly. She decided she could trust him and told him she had been to Luçon to find news of her father and brother but had learned nothing. The stationmaster took pity on her.

"Stay in my office till the next train. You'll be all right here. The next train is not for another two hours. I'll phone my wife to bring you something."

Although Rose thanked him and said she was fine, the stationmaster picked up the phone and spoke to his wife who a little while later appeared with a pot of coffee, a cordial drink and some biscuits.

"Join me," said the stationmaster. "I usually have something about now," he added somewhat unconvincingly though Rose did not notice. She realised she did need something to help calm her and gladly accepted the stationmaster's offer.

She had thought about walking home from Triaize; it was only five miles or so, a distance she would normally think nothing of walking. But she felt obliged to wait as the stationmaster had been so kind and had promised the German officer he would see her on the next train. In any case she still felt shaky and in no mood for the trek even though walking would probably get her home a little earlier. She knew her mother might start to worry but she could do nothing about that and settled herself for the wait. After a while a thought crossed her mind that brought a half smile to her face. Always taught by her father to tell the truth, she thought he would be pleased she had managed to thwart her German interrogators without telling an out-and-out lie – he would chuckle at that.

The mood at home that evening was bleak since there was disappointment all round when Rose finally arrived back to find no father or brother waiting to greet her and she herself had no good news to impart. And to make matters worse, Rose's mother told her a neighbour had called round to say that Alphonse Gouraud and his son had been arrested earlier and that the talk in the village was that her father or brother must have denounced the Gourauds. The neighbour also said that some people were afraid there would be reprisals for the whole village. It was just gossip, nothing more, her mother said trying to reassure her. It was a terrible blow to hear the Gourauds had been taken. But what really upset Rose was that people should malign her father so and her mother's efforts to play it down as mere gossip had little effect.

As they were all about to retire, Rose's mother rather suddenly announced, "We must all pray for their release at Mass tomorrow, the Gourauds too. They need our prayers. We shall seek God's help." Rose knew her mother never missed church on Sundays and despite all that had happened it seemed tomorrow would be no exception, her mother's announcement dispelling any doubt.

Dressed as usual in their Sunday best with heads covered, Rose and her mother went to Mass; Rose's grandmother joined them having gone to her own home first to change for church. They placed lighted candles in front of the statue of Our Lady each saying a silent prayer. Normally after the service there would be clusters of parishioners outside the church exchanging news and gossip. Rose's mother would normally be amongst them but today most of the congregation moved off as Rose, her mother and grandmother came out of the church. The atmosphere was tense and awkward, glances towards them were brief, heads lowered in embarrassment at either not knowing what to say or wanting to avoid eye contact. At least the priest came over to them. He said he knew of their troubles and that he would visit them.

Rose's mother thanked him and as the priest moved on to another group, sensing they were being cold-shouldered by a number of the congregation, said loud enough for others to hear, "We should get back." At which she set off at a faster pace than usual leaving Rose and her grandmother to catch up.

The next morning Rose was busy helping her mother clean the kitchen when the dogs began to bark at a visitor coming across the yard. Renée went immediately to the door and saw it was Estelle Bon approaching.

"It's only me, Renée," she called.

"Estelle, how good of you to come," Renée welcomed her friend and they exchanged the usual greetings. "Come in, come in." After greeting Rose, Estelle Bon sat down at the table with Renée and the two began discussing in earnest the events of the last few days while Rose listened in on the conversation as she continued with what she was doing. It was obvious that Madame Bon had great sympathy with the family's plight and offered all the help she could give. It was also clear that she held in contempt those in the village who spread malicious rumours about Fernand denouncing Alphonse Gouraud. She had witnessed the scene at church and felt ashamed at the behaviour of some she thought she knew well. Feelings in the village were running high, she said, but told Renée not to worry as very many supported what Fernand had done, they were just afraid to show it publicly. Rose could see her mother was greatly comforted by Madame Bon's words and unswerving support. Reiterating her promises of help Madame Bon took her leave.

A little while later the dogs started barking again, more excitedly this time. Rose stopped wiping the table and her heart quickened at the prospect of news. Listening as she dried her hands, she immediately recognised a familiar voice ordering the dogs to be quiet and her heart raced even faster.

"It's Fernand, Maman! Fernand's home!" she called out elatedly and almost before she finished drying her hands her brother appeared in the doorway tired-looking and dishevelled.

"I'm back," he said, his tone almost matter of fact. "They released me." Before he could say anything else Rose and her mother rushed to hug him, all three in an embrace which lasted and lasted.

"My son, my son!" his mother kept repeating. Eventually, as she released him she asked, "What of your father?"

"No news, Maman. I asked to see him, several times, but they wouldn't let me or tell me anything. They just put me in a car back here. I asked the soldiers again at the café before they let me go but all they said was that I was to stay on the farm and not go anywhere. We were taken to the military barracks at Fontenay-le-Compte but I didn't see Papa after we were put in separate cells."

Gradually his story came out. He was never much of a talker and hated being asked question after question but bit by bit he told of his ordeal. There was no denying the fact that the airmen had been found at the farmhouse and the Germans knew he had rescued them from drowning in the bay, information that must have been given by the two council workers who were at the dyke; he saw them at the café when he and Papa were taken there. There was a brief interrogation at the café but he did not let on what happened after the rescue and then he and Papa were taken by car to Fontenay-le-Compte but he did not know what happened to the airmen. He was put in a small cell, he said, and to his surprise nothing else happened that day. The next day though he was questioned time and time again but he kept to his story that he knew nothing other than the rescue and the airman arriving late at the farm. He said the Germans asked lots of questions about why Papa hid the airmen, who Papa's friends were, who his own friends were, was Papa a communist, were the family Jewish. It seemed to him as though they suspected Papa was in some sort of resistance group like those rumoured to be in the north of France. Another interrogator tried more questions the next day, he said, but again he told them that all he and Papa did was to rescue the airmen and give them some food and shelter because they were in a bad way. The Germans had said it would be best for Papa if he told them the truth because Papa was in very serious trouble. Over and over again he told the Germans he did not know they had done anything wrong; they had not heard any announcement and did not read newspapers. And he repeated many times that he did not know what Papa intended to do with the airmen.

"They wanted names but I didn't tell them anything. It was difficult. They asked lots of questions," he said. He could not know what the two airmen might have said or indeed what Papa had told his interrogators, he explained. "But I didn't denounce anyone. No one! I don't know how I managed it, but I did," he said, emphasising the point.

"But listen," he said, "as I was leaving the café when they told me I could go, Monsieur Brard the dairyman was being brought in. And I heard just now from my friend Olivier when I saw him in the village that Alphonse Gouraud and his son Michel have been arrested. That's bad. Apparently Papa was seen that evening on Alphonse Gouraud's cart and the Germans searched his house and yard and arrested them. That's what's being said in the village anyway. But I wasn't questioned about Alphonse Gouraud or Monsieur Brard."

In the end, he said, they seemed to tire of questioning him and let him go. He hoped Papa would also be released very soon.

"Poor Papa, still locked up. How did they treat you? What about your shoulder?" asked Rose who had been hanging on his every word.

"The shoulder's just bruised – it will be all right," he replied. "But I'm glad I wasn't in that cell any longer; being locked in was the worst. Papa will cope, though, I'm sure," he said to reassure his mother. He had deliberately played down the worst parts of the last few days for fear of his mother worrying about his father more than she already was. Rose was curious to know what it was like in the prison cell but held her questions for later.

The following morning the local priest called as he had promised. He said it was encouraging that young Fernand had been released, and offered words of comfort and prayers for the release of Rose's father saying the family may call on him at any time should they need during these difficult days. Rose listened to his words carefully and she began to get irritated. Not once, she noticed, did the priest condemn the Germans for their actions and brutal invasion of their home. And she wanted to challenge him because no one in the Church seemed to be speaking out against the war, the killing and destruction. She was incensed, itching to speak her mind but with difficulty she held her tongue out of respect for her mother, seeing her mother's reverence towards the priest. He did however agree in response to her mother's request to have a quiet word in the ear of one or two people who may be able to have some influence in obtaining her father's release but he could not guarantee any results. That mollified Rose a little but she still seethed inside at how weak she thought the priest was; he did not even pay tribute to the family for their Christian acts in saving and helping the poor airmen. She bit her lip and went out of the house as the priest left for fear of upsetting her mother with her frustrations.

A little later she heard her mother call her. "Rose, there is someone here to see you." For once her mother sounded cheerful and Rose dropped what she was doing and hurried over to the house. The visitor was Monsieur Tessier, Rose's teacher in her last year at the local school.

"Hello Monsieur Tessier," said Rose pleased to see her old teacher whom she really liked and who had pushed her to get into High School.

"I hear you are doing very well at your new High School," said Monsieur Tessier. "I'm glad to hear it, but not surprised. I always said you would do well. Keep it up."

"Thank you," said Rose, a little embarrassed at his praise.

"I came to tell your mother that I don't believe all these rumours going around the village about your father. People are scared of reprisals and are not thinking properly. Your father acted honourably to help those airmen without thought for his own safety. I was telling your mother that when all the facts are known he will be honoured for his actions. Your family has my support and I will help you all I can."

"Monsieur Tessier suggests I write a letter to the authorities seeking your father's release," said her mother. "He thinks we should take it to the Town Hall to send. I can't possibly compose such a letter. Will you write down Monsieur Tessier's ideas and come with me to the Town Hall? We should do it now."

"A letter! Yes, of course. I'll get a pen and paper," said Rose keen to be taking some positive action for her father.

Together with Monsieur Tessier and her mother, Rose wrote out a draft letter. Keep it simple, no need to mention young Fernand as he was now free, was Monsieur Tessier's advice. It should be addressed to the very top man, he said, to the French Ambassador to the German Occupying Authority in Paris no less! The Mayor's office should help you, he said, by sending it through the proper channels. Not long after Monsieur Tessier left young Fernand came in from the fields. He approved of sending the letter but was doubtful it would do much good.

The letter written, Rose and her mother walked into the village and climbed the steps to the Town Hall, their serious faces reflecting the important business of their visit. After explaining their purpose to the receptionist they were ushered in to see the Deputy Mayor, Monsieur Caillaud. At first he was somewhat frosty towards them saying bluntly he had no news of Monsieur Neau. He then tried to prevaricate over the letter, but seeing the determination of Rose's mother, a resolve born out of Monsieur Tessier's strongly expressed backing, he called in his secretary and asked her to type the letter Rose had proffered. While this was being done Rose and her mother were requested to wait in the reception area. A short while later they were called back in and the Deputy Mayor passed over the typed letter for Rose's mother to read and sign. Rose's mother immediately passed it to Rose.

"Please check it is correct," she requested, her voice flat. Rose knew her mother could read perfectly well but guessed she was nervous of signing a letter to such an important person. Rose began to read it. It was headed with the date and the village name followed by:

> *'Madame Fernand Neau, farmer, to His Excellency Monsieur Fernand de Brinon, French Ambassador in Paris'*
>
> *Dear Minister,*
>
> *On 24th July last, during an aerial battle over La Pallice, several English bombers were brought down.*

Two English airmen parachuted down and my husband, Fernand Neau, aged 40, a farmer at St. Michel-en-l'Herm wrongly gave them shelter.

My husband knew nothing of the consequences of doing this; he was simply performing a charitable act in helping two weary airmen: he would have done as much for German airmen in the same situation.

Nevertheless he was arrested that same night and taken to prison.

This is why I beg leave to request that you intercede on my husband's behalf with the German authorities.

Yours respectfully'

"It's fine, Maman" said Rose returning it to her mother. Her mother took the pen offered to her by Monsieur Caillaud and very carefully signed the letter.

"I will send it tonight to the Préfet's office at La Roche-sur-Yon for despatch to Paris," confirmed Monsieur Caillaud, standing up to indicate the end of the meeting.

"Thank you," said Rose's mother quietly and politely as she too rose from her chair. Satisfied they had done as much as they could they walked home in silence trying to appear stoical in public at least. Casting an occasional glance at her mother's strangely solemn face, Rose thought the strain was beginning to tell. She sensed the hurt and suffering, even humiliation, there must be behind her mother's outwardly and unusually austere demeanour. As they walked, Rose unconsciously found herself praying, not out loud and not necessarily to God, but silently to herself, 'Please, please let Papa go. … Please, let this all end.'

Chapter 10

The next morning saw Rose feeling a little brighter and happier. The more she thought about her brother's release the more she convinced herself the family's nightmare would end soon. Surely, she told herself, the Germans would not have let her brother go unless they had finished all their questions and his release must mean they were not looking too seriously now at what the family had done. If they let young Fernand go in the knowledge he had been so involved, then it was only a matter of time before they released Papa too. Her mother's letter via the Mayor's Office should surely help. Maybe they were just deciding what should be done with Papa and bearing in mind her brother was let off scot-free, perhaps Papa would be let off with nothing more than a warning; she hoped so. Extending her reasoning, it was obvious that she and her mother were, thank goodness, no longer under threat of arrest. The fact that the authorities had not allowed young Fernand to see Papa on his release was just part of their vindictiveness, she concluded; just being hurtful because they could be. Then, with Papa home life could get back to normal again which she so desperately wanted. All these thoughts buoyed Rose's spirits for the first time in many days and put a hopeful spring in her step which her mother quickly sensed, lightening her own mood in turn.

Young Fernand had already left to work in the fields seemingly no worse for his ordeal and Rose busied herself around the house and the yard. Again the day was fine and warm and Rose was diligent in her work as she wanted her father to be pleased that everything on the farm had been done properly in his absence.

Wednesday being market day, Renée was as usual going to walk into the village to see what there was to buy this week. Usually she would be an early customer in order to get the better produce but today was not normal; she had much on her mind. In her better mood the idea occurred to her she might get something special for her husband for when he came home, a little treat. She had a few extra coupons but she did not have much money – she would just have to see what there was available. Just as she was about to leave she heard a voice outside call her name. She recognised the voice; it was her friend Estelle Bon, whose figure then appeared at the ever open kitchen door.

"Estelle, come in," said Renée, pleased to see her. But Madame Bon had a worried look on her face and was rather out of breath. "What is it?" asked Renée on seeing her friend so anxious.

"I'm glad I caught you," said Madame Bon after pausing briefly to compose herself. "Were you off to the market?"

"Yes," said Renée. "What's the matter?"

"I've just come from the market and maybe it's better you don't go."

"What is it?" asked Renée anxiously.

"Oh, Renée," she said, "one of the local councillors, Madame … I can't remember her name … is going around trying to get signatures for a petition to the German authorities. She asked me to sign and when I read it I couldn't believe it. It's about the arrest of your husband and Monsieur Gouraud. It's dreadful, and I told her in no uncertain terms that I would not sign." Madame Bon was getting agitated and puffed up with indignation but Renée was as yet none the wiser at what was concerning her friend so.

"Come in and sit down and tell me what it's about," said Renée on edge.

"They are trying to get as many of the villagers as they can to say they do not support what your Fernand did and that he alone should shoulder the blame. They are even trying to say that he and Monsieur Gouraud are on bad terms and that Monsieur Gouraud wouldn't possibly get together with Fernand to help those poor airmen. It states Monsieur Gouraud could not have been involved and calls for him to be freed, but not Fernand. When I saw it I went straight home to Maurice who said they were all afraid of the Germans and he said I was right to have nothing to do with it. So I came here to warn you so you did not have to face that woman councillor. I don't understand it but she told me it was the Germans who suggested to Madame Gouraud to get this petition up and that she, the Mayor and Deputy Mayor had all signed it. Maurice says they all signed it because Monsieur Gouraud is a big wig and his wife is well connected. The talk in the village is that Monsieur Gouraud was just as involved as your husband. So how can they blame it all on Fernand? It's wrong, and my Maurice agrees. He says they are cowards, afraid of reprisals."

Renée, shocked at Madame Bon's revelations, sat unable to speak, completely bewildered by the turn of events. Then she realised why Monsieur Caillaud, the Deputy Mayor, had been so sheepish yesterday; he knew this was going on.

"I thought it better you should know this before you go into the village," Madame Bon continued. "I'll go for you if you like." She paused as she could see what effect her news was having on Renée.

"I can't believe it. … Why are they doing this to us? I thought some people at Sunday Mass were avoiding me. And Monsieur Caillaud looked ill at ease when we went to see him yesterday. But why? Everyone should be trying to get both of them released, surely."

"People are just worried about everything. Even Maurice gets stick from some folk because he sometimes has to mend German vehicles. But what can he do? If he doesn't, they will shut down the garage and no one will get anything mended. Try not to worry. Maybe they'll not get many signatures and then they won't be able to present it to anyone and they'll be the ones to look silly. Let's hope so. Let me go and get some things for you from the market if you like."

"That's kind," said Renée. She felt beaten down again, drained as if there was not much fight left in her. How could she go on like this, just when things were beginning to look better with young Fernand now home?

She took up Madame Bon's offer and with some words of comfort Madame Bon set off. A short while later Rose came into the kitchen to find her mother sitting at the table with her head in her hands.

"Maman, what is it?" said Rose startled.

Her mother had initially thought not to tell Rose about the petition but changed her mind seeing how grown up Rose had been over this whole affair. She told Rose of Madame Bon's visit and of the tenor of the petition.

Rose immediately became infuriated at the blatant unfairness of it and wanted to go into the village to confront the councillor. But her mother told her not to go, that it would only cause trouble because these were important people elected by the village. Maybe Madame Bon would be right and few people would sign it, she said. Rose felt like ignoring her mother she was so upset and angry, but her desire not to upset her mother seemed more important and she sat with her for a while telling her how she was convinced it would all end soon, trying to be upbeat and positive. Inside though, she was incensed that the family could be so betrayed by their own people and promised herself that as soon as possible she would aim to set the record straight.

Later young Fernand came in to see if there was any news of his father and was disappointed to learn there was none. When they told him of Madame Bon's news about the petition, he was very angry as he had made such efforts to repair the family's reputation after the beans episode.

"Cowards!" He spat the word. "They can do what they like, but they'll have to face Papa when he's back. Then they'll regret it."

There was much to do around the farm at this time of year which needed everyone to lend a hand. Young Fernand was working very hard spending long hours out in the fields, with Rose and their mother helping after the other tasks around the house and yard were done. The harvest should produce a good surplus to sell but it was vital the family gather it in to ensure they could survive the winter. Young Fernand was never shy of work and now he appeared to Rose to immerse himself even more than usual in the farm, taking his responsibilities very seriously. Temporarily of course he had control of the farm at such an important time yet he was mostly quiet, only discussing in the briefest terms what needed to be done, how and when. His general tone was matter of fact, even with his grandfather who came over every day to lend a hand. Rose noticed he handled

Hector, the horse, somewhat abruptly instead of in his customary fond and encouraging manner. Rose had so many questions she wanted to ask him about his arrest and imprisonment but his mood was non-communicative and she held back. In truth she recognised the imperative of the harvest provided a distraction, albeit a distraction of great necessity, for all the family who were glad to be kept busy.

At their midday meal on Friday Renée told Fernand and Rose the parish priest had called round earlier with some news, not wonderful news but news nevertheless. Papa was all right, he had said. Papa was still being held at Fontenay-le-Compte, according to the priest's sources, as was Monsieur Gouraud, but they were not allowed visitors nor was there any news as to when they might be released. There was no point in any of the family going to try and see Papa, the priest believed, as it was a long way and they were unlikely to learn anything. He was doing what he could diplomatically and he was praying, as no doubt they all were, for their quick release. As soon as he had any more news, the priest had said, he promised to return.

"What about the petition?" asked Rose insistently. "Is he trying to stop that?"

Her mother replied that the priest had said he was aware of the petition but could not interfere; nonetheless despite this awkward situation he expected he would see the family at Mass on Sunday. Rose wanted to rant against this spineless priest, as she saw him, who would not even intervene against this absurd petition. But she contained her anger so as to avoid an argument with her mother whom she knew would have nothing said against him because 'he was a man of the cloth'. Instead, Rose said to herself she was glad to have missed his visit and started to think of a way to avoid attending Sunday Mass, so bitter did she feel. Still it was good news of sorts about her father. We must be patient, she told herself.

The following day while she was in the kitchen garden picking lettuce and tomatoes she could not stop thinking of her father. She was still convinced he would be home soon. She even began to hope, perhaps to expect, that he would be home each time she got back to the house. Or better still she would hear his call as he came to find her. Then everything would get back to the way it was; the war and the Occupation would not go away but with Papa back everything would be all right. She might then be able to start some of her holiday school work, seeing herself sitting under the apple tree there in the kitchen garden blissfully absorbed in her books.

Resentfully Rose did attend Mass on Sunday with her mother and grandmother. Both had pointedly stated they should all go despite any possible unfriendliness. Young Fernand said he needed to work and that he could manage without Rose and with that her plan to miss Mass evaporated. During the service she went through the motions but her mind was elsewhere, restlessly ranging around the many religious issues she had in her head; why did the Church not condemn the death and destruction taking place in France, why did God allow such hatred and cruelty, why did the priest not stand up for what was right? She did pray earnestly for her father though and longed for her prayers to be heard.

They had sat in their usual pew, but a few averted eyes, some perfunctory greetings and the odd awkward shuffling made the atmosphere decidedly unpleasant and Renée decided to leave as quickly as possible afterwards.

As they were leaving the church after the service the priest came up to them and said in a low voice that he was sorry he had no more news. Her mother thanked him and then ushered Rose and her grandmother hastily homeward. Rose had wanted to speak with some of her friends after the service to find out what they knew of the petition, to speak out for her father and to gauge the true mood of the village but she was denied the opportunity by their hurried departure. Tomorrow, Rose said to herself, tomorrow she would talk to some of her friends to put the record straight. Of course Papa could be home tomorrow and what a joy and celebration that would mean – in which case putting the record straight would be for another day.

The following afternoon, Rose was helping her mother and grandmother in the kitchen. She was waiting for the right opportunity to ask her mother if she could go into the village to call on her friends, planning not to reveal the true purpose of her visit. Young Fernand was just getting ready to leave for the fields when they heard the sound of engines in the lane and they all stopped what they were doing and listened. Several vehicles appeared to stop outside the house with engines running. Rose's heart raced; was this Papa coming home? But when the dogs started growling she knew something was not right. Rose, her mother, brother and grandmother looked at each other nervously then slowly made their way out into yard, into the bright sunshine. In the sudden tension they did not speak.

Moments later a dozen soldiers spilled into the yard kicking the dogs aside, helmets on, rifles and pistols at the ready, shouting, "Hände hoch!" as they surrounded the family forcing them against the wall of the farmhouse. No one actually put their hands up but they flattened themselves to the wall in obvious submission. For a second everyone was still, then Captain Schulz strode through a gap in the line of soldiers and surveyed his captives. He seemed satisfied calling over his sergeant and pointing to young Fernand and then to Rose.

"For questioning," said Captain Schulz, his only words.

Two soldiers stepped towards young Fernand who started to plead that he had already been questioned but the guards took no notice and forcibly pushed him towards the gate and the waiting vehicles.

"Leave him be," shouted Renée. "He's already been questioned." But her protests too were ignored.

Two other soldiers approached Rose, one of whom grabbed her arm and steered her also towards the gate. "No!" screamed Rose as loud as she could.

"Leave her alone! Let her go! Let her go!" shouted Renée trying to intervene only to be roughly pushed back.

The soldier's grip on Rose was hard and it hurt her but she managed to look back in anguish at her mother and grandmother standing by the cottage frightened and so helpless. They knew there was nothing they could do to stop the soldiers. With both of his captives outside in the lane Captain Schulz turned away without a glance at the two women and strode out of the yard to his car.

Rose caught her brother's eye. "Don't worry. It'll be all right," he called as he was pushed into the car in front trying to be strong for his sister. She was bundled into a second car, a soldier either side of her on the rear seat. All she could make out of her brother was the back of his head in the rear window of the car in front. Behind was a truck for the remaining soldiers. Without delay the small convoy set off in a cloud of dust turning back towards the centre of the village as Renée and her mother stood at the gate watching in despair and disbelief. Rose sat there, numb, squeezed in between these two helmeted soldiers hating the very touch of their uniforms against her. She began to tremble with fright as questions filled her head. What do they want? Where are they taking us? Why now? She wanted to shout the questions out loud but she knew it was futile from the impassive faces of the burly soldiers either side of her.

Rose thought they would be taken to the café but to her dismay the convoy sped through the centre of the village without stopping and headed out on the road to Triaize. Again she wanted to ask, 'Where are you taking us?' but she was too scared to say anything. There and then she made up her mind to remain silent, not to answer any questions, to be totally uncooperative if this is how they were going to treat her. She determined she would be obstinate, stubborn, unbending, defiant, all the things which would frustrate and irritate them. But this naïve spirit of resistance quickly began to evaporate as the convoy continued on through Triaize, through Luçon and onto the Route de la Roche heading further north. Why had they not turned onto the road to Fontenay-le-Compte where Papa was being held? Where were they taking us? Rose became even more anxious as she had not been beyond Luçon before. Were they taking us all the way to La Roche-sur-Yon? She knew of La Roche-sur-Yon, the administrative capital of the Vendée region but she had never been there. Why would they take them all the way there just for questioning? As the convoy sped on she could not help but become more and more worked up, to the extent she could contain her distress no longer.

"Where are you taking me?" It was almost a shout; and the soldiers on either side of her jolted out of their thoughts but neither they nor the driver responded. "Please tell me. Where are we going? When am I going home?" demanded Rose again, suddenly sitting more upright, her body tightening and her voice wavering with the frustration. The guards moved to hold her arms as the driver, who was much older than the two guards in the back, tried to calm her.

"It's best to keep still or they will get you a handcuff," he said in passable French. Rose burst into tears, a mixture of distress, anger and frustration. She sobbed for a while until she gradually calmed down and sat back into the car seat. She reached into the pocket of her dress for a handkerchief but the guard grabbed her hand and held it in a tight grip.

"I need my handkerchief," Rose appealed. The driver said something in German and the guard relaxed his grip allowing Rose to reach for her handkerchief to dry her eyes. For the rest of the journey she sat still. So much was swirling around in her head it was difficult to focus on any one thought and in the end, almost thinking of nothing at all, she stared ahead.

An hour after their arrest, the convoy brought Rose and her brother into La Roche-sur-Yon. Rose began to pay more attention now, looking through the car windows at the unfamiliar town with its factories, shops and wide streets lined with tall buildings. It was soon clear this was a much bigger place than Luçon and Rose was reminded how she found the size of Luçon daunting the first time she went there. Eventually the convoy swept into a military barracks, just like the one she had visited at Luçon. It was intimidating to be surrounded by so many soldiers and military vehicles of all sorts. They passed a row of fearsome Panzer heavy armoured cars as they were herded, her brother in front, across a yard towards a side door to the main building, a large Swastika flag flying from its mast. As they were made to wait in a corridor in silence, Rose felt very vulnerable and sought some reassurance from her brother. She managed to catch his eye but before they could make any exchange a soldier moved and cut off her line of sight. Then they were taken into a large almost empty room where she was astounded to find Monsieur Brard, the dairyman, an older man she thought she recognised as the Mayor of St. Michel-en-l'Herm and a boy a bit younger than herself who was vaguely familiar. They were sitting on chairs well apart set against the walls of the room which had a guard at the door. The room echoed at the footsteps of the soldiers who ushered in Rose and her brother who themselves were told to sit on chairs well apart like the others and ordered to keep absolute silence. Petrified, her eyes red from crying, Rose looked across at her brother seeking some further reassurance, some explanation of what was going on. But he gave the merest shrug of his shoulders as if to say he did not know what was happening either. He then raised his eyebrows and mouthed, 'Are you all right?' to which Rose gave the slightest nod of agreement although the look on her face told him a different story. She cast her eyes around at the others assuming they were all there for questioning too. Only Monsieur Bodin, the Mayor, gave her a weak smile of recognition. It then occurred to her that maybe her father was somewhere here too.

There they all sat for what seemed hours; no one came or went. Occasionally they could hear noises outside the room and Rose thought the interrogations were about to start but then nothing happened. Nerves played on the old Mayor who, embarrassed, needed to ask several times to go to the lavatory which he was allowed to do but always accompanied by a guard. Later when the guards changed over they were brought a cup of tea and a baguette each at which point the Mayor demanded to be told what was going on only to be ignored. No one spoke; occasionally Rose looked at her brother and the others but she gleaned nothing from their glances. Monsieur Brard seemed the most agitated of them all; the boy sat rigid with his hands clasped between his knees, a frightened look in his eyes. She tried to work out who this boy was; perhaps he was Monsieur Gouraud's son Michel, she thought, brought in again for questioning like her brother. He would have been in a lower class at her old school which is why his face was familiar although he must have changed a lot since she last saw him.

Ever since she was taken from home Rose tried to convince herself she would be back by the evening; after all there was not a lot the Germans did not know about the affair by now. She had no real idea what the questioning would be like but the more she thought about it she imagined she would only be providing confirmation of what was already known and as such it would be over quickly. Indeed she did not really understand why they wanted to question her at all, which made all this brusque treatment doubly unnecessary and very aggravating. So she sat, seething underneath, just about under control.

The clock high on the far wall indicated seven o'clock. It looked as though it could be a long evening ahead because they had not even started questioning the first of them. Then suddenly the door opened and an officer took a few paces into the room, stopped, looked round at them all and made an announcement.

"Your case has been transferred to Paris," he said with no explanation. "Arrangements are being made for you to be transferred there tomorrow. You will stay here tonight. That is all." He turned and strode out before anyone could gather their thoughts. Monsieur Brard was the first to speak. He got up.

"Paris! But I must get back to my wife and children. I have to be up early in the morning for my rounds!"

The guard at the door took his rifle off his shoulder in readiness and shouted, "Sit. No talk."

In shock, Rose had put her hands to cover her mouth and looked across to her brother who appeared equally shocked and confused.

A short while later, one by one they were taken out of the large room, Rose being shoved into a small room bare except for a table and a chair. The door was locked behind her. She stood in the middle of the room for some while stunned, unable to move and unable to take in what was going on. Eventually she sat down and realised she was trembling. There was a window that looked out on to a blank wall; it was strong-looking and locked, not that she had any ideas of escape. She had never been shut up like this; it was horrible and she felt so unhappy. Later, when it was getting dark the door opened and an orderly dropped a straw mattress and a blanket on the floor then withdrew locking the door again. Bewildered and disoriented she had been trying to think how she could avoid being sent to Paris but nothing seemed likely to work: these barbarians just rode roughshod over everyone. Realising how helpless she was and feeling alone she curled up into a ball on the lumpy mattress and cried. Eventually she fell into a shallow sleep.

The following morning Rose and the others were escorted to the main railway station and onto the platform. There to Rose's total amazement she glimpsed her father and Monsieur Gouraud guarded by a number of soldiers.

"Papa! Papa!" she cried as her heart soared at seeing him. She started towards her father but she was grabbed instantly and held firmly by one of her escorts. Her father turned to see where the cry came from.

"Papa!" she cried again but the raised hand of her guard stopped her calling further. Then to her horror as her father came into full view she could see he had his arms handcuffed behind him and the euphoria she felt at seeing him was immediately dispelled by the sight of her father shackled like a common criminal. His eyes met hers and his face lit up with a smile, and again when he spotted young Fernand. But the smile was fleeting and it was as though he wanted to avert his eyes in embarrassment and shame, yet could not. His eyes still had a glimmer of her father but the demeanour was not his; it was of someone cowed and defeated, and her heart sank at the sight. It was at that moment she realised just how serious the situation was for all of them.

The moment was broken by the sound of a train arriving. Since seeing her father Rose had been unaware of everything else but now the puffing and clanking of the big express engine brought a hustle and bustle all around them as waiting passengers prepared themselves. Rose and the others had been kept well apart from her father and from Monsieur Gouraud who was also handcuffed. When the train stopped two soldiers barred passengers from boarding one of the carriages while another cleared it of the passengers inside who, disgruntled, had to get off and find a seat elsewhere. Then one by one Rose's father, Monsieur Gouraud, The Mayor, Monsieur Brard, young Fernand, Rose and finally the boy were ordered aboard the empty carriage, spread around so communication was impossible, each accompanied by their own guard. She could see the back of her brother's head but not her father. A loud whistle signalled the train's departure and slowly at first it rumbled out of the station.

On another day, in a different situation, Rose would have been fascinated by the journey; today however there was no excitement only a sort of numbness brought on by the rollercoaster emotions of the last twelve hours and the hammer blow of seeing her father so demoralised. She tried not to think of her father too much, it upset her so. She recalled looking around at the others earlier this morning on the way to the station – it was Monsieur Brard who seemed in the worst state; the Mayor looked pale and poorly; her brother gave little away as usual; and the young boy looked as though he had cried all night. What were they doing dragging him away? He was even younger than she was. What could they possibly want from him that they needed to treat him like this? Such thoughts turned her mind to her own circumstances. Why on earth do they need me in Paris, just to ask some questions? What was wrong with the Café Pilnière? She remembered a friend at school who said her father once told her the Germans were deliberately cruel and did spiteful things to the French just to crush them, to show them who is in charge. Is that what they're doing to us, she wondered?

The train journeyed on, sometimes going fast, at other times crawling for no apparent reason, and stopping many times. Rose recognised the names of some of the stops, major cities like Nantes, Angers and Le Mans. At Nantes they had to change trains and while they waited a soft drink and a tepid croque monsieur appeared, apparently insisted upon and paid for by the Mayor. Rose was famished; only a small roll with a piece of cheese had been provided for breakfast. The break also allowed the German guards to change over. For much of the time Rose was preoccupied by thoughts of her father, upset and worried by his demeanour. She was conscious he was near, that they were on this journey together, yet forced to sit apart and unable to comfort each other. As the journey resumed Rose's new guard sitting opposite her was a fresh faced young soldier, younger than her brother she thought, whose manner was awkward as though he was self-conscious at his duty guarding such an innocent looking girl. He averted his eyes every time Rose glanced at him. The more Rose observed him the more her initial and instinctive hatred of him waned; he was hardly shaving she noted and his uniform and forage cap were on the large size for him. Was there a look of François about him, her 'hoped for' boyfriend at school ...? Such distractions from her mood helped to pass the time. A question she was tempted to ask her young guard was how soon would they reach Paris, but she knew he would not answer even if he understood the question. After the long stop at Angers the carriage had become very hot but the young guard, under orders probably, would not allow her to open the carriage window although he looked equally uncomfortable. From late afternoon Rose expected they were nearing Paris and wondered what it would be like, if it was really like the pictures she had seen in books and magazines. Fleetingly she imagined the Eiffel Tower and other famous attractions but the guard in front of her was a constant and ominous reminder that Paris, journey's end, held for her, her father and brother only uncertainty and foreboding.

By evening as the train slowed Rose looked in awe at the passing scene outside – buildings, as far as the eye could see, tall, densely packed, with occasional burned out shells, evidence of the war. But from her carriage window she could not make out anything famous. Nevertheless, this must be Paris, she said to herself, and a shiver ran down her spine.

Chapter 11

As the train pulled in to Gare Montparnasse Rose's apprehension increased significantly. They were all taken from the carriage, marshalled along the platform and across the wide concourse; Rose's father and Monsieur Gouraud, both still handcuffed, were kept in a separate group behind the others. Rose's eyes followed the huge supporting columns up to the vast, high vaulted roof of the station; everything about the place was gigantic, bigger even than the cathedral at Luçon, way beyond her experience. And the people – she had never seen so many people, all purposefully making their way here and there, feigning disinterest in the groups being escorted towards the main exit. Only the many soldiers about openly took any notice. Outside the oppressive heat of the day still lingered and it took a moment for her eyes to adjust to the evening brightness. There was a large plaza in front of the station with tree-lined roads leading off in all directions. Behind them was the impressive, solid-looking façade of the station with its clock high on top showing eight o'clock. As the two groups were herded to the side of an elaborate bus shelter Rose caught her father's eye. He smiled weakly. He looked so forlorn, so out of place among the smart-suited Parisians bustling along no doubt with important business. He wore the clothes he was wearing when arrested, his working clothes and his favourite old, battered leather jacket. Without his habitual cap, his white forehead showed up against his nut-brown face making him look every inch a farmer. A small, drab-painted bus with a German guard driving stopped in front of them. In this they were driven off, but only for about five minutes when the bus came to a halt in front of a pair of very large, heavy doors set into a long, high, blank wall. Above the imposing gateway Rose saw the words, 'Prison Militaire de Paris'.

"A prison!" she murmured, horrified. "They have brought us to a prison! There must be some mistake."

“There was no mistake,” the admissions warder for the women’s wing of Cherche Midi prison flatly informed her. “The authority is here,” she said, tapping the document in front of her, adding that it stated she was to be held in prison until her interrogation was complete.

“Who said so? When can I go home?” beseeched Rose. The female warder ignored her questions adding to Rose’s anger and frustration, but she did query Rose’s age.

“It says here your date of birth is 23rd February 1925. Is that correct?” Rose confirmed it was.

“That makes you just sixteen.” The warder looked surprised and paused a moment to consider Rose’s young age. Her manner softened somewhat but she continued to complete the formalities.

In an anteroom Rose was searched and checked physically by a nurse who asked if she had any ailments. Rose told her she suffered from kidney disease at which the nurse said a doctor would see her shortly. These procedures were brief and ten minutes later Rose was in a cell, the thick door slammed shut behind her and the key turned in the lock. Then all she could hear was the receding sound of the guards’ boots on the corridor floor until there was silence.

Rose’s head was in turmoil. Surely this was not happening, not to her? If only the airmen had come down somewhere else; if only the Germans had not come to the house when they did, none of this would be happening. Why did Papa not hide the airmen in the fields like her mother had begged? This must be a bad dream from which she would wake up at any moment. Frightened, bewildered, lost and now alone in this place, Rose could no longer hold herself together. She lay down on the rough mattress and sobbed uncontrollably for hours. Even when she ceased sobbing she just lay there feeling utterly despondent and miserable, more miserable than she had ever been in her life. By then it was dark and even the bare light hanging from the ceiling had been switched off. She felt empty, so low that she paid no attention to the faint voices she heard at times. Her wretchedness consumed her; she had no thoughts for anyone else. In the dark she felt frightened and alone. Soon hunger was added to her woes but eventually exhaustion and shock overtook her and she drifted into a fitful sleep.

She awoke with a start at noises in the corridor. Early light was filtering through a high barred window. Waking brought depression and hunger in equal amounts. She looked at her watch; it showed seven o'clock. The key turned in the lock and the heavy door swung open and anticipating food Rose quickly sat up on the edge of the bed eager for some breakfast. Outside the cell was a female trusty, a prisoner who was allowed to help with some basic tasks in the prison in return for better conditions. The trusty stood by a large trolley accompanied by a guard. Anxiously Rose looked at the trolley but could not see any food only jugs, pails and a very large lidded bucket.

"You've nothing to eat?" asked Rose perplexed.

The worldly trusty seeing a very young and naïve new inmate gave Rose a sympathetic smile. She then explained this first routine of the day, instructing her to empty the slop pail, to sweep the cell and to exchange her jug for a jug of fresh water; she then added that food would come later, at about ten o'clock. When Rose started to complain she was hungry now the woman cut in advising her in a kindly voice it was better not to make a fuss in here, just do as she was told. Making a fuss would change nothing and only lead to trouble.

The guard, who obviously had insufficient French to understand all the trusty had said, nervously barked out, "No more talk!" So Rose took the brush offered and quickly swept the floor, exchanged the jug of water and indicated the pail had not been used. The cell door slammed shut before Rose could thank the trusty for her advice.

Rose stood facing the door for a while. In the end she turned slowly and sat on the bed with her head in her hands feeling trapped and confused, hardly able to think until gradually she became more conscious of her surroundings and she started to look around. Her cell had grubby whitewashed walls and was no more than eight feet by five feet with a high ceiling. From the ceiling hung a bare light bulb well out of reach but there was no switch anywhere to operate it. There was a small barred window high on the wall opposite the door that allowed sight of a sliver of sky only, no more; and there was a closed fanlight above the door. The solid-looking, dark brown door was unfurnished except for a small ledge in the middle with a hatchway that opened outwards for food to be passed through. Above that at eye level was a spy-hole with the shutter on the outside. Rose examined the iron-framed bed which was not dissimilar to her bed at home except the springs had been removed and replaced with short planks of wood. The thin straw mattress smelt distinctly unpleasant. In one corner by the door was a meagre table on which were a brown enamel basin, the jug of water, a beaker and a spoon. Underneath the table were a wobbly stool and the slop bucket with an ill-fitting lid. Is this really my world for the moment, Rose asked herself? Is this … this room which is no bigger than Maman's larder, is this where I am supposed to stay? Can people really survive in this tiny space, locked away for years? Rose had read stories of people incarcerated in prison for years, so it must be possible to survive, she thought, but how? The idea sent a shudder right through her. And then to buck herself up she reminded herself she would be there maybe only for a few hours, or a day or so at most, before she went home after answering their questions.

Hunger intruded again. Pangs of hunger nagged away at her and Rose's only thoughts were of getting through to ten o'clock when the trusty said food would arrive. She drank some water hoping it would help but not knowing how long the jug of water had to last she drank only enough to slake her thirst. The cool water managed to assuage her hunger just a little and made her feel marginally better. She kept looking at her watch but time seemed to have slowed to a snail's pace. Nevertheless this enforced wait brought home to her just how precious her watch was to her and she hoped they would not take it away. Did they allow watches in prison, or had they made a mistake and missed that she was wearing one, she wondered? Or maybe it did not matter as she was not due to be held for long. Whatever the case she determined to keep it if at all possible and put it in the pocket of her dress out of sight. In its way, she thought, retaining her watch was a minor triumph over her captors; a thought which brought a brief satisfactory smile to her face.

Despite the satisfaction this small victory brought, Rose had never known time pass so slowly but eventually as ten o'clock approached she heard encouraging noises along the corridor. The anticipation of food was almost unbearable, to the point that when the trolley stopped outside her cell Rose was already standing impatiently by the door. The little hatchway opened and a roll of bread was pushed onto the ledge followed by a bowl of soup; all done in silence. Rose waited a second to see what else there was to come but the hatch slammed shut and the trolley moved on.

Greedily she grabbed the roll and stuffed it in her mouth taking a huge bite. The soup was watery with a few bits of vegetable floating in it along with some other unidentifiable pieces. It was tepid and in no time both the soup and roll were finished. The rations, paltry though they were, had a remarkable effect on her, boosting her spirits no end and turning her mind to what might happen next – her interrogation. That could be any time now, she thought, but she had no real idea what it would be like, where she would be questioned or by whom. She desperately hoped it would take place very soon so this nightmare could be over and she could go home. Of the questioning, naively she could only think it would be more or less straightforward, about the airmen being at the house and what her father intended for them. That should not take long and then she would be released just like her brother was earlier. There would be no punishment she assumed; her part was hardly enough to warrant anything more than a telling off, surely? She expected her brother, like her, to be released quickly also. Maybe strictly speaking her father had broken some Occupation rule but no one had been hurt, nothing destroyed or damaged, the airmen had been captured, sadly, and it was all over in no time and so her father's penalty should not be much. She had heard of harsh punishments for espionage and the killing of German soldiers but these events were mostly in the north of France and in Paris. Their brush with the German military was nothing like that and by her thinking should hardly warrant retribution. Without doubt that is what will happen and we will all be able to go home, she tried to convince herself – but there was a counter argument that kept butting in.

This counter argument painted a bleaker outlook, one she could no longer simply dismiss, born out of the sight of her father in handcuffs which had really upset her; an image she could not get out of her mind. And the Germans had brought all of them to Paris and put them in prison. Why would they do that unless they considered the matter more serious? She remembered what her school friend's father had said, that the Germans made examples of people and treated them harshly simply to create fear in others. Before today it had been easier to discount such gossip, but no longer. Now in her prison cell, all these darker thoughts came unbidden to the fore and would not be suppressed. Still, on balance she remained optimistic all this would be over soon. She thought of her father. How would he be coping? There were family stories of her father involved in all sorts of scrapes when he was in the army and Rose knew he would stand up to authority. And over the theft of the beans she could see that he had done what he thought was right despite the consequences, as he was doing again now. He would not like being cooped up though; he loved the outdoors and the freedom of being his own boss – but he was strong and would manage, at least for a while. Her brother on the other hand would find this hard. He would be building up resentment, she thought, and find being caged like an animal difficult to accept. She worried more for him than her father. Then her mind turned to her mother, her poor mother. She would be distraught not knowing what was happening, not knowing even where they were. Rose remembered how her mother had been when Papa and her brother had been taken the night the Germans came to the house. How would she be now that all three of her family were gone? She could not possibly manage the farm on her own at the best of times let alone in the middle of the harvest. She must be worried sick. The more Rose thought of her mother, the more anxious she became about her; even more concerned for her than for her father and brother.

The sound of heavy footsteps outside her cell jolted her from her thoughts and she held her breath as a key turned in the lock. Was this the call to her interrogation? The door opened and in walked a formidable looking female warden dressed in a black shirt and skirt. She eyed Rose and for a second was taken aback at seeing such a young girl in the cell, then recovered her composure to deliver the prison rules and regulations, the purpose of her visit.

"You must stand when a German addresses you," she ordered, then paused for Rose to stand up which she did. "Whilst you are here for interrogation you will not be allowed visitors, you may not write or receive any letters, you shall have no food from outside, no cigarettes, no books or newspapers and will not be permitted to work. At all times you will obey instructions and make no disturbance. All violations will be punished. You may receive additional clothes from your family. That is all." With that she turned to leave.

"Wait, please," said Rose grasping the opportunity to get some much needed information. "When will I be questioned? How are my Papa and brother? Has my mother been told we are here? I …" She wanted to ask more but the warder just ignored her, strode out and the cell door banged shut leaving Rose's words to echo around the walls. Exasperated and never having suffered such ill-mannered treatment she called out pleading, "At least tell me how long I shall be here?" That too was ignored.

Rose turned around as if to appeal to someone in the cell but it was a futile gesture, only the walls stared back at her in silence. The whole episode with the unfeeling warder just confirmed Rose's understanding of how vulnerable she was to this regime which could take her from her home, remove her hundreds of miles away, lock her up in a prison made for thieves and murderers, deny her access to her family, without proper food, and on top of all that give her no information other than rules and regulations. In the past Rose's impatience and sense of injustice had got her into trouble, particularly at school, now that trait of hers was being stretched to the limit. The unfairness of it, not being treated properly, this terrible place with the hunger and isolation; everything was already getting to her. But then her helplessness meant she could do nothing about her situation, only seethe inside. It occurred to her, however, she was not alone in this place and reminded herself that her brother and especially her father were not far away. Such thoughts gave her some small comfort.

More practical issues eventually wormed their way into her thoughts. It was high summer and it was hot, very hot. At home the weather would be very agreeable with a gentle Atlantic breeze to cool the heat of early August but for Rose in her prison cell in the middle of Paris it was stiflingly hot and airless. She remembered she had slept last night in her clothes without a blanket but of course she had no change of clothes and was obliged to remain in the dress and underclothes she arrived in. She had no flannel or soap to wash with or detergent to rinse out any clothes, no brush or comb for her hair, no toiletries of any sort. Before boarding at the High School, Rose had been far less conscious of herself and being a rural farm girl was used to the mud and grime of farm living and work. The other girls in the school dormitory though quickly made Rose more worldly-wise. She became much more aware of her good looks, readily accepted the fashion help and advice of the 'town' girls with their cosmetics and accessories, and tried to look as chic as possible on her limited resources. And there was the added incentive of looking attractive to secure the attention of François. By the end of her first year at High School, Rose was definitely no longer the naïve country girl. Nevertheless she felt she could just about tolerate, perhaps for a few days, the primitive conditions she now found herself in, unpleasant though they were. It was only about five years ago that the farm had been connected to the village water supply and mains drainage, so a jug of cold water to wash with and very basic toilet facilities had been the norm for her not that long ago.

There was a noisy commotion down the corridor, shouting and doors banging, and then her door was unlocked and flung open.

"Exercise time!" announced the guard. But as Rose did not understand what this meant she remained sitting on her bed looking blankly at the guard. "You must stand," snapped the guard. "By the door, here. No talking!" Rose, remembering the trusty's advice, did as she was told and looked around surprised to find several women standing by their cell doors and gradually more joined them further along the corridor. Why were they all in prison, she wondered? The first women moved off in file keeping a distance apart from the next and Rose followed suit. Going down the stairs to the ground floor the woman in front of her slowed a little and quietly called back.

"You're new, aren't you?" she whispered. "I'm Marie."

"I'm Rose," said a surprised Rose joining in the subterfuge.

"Get a bit closer to me at the far side of the yard," Marie whispered, then moved away. The file of women accompanied by a number of guards walked slowly out into the large quadrangle in the middle of the prison, formed by four wings three storeys high. Rose blinked at the strong sunlight but it was good to be in the open air if only to walk slowly around the quadrangle enclosed by the high walls. Rose had been curious to know who else was held in the prison but the sight of her fellow inmates depressed her. There were only women in the courtyard, no men, no Papa, no Fernand. The women were mostly pasty faced, dishevelled, moronic-looking, trudging along in single file showing little interest in their surroundings. Rose noticed the guards lazily stayed by the entrance and when she reached the far side Rose closed a little on Marie as she had suggested.

"Marie," whispered Rose to let her know she was close.

"Are you all right?" was the response.

"Yes."

"You look very young. How old are you?"

"Sixteen."

"Only sixteen!" Marie exclaimed, then as they turned the corner, "Move back now."

The conversation renewed when they reached the same spot next time around. In response to Marie's enquiry Rose said she was just in for questioning about some British airmen and would then be released. Marie said she had been there for three months but not why which made Rose wonder what she had done. Might she be talking to a murderer? But Marie sounded well spoken and her somewhat crumpled dress appeared to have been expensive which only added to the mystery. On the next round Marie had some advice.

"Trust no one. Tell them nothing. Sign nothing."

As the file shuffled back into the building Marie whispered that she would call Rose later from under her cell door when the guards were gone. A few minutes later Rose was back in her cell, the door slammed shut and the key turned, exercise time over. She almost had to pinch herself to make sure what she had just witnessed was real. This is crazy, she thought, like being at school whispering at the back of the class when the teacher's back is turned or passing surreptitious notes to another classmate. Yet hearing a friendly voice, knowing there was someone else on her side, meant a great deal to Rose lifting her spirits, outweighing the grimness of the prison façade and the wretchedness of the other prisoners. She pondered on Marie's remarks about trusting no one. What did she mean? It was a warning, no mistake. Did it mean not everyone was what they appeared to be? She must ask Marie later; but could she trust Marie? She seemed nice enough. And what was she to make of the other warning to tell nothing? Presumably Marie meant divulge nothing to her interrogators. But how can I stay silent, Rose worried? The airmen were found in the house. How can that be denied? The warning unnerved her. Was there something she had not thought about, something that Marie knew that she did not? She must ask Marie to explain.

In time hunger began to nag again. Every now and again there was the sound of heavy boots along the corridor but each time the sound faded as the guard walked on by. All was quiet; no food arrived. One o'clock came and went; two o'clock likewise. It was not till four o'clock that the small hatch in her cell door opened and a piece of sausage with some bread spread with margarine appeared. The hatch shut. Rose inspected the unappetising-looking rations. It was pretty awful and so dry she had to wash it down with some water which having sat in the hot cell all day was tepid. Surely there is some supper to come later, thought Rose; that cannot be all they feed us on. Then she remembered last evening when there was no supper and she became indignant that prisoners could be treated in this inhumane way, particularly people like herself who really should not be there at all. This latest sense of indignation and unfairness was just another swing in her mood since arriving at Cherche Midi. Everything was new and strange; Paris, prison, privation and the smallest thing was likely to trigger a lurch from confidence and hope to insecurity and dejection. Her world was completely out of control and her head was spinning. Calm down, she told herself, getting worked up will not help. Think of something else. Think of Papa, of Maman and Fernand; you must always think of them she told herself.

For the next couple of hours Rose's mind wandered. She was impatient to get this questioning, or whatever it turned out to be, over and done with so she could get out of this place and go home; impatient not to lose any more of the summer holidays. It was still light when she heard the regular turning of keys in locks all along the corridor, the check that all the cells were properly locked for the night. Her own cell door was tried which unnerved her but nothing happened. A little later when the sound of the guards' footsteps had faded away she heard a slow tap-tapping which seemed to come from some pipes somewhere. She heard the faint sound of voices and remembered Marie saying something about talking under the cell door after lock-up for the night. She went to the cell door, knelt down and could see there was a small gap between the bottom of the door and the doorstep. She leant closer to the gap.

"Rose. Rose. Can you hear me?" It was Marie's voice.

"Yes, I can hear you."

"Stand on your stool and reach the fanlight above the door. It appears shut from the outside but you'll see the catch is jammed and there's a bit of string on the catch. Hold on to the string and push the fanlight gently and it'll open. Try it now."

Rose followed Marie's instructions and it worked just as she had said. Rose could easily see Marie in her open fanlight opposite and when she turned her head she could see a little way either side along the corridor.

"We can talk better now. When the pipes are tapped twice it means a guard is coming. Pull the string to close the window. Four taps means the all-clear.

Rose was amazed at all this organised and clever subterfuge.

"What news do you have from outside, of the Russian front? Everyone here is always hungry for news."

"I'm sorry I don't know anything. I am a student from St. Michel-en-l'Herm in the Vendée."

"Oh! Is that a big place?"

"Just a village. I live on a farm."

There was a pause which allowed Rose to pose the questions she had thought about after their exchanges during exercise.

"What did you mean earlier by 'trust no one'?"

"The Gestapo have spies everywhere. Not everyone is who they seem; the guards, the 'trusties', even people in the next cell like me could all be spies for the Gestapo. Don't tell me anything you don't want them to know. Even if I am not a spy they may torture me to get information on you."

Rose was shocked at what she was hearing.

"Are you serious?" she asked incredulously.

"Oh yes. Trust no one."

"You also said not to tell them anything. What do you mean?"

"They will use every trick and more besides to get information from you; names, addresses, organisations. Don't denounce or implicate anyone, deny everything, tell lies, anything, but don't give them anything useful."

The conversation ranged over the prison regime and routine, and Rose said she had no toiletries or change of clothes only to find out that was common in the early days of someone being held. Sometimes, Marie said, those being released donated such things to those without. She would pass the word around. Rose asked how she could get news of her father and brother but as Marie was about to answer there was a quick tapping on the pipes that ran above the fanlights the length the corridor. All went quiet.

Rose lay on her bed mulling over Marie's warning of the Gestapo. She knew little of the Gestapo other than their reputation for being secretive and brutal. Marie's stark words, however, set Rose thinking she should decide now what she should and should not divulge at her interrogation. What should she do? Say absolutely nothing? Could she manage to keep that up? Or lie about everything? She never was good at telling lies and nearly always got caught out. What did they know for certain? That was the question. She would try and work that out and then try and tell them only what they already knew. She spent the rest of daylight turning over these questions in her mind, trying to think what they would ask her, rehearsing answers. Before Marie's warning Rose had reckoned she could cope with the interrogation which would probably be conducted by some sort of German policeman. It had not occurred to her the Gestapo might be involved and the thought scared her – everyone was scared of the Gestapo.

A week went by, a week of unbroken hunger, oppressive heat, frustration at no interrogation, boredom, and unhappiness at having no news of her father or brother. The time passed slowly, punctuated only by the routine of the prison which changed only on Saturday and Sunday when lock-up was at midday. Each morning she hoped and prayed she would be released, but when nothing happened she became depressed and the only thing to look forward to was the evening chat through the fanlight after the guards had gone. Her privation was relieved one day by the bequest of some soap and a comb by a departing prisoner, passed to her via a trusty; a most welcome gift. But then one morning before exercise her door was unlocked and a guard she did not recognise said she was to come with him. Immediately suspecting she was being taken for questioning at last Rose came over in a cold sweat. Meekly she stepped outside her cell where there was an escort of three more guards. How absurd, she thought, that it needed four armed guards to escort her. To her surprise she was taken out into the prison yard and bundled into the back of a small truck then ordered to sit on the bench along one side in between two of the guards. The other two guards sat opposite and obviously enjoyed eyeing up a pretty young prisoner for a change. They must be taking her out of the prison, but to where, she wondered apprehensively?

"Luftwaffe Tribunal, rue du Faubourg Saint-Honoré," called one of the guards to the driver. During the journey which took no more than ten minutes Rose's heart was pounding and she clenched her hands tightly in her lap. She stared out of the back of the truck distracted briefly by the beautiful tall buildings of Paris and the sights of everyday life tantalisingly close but denied to her. They drove across a bridge over the River Seine and crossed the Place de la Concorde before turning into the narrow rue du Faubourg Saint-Honoré with its elegant buildings and smart shops. The truck stopped outside a very modern looking five storey building with large arched windows fronting the street and a tall arched glass doorway in the middle. A huge Swastika flag hung limply in the Paris heat from a flagpole set horizontally from the small balcony above the main door. As Rose got down from the truck she looked around but none of the Parisian folk going about their business took any notice of her and her escorts. She was ushered up a set of stairs to the first floor and told to wait in an anteroom with one of the guards still in attendance. There they waited for some time before an inner door opened and a civilian told the guard to bring Rose in. The guard followed her into this next room, closed the door and stood by it. The room was large with a polished wooden floor but the only furniture was two sets of a desk and a chair at right angles to each other and a further chair in a corner. Rose stood there shaking and very apprehensive but she steeled herself with the thought she would soon be going home. The civilian indicated Rose should stand in front of the larger desk and then sat down at the other desk and made a phone call. Moments later an officer in grey-blue uniform with a shiny belt and polished boots entered and walked smartly to the large desk and sat down. He had a round head, thinning hair and glasses, cerebral looking. He eyed Rose up and down and turned to the civilian who gave him Rose's name.

"Mademoiselle Neau," the officer said. "I am Major Scherer, Luftwaffe Prosecutions Officer. You are here to answer my questions regarding the capture of British airmen Flight Lieutenant McLeod and Warrant Officer Finlayson on 25th July. First the clerk will take particulars." At that the civilian began with the usual full name, date of birth, address, parents and occupation. When Rose gave her date of birth, 23rd February 1925, the clerk queried this.

"That makes you aged sixteen?"

"Yes," confirmed Rose. The clerk looked across at the Major as if to question whether the interview should continue in view of this person's young age. The Major made no signal to stop. When all the details were recorded the Major began; his French understandable, though spoken with a heavy German accent.

"You know why you are here. I know you will want to help your father and brother and the best way to do that is to cooperate and tell the truth. You do want to help you father and brother, don't you?"

Rose nodded and gave a weak, "Yes." She was trying very hard not to let her nerves show.

"Tell me everything I need to know and you can go home."

The Major's tone was crisp but quiet and from his uniform and title Rose guessed he was not from the Gestapo which relaxed her just a little, still she found the whole affair and surroundings very frightening and intimidating. At first his questions were innocuous, where she went to school, what subjects did she like – she omitted English from the list of her favourite subjects – what did her father and brother do for a living, what did she want to do after she left school. All of these were easy to answer quite truthfully if not wholly. But eventually he turned to the events of the 24th July. Witnesses have said how brave her brother was to rescue the airmen from the sea, he said. What did she know about the airmen being rescued by her brother, he asked?

This was Rose's first dilemma, should she confirm her brother's involvement in the rescue? The Major seemed to know about it and there were the council workers who saw the rescue, and even the airmen may have said what had happened. But in her rehearsals she had decided to deny everything except that the airmen were found at the house, and so, knowing she was entering dangerous territory, said she knew nothing.

"Nothing!" retorted the Major raising his voice a notch. "Your brother told you nothing of his heroism? The airmen said nothing to you about their ordeal? I don't believe you. I say again, what do you know?"

Rose was not practiced at deceit and felt so self conscious she was sure he could tell she was lying. Unused to direct confrontation she found herself wavering but, having committed herself to this path of deception, held her line.

"Nothing," was her one word reply.

The Major decided to change tack. He wanted to know how the airmen got to their house. The house was a long way from where they landed and one was injured. How did they reach the farmhouse? They must have had help. Rose did not know. But, the Major said, Rose was seen with her father and Monsieur Gouraud coming back to the village from the dyke that evening. Rose said she had gone with her father to see the repairs to the dyke and Monsieur Gouraud had offered them a lift back.

"You didn't see the airmen at all that evening?" questioned the Major.

"No," said Rose as firmly as she could, knowing she was getting deeper and deeper into this deception.

"But we know the airmen were hidden on Monsieur Gouraud's cart."

"They must have hidden there without anyone knowing then," said Rose giving one of her practiced answers, feeling her rehearsals were beginning to pay off.

"H'm. So how did the airmen end up in your house? You don't deny they were found in your house do you?"

"No," said Rose. "But I don't know how they got there. They were there when I came downstairs. My father said they needed help."

"And when was this?"

"I don't know. Late."

"What help was your father intending to give these airmen. What was he intending to do with them?"

"I don't know – he didn't say. They were in a bad way and all he said was they needed help."

The Major changed tack again. He suspected her father was part of an underground movement helping escaping British airmen and he spent some time asking Rose about her father, his politics, his friends and associates, even about his finances. Rose was perplexed by this line of questioning as she could not see the connection to the rescue of the airmen but she found she could answer nearly all the questions truthfully and fully simply because, as far as she aware, the truth was that her father's only motive was compassion. As such she felt the interrogation was turning in her favour although she noticed the Major oddly became more and more frustrated. He saw her naïve answers as deliberate obfuscation and that the interrogation he thought at the outset would be easy and productive was drawing a blank. At this point his patience ran out.

"You expect me to believe your brother rescued these British airmen but did not tell you; they were hidden on the cart you travelled on but you did not know; they turn up in your house but you have no idea how. You tell me your father helped them out of kindness only. Young lady you are wasting my time with these lies. This situation is very serious. You know you are required to tell the authorities immediately of the presence of any enemy airmen yet everyone in your family failed to do so despite numerous opportunities. I have to ask myself why."

"I am a student. I have been away at school working hard at my studies. I don't know about reporting airmen," Rose pleaded.

"Punishments for this crime can be very severe unless we have full cooperation. I do not think you are cooperating. I give you one last chance to change your mind, to help your father and brother."

"I can't tell you any more," Rose implored, desperately sticking to her story although by now she was close to tears with the strain.

"Take her out," the Major tersely ordered the guard. Rose was made to sit in the anteroom without explanation of what was to happen next. She gulped back her tears and sat shaking in trepidation of what they might do to her, her mind confused at the way the interrogation had ended, her head whirling at the deception she had embarked upon. One of Marie's words came to mind, one that had struck a chord with her – the word 'denounce'. Since the Occupation, Rose had heard that word used many times with its connotation of the worst kind of cowardly informer. How could she denounce her own father and brother? She must resist. But silently she prayed, please, please bring this to an end. After a long wait the civilian clerk reappeared and said she was to come back into the room. The Major was still seated at his desk but said nothing initially.

"You must sign this statement," said the clerk sliding a document across the table towards her. Rose had not expected this development, but remembered Marie's advice to sign nothing. She picked up the three pages of type and straight away saw it was written in German.

"I can't sign this," she stated. "I don't understand it."

The Major interjected. "It is a record of what you have just told us. It is in German as it is for the tribunal. You must sign it now then I can order your release. Your father and brother have signed theirs." Rose did not trust him or believe his last statement.

"My Papa will not let me sign anything unless he has approved it and he won't approve it if he can't read it," said Rose standing her ground. She laid the papers back on the table. "It has to be in French and I need to meet with my father." She deliberately spoke very fast hoping the Major could not follow. She succeeded, forcing the Major to turn to the civilian for a translation.

"Sign!" he barked and when Rose made no move, he shouted, "Take her back. Maybe a further spell in solitary confinement will bring her to her senses." Exasperated, he got up and stomped out.

Chapter 12

Abbé Franz Stock sat at his desk in his office at 23 rue Lhomond in Paris staring momentarily at the piece of paper in his hand, a typewritten list he had just taken from an envelope. He had known what the envelope contained when it was given to him a few days ago which was why he had not opened it straight away – there had been more pressing matters. Now he must catch up but the content of the envelope did nothing to improve his sombre mood. It was a list of new inmates from the previous week to the Cherche Midi prison and it was the length of the list which caused him to pause and sigh, lamenting the ever increasing number of prisoners. His attention however was caught by something unusual in the list; three surnames the same. Just as he finished reading the details of these three names his sister appeared in the doorway.

"Before you go, I have some things for you to take," she said. Franz smiled; what would he do without his dear Franziska.

He had been back for a year now as Rector at the German Catholic Mission in Paris. His earlier spell there had abruptly ended the day he returned from one of his visits to his beloved Brittany only to be advised by the German Embassy to leave Paris immediately. That was in late August 1939. He and Franziska caught the first train out of Paris the following morning and for the next year at the family home in western Germany he watched with great sadness as Europe was plunged into war yet again. For the past ten years or so he had dedicated himself to peace and reconciliation between France and Germany, his personal mission. But then he had been forced to watch helplessly as his hopes and dreams were shattered by the returning sound of heavy guns across Europe.

His parents were hardworking Catholics and at an early age he was drawn towards the priesthood. His ambition was nearly thwarted by an only average attainment at school plus ill-heath but once his mind was made up, determination and hard work saw him complete his training and he was ordained at Paderborn in 1932. Many of his ideals were set in his late teens when he was an enthusiastic and active member of a Christian youth group which had an emphasis on outdoor activities. With this group he attended many rallies where influential speakers gave lectures on the pursuit of peace and the reconciliation of conflict. He travelled often to France with this group and came to love the country and its culture, so much so that he pressed to take a year of his seminary at the Institut Catholique in Paris. Until then it was unheard of for a German to attend the Institut and because he was a German he often faced prejudice there, yet he saw this as another challenge to overcome, succeeding generally through his gentle demeanour and his genuine passion for harmony between the two countries. His time at the Institut was to be significant; he made many friends and important connections, he became fluent in French and the year he spent there cemented his love of France.

For two years after his ordination he was the priest to local parishes near his home but then, as a result of his earlier connections, he was given the opportunity to become Rector at the German Catholic Mission in Paris which he jumped at, taking his sister with him as his secretary and a family friend, Elizabeth, as his housekeeper. He threw himself into the Mission's work adding his own influence promoting peace and reconciliation. He was also able to reconnect with his many French friends both inside and outside the priesthood. But as war approached his pro-French activities drew the attention of Hitler's secret police in Paris who maintained a watching brief on him. This watching brief resumed when he was asked to return to Paris after France was defeated. He reopened the Mission in October 1940, though now his flock was very different, made up of German military personnel, diplomats, bureaucrats and other civilians drafted in to support the Occupation. Soon he began informal visits to the nearby prisons of Cherche Midi and La Santé and to a third, large prison at Fresnes to the south of the city, all of which the Germans had taken over to hold political prisoners and those acting against the Occupation. The Abbé knew some of the prisoners, former friends and expatriate Germans living in Paris who had fled Hitler's Germany before the war. But when he tried to see some of the hundred or so Paris students arrested and imprisoned during clashes with the Occupying forces on 11th November 1940, all his visits were stopped. He appealed to higher authorities and through the offices of the Wehrmacht Chief of Chaplains he quickly received a formal prison pass. Weeks later he was formally appointed Chaplain to the prisons to take care of their growing population. This was to be a turning point for the priest known for his open and placid manner. From then on his prison flock consumed most of his time, comforting the desolate, praying with those in despair and accompanying the condemned to their execution.

In the New Year as a result of his appointment as Chaplain he was commissioned into the Wehrmacht with the rank of major which enabled him to move freely around the prisons. Until then he had been hindered by the guards and even mocked by some of them as being a friend to the prisoners. With the rank of major he was a superior officer and almost all of the hindrances stopped – the guards knew a bad word from Major Stock would condemn them to harsh discipline.

This appointment to the rank of major had other implications for Abbé Stock, one with which he constantly wrestled. In accepting the appointment he was in effect joining the very organisation which had waged war against France and yet he had spent the last decade trying to mend the differences and prejudices between France and his native country resulting from the last war. He was only able to reconcile this dilemma by rationalising the needs of his prison flock as being much greater than his own sensibilities – that he was far better able to care for them pastorally by accepting the appointment than not.

Still he constantly felt uncomfortable at belonging to Hitler's army and never used his rank for personal advantage, ignoring rather than admonishing a junior guard here or there for some ineptitude or stupidity. He refused to wear military uniform; instead he wore his usual cassock with just a red armband to signify he was an auxiliary officer. He had been aware of the Gestapo's interest in his pro-French activities and he was circumspect about whom he met and where. However he was not going to abandon his personal mission and he believed, rightly or not, the appointment gave him a small measure of protection from those suspicious of him. Often he would work behind the scenes to try and secure the release of a particular prisoner or a reduction to their sentence, rarely with success but all the sweeter when succeeding. Yet he knew his rank would not save him if his other, more dangerous, clandestine activities were to be discovered.

"I have some things for your satchel; some strudels I baked, some notepaper and pencils, only a little chocolate I'm afraid and two books," Franziska continued. "Do you know what time you'll be back tonight?"

"You've been busy as usual," said Franz. "I can't say what time I'll be back. I have a lot of visits to catch up with today." He held up the list of new inmates as evidence of his workload.

His satchel went everywhere with him as it carried his Bible, prayer book, his Mass kit and other items for his ministry. At the very beginning when he was a mere visiting priest the prison guards would inspect it but after a time they became so used to seeing him with it they no longer bothered, conscious of its sacred contents. When he thought he was safe from being found out he secreted inside it some sweets, chocolates, bits of paper and pencils and anything else small that would help relieve the suffering of the prisoners for whom he felt great compassion. Later in the colder weather he would hide larger items like books in his coat pockets and in secret pockets sewn by Franziska inside his cassock. Sometimes a prisoner's family who were denied access would visit the Mission and give him tiny notes which he would take into the prison hidden in his satchel or a pocket, or even sometimes inside the strudels Franziska baked. He was prepared to take such great risks because he saw how much pleasure these notes and simple everyday items brought to the prisoners but he had to be careful not to raise suspicions. Ironically his appointment to the Wehrmacht made this smuggling easier for him as he would not be challenged and searched by the guards unless ordered to by a suspicious Gestapo officer. On the other hand, though, he knew if he was caught his punishment would be severe. He would also pass verbal messages to and fro between the inmates and their families and he became practised at remembering each message and who it was for. These messages and notes were a lifeline for the prisoners and their relatives, allaying fears and giving reassurance where before there was just a wall of silence.

Not everyone welcomed the kind and sensitive priest into their cell, even those who had requested a chaplain, for they expected a French priest not a German one. He encountered all sorts of reactions from polite refusal to outright hostility, often because the prisoner was a communist, an anti-cleric, a Jew, a lapsed Catholic or of no religion at all. Occasionally otherwise staunch Catholics refused his priestly services saying they would never make their confession to a German. Many of those who did receive him were cautious at the outset not only because he was German but also because it was known the Gestapo used false priests to obtain information. These obstacles, however, did not deter Abbé Stock from his work and he was often able to break down a prisoner's reserve through his quiet personality and his overt sensitivity to their suffering. The tit bits and news he brought in from the outside helped establish a trust which allowed a spiritual relationship to flower and, for most of those who allowed him to enter their wretched lives, the fact he was a German was almost totally forgotten. Inside these Paris prisons was a world devoid of humanity; it was only Abbé Franz Stock who brought a human face to those prisoners who received him. He was someone who behaved towards them with charity and kindness; he showed such sympathy and compassion that they felt he bore their suffering with them and he offered much needed spiritual support and guidance. Everything he gave was given without favour or reservation to those who found themselves desolate and forsaken, separated from family and friends – or worse, in their final moments at the execution stake.

"I must make time to visit these three here on the list, Franziska" he added. "All from the same family most probably; father, son and a young daughter. The daughter appears to be only sixteen years old. How can it possibly be necessary to detain a girl of sixteen?"

Franziska understood the question to be rhetorical but also noted the exasperation and embarrassment with which her brother posed it. Franz would tell his sister little of his prison visits, not just because the contract he signed when he was commissioned into the Wehrmacht contained a clause requiring him to keep strictly confidential all official military matters but also in case his activities should be investigated in which case the less his sister knew the better. Of course as a priest he was used to keeping the secrets of the confessional as well as many other issues that came to his ear in the course of his duties, but his prison work created a huge burden for him to carry alone as he was unable to share, even with his sister, the horrors he saw on a daily basis and which tore at his heart. Such a burden would weigh heavily on the most experienced of shoulders but Abbé Franz Stock was only thirty-six years old.

In her cell Rose sat on her bed hunched up in a foetal position in the corner furthest from the door trying to block out the events of the last few hours. She had arrived back at her cell shaking uncontrollably and had gradually edged into the corner drawing her legs up tightly. Eventually the shaking subsided but she remained there with eyes shut wishing over and over again that the world would go away and leave her alone. Her frame of mind was finally altered by the arrival of food, her afternoon ration of bread and, this time, a piece of cheese. Unusually she sat and stared for a whole minute at the food pushed through the small hatch onto the narrow ledge before she slowly uncurled herself and made her way over to pick up the meagre rations. Ravenous hunger normally meant a rush to grab any food the second it appeared but she had been so affected by her treatment at the morning's interrogation her usual state of permanent hunger had been suppressed. She nibbled through the food, washed it down with a little water then sat on the edge of the bed feeling somewhat calmer and wishing her father was there. She needed to make sense of what had happened to her but her head was muddled. If Papa were here, she thought, he would know what to do. Oh, how she wished he was with her now. But she must think, think clearly, she told herself; it was difficult, but she must be strong and try hard.

The abrupt and threatening dismissal by Major Scherer ending her interrogation had shocked her, but she still felt sure she had done the right thing by remaining silent about her brother's rescue of the airmen and their ride hidden under the hay of Monsieur Gouraud's cart. Somehow, though, the Major seemed to know the full story which puzzled Rose. She went over and over again in her mind what she could remember, trying to gauge whether he really did know the truth or was guessing. From what she could recall she could not find any inconsistencies between the Major's account and what actually happened. Did that mean someone had told him? If so, who? Not her father or her brother she was sure – her brother had been emphatic that he had not denounced anyone during his first interrogation at Fontenay-le-Compte so he would not have talked now. She did not really know Monsieur Gouraud; could it be him? What had the airmen said? When they were arrested at the house it appeared they just gave their names and a number, but it had all happened too quickly for her to take in. What might they have said since? And what of Monsieur Brard? Rose did not know him well either other than he had been the local dairyman for years. Had he told what he saw? If the frightened boy was indeed Michel Gouraud what did he know of his father's involvement and what had he divulged? Perhaps the Major had gleaned bits and pieces from some or all of them and been able to piece together the correct sequence of events.

But what if the Germans really did know the full story, Rose asked herself? If so her stand would be in vain and she might be punished for her obstinacy. And should they know the truth because others had cooperated, then those others might get off lightly. If on the other hand the Germans already knew the truth and she herself cooperated, then nothing she might say could harm her father. According to the Major her cooperation would end this nightmare and she would be allowed to go home.

Despite the counter arguments the persistent refrain going round in her head was that she could not, must not, denounce her father whatever the consequences for her. Should the Germans find the truth from other sources, so be it; but not from her. Such resolve though was easy to say but could she maintain that resolve in the face of the Major's tantrums and threats of punishment? Of that she could not be sure because the prospect frightened her so much. Could she survive this awful place, these cruel people who seemed to care nothing for her or her family's suffering? Had she the necessary strength to cope? If not, then where would she find the extra courage she would need? Papa, my Papa, he would help me, he would know what to do, she said to herself. She looked up through the window and out at the sliver of sky beyond as if her father was out there listening, and she silently beseeched him, 'Papa, I wish you were here, here with me now. I need you to help me. I don't know if I can get through this without you.'

All these thoughts were still milling around in her head when the keys were turned in the lock for the night. When the guards had finished and gone the early evening chatter along the corridor began.

"How are you Rose? We missed you at exercise. Were you interrogated?"

"I'm all right, Marie," Rose answered. "Yes, I was interrogated and they said if I told them everything I could be released, but I didn't. Then they wanted me to sign some paper but it was in German so I refused and they sent me back here. I was frightened and now I don't know what will happen to me."

"You did well. It is a trick they use to say they will let you go if you sign their papers. They will probably try again. They did that with me. Did they hurt you?"

"No. They shouted at me but didn't hurt me."

Rose listened as best she could to some of the other prisoners but the talk was of people and places she did not know. Marie explained they were talking about writers and Paris intellectuals so Rose returned to her bed. Until then every day she had anticipated being released, going home, helping her mother, catching up with her schoolwork; but now back in her cell after her encounter with Major Scherer her release no longer looked imminent. She began fretting about her schoolwork, that she could not get on with the exercises she should complete in the holidays and would fall behind. What would happen if she was not able to do the work before she went back to school at the beginning of September? She would try to catch up as quickly as she could and surely the teachers would be sympathetic. She tried to remember the various pieces of work. If only she had her English text book with her now she could do lots of work with all this time on her hands. Maybe Marie knows some English she thought. She was about to ask her when she heard a cheery, "Goodnight," and, "Goodnight everyone," as the evening conversations came to an end.

"Goodnight, Marie. Goodnight everyone," Rose joined in having clambered on the stool.

"Goodnight Rose."

She pulled up the fanlight with the string until it appeared closed and tucked the string out of sight.

This ritual of illicit chattering each evening followed by wishing everyone goodnight reminded Rose of the dormitory at school after lights out when as often as not someone started messing about, being naughty, rebellious and breaking the rules. But in prison the human contact was such an immeasurable comfort that Rose looked forward to the evenings although she rarely contributed much. There were interruptions when a guard appeared on his rounds, then everyone would be silent until the all-clear signal was given. The main topics were about the war and the Occupation and everyone was hungry for news from the outside; any new arrival was immediately questioned on the latest developments. Rose mostly listened because the others were much older than her and, like that evening, the conversation was often centred on the Occupation of Paris where nearly all the prisoners appeared to live. The latest news of De Gaulle was always discussed in great detail generating much fervent talk of liberation which raised everyone's spirits. One topic Rose discovered was taboo and that was food since everyone was permanently hungry. Marie was the only one Rose chatted with at any length. She was a lecturer at one of the universities in Paris she told Rose and had been arrested because the Gestapo were interested in some of her colleagues. It all sounded a bit vague to Rose but she guessed Marie was being discrete about the reason for her arrest so did not probe further.

Early the following morning Rose's cell door was unlocked and swung open.

"Come!" the guard instructed. A chill immediately ran through Rose as she anticipated a further interrogation. But instead of being taken to a waiting vehicle in the yard she was ushered along a corridor on the ground floor and into a waiting room with Medical Reception in French on the door. Shortly another door opened and a nurse called Rose's name and asked her to come into the consulting room. There stood a kindly looking elderly man in a white coat who introduced himself as Doctor Papin saying he was to examine Rose for her fitness to remain in prison as she had indicated on admission she suffered from a kidney disease. Rose had forgotten the admissions nurse had said a doctor would see her mainly because she did not think she would be in prison for long. Doctor Papin questioned her about the history of her complaint and she explained she mainly managed it through a low-protein diet. She had some prescription pills in case of need but of course she did not have them with her in the prison, she said. During Doctor Papin's examination it dawned on Rose that she might be able to persuade him to get her released on medical grounds so she added that her doctor at home had told her that if her condition got out of hand it could be serious for her. She felt justified in saying this as it was not a direct lie; her doctor had said something to that effect although he was referring to possible later stages of the disease. Rose said her doctor had also told her stress must be avoided as it could worsen her condition. She was very anxious about her situation, she confided, as she did not have her pills and she was afraid the poor food in the prison would cause her harm.

"I'm very frightened and worried. I don't really understand why I am here as I've done nothing wrong. Can you help me Doctor? I need to go home to my Maman."

"Your file says you are sixteen years old. Is that correct?" the Doctor asked looking up from the paperwork.

"Yes. I should be going back to school at the beginning of September."

"H'm," the doctor mused then stated, "Prison is not the right place for you, young lady. I am prepared to recommend you be released on medical grounds. But be warned, my opinion is not always acted upon straight away. In the meantime I will mark your file that you should receive more nourishment in your rations. Should your condition suddenly worsen you must ask immediately to see me again. Do you understand?" Rose's spirits were soaring.

"Yes, Doctor. Thank you," she gasped, hardly believing what she had just heard.

For the rest of the morning Rose was elated at the unexpected turn of events. Last night she had despaired she could not cope in these harsh conditions and had silently prayed for her father's help. The thought occurred to her that perhaps Papa had answered her prayers in the shape of Doctor Papin. For the very first time since entering Cherche Midi prison Rose was smiling; even the drabness of her cell appeared less severe. How long would it be before the medical release came through, she wondered, how long before this ordeal was over? Although the Doctor had sounded a note of caution about when his recommendation might be acted upon, could it be in a day or two perhaps? Maybe she would escape further interrogation, in which case her defiance would be vindicated and she could walk tall. On her way back to her cell she decided not to tell anyone, it did not seem fair to crow, yet it was particularly difficult not to say anything to Marie who had been so supportive. The hunger was still the same though, but then the Doctor had ordered she should have better rations so even the rest of her detention ought to be more bearable. Without telling Marie her real purpose, which was to know the exact date Doctor Papin gave his recommendation, she asked Marie later that morning as soon as the coast was clear if she knew what the date was. Marie did not but the question went up the corridor and the answer came back; it was Tuesday, the nineteenth of August.

"Oh! It's Papa's birthday in two day's time," Rose realised excitedly. "Is it possible to get a birthday message to him, do you think Marie? Maybe to Fernand too?"

"We can try," said Marie with her usual encouragement and the request was passed up the corridor to see if a route could be found, perhaps via a trusty. Rose loved birthdays and always made family birthdays a special day, baking a cake with her mother, decorating the house and extravagantly wrapping her present which of necessity could only be modest. It would be wonderful, she sighed, if Papa could get a 'Happy Birthday' message from her; if she wished hard enough it might, just might happen …

It was stiflingly hot and airless as usual in the middle of the afternoon and Rose lay on her bed imagining the joy of her journey home, hugging her mother and rushing around the farm relishing the freedom of the open air, clean hair and clean clothes. Suddenly she was startled by the key turning in the lock of the door and the door was swung back. She froze as her first thought was that she was about to be taken for a further interrogation which, after the outcome of the morning's events, she had hoped to escape. But instead of the guards ordering her out, there, framed in the doorway, was a priest.

"You must be Rose Neau," he said in a quiet voice.

"Yes," said Rose after a moment's hesitation, taken aback by the priest's unexpected appearance.

"My name is Father Stock. I'm Chaplain here. May I come in?" He stood there looking directly into her eyes, waiting for her reply, his stance and whole demeanour unthreatening.

"Yes," said Rose, again somewhat hesitantly, responding respectfully as if the local priest had called by at home yet surprised and puzzled there should be a priest in the prison. She started to stand up as Abbé Stock stepped into her cell but he immediately gestured her to stay sitting and he drew up the stool close and sat down.

"The guard outside is a good Catholic and he will not try to overhear what we say," he said quietly. "I am told you are a practising Catholic and as Chaplain here I can bring you communion, here in your cell. I will call as often as I can if you wish."

Rose picked up on his remark that she was a practising Catholic. How did he know that, she asked herself? The answer soon came.

Abbé Stock lowered his voice further. "I have just been to visit your father and brother. They are bearing up. Your father has a message for you. He says he loves you and try to be brave."

"You've seen Papa and Fernand?" Rose said excitedly. Abbé Stock put his finger to his mouth to indicate she should whisper. "How are they? Are they all right? Can I see them?"

"They are bearing up as I said. Do you have a message for them?"

Almost unable to contain her excitement Rose whispered, "Yes. Yes. Say I am well. Say 'Happy Birthday' to Papa."

"I'll tell him," he said allowing a little smile as he saw her eyes light up. "I'm told you are only sixteen years old. Is this true?" he asked wanting to check his understanding.

"Yes."

It hurt him to see someone so young locked up in this way, by far the youngest of his 'parishioners'.

"Then it must be especially hard for you being here." He paused, looking somewhat embarrassed. "I have many visits to make," he continued. "Before I go, do you wish to receive communion or to be blessed, my child?"

"Bless me, Father," she answered. Given this unexpected choice Rose, somewhat flustered, asked just to be blessed. Indeed it struck her that God had been totally absent from her thoughts since her arrest and her first notion was to refuse both communion and a blessing but out of respect and politeness she thought she should accept at least one. Abbé Stock rose and blessed her then repeated his offer that he could call again if she wished. Rose said, yes please, she would like him to call, forgetting she expected to be released at any moment. He said he would visit again soon then made for the door and on reaching the doorway he half turned, looked into Rose's eyes and with a simple conviction assured her, "God is with you." With that he was gone and the heavy cell door clanged shut.

His visit was over so quickly yet it held so much for Rose. She was left with the lingering impression of this tall, handsome young priest in flowing cassock, with blond hair, a high forehead and a soothing ease about him. But of all his features it was his eyes that were the focal point of her image. They were an intense blue and Rose felt she had been held in their soft gaze, captured, almost mesmerised by the kindness they radiated. She dwelt on this dream-like picture for a few moments until reality and the exciting news of her father and brother took over.

'My Papa!' she thought. 'He has seen Papa.' She twirled around totally forgetting where she was. "He has seen Papa!" she whispered to herself. "Papa is all right, and Fernand too." Happiness flooded through her at the thought. She began to go over the other things the priest had said. Papa's message? What was Papa's message, again? He loved me and that I should try to be brave; that was it. Be brave? What did he mean by that, she wondered? Was it an encouragement to face up to her ordeal? Or did it mean she should not denounce anyone despite everything? Perhaps it meant she should stand up to her captors? Maybe some or even all of those, she thought; certainly her fearless Papa would not flinch from any of them. For a while she felt a sort of lightness, a joy that lifted her from her situation. Not even the arrival of her afternoon morsel of food could spoil her mood and again for once, despite her hunger, the pittance was nibbled instead of being gobbled down. Then she remembered the morning and Doctor Papin. What a day it had been now that she was closer than ever to being released and now that she knew Papa and Fernand were all right! She could hardly contain herself, wanting to tell Marie of Abbé Stock's visit but still she felt she should not mention her visit to Doctor Papin.

Later, Marie sounded genuinely pleased at Rose's news of her father and brother and cheers went up along the corridor as the news was transmitted from cell to cell, all of which added a further boost to Rose's spirits. It was customary for good news to be shared as it provided a morale boost for the whole corridor. But Marie was less sanguine about Abbé Stock's visit. She herself was not religious and had refused, politely she said, his offer of ministrations. Others, even Catholics, she said, were very wary of him either because he was a German or they feared he was a stooge.

"A German!" said Rose incredulous. "He is a German priest?"

"Of course," said Marie. "They wouldn't allow a French priest to roam their prison. Be careful, Rose. Be certain the messages from your father are genuine; he might be trying to gain your trust. Don't tell him anything you would not tell your interrogators."

Marie's words demolished completely her high spirits and for the rest of the evening and into the night Rose played over and over again the visit of the priest and Marie's warnings. At first she was cross with herself for accepting the priest for what he appeared to be; for not questioning who he might really be and for not being on guard. But she could not shake off this impression he left her with, of someone who cared, who showed her warmth and compassion, who gave her hope for more news of her father and brother. Be brave, he said was her father's message. She believed him; Papa would have used such words, she told herself. But he was a German! How could she not have suspected that! He acted as if he was a Frenchman and he spoke perfectly correct French; yet on reflection he spoke in a way that was lacking in some way, not totally colloquial. And, of course, his name was a give-away that she missed altogether, how silly. Regardless of Marie's words of caution, she was drawn to him for reasons she could not fully explain or justify but she realised she had never met anyone who had had such an immediate impression on her. Does it make any difference that this priest is a German, she questioned? Her mother would see his priesthood first, no doubt; but would his nationality not matter at all to her mother? Rose could not answer this question. These reflections in turn led her to think about her mother. She chastised herself for not giving more thought to her mother's suffering which was just as much as her own, not knowing where her family was, when they would be back, left to cope with the farm at the busiest time of the year. Perhaps Grandmaman and Grandpapa have moved in with her to help her manage and no doubt Uncle Bernard would come over to lend a hand too but she must be sick with worry.

Rose's mind was unstoppably active as she lay on her rough bed enveloped by darkness and silence. It was wrong, she told herself, not to think of her mother more than she had of late. Somehow her father and his suffering loomed large in her mind, much more than that of her mother or even her brother. Why was this, she asked herself? Did she love her father more than her mother or brother? The thought had never occurred to her before but presented with such questions in the black of the night and unable to shut them out of her mind she was forced to confront the possibility that perhaps she did. It was not that she did not love her mother or her brother, but that her father was easier to love. At least that is how she could explain it to herself. He was warm, cuddly and gentle with her, always looking for fun, protective and supportive, never too stern. Her mother on the other hand was more serious, not cold, but not as warm as Papa and she would confide in Papa in preference to Maman. Rose knew she owed a great deal to her mother especially in terms of her education – Papa alone would never have influenced her and urged her to progress to senior school which had now become the most important aspect of her life. And it was Maman, of course, who had been largely responsible for her day-to-day upbringing as a child. Yet, was it wrong to love one parent more than the other? It did not seem right. Rose remembered at school sometimes her friends would talk of their parents and some expressed a preference for one over the other, usually the parent who was less strict. But was that the same as really loving one more than the other? In the end Rose could only satisfy her dilemma by rationalising that she loved both Papa and Maman by the same amount but in different ways.

There was another person who occupied her mind – the Abbé. Their meeting had been brief but the impression he left endured. In thinking about him she arrived at the conclusion he was unlike anyone she had ever come across before; there was just something …, a sort of charisma she could not really put her finger on. He had said he would come again: she hoped he would.

Days passed without event. To start with her heart quickened with anticipation each time she heard footsteps approaching. Would they stop at her door? Was this the moment she would be released? But when the footsteps did not slow down the flame of hope began to die and quickly went out altogether as the footsteps went on by. It was still stiflingly hot; the hunger never ceased and the bugs that scuttled in the corners of her cell seemed to multiply. Her clothes were dirty; she felt dirty. She had not washed properly since her arrival and her hair was matted and smelt. She became agitated. Why had she not been released as Doctor Papin had said? It was not right she should be kept here when he said she should be released. Why does no one tell her what is happening? Her mounting frustration festered inside her, the excitement and hope of a few days ago dissipated, replaced by a growing anger at her continued detention.

When eventually some guards stopped at her door and threw it open any hope of release was immediately quashed with the command, "Come! Interrogation!"

Rose soon found herself back in front of Major Scherer.

"I hope you have used your time wisely and have decided to cooperate. I can then order your release just like your friends Monsieur Bodin, Monsieur Brard and the boy Gouraud. They have all cooperated and of course have been released immediately. They are all home by now. You too can be home tomorrow if you satisfactorily answer my questions."

Rose butted in. "I should have been released by now. Doctor Papin said I should not be in prison on medical grounds."

"Doctor Papin does not decide," barked the Major. "Cooperate now and you go home. Refuse and the matter will be taken out of my hands."

Rose's plan of playing the Doctor Papin card did not seem to be working. She had earlier decided on that tactic should she be taken for further questioning and, encouraged by her father's message, she had also decided not to reveal any more information or sign any papers.

"Sign here," ordered Major Scherer pushing a paper across his desk at her. Rose steeled herself and made no move. "Sign!" he shouted. Rose, scared stiff and holding back tears, stood her ground. There was a moment's tense standoff before the Major gave up. "Take her away," he said angrily with a dismissive wave of his arm. "The Gestapo can deal with her."

Chapter 13

"A letter for you, Madame," announced the postman at the kitchen door. Renée looked up from the stove immediately apprehensive at the arrival of a letter. The postman was a rare visitor to the Neau farm and more often than not a letter carried bad news. "I hope it's good news," the postman added trying to be cheerful. Everyone in the village knew the Neau family's circumstances. Renée sat down at the table and examined the envelope. It looked official with a local postmark. Since the arrest of young Fernand and Rose she had received no news of where her husband or children were being held despite her efforts to find out. With hands shaking she nervously opened the envelope and unfolded the letter. It was from the Mayor's office, signed by the Deputy Mayor and informed her that Fernand Neau, his son and daughter had been taken to the Cherche Midi prison in Paris where the Mayor and two other citizens of the village had also been held and questioned in connection with the discovery and capture of two British airmen at her house. The Mayor and the two citizens were released two days ago and had returned to the village but as far as the Mayor knew the three Neau family members were still held in the prison in Paris. It was not known when they might be released but hopefully it would be soon. In the meantime, it was suggested that Madame Neau might like to write to her family and send parcels as they would benefit from extra clothes, toiletries and food. The letter ended by saying the Mayor had unfortunately relinquished his duties for the time being due to ill health but any further news received at the Mayor's office would immediately be passed on to her.

Renée sat stunned at the contents of the letter. Paris! In prison in Paris! She re-read the letter and still could hardly believe what she was reading. Relieved to have some news at last she gathered her thoughts. Stoically, she decided action was necessary straight away and she called out to her parents who were feeding the chickens and collecting eggs. In no time they were making up parcels while Renée wrote letters to her husband and children. She also decided that as the Mayor was indisposed she would visit instead Monsieur Tessier, the schoolmaster, to seek his advice. Monsieur Tessier was pleased she had had some news at last but was rather disturbed at its nature although he did not let on how concerned he was. He suggested she write again to the Ambassador and offered to help. After a brief discussion on the content she drafted some words which she handed to him for a final check. He read:

> *To Monsieur de Brinon, Ambassadeur de France.*
> *I had the honour on 30th July last, of sending you a request on behalf of my husband Fernand Neau who was arrested on 25th July.*
> *I would like to continue with this request and add to it today as both of my children have now been detained since 4th August in Cherche Midi prison.*
> *Please may I ask for your goodwill on their behalf.*
> *My son Fernand is only twenty years old and Rose is sixteen. She has to sit an exam in October. Will she be able to? She is weak. She has been treated for a kidney disease for a year. She needed specialist help and is following a strict regime. I really worry that being locked up will have detrimental effects on her health.*
> *Alone here, I do not know how they are being affected and as a mother who loves them dearly can only seek your intervention.*
> *Yours etc.*

When he had finished reading Monsieur Tessier said, "That's fine. Take it now to the town hall for them to send off as before."

When Rose was next taken for interrogation the driver was told to go to rue des Saussaies and the men who confronted her in a dingy half-basement room wore dark suits not uniforms. A single ceiling light cast a pale glow on a largely bare room, the only furniture being a small table and a chair pushed carelessly towards one corner. The guard made her stand in the centre of the room under the lamp and then left. Rose eyed the two men who were in hushed conversation in German looking at some papers on the table. One lit a cigarette, the smoke from which drifted in the airless room. After Major Scherer's final words Rose expected her chances of an immediate release would be slim and the threat of the Gestapo had left her in of a state of persistent foreboding. Now she stood in this room, this dungeon, and she could hardly breathe she was so terrified. She could not stop herself shaking and her mouth was dry. One of the men took a glance at her and that seemed to raise some more debate between them. Eventually one of them started a slow walk around her while the one smoking remained perched on the edge of the table staring coldly at her. It was the man on his feet who spoke.

"You are Rose Neau?" he said in halting French with a heavy accent.

Rose nodded, trying to confirm her name but the words just would not come out.

"You have helped British airmen, no?" he said from behind her.

"They needed help," she mumbled, her head bowed.

"This is a very serious matter, you know. You are here to answer our questions. You must answer our questions or ... Well, I'm sure you are a truthful girl. But before we get to the airmen, I want to know about your father. Tell me about his friends, about any strangers that have visited your house lately. Tell me why your father wanted to help these airmen. Was it because he has friends who are against Germany?"

Since her dismissal by Major Scherer, Rose had been rehearsing over and over again the answers she had given to the Major in the hope she would be able to keep to her story but she had not anticipated questions about her father's friends and was somewhat nonplussed by this approach to the extent she could not think of an immediate response.

"You must answer," the man said, in a slightly raised voice.

"He ... he has lots of friends," stammered Rose.

"I want names," the man ordered, his voice more urgent.

"Everyone knows my father. He knows all the farmers and everyone. He grew up in the village. He helps everyone; he's always helping people. That's why everyone knows him."

"Who are his special friends? Who has come to your house recently, maybe at night to talk to your father? Who does your father visit? I need names."

"I don't know …" said Rose getting confused. "He knows lots of farmers, … Monsieur Jullien … Monsieur Chopeau, and the dairyman Monsieur Brard, the man who has the garage Monsieur Bon, and the café man Monsieur Pilnière. Lots of people know my father." Then she blurted out, "Look, Doctor Papin says I shouldn't be here. You must let me go."

"The doctor decides nothing and we have many more questions before you can go anywhere. Who has come to the house recently, someone new, a stranger, someone your father doesn't talk about much?" The man was much closer now, his face showing growing annoyance.

"No one. No one has come. I've only been home from school a few days so I wouldn't know but I don't think any strangers would come to the house to see Papa. Maman wouldn't like it."

The questions came quick and fast and Rose had no time to think. She was panicking she was going to trip up but the longer the questioning went on the more she realised she was able to answer truthfully to everything the man asked. Sometimes she was simply unable to answer and in saying so it was the truth. The man kept asking the same questions over and over again, sometimes in a different way and all the time Rose's answers were truthful. Yet the man became more and more frustrated.

"Did your father go away, to the next village or town to see people? Was he secretive about going away?" There was an edge to his voice now.

"Papa never goes away! He has his farm. He has to be on his farm. He is a good farmer. He works hard from morning till night, especially now it is harvest." There was a touch of defensive indignation in Rose's answer which brought an angry riposte from the other man who stood up, cigarette still in hand.

"He has time to harbour enemy airmen!" he shouted as he strode over towards Rose who was startled and shied away. He was pointing the cigarette at her but suddenly lifted his other arm and swiped her with the back of his hand slapping her cheek hard.

Rose screamed and ducked away, her cheek smarting from the blow. She started to cry and wiped her hand over her lips – there was blood on her hand.

"Don't hurt me!" she cried out as she cowered in case the man attacked her again. He stood leaning over her for a moment then turned back to perch on the desk drawing again on his cigarette.

"My friend is very impatient," said the first man in a mock explanation for the attack. "Here, sit down," he said dragging over the chair, feigning concern. "He only wants to get to the truth but his methods are not so subtle. My friend has done you a favour really: you will do well to learn his lesson. If you have to come back again I cannot promise he will be able to control his temper which is not as bad today as it usually is. Now, let's start again."

Rose sat on the chair snivelling, her cheek and lip sore. No one had ever hit her like that before, not Papa, not Maman. They had administered the odd reproachful smack on a leg when she was much younger but this was a vicious blow that stunned her and made her head reel. She could not understand why they were doing this to her. She was telling the truth. Why didn't they believe her? Please let them stop, she pleaded silently.

"Your father and your brother have told us things which we must confirm or we cannot believe them. We want to believe them which is why we need your help. You do want to help them, don't you?"

Rose nodded. She was trying to compose herself but was still unable to talk and sat there her shoulders shuddering as she wept not only from the pain but the shock of being hurt in such a manner and the anticipation of being attacked again.

The questioning started again, going over the same ground as before but the man also wanted to know about her father's army friends, whether they contacted him or he them. Who had told her father to take in the enemy airmen? Who was her father going to pass the airmen on to? Again and again Rose gave truthful answers that gave her inquisitors no real information. Again the man became more annoyed and threatening. Rose could take no more and shouted at him.

"Leave me alone, can't you! I've told you all I can! Why don't you believe me? Just leave me alone." She dissolved into tears once more and her head slumped onto her chest. She closed her eyes and put her hands over her ears as if to shut everything out. As she did so she heard the sound of the table being pushed away and she feared the cigarette man was about to hit her again. She looked up to see him moving towards her but the other man intervened.

"Wait!" he said in French. "Enough. Enough for now. I think she needs a little time to come round to our way of thinking." Addressing Rose he said, "I am sending you back now, young lady. You will be brought back here at eleven o'clock tonight by which time I hope you will have decided to cooperate. I will not be here tonight ... but my friend will be. Think very hard meanwhile. Think of your father and brother. It will be very hard on them if you don't cooperate."

Back in her cell Rose lay down and cried for a long time. Her face hurt but her mouth no longer bled. She felt utterly miserable, trapped and vulnerable. These people seemed to be able to do what they liked with her, she thought, and no one knows; even Doctor Papin is ignored. Later Marie tried to cheer her up and encourage her but Rose was in no mood for chat preferring to sit on her bed hunched up in the corner brooding on the threat that eleven o'clock held. Every now and again she tried to convince herself that her interrogators would understand she could not help them and they would leave her alone. Curiously her light did not go off at the usual time, not that it mattered because she could not possibly sleep she was so fearful, and then near to eleven o'clock she heard footsteps approach which set her heart racing. But all that happened was the shutter on the spy-hole in the door was slipped aside, an eye appeared momentarily then disappeared and the footsteps receded. That happened twice more until about two o'clock in the morning. This time after the guard had checked her through the spy-hole her light went out. Did this mean they were not coming for her? Why had they not come for her? It was some time before she could sleep.

The following day Rose was in trepidation each time she heard footsteps in the corridor, gripped with fear until the footsteps passed on by. Eating was painful but she managed by being careful, eating on one side of her mouth though the food was no better than before she saw Doctor Papin. Then at lock up time the guard opened the hatch and told her the interrogation would be at eleven o'clock that night and her light stayed on. Having been jumpy all day, Rose was now even more on edge; unable to settle, she paced up and down her cell. It was a tempo she had become used to – three paces, turn; three paces, turn. Eleven o'clock came and went, and like the previous night her light went out at two o'clock without anything happening. The effects of this permanent state of tension were beginning to show when she awoke the next morning feeling drained and disorientated, her head fuzzy. The morning exercise helped clear her mind a little but for most of the day she lay on her bed sleeping on and off. That evening Rose explained the series of events to Marie who said it was a common practice of the Gestapo, aimed at breaking a prisoner's will. She said many on the corridor had had similar experiences. That explanation seemed to help Rose out of her torpor even though the threat of being hurt still haunted her. She relaxed a little and her mind began to wander. One question she pondered over was how long had she been in the prison. Three weeks or thereabouts, she thought, but she could not be sure as the days seemed to merge into one another and she had found it difficult to keep track of time. So much had happened to her yet there had been days on end when absolutely nothing had occurred other than the rhythm of the prison to which she had gradually become accustomed. The sound of the guard's boots on the corridor floor as they made their rounds, the wait for the next meagre meal, the morning slop-out, the exercise yard, the evening lock up, chats and lights out all provided a sort of regularity that helped the empty days tick by, hunger her one constant companion. The oppressive heat of the day was only relieved by the relative cool of the night but even that could not rid her of the awful smells that lingered.

After exercise the next morning, just as her cell door was about to clang shut it was opened again and the chief warder took a step inside. Rose turned in surprise.

"A parcel for you. You are very lucky," she said without emotion tossing a crumpled package onto the bed.

Stunned by this unexpected turn of events it took Rose a moment or two to react by which time the chief warder had disappeared and the door shut. The brown paper parcel had fallen partly open as it landed but Rose could make out her mother's handwriting on the label. She dived excitedly at the parcel opening it out and quickly rummaging through what appeared to be mostly clothes to find out what else was there. Where is Maman's letter? There must be a letter! Maman always put a letter inside the parcels she sent to her at Luçon. She searched and searched, but there was no letter. She looked at the contents now spread around, not believing there was no letter. But Maman always wrote! Then it dawned on her the parcel had already been opened. They have taken Maman's letter. How could they! Her initial joy at the arrival of the parcel turned to bitter disappointment, but gradually she accepted she was unable to do anything about the missing letter and began to go through what her mother had sent. There were two dresses, some underwear, one of her favourite cardigans, a tiny tablet of soap, what looked like shampoo in a bottle, her hairbrush, some socks and her stout school shoes. Also Rose could see a slab of her mother's fruit cake showing under the torn wrapping. Food! She took the cardigan and drew it to her face. It smelt of home, that unmistakable smell of home. As she inhaled, the joy she first felt at receiving the parcel returned. She laid out the dresses; one was rather old and a bit frayed and had been relegated to wearing around the house but she had always liked the pattern of the material. The other one was a much nicer dress which she would wear at school and she wondered why her mother had sent that for her to wear in this awful place. Then she checked all the pockets in case something was hidden in any of them, but she found nothing. She held the soap to her nose; it smelt so good, an aroma of cleanliness amongst all the foul smells of Cherche Midi. What to do next, she wondered, eat or wash and change? She decided not to decide immediately, wanting to savour the moment, the luxury of having a choice! In the end she chose first to smooth out the two layers of brown paper, examining both sides for any hint of news from home. She ran her finger over the handwriting on the address label and felt close to her mother for the first time since her arrest. Looking at the size of the wrapping paper Rose became certain the warder had taken not only her mother's letter but some other items as well. What was missing? What would her mother have packed for her? A treat no doubt; her mother always sent her a treat of some kind when she was at school, perhaps some chocolate if she could get some. Maybe there was some other food or even a school book missing from the parcel. Rose was convinced the warder had stolen it all.

Nevertheless the arrival of the parcel meant so much to her in so many ways. She knew all along her mother was thinking of her but here was tangible evidence in the form of some very practical items her mother had deliberately chosen to help her. If only she could read the letter her mother had sent with the clothes; there would be all the news of home, how they were coping with the harvest, maybe even some news of Papa and Fernand. Even without the letter the parcel represented contact with the outside world. It made Rose realise she had thought of nothing but herself during these last few traumatic days, that the outside world had receded almost totally from her mind and that made her cross with herself. How could she forget Maman and the family and all the problems they had? And she also realised she had not thought of her father or her brother for days. How could she not think of Papa? How much was he suffering? How selfish was she being thinking only of herself? Since it must be nearing the end of August she should be thinking about school; she should have finished her homework by now. She should be enjoying the wonderful summer weather, being out in the fields, sometimes helping Papa, sometimes cycling under enormous blue skies with her friends perhaps to the beach. She gathered up the clothes and clasped them tightly to her as she thought of home and the farm, of Maman and the smell of cooking in the warm kitchen. For a while she sat on her bed, rocking, allowing a warm glow to permeate every inch of her. But almost inevitably, hunger interrupted. The cake! What should she do with her mother's special cake? It was a generous piece that she could make last yet the temptation was so great she wolfed down a good chunk there and then. It tasted just wonderful. She would decide how to apportion the remainder later, for now she was desperate to wash and change into her new clothes. She must look frightful, she thought, not having seen herself properly for all this time; the only reflection she had seen of herself was in her bowl of water. Her appearance, though, had been the least of her worries. She did her best to keep herself and her clothes clean but it was impossible in the August heat without proper washing facilities and toiletries; a common problem it seemed as everyone around the exercise yard looked equally unkempt. Certainly these last few days her hygiene efforts had been minimal. The contents of the parcel gave her the motivation to freshen up as best she could but that was not easy with only limited water and a small bowl. The more water she used to wash herself and her hair with, the less water there would be for drinking. Still, it would be worth it, she told herself, even if she could not rinse her hair properly. Her hair normally needed rinsing thoroughly several times if it was to look its glossy best.

Later, washed, changed and her hair brushed, she felt a new Rose both physically and in spirit. The boost the parcel from home had given her was immense; it was not only the clean clothes and extra food, it was manifest of her mother's love and devotion and proof there was a world outside. But most of all it gave her hope as she was now certain her mother would be making efforts to secure her release just as they had both done for Papa. And of course both Papa and Fernand will have received parcels so they too will be elated and more hopeful. She would have so much to tell Marie that evening.

As expected Marie said how pleased she was for Rose but suddenly she stopped talking.

"What is it?" asked Rose.

"Shush! I want to listen," said Marie sounding serious.

The chat from the prisoners in the nearby cells seemed to be about some alarming news that had filtered into the prison and was going around like wildfire. Apparently a German Naval

Officer had been killed in the Paris Métro by a resistance group and the Occupation authorities were ordering reprisals. Notices had gone up all over Paris about it. The talk was that those in prisons would be held hostage and a number would be shot if the culprits were not handed over. Everyone agreed it was a chilling development. Was it true, someone asked, or just a ruse to scare us into denouncing our friends? It was true, came the answer. Instead of the usual banter and distractions of the evening chat, the atmosphere along the corridor went cold and the discussion quickly dried up when the severity of the news had been digested.

"What does all that mean, being held hostages? Why is everyone so concerned?" asked Rose who had found the discussion difficult to follow and understand.

"Try not to worry," said Marie kindly, trying to shield Rose from the full import of the news. "There are always rumours going around. It's probably nothing."

As the corridor fell silent a deflated Rose sat down on her bed, the cheerful mood she was in less than an hour ago had turned sour, replaced by new fears and added uncertainty. Could it really be that she, her Papa and Fernand were all now in greater danger? Surely they cannot hold people hostages just like that, she questioned? There must be some law that says they cannot do just what they like; it's not even their country.

The joy and hope her mother's parcel had brought had been short lived. Why is it, she lamented, that even when something nice happens in this horrid place, however small, it's quickly spoiled? It's not fair. Every tiny glimmer of hope is stamped on, squashed, extinguished.

It was several days before she was taken again to rue des Saussaies; and it was during the day, not late at night as they had threatened. The interrogation followed the same pattern as before with the same two men only this time it was the man with the cigarette who asked the questions and all the time he held a sort of lengthy rubber truncheon. At first he banged this on the table to scare her but Rose was already extremely frightened of him after last time. The questions, repeated time and time again, were all about her father. Who were his friends? Who came to the house to see him? Was he away a lot? Where did he go? Who did he meet? Did he favour the Communists? Was he a member of the Communist party? Did he have a gun? What sort of gun? Where did he keep it? What did he tell you he was going to do with the enemy airmen? How long were they to stay at the house? Who were they going to be passed on to? The questions were interminable. She had already answered most of them and there was nothing more she could add. The cigarette man became more and more enraged, haranguing her that she was lying.

"I'm not lying," wailed Rose. "I'm not!"

At that he stepped forward and hit her hard across the back of her legs with the truncheon.

"Tell me the truth!" he shouted in her face.

"I am! I am" Rose shouted back, tears swelling in her eyes. "Don't hit me!"

"Your father has told us things which mean you are telling us lies. Your brother has told us things which mean you are telling lies. Tell us what we want to know or it will be worse for you."

The questions resumed, later they were more about Rose herself; where she went to school, her friends, her political views, all of which she was able to answer without any concealment. Her legs were smarting where she had been hit and with the barrage of questions and shouting she could hardly stand any more but she gritted her teeth determined not to cave in against the cigarette man's onslaught. She found it much easier to cope with the questions about herself which gave her confidence she might not be hurt any more. But the man returned to questions about her father which made her tense up once again. Losing control she turned and shouted angrily at the man, stamping her foot.

"I've told you everything! Just leave me alone!"

The man came behind her brandishing the rubber truncheon again. This time he hit her repeatedly across the back of her legs but before he could finish Rose collapsed on to the stone floor crying out with pain, then lay crumpled holding the backs of her legs with one hand and shielding her head with her other arm, sobbing uncontrollably. The man stood back considering what to do. The other man, the one who had questioned her the first time, came out of the shadows and told her she must stand for questioning or his friend would get more violent.

"Don't hurt me! Don't hurt me!" she pleaded between sobs, unable to raise herself and fearing more blows. She heard the two men talking in German obviously discussing their next move then, surprisingly, they left the room. A guard came in a few moments later.

"We go," he said but Rose did not have the strength to move and he yanked her half up and dragged her out of the room, under orders to return her to Cherche Midi.

For days Rose moped about her cell, mostly lying on her bed on her side because the pain and soreness from her beating prevented her from sitting properly, a wretchedness enveloping her which she could not shake off. Again her thoughts turned in on herself. Here I am in this stinking, stifling horrid cell, with only bugs for company, being treated so cruelly, not knowing when it will end. And for what, she kept asking? Why don't they believe what I tell them? I have answered their questions over and over again. What more do they want? What more do they think I know? She felt more frustrated than ever and wanted to strike out but it was pointless and futile, caged there isolated in her tiny cell, its oppressive atmosphere adding to her sense of complete helplessness. For the first time she began to sense real loneliness. Her mother would be praying night and day for all of them and so should she herself, but as her world just seemed to be spiralling ever downwards, she questioned whether anyone's prayers were being answered. Was all this her punishment for doubting God? Had He abandoned her because she doubted Him? Her mind filled with questions, yet no answers came. Thoughts of Joan of Arc entered her head but she knew her heroine's courage was born of unquestioning faith so how could Rose, with all her doubts, draw strength from such a saint? What was it the Chaplain had said? 'God is with you.' He seemed so certain of it. Maybe he knows better than her; he should do, after all he is a priest. Could she trust him though? It was all so difficult to understand, her head was so muddled.

When Abbé Stock did visit Rose a few days later he could see immediately she was troubled; he had seen that look many times in the past year. Although she smiled at seeing him it was her eyes that were the giveaway – he could always tell from the eyes. He prepared himself to spend a little longer with her and he had something with him which he knew would be an enormous fillip to her morale but there was a danger. He could not trust the guard at the door to turn his back; he was new and appeared diligent and the Abbé was unsure whether this guard would report everything he saw and heard or not.

Rose's mood lightened when she saw him, her weak smile though was not enough to remove the anxieties showing on her face, a face which was tanned and healthy-looking when the Abbé first met her but now wore the familiar prison pallor.

"How are you, my child? Your lovely smile welcomes me but you are suffering I can see. Come; tell me what it is that worries you so much." Abbé Stock sat on the bed and patted the space next to him urging Rose to sit close which she did, although she perched right on the edge of the bed as her legs still hurt.

At his voice, at his manner, at his show of concern, any unease Rose had harboured towards the Abbé completely melted away. She relaxed somewhat; but only to the extent that the introspection which had characterised the past few days gave way to an uncontrolled outpouring of emotions in an unexpected release, like an overfilled cupboard being suddenly flung open and the contents spilling out everywhere.

"We have done nothing wrong! Papa and I and Fernand. We have done nothing wrong yet we are in here, shouted at, beaten and starved, kept apart not knowing what will happen to us. It's not right. All I did was help Papa. They say they will let me go if I answer their questions which I have. But they beat me and keep me here. Doctor Papin says I should not be here but they ignore him. I don't know what will happen to me, or Papa or Fernand. Why did God let this war happen; so many people killed, so much misery and destruction? Why is this happening to us? Why is God letting this happen to me? Is He cross with me, punishing me because of my doubts?" She turned her head to the Abbé. "Has God abandoned me? You said God is with me. How can I know when I am a prisoner here in this horrid place?" Her head slumped in her hands and she sobbed. Her volatile reaction to his sympathetic invitation surprised even her; surprised her that she could speak with such candour to a priest, that she could open up so freely, that in front of a priest she could be critical of God. But she had so much anger inside her that the urge to vent her feelings was too much for the usual niceties, the reticence and the unquestioning respect that surrounded the priest at home or those aloof priests at the cathedral in Luçon. The flood gates could hold no longer.

Abbé Stock placed a caring hand on her shoulder.

"There is much in this world we cannot understand. But we can be certain of God's love. He is here with us now. I hate war as much as you and pray to God to relieve your suffering and the suffering of others. But we have to accept that God gave us all free will, a free will to follow a path to Him or to take a different path. Your father had the free will to help those airmen and he took the path of mercy – feeding the hungry, giving drink to the thirsty and sheltering those in distress. You helped your father in his mission of mercy. God gave your father the free will to do what he did knowing the risks he was taking. But others would have done nothing and walked by on the other side. Others still have turned away from God altogether and pursued a path of evil. Remember Jesus too suffered on the Cross. Being a Christian is not easy. There are many questions we cannot answer. But through our faith we place our trust in God. Your poor mother must be suffering as Our Lady suffered."

Rose was calmed by his words. She raised herself to look at him.

"I'm sorry," she blurted, feeling rather contrite after her outburst.

"Before we talk further let us kneel and say the Hail Mary together," he said taking something from his satchel. He held out his hand for Rose to take and together they knelt down, his back to the door so as to block the guard's view as much as possible. Rose faced him bowing her head.

"Let us pray holding hands together," he said very quietly. With her hands covered by his hands he commenced.

"Hail Mary, full of grace. The Lord is with thee." As he recited, Rose felt him squeeze something into her hand. A little startled she opened her eyes and parted her hands slightly revealing a scrap of paper.

"Blessed art thou among women," he continued and when he finished he indicated with his eyes that she should look into her hands very carefully. Understanding the subterfuge Rose slowly opened her cupped hands holding them close to her and looked at the small crumpled piece of paper. There seemed nothing on it so she turned it over and smoothed it out still shielded in her hand. What she saw took her breath away. There on the paper in faint pencil were the words '*For my little Rosette*' in her father's unmistakable handwriting. Overwhelmed with emotion, she stayed kneeling looking into Abbé Stock's eyes and tears began to roll down her cheeks.

'Papa!' she mouthed. The Abbé gave the merest nod of confirmation.

"Our secret," he whispered.

She desperately wanted to ask about her father and her brother but Abbé Stock quickly moved on in case the guard should hear something he should not.

"I have a favourite hymn from when I was young," he said. "It appeals to Mary for help to relieve our suffering. Mary understands our suffering on earth because she too suffered when Jesus was crucified. It does not translate well but it goes something like this." He sang quietly:

"O Morning Star, I greet you
O Mary, Help!
Sweet Mother of God
O Mary, Help!
O Mother, in all our trials here below
Mary, Help us!"

Rose was mesmerized by the Abbé's gentle singing. It granted her a few moments of untroubled bliss.

"It is lovely," she said hardly able to believe a priest had sung just for her and rather surprised to find herself speaking to him with such familiarity.

"Pray to Mary, Rose, and to your guardian angel," said the Abbé. "You have a guardian angel, don't you?"

Rose nodded. “I will,” she said. Looking over the Abbé’s shoulder she noticed the guard had stepped away. She leant close and whispered.

“Tell my father I have his message. Tell him I will be all right. Tell him I have had a parcel from Maman, but no letter. Bless me, Father.”

He blessed her and they both made the sign of the Cross.

“Please come again,” pleaded Rose as he stood and picked up his satchel.

“I will. Remember, God is with you.”

As soon as the door banged shut Rose opened her hand to reveal again the precious piece of paper. She could hardly believe what she was looking at. After all this time a direct contact with Papa. She was so overjoyed. Papa must be all right! She traced her finger over his writing; the big ‘R’ of Rosette and the hurried line across the double ‘t’. She must find somewhere to keep this precious note safe and hidden to ensure it would never be taken from her. In the end she decided to secrete it under the loose inner sole of one of her school shoes. It was a most wonderful addition to her growing list of possessions; her watch, a change of clothes and shoes, her hairbrush, toiletries and now a note from Papa.

Chapter 14

Much of the chatter after lock-up was above Rose's head with talk of politics, art and literature all centred on Paris. Names of people, places, plays and publications that Rose had never heard of were regularly bandied about which made her feel somewhat excluded even though Marie tried at times to explain what was going on. There was however one aspect of the conversations which attracted Rose and that was the fervent patriotism shown at every opportunity, be it news of a speech by de Gaulle, some setback for the German military or a show of defiance. Often the chatter about such matters would be concluded with a rousing chorus of La Marseillaise all along the corridor in which Rose always joined enthusiastically, not always fully understanding why it was being sung but feeling better for adding her voice. Sometimes when the guards heard the singing they would come running, shouting for everyone to be quiet and threatening reprisals. Just recently there had been several pieces of news filter through to the corridor from outside which had led to spontaneous outbursts of patriotism. In one instance apparently, a Vichy politician had nearly been killed and appallingly some prisoner hostages had been shot in reprisal. But the news that an inmate of the prison, someone called d'Estienne d'Orves who everyone else apart from Rose seemed to know, had been executed along with two others caused immense sorrow on the corridor. It was said he had been sent from London by De Gaulle to spy on the Germans but was betrayed and had been under sentence of death since May. According to Marie who seemed to know a lot about him, he had not expected to be pardoned. La Marseillaise was sung with great feeling that night. These demonstrations of defiance and patriotism whilst momentarily raising Rose's spirits also had the effect of feeding the festering bitterness she felt at her treatment, a resentment which was near boiling point.

Unexpectedly one morning Rose was given the opportunity to wash her hair and shower in the bathroom. This was staggering for she had not heard there was such a thing as a bathroom in the prison let alone having the privilege of using it. The governor, she was told, who had introduced the morning walk to improve the health of the prisoners also wanted to improve hygiene; hence everyone was to have a bath or a shower once a month. Today was her turn and the female warder accompanied by a male guard escorted her to a bathroom on the first floor. The facilities were crude but only a little more basic than she was used to at home and soon Rose was washed thoroughly and smelling clean for the first time since she was arrested. As she was collecting her toiletries she was able to see out of an open window onto the yard below. What greeted her eyes rooted her to the spot. A couple of German soldiers, idly whistling, were washing out the back of a truck which had an empty simple wooden coffin propped up against it. But the pools on the ground around the truck ran red with blood and Rose could only think the lorry had just returned from another execution. Anger and revulsion welled up in her and without stopping to think what she was doing she started to sing La Marseillaise as loudly as she could. The soldiers abruptly stopped what they were doing and looked up just as the warder yanked her away from the window ordering her to be quiet. The guard rushed in and together with the warder manhandled Rose out into the corridor and back towards her cell. Her bottle of shampoo had fallen to the floor but the guard merely kicked it away. Moments later Rose was flung on the floor of her cell with the words, "Don't forget you're a hostage too."

Instead of feeling the pain of hitting the hard surface and ruing the loss of her shampoo Rose felt a curious sort of strength, a satisfaction resulting from the sudden courage that came to her to take a reckless tilt at her tormentors.

A short while later her cell door was violently flung back and two soldiers burst in, pistols at the ready.

"Get all your things and come! Now!" one of them barked at her.

Rose cowered at the end of her bed, shaking with fear.

“Where are you taking me?” she pleaded, her voice trembling.

“You have to be punished. Hurry!” shouted the soldier.

Rose whimpered, “What are you going to do to me?”

“You’ll soon see,” growled the other soldier who then made a slicing motion across his throat.

“La Santé,” the soldier in charge directed the driver of the waiting staff car. Rose had been bundled into the back and sat petrified jammed in between the two soldiers. She clutched her meagre bundle of belongings and looked straight ahead hardly able to think. As the car moved off through the huge main gates and out onto the sunlit street she was so tense she was not aware how tightly she gripped her small collection of precious possessions. She wanted to ask again where they were taking her and what was to become of her but her jaw was clenched tightly shut, like all of her body, rigid with fear.

The car turned in the opposite direction to her previous journeys and after a few minutes Rose recognised the immense façade of the railway station where she had arrived in Paris and for a second the faint hope flickered that she was being taken to the station to catch a train home; but the car sped on, shortly turning into a narrow street the name of which Rose caught as the car swung round. They had turned into the rue de la Santé and moments later the car slowed as it approached an imposing tall arched gateway in the middle of a long, high blank wall. Rose shuddered. What was this place? The car stopped outside the gateway allowing her sight of the sign on the wall: Prison de la Santé. Another prison! But why was she being moved to another prison? To be punished? That was what the first soldier had said; but what punishment? The second soldier had made that sinister cut-throat gesture; what did he mean? What did it all mean? She became extremely apprehensive. With one soldier out of the stationary car calling for the gates to be opened the possibility of an escape flashed into her mind; but it was impossible. There were more armed guards at the gate, and even if she did manage to jump free from the car, in a trice there would be half a dozen rifles pointing at her and since the road was straight in both directions there was nowhere to take cover. Ordinarily she could run like the wind but now she was weak and she knew it would be pointless to try.

Inside the massive walls of the prison the cell wings loomed large, just as ominous and oppressive as at Cherche Midi. The admission process was similar except this time the leading soldier handed over a dossier to the female warder seated at her desk who glanced at it briefly, scanning down the first page.

"You are Rose Neau?" she asked, her expression changing to surprised curiosity when she realised the new inmate before her appeared very young indeed. "How old are you, Rose?" she said, her tone sounding concerned; not the usual impassive demand. Rose was standing in front of the desk still clutching her bundle, her stance awkward under the tension.

"Sixteen," she replied in a quiet voice, her mouth so dry she struggled to get just the one word out.

The warder, a large round faced Austrian woman hardened by many years working with female prisoners, found she was unusually affected by Rose who was younger than anyone she had had to detain in the past. Surely, she thought, this young girl need not be held under such harsh conditions, despite the reasons for her detention stated in the file. She called another warder into the room and told her to take over at the desk, saying she would take this latest inmate to the cells herself.

"Come," she said to Rose in a tone that was more an invitation than the usual barked order. Sensing a touch of compassion in the warder's voice Rose's tenseness eased just a little as she followed her through the door which led into the main hub of the prison, a tall circular hall. It was three storeys high, off which ran a number of corridors like the spokes of a wheel, four wings of which had row upon depressing row of cells on each level. Rose was led by the woman across the hall and along a ground floor corridor, deeper into the prison through a series of iron grille partitions. Each grille door clanked shut behind her until they reached another cell block. They climbed to the second storey and along yet another corridor where the third cell door was open.

"In here," the warder said gesturing Rose to go in, her manner subdued. Rose took a couple of steps inside and then turned.

"Why am I here?" she asked meekly.

The Austrian woman found she was unable to answer Rose's simple question. Try as she might during the short walk to the cell she could not help thinking she should not be locking up this young girl. She knew she ought not to get emotionally involved but she could see a close likeness in Rose to her own darling daughter whom she had not seen for over six months now. The parallel of her only daughter being imprisoned in such an awful place was too much for her to bear. Choking back her own emotion she said nothing, turned away and closed the cell door.

Rose slowly lowered herself and sat on the edge of the bed, the back of her legs still sore from the beating, and gently placed her bundle beside her. The warder's lack of response to her question just added to her trepidation about her fate which, if all the signs of the last few hours were taken into account, looked far, far bleaker than ever it had since her arrival in Paris. Was this where she was now going to be held? It certainly seemed as though she was not going back to Cherche Midi. What was the purpose of being moved to this prison? What punishment lay in store for her? Unusually, the woman warder gave the impression she could be kindly; but everything else about the place was foreboding.

Rose looked around her new accommodation. It was little different from her previous cell but this place had a certain chill to it; it was stale-smelling as though it had not been opened for some time, and there was the whiff of dampness in the still air. It was only mid-September yet involuntarily she shivered, perhaps as much from her sense of apprehension as from the atmosphere of the cell. There was a heavily barred window high on the north-facing outside wall with a small section that could be opened but Rose could hardly see the sky through it. No sun ever penetrated here as that part of the building was in permanent shadow. In one corner by the door there was a small table with a water jug and bowl just the same as Cherche Midi, together with a wooden stool which was chained to the wall. In the opposite corner by the door was a latrine, no more than a hole in the concrete floor. The cell was the same size as the one at Cherche Midi but one aspect that made it feel smaller was the absence of a fanlight window over the door; and the door itself appeared tight-fitting all round. 'No chatting along the corridor here. How I'm going to miss that!' Rose said to herself disconsolately. One slight benefit she later discovered was that the metal frame of the bed could be folded up against the wall to provide more space. She scanned the room again and it unnerved her – not that it was worse physically than her previous cell; it was more that the whole ambience of the place was somehow sinister. She quickly convinced herself that La Santé was going to be even worse than Cherche Midi. Then she was worried that no one might know she had been taken there, especially Papa and Maman; maybe she would not see Abbé Stock again. And she would miss Marie. All these thoughts began to overwhelm her and she started sobbing and lay down on the thin, uncomfortable mattress. That night after lock up, to take her mind off the day's events she tried to imagine the normality of being back at school, back in her class, studying hard for the exams due next month. But the world outside now seemed so remote, so totally out of reach, almost unreal.

At the breakfast table Franziska poured her brother a cup of coffee. She admired Franz immensely but she also worried that he did far too much, for most nights when he eventually arrived home he was exhausted not just physically but mentally too. She fussed and nagged him to take things easier but he took little notice. First thing that morning he had seemed in a pensive mood but now having just come from the small chapel at the mission where he prayed before breakfast his mood was lighter as though his prayers had helped resolve something that had been troubling him.

"I've been thinking about that young girl in Cherche Midi," he said, "and I've decided I must do more to help her. Do we still have any of those small New Testaments in French? I think I'll take one in for her if we have. She needs encouragement to find the faith and trust she has lost."

"I'll look now," said Franziska knowing what he wanted. Before the war the mission held a small stock of miniature New Testaments in both French and German which they would hand out as gifts to visitors or to the needy. More recently her brother had taken several of the French versions in for prisoners despite the risk of being found breaking the prison's strict rules banning certain inmates from having books. She looked in the cupboard to find only one copy in French remained.

"The last one," she announced. "We haven't any money to buy any more even if there were any to buy now."

Franz looked up at his sister and said with a smile, "No doubt our Security Service friends who keep an eye on me would find it interesting if I were to buy any more. This last one though couldn't go to a better home."

A short while later he wheeled his bicycle out onto the rue Lhomond and pushed off down the road, his satchel in the basket over the rear wheel and the tiny New Testament tucked into a secret pocket in his cassock. He felt a touch of autumn in the breeze on his cheeks.

At the same time as Abbé Stock was setting off from his home Rose was escorted into an office in the main administration block of the prison and told to stand in front of a large desk with various piles of papers on it in disarray. The guard who had escorted her stood at the back of the room in silence and there they both waited for several minutes during which Rose became more and more petrified thinking some sort of painful punishment was about to be meted out to her. A rather portly intelligence officer entered and made his way round the desk to his chair and sat down. He looked much older than all the other soldiers Rose had come across, almost fatherly in appearance, and when he put on a pair of glasses he looked more like a retired teacher than a German army officer; but in reality his role was a sinister one – to gather intelligence on French Jews and communists. He consulted a list and then picked up a folder from one of the piles.

During the wait for the officer to appear and now in the silence as he read the file, Rose's emotions tumbled and turned and despite the danger she felt she was in, or perhaps because of it, her mood became defiant, almost as though she felt she had nothing to lose. Before the officer had finished reading she could contain herself no longer.

"Are you going to kill me?" she blurted out without thinking. She had not meant to say it at all, but it just came out sounding like a dramatic challenge. Startled, the officer dropped the file on his desk and looked up.

"No, no. Goodness, no," he stammered. "I'm just going to ask you some questions." He paused. "You look very young and very pale," he said, somewhat taken aback to find his interviewee was a mere girl. "Try not to worry."

He said something in German to the guard who brought a chair over. "Sit down. I won't harm you." He said something else to the guard and reached into his pocket, took out some money which he gave to the guard who then left the room.

"I need to record your family background. Just for the file, in case it needs to be taken into account," he said. His French was passable and his manner surprisingly friendly. "You must tell me the truth, of course, and what you tell me will be checked. I'm sure your parents have brought you up to tell the truth and if you answer my questions properly this will soon be over. Bear with me one moment," he said and proceeded to pick up and review the file he had dropped a moment ago. Rose found that during the silence that followed her courage began to wane but eventually the officer began to question her about her family, where they came from; where the family name was from; did they have relatives in eastern European countries or the Holy Land; was there a synagogue where she lived and did her family visit it?

To start with Rose was puzzled by his line of questioning. What did he want to know all this for? Surely it was nothing to do with why she was being held in prison? But gradually, and chillingly, she realised he was trying to find a Jewish connection. However, as she remembered Papa talking proudly of the Neau family having lived in the west of France for centuries and because she could not think of anyone she knew who was Jewish, she calmed down and grew in confidence. At that point the guard returned and handed the officer a packet of biscuits.

"You must be hungry," said the officer. "Everyone in here is hungry. Please, take a biscuit. Two or three, if you like." He tore open the end of the packet and leant over to offer her some. Rose eyed the biscuits and her mouth watered. The temptation to grab and gobble up as many as she could was enormous; she had almost forgotten what it was like not to be hungry. But she was wary of his generosity and in her mood of defiance she resisted.

"Are you sure?" he asked.

"I am sure," said Rose with emphasis. What he said next puzzled her for a moment.

"You are a very organ young lady, I must say," he said aiming to appear affable. "I'll leave them there in case you change your mind."

What could he mean, 'a very organ young lady?' Then she realised he had meant to say, 'a very proud young lady,' confusing the similar French words for 'organ' and 'proud.' She smiled, almost giggled, at his mistake and although tempted to correct him thought better of it.

He resumed his questions, asking her about her school. Was it a Jewish school; did she have any friends who were Jewish or teachers who were Jewish? Was there a synagogue in Luçon? Did she go there or know anyone who went there? Rose was glad she had nothing to hide as she had heard of the growing persecution of French Jews by the Germans which she thought was very wrong and cruel. He wanted to know about any communists in her village or if strangers had come to the house or whether absences of her father or brother were unexplained, ground that had been covered in previous interrogations. Some of his questions were repeated in a different way, other questions Rose could not see were of any relevance.

The intelligence officer was no fool. At times he deliberately put on a friendly, bumbling guise to disarm the person under interrogation, which on this occasion worked as Rose did not suspect anything and did not pick up on his subtle techniques or trick questions. As he rather suspected at the beginning though there was no intelligence of any value to be had from Rose. Despite her obvious nervousness he concluded she was not lying. He noted her answers were entirely consistent, her body language was not suspect and she regularly maintained eye contact with him; all signs that she was not trying to conceal anything. But he was happy to string out the interrogation as he had a young girl sitting opposite him, an unexpected if temporary pleasure. Although rather dishevelled and pallid he guessed in better times she would appear quite pretty. Time was, nevertheless, pressing and there were more serious matters for him to attend to. Finally he pushed back his chair preparing to leave.

"What is going to happen to me?" Rose asked plaintively, desperate for any information and hoping this kindly officer would take pity on her.

"I'm sorry, young lady, I can't help you. Such decisions are in the hands of others," he replied quite sincerely, knowing from the file no decisions had yet been taken. Normally he would deliberately ignore such a plea whether he knew the answer or not – keeping detainees in ignorance and in isolation was part of the dehumanisation process, aimed at crushing them both mentally and physically. But, for once, for this young girl, he had relented. As he left the room and walked along the corridor he wondered if he was going soft in his old age, acknowledging that he had been slightly beguiled by this spirited yet naïve young girl for whom he had gained a touch of admiration. He had certainly not been involved with anyone so young held under such serious charges before, let alone a girl, and pondered her fate. But not having come across anything like her case in his experience he reached no firm view and whilst he rather hoped she might receive some clemency, he doubted it.

In the following hours Rose lay on her lumpy bed mulling over and over the episode with the intelligence officer picking on a word here, a phrase there, a glance or a gesture, looking for hidden meanings, trying to remember all his questions and wondering if any of her answers would count against her or if she should have answered differently. At least this officer had been unthreatening and seemed sincere. Fortunately there had been nothing she needed to hide from him and as a result she had been able to tell the truth. So, she thought, perhaps at last she had been believed but she could not really be sure.

Later, footsteps on the corridor stopped outside her cell and the key was turned in the lock. The cell door opened and the kindly warder appeared.

"You have a visitor," she announced stepping aside to reveal Abbé Stock standing in the gloom. Rose's heart soared as she got up from her bed to greet him.

"Please. Oh, please come in," said Rose. "I didn't expect to see you again. How did you know I was here?"

"This is part of my parish too and I get told of new arrivals," he replied. "How are you, my child?" For Rose just the simple humanity of him asking how she was lifted her spirits. She looked up and his eyes were as before full of gentleness and concern. It was as if an aura of light shone from him, eclipsing all her misery and the harshness of her surroundings.

"Have you seen Papa and Fernand? Are they all right?" she asked. "Will you tell them I have been sent here? I'm so worried no one knows where I am."

Abbé Stock looked over his shoulder and smiled. He had arranged with the Austrian lady, a good Catholic, to have a few minutes alone with Rose. They had discussed Rose on the way to the cell and he knew she was somewhat sympathetic towards her.

"Your father is strong," he said having checked they were alone. "He is like an ox! He asked me to pray for his family which I do. Your brother, I think, is used to the outdoors; he is finding it more difficult. Sadly, I have no other news but sit at the end of the bed, my child, as I have something for you." He pulled the stool over as far as the chain would allow, sat down and delved into his cassock. He pulled out the tiny book which he offered to her. "It's a copy of the New Testament. Hide it from the guards or they will confiscate it. Read it whenever you can and it will give you strength and comfort and bring you closer to God."

Rose took the book gently as if it was a delicate flower. She was curious; she had not seen a book that small, so small it was not much larger than the palm of her hand. On the spine in gold lettering were the words, 'Nouveau Testament'.

"Thank you," said Rose tentatively as she was uncertain how to react. She felt a mixture of surprise and delight, but something else as well which she could not immediately identify. Perhaps it was a touch of embarrassment that her Bible studies had waned to nothing and the beautiful white leather Bible given to her by her mother at her confirmation was in its case in her bedroom cupboard untouched for several years now.

Under his gaze though she was encouraged enough to ask hesitantly, "What should I read first, do you think?"

"In times of trouble I comfort myself with the words of Saint Peter from his First Epistle. He wrote that because God cares for you, you can pass all your troubles onto Him. Find that, it will help you too. And if you read the Gospel According to Saint John you will find Jesus' story likening himself to a vine: 'I am the vine, ye are the branches. He that abideth in Me, and I in him, the same bringeth forth much fruit.' He is telling us that being at one with Him offers us strength and hope; that without Him we can achieve nothing.

"Shall we pray?" he said after a brief pause. Together they knelt and he led them in prayer, seeking God's help for Rose and her family in their suffering, at the end of which he blessed her.

Hearing footsteps on the corridor Rose quickly dropped her latest possession into the pocket of her dress, giving the Abbé a conspiratorial look.

Moments later he was gone; but his aura lingered, manifest in a kind of inner light, a lightness of heart. She felt 'different'. It was as though the Abbé had thrown a heavy cloak over all her worries, smothering them, shielding her from them. She felt unburdened, calmer, more composed. These inner feelings lasted but the physical world soon intruded and she realised yet again how hungry she was and noticed it was colder. She shivered and reached for her cardigan.

Later that evening after lock-up she decided it was safe to look at her New Testament which she had hidden amongst her pile of spare clothes soon after Abbé Stock had left. The book was tiny, beautiful, less than five inches by three inches, quite thick with dark hardback covers. Both front and back covers were heavily embossed with an intricate and delicate design, the spine also. Intrigued she opened it up and looked inside at the first pages. Even though the light was gloomy it was not too dark to read. The title page read, 'Le Nouveau Testament de Notre Seigneur Jesus-Christ, Version du Chanoine Crampon'; the following page listed all the books of the New Testament with the number of chapters; then, without further introduction the next page was the beginning of the Gospel According to Saint Matthew. The print was small but perfectly readable even with two columns to a page and she marvelled that the whole of the New Testament could be contained between the covers of this tiny book. She felt quite excited. Until now she had had only her own thoughts for company in her cell but now she had a book that could occupy her for many, many hours. She turned to the last page to see how many pages there were. Five hundred and four! It was too daunting to think she could read all of it. She ran her finger over the embossing and turned the cover in the light better to see its intricacy. She had never had anything so expensive looking and beautiful before. She should look for the words of Saint Peter, the Abbé had said, and so she turned to the contents page and found 'I S. Pierre and II S. Pierre' towards the bottom of the list, five chapters and three chapters respectively but no page numbers. After a few moments searching she found the start of the First Epistle and began to read. But her excitement quickly fell away as the verses were mostly impossible for her to follow. It was so difficult to read and understand and she soon became discouraged. There were however a few verses that she could make some sense of, particularly those verses referring to Christ's sufferings and although she ploughed on, by the end of Chapter Four she was about to give up. But she saw that Chapter Five was short and the final one before the Second Epistle so she decided to read it; and her face lit up at the beginning of verse seven, immediately recognising the Abbé's quotation: 'Unburden onto Him all your anxieties, because He cares for you.' To Rose, alone, afraid and starved of human kindness the words sounded wonderfully comforting. She read them again and again. The light was fading as she finished the chapter, the rest of which made little sense to her. She memorised the page number, closed the book and returned it to its hiding place.

For a while she sat on top of her bed, wedged in the corner just thinking about the Abbé. He occupied her thoughts a lot, had become very important to her, the only person who brought her any hope, the only source of news of her father and brother. How vital this news was to her strength and courage. Their meetings were brief but their effect was lasting. Through his presence, his manner and his obvious tenderness he seemed to share and alleviate her misery and distress, just like the words of Saint Peter. He said how he had found comfort in those words, and, yes, she too felt comforted. And now, through his gift of the New Testament, he had brought her the words of many Saints. Tomorrow, she said to herself, she would start reading the Gospel According to Saint John as he had suggested. She kept thinking too of his parting words, 'God is with you,' said personally to her with such sincerity and certainty that she was left in no doubt of his total conviction. Was she wrong to doubt God when he was so convinced, she wondered? If only he had been her priest at home. She could talk to him openly; he seemed to understand her.

That night before she went to sleep, for the first time for a very long time, she prayed. Remembering the Abbé's earlier encouragement she offered to her guardian angel the simple daily prayer she had learned by heart as a young child. Silently she recited, 'Angel of God, My guardian dear, To Whom His love, Commits me here, Ever this day, Be at my side, To light and guard, To rule and guide. Amen.' Then as an afterthought she added, 'I'm sorry to have left it so long.'

The following afternoon Rose's composure of the day before was soon quashed as she was taken to a far part of the prison by a burly female prison officer she had not seen before and who gave no word of what was to happen. With one hand the officer clasped Rose's upper arm tightly hustling her along so quickly Rose was half running. Ominously she carried a rubber truncheon in the other hand. Rose was gripped by a numbing terror at the thought she was about to receive her threatened punishment. She was taken down some steps to a dank basement area with bare walls and weak lights. They turned in to a side room where Rose was told to take off all her clothes. She was about to object but the officer stood facing her threateningly tapping the truncheon in the palm of her hand. It was cold and, embarrassed, Rose stood there naked with her arms covering herself as best she could. The officer grabbed Rose's arm again and dragged her towards an inner door which she opened and yanked her to the middle of the room. They stood there, Rose's arm hurting in the tight grip. It was a large windowless room, very dimly lit with a sizable bath along one wall filled with water, the surrounding floor still wet as though much water had been spilled from it recently. On the other side of the room was a padded table like a doctor's couch with a bank of lights suspended above it. Two men stood leaning on the couch talking in low voices, speaking German. They had looked up when the prison officer and Rose had entered the room, stared at Rose and continued their debate with much gesturing.

Rose stood there, her arm still grasped tightly, humiliated by her nakedness and utterly petrified. Of all of her experiences since her arrest, this situation held the most menace, the most terror. She could not make out why there should be a bath and this doctor's couch in the room or what they might be used for, but the whole atmosphere was heavy with threat and Rose was convinced something terrible was about to happen to her. Shivering and shaking with cold and fright she looked up pleadingly at the prison officer but the woman ignored her, looking straight ahead expressionlessly. Rose did not recognise the two men who wore civilian clothes but quite obviously it was they who were in charge and the woman officer stood silently awaiting instructions. It seemed to Rose from their gestures the two men were deciding whether to use the couch or the bath but since Rose did not know what either was used for she waited in trepidation, feeling faint, occasionally swallowing nervously. Her instinct was to struggle and fight but she knew it was useless and may only lead to more pain and humiliation.

After a moment or two of further discussion the men stood up straight and one tapped the couch indicating their choice. The woman pushed Rose towards the raised couch which had cuffs to strap down both wrists and ankles. With only token resistance Rose was strapped on to the table which was then raised a little higher. It was only then one of the men addressed her speaking in French, his face so close to hers she could feel his breath on her cheek.

"This far you have not cooperated with your interrogators and you have withheld important information about your father. We know he is part of a resistance organisation whose aim is to kill German soldiers, destroy important installations and to smuggle enemy airmen back to England. We need to know who his contacts are, where his orders come from, where he passes messages."

"He isn't! He isn't!" Rose blurted out, exasperated at the man's totally incorrect premise. "I keep telling you. He is not part of any organisation. He is a farmer. He looks after his farm and his family. He's not what you say." Her voice was shrill with emotion and desperation.

"If you continue your lies, you must be made to tell the truth," the man threatened, at which point the bank of lights above Rose was switched on flooding her in a bright, white light. The dozen or so powerful bulbs were set in a shallow concave casing suspended from the ceiling immediately above her, the harsh glare from which blinded Rose who turned her head to one side to avoid it. "These lights can be very hot," said the man in her ear. "Start talking or my colleague here will lower the lights."

"Please don't hurt me! Please!" Rose wailed. "I've told you all I know." Suddenly the lights jerked lower and Rose could feel their searing heat. "Papa doesn't belong to any organisation. He said the airmen needed help; that's all. Don't hurt me! Please!" The light jerked lower and hovered just over her body, so close that if she had moved she would have been scorched instantly.

"Tell me!" shouted the man.

"I've told you all I know," Rose yelled back through gritted teeth as she tried to bear the pain. The heat on her skin built rapidly and she started to cry in terror of being horribly burned.

Seconds later the lights were lifted away and extinguished, leaving Rose with a severe and painful stinging sensation over much of her torso. Although relieved the hot lights were out, she sobbed and was shaking uncontrollably, not daring to look at herself for fear of what she might see. The man said something in German to his colleague and Rose heard footsteps receding.

"Tomorrow you will talk," Rose heard the man call back as they left the room.

The woman prison officer undid the clasps and told her to get up. Gingerly at first Rose swung her feet over the side of the couch and as she did so she could see much of her body was badly reddened. Her skin felt tight and sore. She tried to stand but her legs gave way and only the woman's grasp stopped her collapsing. She took a few moments to steady herself and eventually, with help, she walked haltingly back to the room where her clothes were. She dressed herself but her clothes chafed painfully on her skin, as if she was suffering from acute sunburn.

The officer took her across the corridor, unlocked a cell door and told Rose to wait in there. To Rose's surprise there was a young woman inside seated at a table. The cell was much larger than she had seen before with room for two beds. The young woman seeing Rose in difficulty got up, came over and helped her to the chair.

"You look terrible," she said. "Are you all right? Here, come and sit down. Have some of my water."

"Thank you," murmured Rose before taking a sip of the water offered, still trembling from her ordeal.

"You look awful. What have they done to you?" said the young woman with concern. "Would you feel better lying down?"

"I think I do need to lie down," Rose said feeling faint and the young woman helped her to the nearest bed where she eased herself down on her back. The young woman, who said her name was Yvette, pulled the chair over, sat close and stroked Rose's hair.

"There, there," she soothed. "You poor thing. It's all over now. They will be taking me next. They keep beating me too and I don't know if I can resist any longer, if I can hold out." Rose just wanted to be quiet, nevertheless she was grateful for Yvette's kind attention but the young woman leant closer and whispered, "Did you tell; did you denounce anyone? You can tell me. I won't let on to a soul or blame you. If you didn't you must be very brave, you are so young. Tell me how you fooled them so I can do the same."

Rose turned her head and said weakly, "I've told them everything but they still don't believe me. That's why they keep hurting me. What can I do? I can't stand any more; but there is nothing more to tell." She started sobbing again which only made worse the chafing of her clothes where her skin was so tender.

Yvette tried to calm Rose, wiping her forehead with a damp handkerchief. She told Rose she was a patriot and had been involved with a group that blew up a bridge and a German ammunition dump. She had been captured and now the Germans wanted to know all the names of those involved. She had held out so far but didn't know if she could any longer. Had Rose managed to keep her secrets, she asked again. She could trust her; she was her friend.

Rose stopped crying and lay absolutely still so as not to aggravate her sore skin. "They want to know if my Papa belongs to a resistance group or something. But Papa doesn't. Can't they see that? What more do they need to believe it? I don't know what will happen to us if they won't believe us."

"You poor thing," said Yvette again. Then, strangely, she got up and went over to the cell door, banged on it with her fists and shouted, "Bastards!"

Moments later the door was unlocked and the woman officer told Rose to get up and come with her, ignoring Yvette. Slowly Rose stood and walked cautiously towards the door.

"Good luck. And thank you," she whispered to Yvette. As the officer steered her down the corridor Rose, still distressed, failed to notice the cell door was not locked after them. As Yvette stood in the open doorway watching Rose and the warder slowly disappear up the stairs, one of the torturers appeared and walked over to Yvette and the two began to talk.

"What did you find out?" asked the torturer in German.

"She is not hiding anything. There is nothing more to be gained from her," said Yvette.

"That's what I think, too," said the torturer. "I thought the lamps would scare her more than a ducking in the bath; spoil her youthful beauty. No need to do any more with her or the two Neau men or the Gouraud man. They are small fry. I'll recommend they go to a tribunal on the evidence we have. It's enough." With that the two strolled off together.

All evening Rose felt very ill. She lay still on her bed trying to get comfortable and despite the cooler weather she had taken off her clothes as she could not bear them touching her skin. She felt wretched, weak, drained, her mind a blank, wanting to roll up in a ball and make the world go away. For hours she lay there. Occasionally she would hold her hand just above her skin but not touching it and she could feel the heat radiating, otherwise she lay unmoving willing the time away until the pain and discomfort were eased. Because her cell had been empty no afternoon rations had been left and unable to bear her chronic hunger any longer she ate the last crumbs of her mother's cake that she had been saving. After that she slept, but only sporadically and as the night drew colder she was forced to cover herself with the thin blanket despite it rubbing painfully against her skin. In the morning she was roused by the usual noises of the prison coming to life and feeling cold she put on her loosest dress which was of a soft material and thankfully just about bearable. She remembered the man's threat from yesterday, 'Tomorrow you will talk,' but because she was so exhausted in body and in mind she was almost past caring what the day might bring.

During the fifteen minutes or so of the morning exercise period she cast a pathetic figure, head bowed staring at the ground, pacing painfully zombie-like around the exercise square. In the end nothing happened that day, or the next, or for more than a week. The burns to her body gradually healed over time leaving no lasting damage but not before large patches of seared dead skin peeled off. But the healing process was slow due to the conditions and her poor diet.

At her lowest ebb she inevitably sought someone to blame for her wretchedness. Of course the Germans were the main culprit, of that there was no doubt; it was they who inflicted all this pain and held her prisoner so unnecessarily. But she could not help thinking that if only Papa had not brought the airmen to the house, none of this would have happened. If her brother had not got involved in the first place, had turned away as the other workers on the dyke had done, none of this would have happened. Yet she could not lay any blame on her brother – after all he had saved the airmen's lives. Papa though …? Whatever she thought about her father's part, however she considered it, she could not find it in herself to reproach him knowing he was suffering also.

As Rose improved it was not the chronic and constant hunger alone which gnawed at her – that had become the norm – it was the loneliness too. She had grown up a typical mixture of the gregarious child who, as she matured, was also content to be alone with her studies, immersing herself in her books for hours on end but then wanting to join in whatever was happening whether at school or on the farm. At home, she loved spending quiet times with the animals, feeding them, cleaning out or collecting eggs: yet she also enjoyed the really busy times when the whole family were out in the fields working together, as at harvest time. At school she was always one of the main crowd, not a leader, but involved in whatever was going on, having lots of friends and having lots to say in class. But all that humanity had been brutally cut off from her by her imprisonment to be replaced by long periods of solitude punctuated occasionally by a surly guard or warder, or by some heartless and brutal interrogator. The only light of humanity which penetrated her cell was Abbé Stock whose visits she now looked forward to more than anything, and not just for news of her father and brother. At Cherche Midi prison with Marie and the others Rose had felt part of a community, a community with a common adversary. The group only existed because those involved could, cunningly, communicate and although Rose was only on the periphery she had felt that she belonged. She would listen as the group offered encouragement to those who were down, shared news or discussed views. She had joined in their celebrations when there was good news on the war front or when someone had been released. Bizarrely, she had known only a few names, known little of their backgrounds or the truth of why they were in prison and had hardly spoken directly to most of them. People came and went but the community had endured and the key element for Rose was that she had been included, she was one of them; she was someone. Looking back Rose was beginning to understand how much that extraordinary little circle at Cherche Midi had meant to her.

At La Santé it was completely different. Silence held supremacy here. Rose had soon discovered that communication with other inmates was virtually out of the question, perhaps a few whispered words in the yard to the person in front or behind during exercise, or a trusty might hurriedly be persuaded to pass a message, a trick learned from Marie, but any sort of conversation was impossible. At La Santé she was anonymous, isolated and alone, forcibly segregated from the rest of mankind, in exile. Hardly another voice was heard in her cell and for much of the day the silence was total.

After her worst ordeal, every day that passed thankfully eventless allowed her slowly to gain a little in physical strength in spite of the meagre diet. Mentally though she struggled, worrying how much longer she would be able to cope, moping around, her mind vacant or wandering aimlessly. Gradually over the next week or so in her more lucid moments she became acutely aware of how lonely she felt. Loneliness had now joined hunger as her constant companion.

What made her think of it all of a sudden she had no idea but she remembered her intention to look up the passage in her New Testament about Jesus' story of the vine and the branches, to be found in the Gospel According to Saint John the Abbé had said. It was the recollection that she now possessed a book which galvanized her, mainly because the book offered a distraction, would help to pass the time, which in turn would also combat her increasing sense of isolation. She retrieved it from its hiding place certain she would not be seen. 'Matthew, Mark, Luke and John,' she recited to herself. Sure enough her finger soon came to the Gospel According to Saint John in the list of contents: twenty-one chapters in all, she saw. After paging back and forth she eventually found the beginning on page one hundred and seventy-two, and then the end on page two hundred and twenty-two. Fifty pages! 'Oh well,' she said to herself, 'I have plenty of time.' She hoped it would be easier to read than Saint Peter's Epistle, which it was, right from the first familiar words: 'In the beginning was the Word.' Encouraged she read on, recognising stories she had learned at Sunday school: the miracles of the water into wine, the lame man made to walk, feeding the five thousand. Remembering these gave her confidence to continue, until at last, she came to the parable of the vine and the branches. She read the verses several times and believed she understood their meaning, more or less, given the initial help of Abbé Stock's interpretation. There were also other accounts in the Gospel she knew well: the Last Supper and the Crucifixion, and several verses she knew almost by heart from the many hours she had spent sitting next to her mother at Mass: 'For God so loved the world, that he gave His only begotten son, …' and 'Greater love hath no man than this, that a man lay down his life for his friends.' Gradually, with growing confidence she became conscious of what she was doing. She was reading; once again absorbed in a book! Reading was something she had really come to love since she had started at the school in Luçon, not just for her schoolwork but for pleasure too. Reading offered her escapism from the gloom and privations of the war, taking her to far away places and back in time to adventures of heroism and romance. She would read for hours, perched anywhere, utterly engrossed. Since her arrest however it had not occurred to her until now how much she had missed the joy of reading. But with her new treasure of the New Testament she had the means to take herself away from her prison cell, albeit not through a book she would have chosen for herself, yet through a book chosen for her by the Abbé who said it would bring her strength and comfort. While reading the Gospel according to Saint John she was surprised to find she recognised many passages and could follow considerably more than she thought possible; so much so she made up her mind to read the other Gospels, starting with Matthew. Heartened, she also decided to offer the prayer to her guardian angel each night, starting that night.

The evenings began to draw in and the nights were noticeably chilly. Rose made a routine of standing on the stool each morning and afternoon just to see something of the outside world. By day the skies were cloudy and sometimes it rained all day but the change in the weather was a relief from the stifling heat of late

August and early September. The monotony of daily life was interrupted by the arrival of another parcel from home. It had been addressed to Cherche Midi which meant her mother did not know where she was. And again there was no letter but Rose had come to expect the disappointment. The thick brown jumper was definitely needed and her prettiest blouse cheered her up although thoughts of wanting to look pretty had not entered her head for a long time. When she unfolded the jumper to her surprise out dropped her rosary which brought a wry smile to her face. Her mother rarely lost an opportunity to encourage Rose to follow her own strong belief and practices and here she was, 'at it again.' Rose was charitable enough to reflect that this time perhaps her mother did have her best interests at heart! But sight of the rosary however also brought with it a tinge of guilt as her rosary, another confirmation present, had not seen the light of day for a while. Had her mother known that, Rose wondered? Probably, she thought, there was not much that passed her mother by. She felt, and liked, the smoothness of the small wooden beads but she was not moved to use it, not straight away at least. She was nevertheless glad to have it as another reminder of home and she laid it out on the bed alongside the jumper and blouse. Rose bit her bottom lip as emotions welled up at the thought of home. Such was her topsy-turvy world; happy at receiving a parcel from home but saddened by the thoughts it invoked. That evening though as she again felt the smoothness of the rosary's beads the thought of Joan of Arc came into her mind. In her despair and isolation it was difficult to be inspired but Rose thought about her heroine's single-minded bravery, and was encouraged just a little. She, Rose, too would try to be brave …

The weeks passed. Why were they not letting her go?

It was mid October when Rose was again taken to the offices of Major Scherer at rue du Faubourg Saint-Honoré. No explanation was given for this sudden interruption of her solitude and at mid morning she sat on a small bench in an anteroom waiting nervously. Could this be her release, she dared to think? 'Please let it be!' she prayed silently and more earnestly than ever, not daring to think of the catalogue of disappointments she had suffered since her arrest. A bored guard stood uninterestedly gazing out of the window while a series of busy looking senior officers came and went, thick files tucked under their arms. Rose sat and waited. She had been brought from La Santé before the morning food trolley arrived but she dared not ask the guard for anything despite the emptiness she felt in her stomach. After a while a young German soldier was brought in, roughly handled by two heavily armed guards who seeing no other seat pushed the soldier to sit down next to Rose. They then spoke to the guard by the window, obviously leaving instructions about the soldier, before leaving. Rose flinched slightly at having a German soldier sit down so close, almost touching her, and she stared ahead her hands in her lap. She had noticed as the young soldier was brought in how ashen faced he looked and after a while she glanced downwards and saw his hands were trembling. She looked up at him and his eyes had a haunted look about them and he was obviously struggling to maintain any composure. He caught her look and a strained half smile came to his lips. He turned and looked towards the guard at the window on the other side of the room whose attention was drawn to some noisy commotion in the street below, then turned back and leaned nearer to Rose.

"They are to shoot me," he whispered into her ear in broken French. "For disobeying orders. I must join a firing squad. I refuse. For that I will be shot."

Rose was shocked and stunned, not knowing how to respond.

"Surely not," was all she could think to whisper back.

"Oh, yes. It is certain," he said almost inaudibly glancing again at the guard who was still distracted. "I could not shoot a man like a captured animal. I could not. Now they will shoot me."

Rose was surprised to feel empathy for this young German soldier, even felt sorry for him that his principles had landed him in such desperate trouble.

"How terrible! Is there no way out?"

"No. It is done." He was shaking. "Have this," he said pushing his hand along the bench to Rose's thigh. Rose put her hand down hoping the guard would not see what was going on and felt the young soldier put something into her palm. "I don't want them to have it."

Rose brought her hand back on to her lap and surreptitiously opened her palm. It was a wedding ring. Just as she looked back to his face and was about to ask his name, the two guards burst back into the room and shouted an order at the young soldier who immediately stood up. They marched him into the next room and shut the door. Silence returned for a while but it was not long before the young soldier was marched out and although Rose called after him for his name her words were lost in the general noise of heavy boots on the wooden floor and doors slamming. The young soldier did not look back.

Rose shivered at the thought of what that young man must be going through and felt strangely privileged that he should give her his wedding ring which she hid in the turn up of her sleeve where a stitch had come loose. Moments later Major Scherer came out of his room, peaked cap in one hand and his overcoat over his arm. He strode out into the corridor without a word or acknowledgement of her presence. Rose waited. He did not return and she was taken back to La Santé just in time for half a bread roll and a piece of dry cheese which did little to assuage her aching hunger and consequent dizziness. That evening as she lay on her bed she inspected the ring but there was no name. The soldier's wife should have it, not me, she thought; then tried it on her wedding finger but of course it was much too big. Her mood was melancholy, even conceding that not every German soldier was necessarily cruel; that some, like the young soldier today, might be frightened, even principled. She fingered the ring wistfully. Would she have a husband one day, she mused? François, perhaps? She hoped so. She would give him a wedding ring, just like this one.

The following day she was back in Major Scherer's anteroom, waiting, her hopes again raised that this was to be the moment of release, of freedom, the start of normal life returning. After a while she was ushered in and she stood trembling in front of his desk. He looked up, his face impassive.

"I have to inform you that you are herewith formally charged with offences under the Order of 10th October 1940 relating to the giving of shelter to and aiding the escape of two British airmen on 24th and 25th of July 1941 at St. Michel-en-l'Herm. You will stand before a military tribunal alongside your father, your brother and Monsieur Gouraud who are all similarly charged."

Rose's first reaction was disbelief, then tears welled in her eyes as she took in his words and she began to feel weak at the knees. She was about to protest, but he continued.

"The tribunal will hear the case and pronounce its verdict. You will be granted a defence attorney, may appoint your own attorney or defend yourself as you wish. These charges are very serious and if found guilty you should expect severe punishment. You will be informed of the date of the tribunal in due course. That is all."

Tears rolled down Rose's cheeks and she was shaking with shock and fear.

"No! You can't do this to us!" she cried out. The Major held up his hand and stood up to stop her further protests.

"It is now out of my hands. Save your words for the tribunal." He turned to the guard ordering him in German to take her away.

In her cell Rose sobbed uncontrollably for hours, her hopes yet again cruelly dashed. And now she was threatened with a tribunal of which she had no understanding. How could they treat her like this? How she wished Papa was with her now. He would know how to deal with all this, how to protect her. Her nerves remained on edge, her ear attuned to the slightest noise from the corridor outside. Later, one thought occurred to her that with formal charges laid against her maybe there would be no more torture, but she could not be sure; nothing in this awful place was ever quite what it seemed.

The days drifted by to the rhythm of the prison's daily routine. Temperatures gradually dropped especially at night but she was not given any extra blankets. Her cell became noticeably dank and gloomier. By day Rose habitually wore her thick jumper and was glad of it although all her clothes began to feel damp. Nothing much happened to break the monotony and she found herself sliding towards despair. No one came to tell her about the tribunal, when, what or where it would be and thankfully there were no visits to the underground chamber. In an effort to stay positive she passed the time reading when it was safe and sometimes making up games. One game she liked was to throw a ball she made out of the wrapping paper from her mother's parcel aiming to land it on the seat of the stool at the end of the cell. She quickly became quite good at it. At other times she would see what she could make of the many scribbles etched into the damp plaster on the walls. One was quite clear: 'Imprisoned since 23.4.1941, long live France. Jeanne L.' Rose wondered who 'Jeanne L' was and what happened to her. Another simply read: 'I am hungry …' There were numerous sets of initials – who were they all? Rose was tempted to add her own. At other times she just watched the antics of her cellmates, a varied parade of insects that scuttled to and fro. As the days shortened she learned to sleep longer, sleep being the only antidote to the cold and hunger.

There was a distraction one morning when heavy footsteps stopped outside her door. Rose froze. The door was unlocked and a young man in uniform appeared; he was in uniform but did not act like a soldier.

"The chaplain is here to see you," the young man announced. Rose relaxed immediately and her spirits soared – the Abbé was here to see her, but she was puzzled by the young man. It was not, however, Abbé Stock who entered; it was a short dark haired officer, perhaps younger than Abbé Stock, wearing an immaculate German officer's uniform complete with highly polished boots, with a priest's collar just visible. She had not seen him before and the puzzlement and disappointment on Rose's face was very obvious.

"My name is Abbé Loevenich," the officer said. "I have joined Abbé Stock in his ministry here. I'm on my initial rounds to acquaint myself with La Santé. This is my assistant," he said indicating the young man who had also stepped into her cell. "You look very young, my child. My list says you are Mademoiselle Neau. Is that right?" His French was perfectly correct.

The brief exchanges that followed were rather stilted as Rose did not take to him. Although his face was open and pleasant, his voice was loud and harsh and his uniform proved a major barrier. Abbé Stock wore his priest's cassock: this priest appeared proud to wear a German officer's uniform, as though it was more important than his priest's attire. Rose sensed no empathy, could not see beyond the uniform and she also felt uncomfortable with his assistant hovering behind him. She accepted his blessing but was glad when they were gone. She was so disappointed it was not the sympathetic and compassionate Abbé Stock who had come to see her.

A few days later her cell door was unlocked once more.

"Come, you are to meet with your defence counsel," said the Austrian warder who, whenever she saw Rose, could not help being reminded of her own daughter. Rose duly followed her down to the ground floor and to an interview room in the administration block. In the small, sparsely furnished room already seated at the bare table was a dapper man in his fifties wearing glasses and rummaging in his briefcase. When he saw Rose he stood up and indicated she may sit down in the chair opposite him. He introduced himself.

"Mademoiselle Neau, my name is Jacques Chaumel, Barrister of Fontenay-le-Compte. I have been engaged to represent you, your father and brother at the forthcoming Luftwaffe Military Tribunal," he said. "You may be aware I represented your father at his recent trial over the theft of some beans. A most regrettable affair. Now you have, of course, the option to dispense with my services and to appoint your own counsel or to defend yourself. My strong advice is you should retain my services as your father and brother have done. What do you say?"

Rose was totally thrown not only by his formal approach but by his blunt question about retaining his services. Added to that she also realised that by his very presence matters were now definitely very serious, that Major Scherer telling her she would be placed before a tribunal was no mere threat.

"You have seen Papa and Fernand? Rose asked urgently. "How are they?"

"They are fine. I'll come to them in a moment. I need to know what you want to do," replied Monsieur Chaumel keen to get on with his business.

"I suppose if my father is content to have your services again then I am too," said Rose. "But what is going to happen at this tribunal? No one tells us anything in here."

"The tribunal is a sort of court, only there is no jury as in a French court of justice and the President of the tribunal will be a German military officer who will decide the case and pass judgment. Now the purpose of this meeting is to agree your defence. Firstly, though, the file says you are aged just sixteen. Is that right?"

"Yes," said Rose.

"H'm," mused Monsieur Chaumel. "I will submit that because of your age you should not be in front of the tribunal at all, but that argument is unlikely to succeed, in which case we must have a defence prepared to the charges laid against you, namely that you aided and abetted the harbouring of two enemy airmen and that you facilitated their attempted escape, contrary to the Order of the Occupying Authorities of 10th October 1940. How do you wish to plead?"

The barrister was going far too fast for her; tribunal, charges, pleas, it was difficult for her to follow let alone to gather her thoughts.

"I don't know," she said bewildered, thinking how can she possibly decide such things? "What does Papa say?"

"I have spoken at length with your father and with your brother. They are prepared to follow my advice and plead not guilty on the basis that they were unaware of the Order and its specific prohibitions and therefore it cannot be held they understood the seriousness of their actions. I suggest you plead similarly so we have a united approach. But I must add that the decision is for you and that I am duty bound to pursue your case on your instructions. In your case, as a schoolgirl, I will contend you could not be expected to be aware of the Order under which you are charged and that you were under the influence of your father. I should be frank, though, and say the prosecution will rest their case on the fact the airmen were found in your house which cannot be disputed. As such we must be prepared for you to be found technically guilty."

"Guilty!" interjected Rose. "How can they find us guilty? I knew nothing of this Order. Why can't you get us freed? Even Doctor Papin said I shouldn't be here!"

"That is why we must present all the mitigating circumstances we can, which are substantial, and I am confident the tribunal will be lenient towards you and your family."

Rose became very upset and was about to interrupt again when the barrister held up his hand to stop her.

"You are being held by the German military and they will exercise their powers as the Occupying Authority. There is nothing we can do about that believe me or I would have done something about it by now. What we must do is to get all of you off as lightly as possible. Try not to worry," he said in a kindly tone. "I am here to help you and I believe we have a strong case for leniency."

"It's not right. Doctor Papin said I should have been released on health grounds but nothing has happened," stated Rose emphatically, then added pleadingly, "Is there nothing you can do?"

"Alas not," he replied, his head slightly bowed in acknowledgement of his impotency. "Your father has already questioned me about why all of you could not be tried under French law in a French court which would surely throw out the charges. But I had to tell him this is deemed a military case by the Occupying Authorities because enemy airmen were involved and that decision would stand even if I challenged it."

"Then I suppose I must do what you and Papa say," Rose said reluctantly seeing no alternative but to accept the situation.

"Good," he said and started to run through how he planned to present their defence, ending by saying, "Do you understand? I know it is complicated and difficult for you but we must try our hardest. Just be led by me and you will be all right."

"Thank you," said Rose, "I'm not sure I understand everything but if Papa has agreed it then I suppose it's all right. Please tell me how Papa and Fernand are."

"They are as well as can be expected," he replied rather guardedly being pretty sure they had suffered under interrogation but not wanting to worry her. "You are like your Papa, direct, impatient and questioning of authority but we have to play this carefully and not rub the tribunal up the wrong way. Your brother is quieter, stoical and will cooperate. You will see them at the tribunal and I hope your mother will be able to travel up for the hearing."

"Maman, I will see her!"

"Hopefully. The date for the tribunal is set for the 10th of November. Before then you may be interviewed by the prosecuting officer but just say you have been told by me to say nothing. Remember though, often the dates move so don't get too set on that date for seeing your mother or you may be disappointed. Until then I will work on your case and I am confident of a good outcome. Goodbye for now." With that he got up, gathered together his papers and hurriedly left before Rose had a chance to think of anything else to ask.

Back in her cell Rose thought the whole episode with Monsieur Chaumel unreal. A defence lawyer, a tribunal, charges against her; this could not really be happening to her, could it? Her head was in a whirl there was so much to take in, so many questions she had not been able to ask. But of all Monsieur Chaumel's words it was the date he gave her that offered a glimmer of hope. For the first time Rose had a date – the 10th of November; a date she assumed would bring an end to this hell, wishfully interpreting Monsieur Chaumel's confidence of leniency to mean release and freedom. But then she quickly realised she did not know what today's date was. How silly of her not to ask Monsieur Chaumel! She must find out, but how? She had an idea. Maybe a trusty could help her.

But however long the wait was for the 10th of November to arrive she knew it would seem interminable, just as when she was much younger waiting for a birthday or for Christmas. Only this time the days would be empty and long and the freedom she craved was yearned for much, much more than for any birthday or Christmas ever was. She told herself she could and would hold on despite everything – the cold, the hunger and the loneliness. She must hold on till the 10th of November; then it would be over, they could all go home, she could return to school and life would return to normal. In a flight of fancy she even thought her escapade and ordeal might attract François whom she felt sure was a patriot. Oh François, what a prize you would be!

Nearer the time when the last rations trolley of the day was due Rose sat on the stool right next to the cell door, her head bent to the closed hatch and there she waited ready for the trusty to arrive outside her cell.

"Can you talk?" she whispered urgently as soon as the flap opened.

"Be quick," was the anonymous response.

"I need to know today's date. It's important," whispered Rose.

"Tomorrow," Rose heard, before the flap dropped shut.

The following morning when Rose picked up her bowl of thin broth there was a tiny scrap of paper underneath. On it, written in faint pencil, was '28 Octobre', but no day of the week. Rose would have liked to have known what day it was, but concluded it did not matter. On her fingers she counted out the days until the 10th of November and because it was difficult to keep count she decided to scratch a line for each of the days on one of the walls and then cross one as she went to bed each night. She tried to scratch the plaster with a fingernail but she had bitten them right down, a bad habit she had often resolved to stop, and she could not make an impression. She tried one or two other things including a button before remembering the soldier's wedding ring which worked well on the softest patch of plaster on the outside wall. She scratched thirteen lines. Each day she looked forward to the evening when she could cross off another stroke, her mood improving as the days ticked by. A thought came into her head which amused her. On the last day she would carve her initials at the end of the line of strokes; a fitting inscription to commemorate her stay.

Monsieur Chaumel had led her to expect an interview with some prosecutor but nothing happened. She became more and more excited as the final day approached, not only because she was convinced of her release but she would be seeing Maman, Papa and Fernand. But as time ticked slowly by on the last day, the 9th November, she was disconcerted to find her excitement gradually waned as the day progressed, to be replaced by an unexpected nervousness, being aware subconsciously that nothing ever went according to plan in this place. She occupied herself preparing what she would wear to look her best, particularly for her mother's sake. That night, after carving 'RN' on the wall as carefully as she could, she solemnly and fervently prayed to God that tomorrow would see all of them set free and heading home.

She awoke early having slept restlessly with curious dreams. But at last, the day had arrived. She washed and dressed quickly to be sure she was ready. Then she sat on her bed, her hands in her lap, nervous, full of apprehension of how the day would unfold, less confident than yesterday yet telling herself the sooner it starts, the sooner it will all be over. She kept checking her watch impatiently.

It was not until late morning that her cell door was unlocked to reveal two helmeted soldiers, rifles slung over their shoulders, one with a pair of handcuffs in his hand.

"Tribunal," said the corporal. The other soldier stepped forward as if to handcuff Rose but the corporal intervened, deciding she was no threat. He simply ordered her, "Come!"

Chapter 15

At rue du Faubourg Saint-Honoré, where the Luftwaffe Military Tribunal sat in Paris, Rose was shown into an anteroom and told to sit down. The corporal spoke to the group of soldiers already in the room before he left. Rose sat there uncomfortably knowing she was being eyed by the guards. Anticipating that she would be taken early in the morning to the tribunal, the tense expectation she had felt at the start of the day turned to frustration when nothing happened for a while. Now that tense expectation returned in earnest and she struggled to hold herself in control, aching to see her family again after all this time. The door opened and she quickly looked up. Her father entered but he did not see her immediately. But what Rose saw made her heart sink. Her father was handcuffed, a soldier gripping his arm steering him into the room. But it was his looks that shocked and upset her most. Normally he was robust and swarthy, a picture of health and strength but now he looked pale and gaunt, stooping, his clothes looking a size too large for him.

"Papa," Rose screamed, jumping up and running to him arms outstretched. Before any of the guards could stop her she reached him and flung her arms around his neck, sobbing and murmuring, "Papa, Papa."

"Darling Rosette," he whispered into her ear before a soldier prised her away.

"No talking!" barked one of the room guards ushering Rose back to her chair. After his handcuffs were removed her father was allowed to sit next to her and they looked into each other's eyes. His eyes told her he was still her 'Papa', and he managed a half smile as he nodded as if saying he was all right. He then changed his expression, raising his eyebrows enquiringly, asking if she was all right to which she nodded in reply. She dropped her hand down by her side and slowly moved it across to rest against her father's thigh just wanting, needing, some physical contact, a reassurance that at last she was with him. He placed his hand over hers.

Shortly afterwards the door opened again and this time it was her brother who was pushed into the room, again handcuffed. She noticed his eyes first, somewhat haunted-looking, but otherwise he appeared physically better than her father. Rose stood up to go to him but one of the guards moved to bar her way.

"Can I greet my brother?" requested Rose of the guard to which he begrudgingly agreed.

"Fernand," she said quietly as she greeted him.

"Are you all right," he whispered out of the side of mouth.

"Yes," was all she could say before the soldier grasped his arm and yanked him away to remove his handcuffs. She returned to sit next to her father.

Her brother appeared to her stronger than her father but his eyes were brooding. Suddenly she had a minor panic – how would she look to them? She had tried to make the best of herself, putting on her pretty blouse and least crumpled skirt but her hair which had not been washed properly for some time was lank and lifeless. She felt unkempt and she was conscious her legs were swollen and blotchy. Because she had no mirror she had not seen her face clearly, again only a vague reflection in her bowl of water. Despite her efforts, her mother would surely be upset at seeing her like this.

Her thoughts were broken when Monsieur Chaumel came into the room. Business-like he greeted his clients.

"Monsieur, Monsieur, Mademoiselle." He then addressed Rose's father.

"I am confident of a good outcome, but we must as I explained respect the court and hold our stance. Leave it to me to conduct all matters. I will not call any of you to the witness box. I had hoped the President of the tribunal would be Captain Roskothen who has a reputation for fairness and humanity. Unfortunately I hear the President will be a Captain Junger, a lawyer just arrived from Berlin; regrettably he is an unknown quantity. Your wife is here; she is next door in the courtroom."

Rose's eyes lit up at the confirmation her mother had arrived.

"Normally," Monsieur Chaumel continued, "you will not be allowed to speak with her but I will try to see what I can do should there be an interval. You will be called shortly and proceedings will commence at two o'clock. Because it is an afternoon hearing we may not get a verdict until tomorrow. Do you have any questions?"

"How is my wife?" Fernand asked, not sounding at all himself, Rose thought.

"She is as well as can be expected. She has a friend with her which is good. Is there anything else? If not I must go and prepare." Fernand shook his head. Monsieur Chaumel looked at young Fernand and Rose as if posing the same question; both too shook their head.

While this brief conversation was taking place Alphonse Gouraud was brought into the room and was made to sit away from the others. He nodded to each of them as Monsieur Chaumel left, but Rose sensed the tension in the room rise with his presence. He looked intense, taut; his eyes, fiery beneath his heavy eyebrows, darted around the room.

They did not have to wait long before they were led into the tribunal room, Alphonse Gouraud first, then Fernand, young Fernand and Rose last. They were made to sit in the front row of the dock behind a low wooden railing facing a raised dais on which was a long table with a large red and black swastika flag draped over the front. Fully spread out on the wall behind the table was another large swastika flag. The room itself was large, elegant and airy, decorated in blue, black and green. At each end of the main table at right angles were two more long tables with several chairs, and below the main table inside the horseshoe arrangement was a small table with a typewriter on it. In front of the windows that looked out on the street below were two rows of seats, again set apart from the main floor of the court by a low railing. Here sat Rose's mother with her friend Estelle Bon, the wife of the local garage owner. On the row behind and several seats away sat an older man and a young lad, Alphonse Gouraud's father-in-law and his eldest child Michel. Rose recognised the boy as the one under arrest and brought with them to Paris but as he was sitting in the same area of the court as his mother she presumed he had been released – a good sign.

Rose looked across to her mother with the bravest smile she could muster and received a faint smile in return. 'I'm all right,' she mouthed aiming to give her mother some reassurance. This meeting, so anxiously looked forward to by both of them, was curiously embarrassing, neither knowing what to do separated as they were and unable to talk. Her mother was neat and tidy in her Sunday best coat and hat, but to Rose though she appeared strangely small and out of place in this large courtroom. The strain of her ordeal was plainly etched on her face and obvious to Rose who was dismayed at seeing her mother so pained. Whilst she derived some comfort from being with her family at long last, the circumstances of the reunion were so different from the scenarios she had imagined many, many times during the last few months that for a moment she felt as though she was in a vague and disturbing dream.

Renée was in a worse daze, disorientated and bewildered by the whole affair. She had never been to Paris before, was intimidated by the overtly military court setting and had built up to this moment of seeing her family with a mixture of anticipation and dread at what she would find. Seeing them herded by armed guards into court was hard enough but it was heartbreaking to see the toll their ordeal had taken on them. Her husband particularly looked drained, pale and haggard but what frightened her most was the look on his face. His usual air of self-confidence was no longer there – he looked scared, unsure. Young Fernand looked stronger than his father but she had not seen him so tense before, as though he was struggling to contain an underlying anger. And seeing Rose, her heart went out to her knowing she must have suffered like the others. Yet there she stood, trying to appear brave and obviously having made an effort to present herself as best she could with the nice blouse sent in one of the parcels. Renée thought she had put on a little weight which surprised her. She had feared for Rose more than the others and was thankful to see her no worse; nevertheless, she could not help but see apprehension written all over her daughter's face.

Rose's attention was brought back to the courtroom when a side door opened and people began to appear, several in Luftwaffe uniform and then Monsieur Chaumel and his assistant both dressed in court attire, long black gowns with a collar of two long strips of white cotton. They settled themselves at the table to Rose's left; three men in uniform and a civilian sat at the table to the right and another man in uniform seated himself at the small table in the middle. Standing next to Rose and at each door to the courtroom stood an armed soldier. On the tables were piles of files and carafes of water. Then a door to the left of the main table opened and the clerk to the tribunal called out, "All rise!" Three important-looking officers paraded in and took their places at the main table. The officer in the middle opened proceedings, speaking in French.

"This military tribunal is convened under German Military Law and I, Captain Karl Junger, have been appointed President by General von Stuelpnagel, Military Commander for all of France. This tribunal will now commence. Heil Hitler." He and the others in uniform saluted as 'Heil Hitler' echoed around the room. The clerk announced, "The accused should remain standing, the remainder may be seated."

Rose started to shake and edged forward to hold on to the rail in front of her, intimidated by the number of high ranking Germans, the formality and the whole military scene. All of a sudden she was filled with doubt that these people would listen to their story; that the trial would be fair.

The clerk continued, "For the benefit of the accused where possible this tribunal will be conducted in French. Otherwise an interpreter is here to ensure the accused can understand all proceedings. I will now read out the charges.

"Fernand Ernest Adrien Neau, please step forward. You are charged with aiding the escape of and giving shelter to members of the enemy's armed forces on 24th and 25th July 1941 at St. Michel-en-l'Herm contrary to the prescriptions of the Order of 10th October 1940 relative to the protection against acts of sabotage. How do you plead?"

Fernand looked across to Monsieur Chaumel who indicated he should respond.

"Not guilty," he said shakily.

"Fernand René Neau, please step forward. You are charged with aiding the escape of and giving shelter to members of the enemy's armed forces on 24th and 25th July 1941 at St. Michel-en-l'Herm contrary to the prescriptions of the Order of 10th October 1940 relative to the protection against acts of sabotage. How do you plead?"

"Not guilty," mumbled young Fernand his head bowed.

"Rose Clorinthe Ernestine Neau, please step forward." Rose was already holding on to the rail in front of her which she gripped even tighter.

"You are charged with aiding the escape of and giving shelter to members of the enemy's armed forces on 24th and 25th July 1941 at St. Michel-en-l'Herm contrary to the prescriptions of the Order of 10th October 1940 relative to the protection against acts of sabotage. How do you plead?" Rose looked at Monsieur Chaumel who nodded she should go ahead.

"Not guilty," she said in a quiet voice.

"Alphonse Armand Désiré Gouraud, please step forward." But before the clerk could proceed to read the charge Alphonse Gouraud called out.

"I do not recognise this court. I will not receive a fair trial and I demand to be put before a French jury!" The startled clerk looked anxiously at the President for guidance.

Captain Junger looked thunderously at Alphonse Gouraud and in a raised voice in German railed at him. When he had finished the interpreter stood up and translated.

"The President orders you not to interrupt the tribunal in this fashion or you will be removed and tried in your absence." The clerk then continued.

"You are charged with aiding the escape of members of the enemy's armed forces on 24th July 1941 at St. Michel-en-l'Herm contrary to the prescriptions of the Order of 10th October 1940 relative to the protection against acts of sabotage. How do you plead?"

Still standing, a defiant Alphonse Gouraud repeated, "I do not recognise this court. In any case I am innocent."

Captain Junger consulted one of the officers at his side and then spoke in German to the recorder seated below him. Then in a clipped tone he addressed Alphonse Gouraud.

"Your objection has been noted. The clerk will record a not guilty plea. The accused may be seated." He then ordered the clerk to continue.

"The prosecutor is Lieutenant Manstein. Messieurs and Mademoiselle Neau are represented by Monsieur Chaumel. Monsieur Gouraud has refused representation."

"Lieutenant Manstein, you may open the prosecution," invited Captain Junger but before the Lieutenant could stand Monsieur Chaumel was on his feet.

"Herr President. I have an important point of order to put before the tribunal."

The Lieutenant who had just about got to his feet glared at him, annoyed at being interrupted as he was about to begin.

A quizzical Captain Junger indicated he may continue.

"I contend that Mademoiselle Neau should not be before this tribunal in view of her young age, sixteen. Her date of birth is 23rd February 1925. As such she is a minor and should be before a juvenile court. I therefore seek her immediate release from this tribunal." Rose's heart rate quickened. He was doing as he said he would. She held her breath. Renée clutched Estelle's arm.

Again Captain Junger consulted one of the officers at his side. After several exchanges the Captain looked up.

"Denied. Proceed Lieutenant." Rose's heart sank as quickly as it had risen although she had been led by Monsieur Chaumel to expect that outcome.

A young looking, immaculately presented Lieutenant Manstein stood up, not a hair out of place.

"Herr President. These are very serious charges indeed and I will show that the two oldest accused, as soon as they became aware of enemy airmen in the area, determined to find them and help them evade capture. I shall therefore be seeking the severest punishment laid down in the Order of 10th October 1940. Let me first outline the background to this case.

"On the afternoon of 24th July last, a force of British Royal Air Force heavy bombers attacked one of our navy's principal battleships, the Scharnhorst, moored at La Pallice, Vendée, causing the deaths of many of its sailors defending their ship. Damage to the ship itself was light thanks to the stout defence of the Scharnhorst and its destroyers and to the magnificent efforts of the Luftwaffe fighters sent to attack the large number of heavily armed bombers, very many of which were shot down. One enemy aircraft came down in the Baie de l'Aiguillon and according to the fighter pilot who followed the stricken bomber only three parachutists were seen to emerge before it crashed, all of which he reported on return to his airfield. One parachutist was rescued from the sea. The other two were seen to come down near the shore of the bay and search parties were mobilised to track them down and capture them.

"I now draw the attention of the tribunal to the statements by two local council workers who were repairing a dyke near to where this aircraft crashed and who saw the two parachutists land in deep mud close to the shore. Their testimonies are explicit and in agreement about what happened next. It is clear the young man Fernand Neau, who was working with the two witnesses, rescued both enemy airmen and took them out of sight of the two witnesses later returning saying the airmen had gone away. This is important as it places the young man Neau at the scene and connects him directly with the enemy airmen. These events were confirmed by the airmen during interrogation with one significant difference. The airmen reported they were hidden nearby by their rescuer, a point I will return to later. Here though I would add that both witnesses state the two airmen, who appeared stuck in the mud, would certainly have been quickly drowned by the incoming tide had they not been promptly rescued. The tribunal should recognise the life-saving actions of this young man whilst not, of course, condoning his later actions."

"The tribunal," interjected Captain Junger, "does indeed commend his life-saving efforts."

Rose was surprised at the praise for her brother and looked across to him but he showed no reaction. The Lieutenant continued.

"I now wish to take the tribunal forward in time, to the early hours of the following day, 25th July, at the house of Fernand

Neau senior in the rue de la Fontaine in the village of St. Michel-en-l'Herm, Vendée, some eight kilometres from the scene of the rescue of the two enemy airmen. I call Second Lieutenant Hans Brandt." Rose recognised the officer who entered the room as the one who had arrested her father and brother.

"The tribunal has the full statement under oath of Lieutenant Brandt and that of one of his men who accompanied him to the house of Fernand Neau on the night of 24/25th July 1941. Lieutenant Brandt, tell us briefly what happened on that night."

The Lieutenant explained how he had been detailed to take a detachment to the Neau house to bring in for questioning the young man Fernand Neau concerning the two British airmen known to be in the area. Routinely he instructed his men to search the property and they discovered the two airmen under the bedcovers in the main bedroom upstairs. His men took the captured airmen away and he arrested Fernand Neau and his son for harbouring them.

"Do you see in this room the two men you arrested?" asked the prosecutor.

"Yes, that man there and that man there."

"Did you encounter any resistance to enter the property?"

"Yes. The young man Fernand Neau attempted to prevent our legitimate entry."

"Is there any way the airmen could have secreted themselves into the house without the knowledge of the occupiers?"

"No. They were in the main bedroom upstairs. There is only one stairway in the house."

"What was the reaction of Fernand Neau senior when the two airmen were brought downstairs?"

"He simply said, 'They needed help.' Nothing more."

"Was there anything suspicious in the possession of these captured airmen?"

"Yes. A little after they were captured a French/English tourist phrase book was seen to be surreptitiously dropped to the ground by one of them. It has a map of France at the back.

"I show the tribunal exhibit A."

Rose drew a sharp breath as she recognised her book as it was held up by the prosecutor. She had forgotten all about it and unnerved she shot a look across at Monsieur Chaumel whose expression seemed to say everything was under control.

"Is this the phrase book?" the witness was asked. He confirmed it was.

The prosecutor sat down and Captain Junger asked Monsieur Chaumel if he had any questions for the witness.

"On entering the house and during the arrests were any of your men injured?" asked Monsieur Chaumel embarking on his planned attempt to mitigate the tribunal's view of the offences.

"No. My men quickly dealt with any resistance."

"What evidence did you find at the house of any preparations having been made to hide these airmen?"

"They were found hidden under bedclothes."

"Hardly an elaborate hiding place," remarked Monsieur Chaumel sarcastically. "Did you find any weapons, explosives or sabotage equipment of any sort?"

"No."

"Did you find any evidence of anyone else being involved in these airmen being found at the house?"

"No," answered Lieutenant Brandt.

"That is all," said Monsieur Chaumel sitting down. Lieutenant Brandt was then excused.

"We now have," said the prosecutor resuming, "the young man Fernand Neau directly connected to the airmen in the early afternoon at the shoreline where their aircraft came down and little more than twelve hours later these same two airmen are found in his parents' house where he is arrested along with his father. Having rescued the airmen from the sea it was the young man's duty of course to immediately alert the authorities as to their whereabouts. He failed to do so, which is in itself an offence. The report of Lieutenant Brandt lists the three accused, Fernand Neau senior, his son Fernand and daughter Rose, all present at the house when the airmen were captured. All are irrefutably guilty of harbouring the enemy.

"The question to address next is how did these enemy airmen travel undetected from the shore to the Neau house some eight kilometres away despite the many army search parties scouring the area. The medical reports on the airmen state that one of them had a severe ankle injury indicating he could not have travelled unaided to the village of St. Michel-en-l'Herm. So how did the airman arrive at the house of Fernand Neau? The answer lies in three witness statements and from interviews with the two airmen one of whom was seen to have on him the tourist French/English phrase book, exhibit A. Asked where this came from the airman said that during the afternoon a man working in the fields nearby approached them and with the help of the phrase book and the map showed them how far it was to the border of the Occupied Zone. He said he would come back again to help them. This man was clearly the accused Alphonse Gouraud."

'No. That's wrong!' Rose breathed, thinking Monsieur Gouraud should not be blamed for giving the airmen her book. But she dare not say anything.

"The first witness statement," the prosecutor continued, "is from Alfred Brard, a dairyman of St. Michel-en-l'Herm. In essence he states that in the evening of 24th July he met three of the accused, Fernand Neau senior, Rose Neau and Alphonse Gouraud, all of whom he knew well, travelling on a hay cart coming across the fields from the direction where the two enemy airmen were rescued. This meeting took place just inland from the shore on the only vehicle track to the village. In his testimony he states that he followed the cart driven by Alphonse Gouraud to the village. On the way they were stopped twice, once by a mobile patrol of soldiers heading towards the bay and again at the entrance to the village by a road block also manned by soldiers. This statement is confirmed by the corporal of the mobile patrol who recognised Alphonse Gouraud – this corporal had earlier requisitioned two lorries from the accused. The soldier in charge of the road block also recorded stopping at dusk a girl on a bicycle and two men on a hay cart. The corporal's statement goes on to say the following day he was ordered to bring in Alphonse Gouraud for questioning. Whilst searching the premises of Alphonse Gouraud, a British Royal Air Force issue watch and a silver English coin – a half-crown I believe it is called – was found on a cart in the yard under some hay. The watch, Exhibit B, and the coin, Exhibit C, obviously came from the pocket of one of the airmen. Also found on the cart was a piece of cloth snagged on a nail that matched the airmen's uniform. Furthermore a patch of blood was noted on the cart. During interrogation Monsieur Gouraud variously claimed that either this evidence was planted or the airmen had hidden on his cart without his knowledge. Both claims fly in the face of logic.

"We now come to the significance of Exhibit A, the phrase book and map, given to them in the afternoon, according to the airmen, some hours after their rescue. Whoever gave this phrase book and map demonstrated a clear prior intent to help the airmen evade capture. This person was Monsieur Gouraud who speaks no English and he would have taken the book with him when he set out in the afternoon on his own to find the airmen. Nevertheless, between Messieurs Gouraud and Neau they hatched and carried out a plan to transport the airmen to their village and hide them.

"Two opportunities presented themselves when the airman could and should have been handed over to military personnel by these two accused. As we know neither opportunity was taken because all along they were intent on secreting the airmen in order to aid their ultimate escape."

At this point Captain Junger politely interrupted the prosecutor and called for a short break. Rose and the others were supposed to remain silent in their seats and surprisingly a welcome cup of weak coffee and a biscuit were brought in for them.

When no one was looking, young Fernand took the opportunity to whisper to his sister, "Are you all right?"

"Just," whispered Rose back. "But it's not right they are blaming the phrase book on Monsieur Gouraud. What should we do?" Covertly he consulted their father.

"Nothing. The airmen are protecting us," was the hasty response.

After that they had to stop as an orderly came to collect the cups and plates. Rose looked over to her mother to catch her attention but her mother's eyes were firmly fixed on her father. Rose sat with her own thoughts, taking deep breaths, worried that the self-assured prosecutor was making a strong case against them that Monsieur Chaumel would find impossible to counter. At the resumption the prosecutor continued.

"The final piece in the prosecution's case concerns the proper execution of the Mayor of St. Michel-en-l'Herm's duties in informing the population of his commune of the provisions of the Order of 10th October 1940 as laid down by the Préfecture structure for civil administration. In early July, each Mayor of the Vendée was given strict instructions to inform all inhabitants of the Order, failing which he may be held personally responsible for any contravention by an inhabitant. With the obvious breach of the Order on 24th and 25th July 1941 the Mayor of St. Michel-en-l'Herm, Monsieur Bodin, was arrested. He has provided an affidavit to the tribunal stating that he complied fully with the instructions in the customary fashion for his commune, namely that an official notice was placed in the local newspaper, in this case in La Dépêche Vendéenne issue of 13th July 1941, and that a prior announcement was made from the steps of the Town Hall to the sound of the drum. It has been independently verified that these procedures took place and that such procedures had been the normal means of official communication for the village for very many years. Monsieur Bodin was therefore released from arrest.

"That, Herr President, concludes the case for the prosecution." With that the Lieutenant sat down, still radiating confidence.

"Monsieur Chaumel, do you wish to open the defence?" asked the President but almost before he had finished Alphonse Gouraud was on his feet.

"No, no! I wish to speak first; I must have my say," he demanded unable to contain himself any longer.

Captain Junger, angered by this further outburst, glared at Alphonse Gouraud and barked at him in German.

"The President orders you to sit down," said the interpreter. Having conferred briefly with his colleagues on either side Captain Junger, looking extremely annoyed, then further addressed Alphonse Gouraud again in German.

"The President says he will conduct this tribunal as he sees fit and he offers the most senior defence counsel the opportunity to open for the defence should he so wish. He says you will have ample opportunity to offer your defence but only if you respect the court. This is your last warning," said the interpreter calmly. A truculent Alphonse Gouraud sat down. Rose noted Captain Junger resorted to German whenever he was cross.

As Monsieur Chaumel rose to speak in their defence Rose edged forward in her seat in anticipation of his opening remarks not wanting to miss a word.

"Thank you," he began, addressing Captain Junger politely, deliberately so in order to give the appearance that the defence would be reasonable and matter of fact. He too was rather cross at Alphonse Gouraud's outbursts which he felt were contrary to the interests of his clients.

"Herr President. The prosecution's contention that there was organisation and planning behind my clients' actions cannot be further from the truth. Lieutenant Manstein has provided no actual evidence of this contention, only inference, and has neither offered nor shown any evidence of motive. Add to these elements the key question in this matter which is: were my clients actually cognizant of the possible consequences of their actions? I note the prosecutor's lack of any effort to demonstrate this, in which case this tribunal should find no difficulty in dismissing the charges against them. Let me elucidate.

"My clients farm a smallholding in a very rural region distant from any administrative centre. They are honest and hardworking but they are not sophisticated in the matters of the Occupying Authority, indeed in their remote area the Occupation has had little impact until very recently other than the shortages which we all suffer. They have no radio, rarely read a newspaper unless an old copy happens to be given to them, and at the time of these events they were busy from dawn till dusk in their fields preparing for the harvest. Because they are largely self sufficient they have no need to make regular visits to the village. The local announcements concerning the Order of 10th October 1940 were made only a matter of days before these events, and as word of these announcements, and the very harsh sanctions they warned of, had not reached my clients they were entirely unaware of any possible severe consequences of offering the two airmen compassionate assistance. Had they known of the Order there is no doubt their actions would have been very different.

"Let me very briefly paint a picture of the area and community where my clients live. It is farmland as far as the eye can see with scattered smallholdings similar to that of my clients, the owners and tenants of which work hard to scrape a living. But if anyone should need help, it is readily given and for free. Everyone helps everyone else; that is how such communities survive.

"Having bravely rescued the two British airmen the young Fernand Neau did not know what to do next and when his work was finished went immediately to tell his father what had happened and how the two men were in a bad way. Without further thought, his father decided to help the airmen motivated only by humanity and a sense of responsibility, his son having saved their lives which the tribunal has rightly commended. The young man described where he had left the airmen and his father called his young daughter to go with him to find them. The daughter had been learning English at school and she would be needed to communicate with the airmen. This pair found the airmen and through the daughter the father offered them food and shelter for the night at his house.

"After dark the airmen made their way to the Neau house by now in desperate need of some medical help, food and rest which the family provided without any thought to what would happen thereafter. The statement by the officer who went to the house in the early hours of the following morning states the airmen were found upstairs in the bed belonging to Monsieur and Madame Neau. It is plain there was no attempt to conceal the airmen, to make a permanent hiding place for them or to make arrangements for their ultimate escape.

"Fernand Neau senior could not possibly have predicted these events, all of which happened in the space of a few hours. To suggest there was some plan and organisation to help these airmen escape capture is fanciful on the part of the prosecution which has offered no actual evidence of such.

"Here I wish to raise an important matter of procedure. The tribunal has been presented by the prosecution with a number of statements and reports only one of which has been given under oath, that of Monsieur Bodin the Mayor of St. Michel-en-l'Herm. I contend these statements and reports, other than that of Monsieur Bodin, are inadmissible and should be ignored by the tribunal. Those who gave the statements or made the reports are not in court to bear witness personally or to have their statements and reports examined and challenged by the defence. Some may have been given under torture, when confused or in biased circumstances, and the so-called evidence attributed to the two British airmen was undeniably obtained under duress, obtained when without doubt they were in severe shock. I formally request the tribunal rule all such prosecution statements and reports be set aside.

"Let me turn to my clients individually – firstly the father, Fernand Neau. He was born and brought up in this remote farming community where he now himself has a small farm and a family. He does not belong to any political party or any such group; all his energies are taken up tending his farm and providing for his family. We hear these days of groups forming in cities such as here in Paris, organising resistance against the Occupying Authorities, destroying trains and important installations or smuggling evading prisoners. My client has nothing whatsoever to do with any such people and no evidence of such has been put before this tribunal. In those events of 24th and 25th July, no one was hurt, no German property damaged or destroyed.

"As to his son Fernand, he lives with his father and mother and works on the farm. He too has no political affiliations or associations. His only role in this affair was a brave one. Were it not for his actions, as we have heard, two men who managed to bail out from a doomed aircraft would have drowned. He sought his father thereafter to see what should be done and was obviously under his father's influence from then on.

"With both father and son missing from the farm at the critical harvest time the farm has suffered greatly. Madame Neau has, with the help of family and neighbours, managed the farm as best she can but the situation cannot continue. Should her husband and son be detained any longer for any reason, she will have to give up the farm and would have no means of support.

"As for the daughter Rose, I find it difficult to understand why the Occupying Authorities found it necessary to detain a sixteen year old schoolgirl in the very oppressive conditions of an adult prison for a number of months when she quite obviously poses no threat to the Authorities. Even more than her brother, she was under the influence of her father and should carry no responsibility. She has a medical condition which led the prison doctor to strongly advise she should be released. She is studying hard and has already missed some important examinations and should be allowed to return to her school to catch up.

"At this point I must lodge a serious complaint at the treatment all my clients have been subjected to since their arrest. Apart from the appalling prison conditions, each of my clients received more than one form of torture and was continually harangued to sign a false confession. They all declined to sign incriminating papers despite intense pressure to do so. They maintain their innocence and I reiterate their not guilty pleas.

"The final matter the tribunal may wish to take into account when reviewing this case is the effect the arrest and detention of the Neau family, as well as that of Monsieur Gouraud for that matter, has had on the inhabitants of the Vendée region. People are deeply disturbed as they perceive ordinary, hardworking inhabitants of the district are being treated in a very harsh fashion out of all proportion to the alleged matter. It is causing deep resentment which runs directly counter to the Occupying Authorities stated aims of treating the French people fairly, with both respect and restraint for the benefit of all concerned."

"Thank you for listening to me, Herr President. I do not wish to call any witnesses and rest the case for my clients' defence."

As Monsieur Chaumel sat down Rose looked across at her father and brother. Relieved, they exchanged weak smiles, acknowledging approval of their lawyer's performance. Rose also noticed the previously fixed expression on her mother's face had relaxed slightly. Rose was particularly pleased that she had had specific mention and thought that Monsieur Chaumel had included all the points she wanted raised. But then she worried what Alphonse Gouraud might say. He seemed very agitated and troubled. The clerk rose.

"Monsieur Gouraud you may speak now in your defence. You may take the witness box but if you do so you may be cross examined by the prosecution."

"I will speak from here," said Alphonse Gouraud, quickly on his feet, his hands shaking nervously. "I am being victimised here. This is not a proper court otherwise you would allow my witnesses who can prove I did not do the things I am accused of. I have been locked up and tortured all this time for nothing and my family suffers. I've been set up, framed."

"Stop!" called the President who then addressed the interpreter in German. After a brief exchange the interpreter turned to Alphonse Gouraud.

"The President wishes you to speak more slowly and clearly as he has difficulty following you, otherwise he will ask me to translate everything you say into German which will slow the proceedings. He asked me to explain, 'set up, framed,' which I said was, 'a conspiracy for someone else to carry the blame or to incriminate someone on a false charge.' Is that what you meant?"

"Quite right," emphasised Alphonse Gouraud. "Because I made a fuss when my lorries were requisitioned they have been out to get me. My lorries were important for my business and they have borne a grudge against me because I didn't let them have my lorries just like that. They are trying to ruin me and my business. When they heard the airmen had been found at Fernand's house they remembered they had seen Fernand on my cart coming from the fields and assumed I was part of some sort of plot. They were determined to get me and torture me. The prosecutor has said I went to see them in the afternoon and gave them a map. This is false and I can prove it but you won't let me bring my witnesses. That day I had lunch at home at half past two. Next I unloaded a cart full of hay and then had a nap."

"An afternoon snooze or short sleep," interposed the interpreter who saw a lack of understanding on Captain Junger's face.

"It was only about six thirty that I left to meet my family in the fields about four kilometres away. I met several people on the way whose names I have given and they told me that two English airmen were hiding by the sea wall. We worked in the field till near eight thirty, seen by more people. I then went alone to my potato field near the sea wall and three or four people cutting grass there saw me. I arrived back with my family about nine o'clock and my son begged me to go and see the English. I took the cart and I saw Fernand with his daughter and offered them a lift back to the village – that's all. There is this report of the English saying a man visited them in the afternoon giving them this phrase book. The book is not mine and I did not visit them. I have given you the names of those people who can confirm my movements but you have not allowed them to come and say so. I asked for the airmen to come here as they could also tell you it was not me who visited them in the afternoon but they have not been allowed to come. You have no one who can swear they saw me with the English in the afternoon or on my cart. My cart was searched when we got back to the village which proves it. Everything else is fabricated. For all I know even the watch and coin were falsely planted on my cart to incriminate me. I wasn't there when they said they found them. Had I known to go and see where the airmen came down was such a bad thing I would not have done it. Monsieur Chaumel is right; not everyone knew of these Orders so how can I be guilty? As proof of my innocence I was released on bail in September, in error I was told later, but I did not run away and hide. I went home to look after my wife who is very ill. That proves my innocence. They came and arrested me again. Since then she has needed two operations and my three young children have had to be cared for by neighbours. My business is being ruined, a business I have built up these last ten years. If Fernand decided to put the airmen under his roof that was his decision and nothing to do with me. He is a good man, a sensible man. Like me he would not have got involved had he known the trouble it has caused. I too have been tortured. This is all wrong. It is necessary I go home immediately to tend to my wife and to restart my business. I am innocent and you must release me now."

With that he sat, almost slumped, down, his rant practically exhausting him it appeared. The whole room fell silent for a moment or two as everyone digested his tirade. Eventually Captain Junger spoke, asking the prosecutor for his closing remarks.

"Herr President. Against the three Neau accused it is an open and shut case – öffnen und schließen bei," he added in German to be sure the President understood his meaning. "The two enemy airmen were found in the house of Monsieur Neau where they had been with the whole family for many hours. That is not disputed and is enough alone to convict the three Neau accused of the most serious breach of the Order of 10th October 1940. Add to this the fact that the father and daughter went to seek out the airmen and brought them to their house shows their intent to help the airmen evade capture. There were numerous opportunities to reveal the whereabouts of the airmen to the proper authorities or to hand them over but none of these opportunities was taken further confirming their determination to make possible the airmen's escape. The Order of 10th October is quite clear, such serious breaches are punishable by death and this is the punishment I call for."

A gasp went around the room. Rose, stunned, teetered on her seat. She could not believe what she had just heard. She darted a look at her father and brother; both looked ashen-faced and shocked. Her mother's hands shot to her face in horror. This was not supposed to happen! How could he say this after all Monsieur Chaumel had said? Before she could think any further the prosecutor, who was still on his feet, continued.

"The exception to this sentence is Mademoiselle Rose Neau who is below the age for the death sentence. She should be deported to work in the labour camps."

Deported to work in the labour camps? The sentence sent Rose's head spinning and she felt dizzy, unable to take everything in. A moment ago it appeared she faced a death sentence; now it was deportation and labour camps. But there was still a claim for the death sentence for her Papa and young Fernand. She started shaking her head in utter disbelief at the turn of events, but the prosecutor had not yet finished.

"For the accused Monsieur Gouraud, it is clear he was complicit in the transportation of the two airmen from the sea wall to the village. He visited the airmen in the afternoon giving them a map. He then went back again and along with Monsieur Neau and Mademoiselle Neau secreted the airmen on his cart. Over several hours he clearly set out to aid the airmen's escape and he too spurned opportunities to hand them over. His actions too constitute a most serious breach of the Order and warrant the death sentence. I have nothing more to add."

Lieutenant Manstein's repeated calls for the death sentence had chilled the atmosphere in the room where the gravity of the moment was palpable. Shocked and shaking, Rose instinctively looked across to her mother for some sign of comfort but her mother had her head in her hands overcome with utter disbelief.

At the invitation of Captain Junger Monsieur Chaumel rose to make his final address.

"Herr President. The Order of 10th October 1940 is directly related to protection against acts of sabotage. In no way can the acts by my clients in July be termed sabotage. No one was injured, no damage done, not even a threat of sabotage. At worst Fernand Neau senior may be considered naïve. Not being aware of the Order, he had no idea of the draconian sanctions and therefore of the risks he was taking. Calling for a death sentence carries with it the onus of absolute proof the accused understood the full implications of their actions. I suggest the onus is even greater when new sanctions are brought in by an occupying authority that are perceived to be significantly more severe compared with punishments for equivalent breaches of the law under existing civil justice. No such absolute proof has been offered here against any of my clients. Under no rationale can my clients' involvement with the airmen be considered a serious breach which leads me to draw the tribunal's attention to section three of the Order. This states that in less serious infringements a term of imprisonment is appropriate and, should the tribunal be unable to dismiss outright the charges in this case, then I suggest a small token term of imprisonment is the course open to it. All my clients have been held in custody in grim conditions for over two months now and this should suffice. They pose no threat to the Occupying Authorities. I therefore call for their immediate release. Thank you."

Rose struggled to follow all of Monsieur Chaumel's speech but thought he sounded convincing. With the arguments ranging back and forth between the two sides and with Captain Junger offering no hint of his thinking she felt confused, in a sort of limbo. But she also felt increasingly nervous knowing the proceedings were now drawing to a conclusion. 'Please, oh please, let us be released,' she prayed. 'Please let me go home. I just want to go home.'

"Monsieur Gouraud, do you wish to address the tribunal with any final remarks?"

"No," said Alphonse Gouraud. "Only to say I am the victim of lies, false imprisonment, torture and gross injustice. I should not have been re-arrested and I need you to release me again now." There was a pause as everyone expected him to continue but he did not. Captain Junger then stood.

"This tribunal will retire to consider its verdicts. It will resume at eleven o'clock tomorrow morning. Heil Hitler." Heil Hitlers were repeated as his entourage saluted then followed him from the room.

It all happened so quickly. As Rose was being led out of the room still feeling shaky she looked back. Her father and brother were not being allowed to follow immediately and she caught their eye and her mother's eye in turn just before passing through the doorway and out of sight. She was left with the impression of three pairs of staring, hollow eyes as she was hauled away down the stairs and out of the building, terrified at the sentences called for by the prosecutor. Then on the way back to her cell, she tried to calm down by reminding herself they could all be released tomorrow. But that only led to anger and resentment that they could be going home now had the tribunal given its verdict straight away. As her cell door closed behind her, she held out her hands in supplication and utter frustration.

"Why can't we go home?" she shouted, half pleading, half demanding to no one in particular, the words almost spat out. "How can you be so cruel keeping us locked up any longer?" she continued but less forcefully, her voice tailing off, knowing full well her outburst was heard by no one. Then she remembered the hollow look in the eyes of her parents and her brother as she was led out. “Why all this?” she wailed, tears welling. “We’ve done nothing wrong!” Overwhelmed by pity, not just for herself but for the rest of the family too, she fell on her bed and sobbed and sobbed.

The next morning Rose was apprehensive entering the tribunal building but when she entered the anteroom her spirits lifted as there were her mother, her father and her brother in a group by the window.

“Maman, Papa!” she called, rushing over. She fell into her mother’s arms and they hugged and hugged without speaking, eventually turning to her father to do the same except the embrace was awkward as he was still handcuffed.

“My darling Rose,” he breathed quietly.

“Monsieur Chaumel arranged this. He has been wonderful,” said her mother casting a close eye over her daughter to see more clearly how she looked. “How are you, Rose? I’ve been so worried.”

“I’m all right now, Maman. Fernand!” she said lastly, turning again to greet her brother.

“Listen,” said Rose’s father. There was something he wanted his family to know. Despite Monsieur Chaumel’s assurances he was worried he may not be released immediately and wanted to leave his instructions. He tried not to sound downbeat. “Monsieur Chaumel is sure we will all be acquitted but if I am to be punished further you must stay together and must look after each other. When this is all over we will be strong again. …” He was about to go on when Monsieur Chaumel rushed into the room.

Somewhat breathlessly he addressed the group. “Good morning, Messieurs, Mesdames. We’re running late I’m afraid but I’m confident we will get the right results so don’t worry. This may be all over in no time. I’m sorry, Madame, but we must leave to go to the courtroom now; it is nearly eleven o’clock.” There were hurried kisses all round before Renée reluctantly hastened out of the room after Monsieur Chaumel.

The tribunal resumed with the usual formalities. Madame Bon was there again next to Renée and the older man and the boy were there too in the same seats as before. Suspense hung heavily in the air, almost tangible. Rose’s apprehension had grown since waking that morning, only interrupted by the brief meeting with her family a few minutes earlier which had raised her spirits so; but now her heart was pounding. The clerk stood and the room fell into complete silence. The tribunal had reached its verdicts, he announced, which will be read out by the President. Captain Junger cleared his throat while shuffling some papers in front of him. He delivered his opening address in German which was haltingly translated by the interpreter.

"Before announcing the verdicts I will address the issues raised by both defences concerning witnesses. As the Occupying power we are, in compliance with international law, the supreme authority with regards to legislative and judicial matters. Military tribunals in an occupied country are not bound by the refinements of the local civil systems of justice. This tribunal is bound only by the regulations of German Military Law, which are not identical to the civil justice system of France but there are common formal principles which may apply where practicable. As to the two airmen, they are held in distant prisoner of war camps and it was deemed impractical with very limited resources available to transport them to Paris. Several military witnesses are unavailable, involved in current campaigns. Tracing and organising civilian witnesses with contributions not deemed material was also impractical. With regard to written statements and records of interviews lodged with the tribunal, their quality and value has been reviewed and judged taking into account the conditions under which such statements were obtained and such records made. I trust that explains the situation.

"The next matter I must address is the claim by the defence that none of the accused was aware of the Order of 10th October1940. I am satisfied the procedures laid down for notifying the inhabitants of St. Michel-en-l'Herm of the Order were properly carried out by the Mayor according to local custom. It is for the defence to prove the accused could not have known of the Order for there to be any mitigation, which it has not. Furthermore it is simply not believable that in a time of war the accused did not have any understanding of the seriousness of what they were doing." At this point he resumed in French.

"Now I turn to the verdicts." This is it, thought Rose leaning forward, gripping her knees tightly. "Fernand René Neau, please stand. You have been found guilty as charged. However the tribunal has taken into account your less serious role in this affair. After rescuing the airmen you could and should have informed the authorities, and similarly when the airmen arrived at your home where you assisted in sheltering them. You are sentenced to three months imprisonment but in view of the period you have already been held in custody you may be released immediately."

Rose took heart at her brother's release and looked across at him and saw his pale face wore a faint smile of relief.

"Rose Ernestine Clorinthe Neau, please stand. You have been found guilty as charged. You played an important role in planning and assisting the British airmen to evade capture and you assisted in sheltering them. I take into account your age and that you may have been under some influence from your father. Therefore I will not deport you to a labour camp but you will serve a sentence of two years imprisonment."

Rose was aghast and her legs almost gave way beneath her. Two years imprisonment! That cannot be right. She stared hard at Monsieur Chaumel, questioningly, pleadingly, her eyes moistening but he did not meet her eyes. Her mind was racing as she dropped to her chair, so much so that she was not listening to Captain Junger as he announced the next name.

"Alphonse Armand Désiré Gouraud, please stand. You are found guilty as charged. Your role was significant and your intentions clear. You were persistent and determined that these enemy airmen should evade capture. You provided a phrase book and map and returned to give them transport to a place of hiding. You are sentenced to death by firing squad."

"No!" shouted Alphonse Gouraud. Both the old man and the boy gasped in horror.

"Quiet! Sit Down!" commanded Captain Junger and indicated to one of the guards to move over. Fuming and shaking Alphonse Gouraud sat down.

Rose too was shaking. It was all going wrong.

"Fernand Ernest Adrien Neau, please stand." Rose watched her father slowly get up; his stare was straight ahead to a point on the floor at the foot of the President's table. "You are found guilty as charged. Your role was the most significant of all the accused. You were determined these enemy airmen should evade capture and went to great lengths to achieve that aim, even harbouring them under your own roof. You are sentenced to death by firing squad. This tribunal will now rise. Heil Hitler."

Renée's anguished cries were drowned out by the noise of chairs being moved, salutes and heavy boots on the wooden floor as the officials left. Rose felt numb and faint and started to shake her head in disbelief. Why had it all gone so wrong? This cannot be happening! Her Papa …

Monsieur Chaumel made his way quickly over to them, obviously concerned. "Don't worry too much. This is normal. I will immediately lodge appeals which I'm sure will succeed. We have to be patient. These things take time. At least young Fernand can go home to help Madame Neau. I must leave you now to start the appeals procedure." He left all too hurriedly.

Through tear-filled eyes Rose saw her mother with her head in her hands, Estelle Bon's arm firmly round her shoulder in an effort to comfort her. Rose moved to her father who stood hunched, head down. She was harshly pushed away by a soldier but called out, "Papa!" He turned his head and their eyes met for the briefest moment before she was hustled out of the room. But that merest glance, though pained, had just enough of her Papa's old spark to tell her he was not completely broken. Although she kept looking over her shoulder until she was driven away she did not get a further chance to glimpse him. Shocked and distressed, and forgetting her own plight, she wondered whether she would ever see her Papa again.

Chapter 16

The evening after the tribunal Rose sat hunched on her bed, wedged tightly in the corner of her cell her knees clasped to her chest. It was as if she wanted to make herself small, to hide, trying to shut out the world. During the short journey from the tribunal back to her cell at La Santé her initial shock, fear and disbelief at the verdicts turned to anger that she and Papa could be treated with such disdain. But by the evening her anger had been dissipated by exhaustion and she now felt completely drained, physically and mentally. Although she cast slowly around her cell her eyes were blank and she was not really looking at anything at all. She simply could not cope with all her hopes having been dashed and with the devastating sentences handed out to her father and to herself, the verdicts delivered by an emotionless and monotone President in just a few minutes. In those moments her world turned from one of optimism into one of shock and distress, from hope to despair, from looking forward to home and normality into spitting anger and bitter hatred at her captors, at anyone in uniform, uniforms representing the cruel and repressive regime tormenting her and her family. But hours of railing at her captors and the Occupying powers, of banging on her cell door with her fists, of crying endlessly slumped on her bed had, in her already weakened state, exhausted her totally. As the afternoon light faded it got colder but it took a while for Rose to feel it. She shivered and slowly put on some more clothes, lay down and pulled the single blanket over her, right over her head so as to shut out the world. In the early hours of the morning a guard rushed into her cell suddenly waking her as he yanked the cover off her, shouting at her that she must not cover herself like that so they could not see her through the spy-hole on their rounds. Rose did not raise her head from the pillow but just stared at him, hatred still in her eyes.

All the following day she was restless. Not only was this nightmare continuing but it was now worse. Her thoughts swung back and forward between herself and her father, between her despair that she could not cope with being locked up any longer and her anguish for her father. Each time she thought of her father she was haunted by the image of him at the tribunal, hunched, pale and thin; not her father at all, but that was the image she was left with and it hurt her so much that choking tears welled up within her. What must he be thinking? It must be unbearable. How would he cope? It was all just so dreadful. She felt helpless and utterly crushed. And Maman; poor Maman, she must be beside herself returning home knowing Papa was under sentence of death. At least she had Fernand back with her now for company and he would set to on the farm, but she thought the sentences were equally as hard on them as for Papa and herself. How would her mother cope with both of them still in prison, Papa's life hanging by a thread? Once or twice even Monsieur Chaumel became the focus for her anger. Why had he misled them with false hopes of freedom? How could she believe him when he said everything will come right? What is this appeals process he talks of and how long will it take? She did not know how she would last waiting for these appeals, let alone face the prospect of two more years in prison.

All this anguish and self-pity drew her into a mood which became darker as the days wore on, added to by the loneliness which the brief contact with her family only exacerbated. Time and again the injustice and cruelty she perceived would prey on her and she would shout out loud that she and her father should not be treated this way and that they should be freed, not locked up in these awful places. She knew her shouting was useless but momentarily it made her feel better although later she began to wonder whether she might be losing her mind.

She worried about her health and appearance too, concerns which had grown in recent weeks but which had been suppressed by the excitement and anticipation of going home. At the tribunal she must have looked frightful and despite her efforts to spruce herself up for her mother she knew she must have appeared dirty and unkempt. Although weak she did not feel ill which surprised her, even though Doctor Papin had recommended months ago she should be released because of her condition. But she sensed her legs in particular and also her arms felt bigger and heavier because, she suspected, she did not have her medicines to keep the kidney condition under control which meant she was retaining more fluids than was good for her. She knew the symptoms to look out for; she was certainly not putting on weight from the thin broth with its few floating bits of vegetable that made up a large part of her diet. Her monthly cycle had stopped too and she worried about what might be happening to her body as well as her mind. She decided to ask to see Doctor Papin again.

At rue Lhomond, Abbé Stock was sitting at his office desk in front of the typewriter, poised to write, when his sister came in with the morning post.

"Ah, Franziska! Can you go to rue des Saussaies for me shortly? I have an urgent letter for Major Beumelburg." A concerned Franziska looked quizzically at her brother and he knew she was wondering why he was writing to the head of the Gestapo in Paris. She hoped it was nothing to do with the risks her brother was taking on his prison visits.

"It's about that young girl in La Santé and her father," he said answering her unasked question. "I've just heard the father and his colleague were condemned to death and the girl to two year's imprisonment. I must add my voice to the pleas for clemency. Their punishment appears harsh and I pray for their families. The father and his colleague are due to go to the firing squad at Mont Valèrien on the twenty-fifth, only twelve days away, so there is no time to lose if it is to be halted. I must visit them all later today."

Franziska knew who her brother was referring to although he never told her the names of the living, just in case questions were asked by Major Beumelburg's men.

"Let me know when the letter is ready and I'll go straight away," she agreed understanding her brother's need for haste.

Later as he walked along the corridor to Rose's cell he asked the guard to allow him a little time alone with Rose whom he expected to find devastated at the turn of events and in need of his ministry more than ever. He had already visited her father and Alphonse Gouraud and found her father despondent, his spirit noticeably sapped. By contrast Alphonse Gouraud was like a caged tiger, taut and pacing up and down. With Rose he was, at least, greeted with a wan smile although he could see she was very dejected.

"My child, how are you? I have been praying for you and your family since hearing the verdicts of the tribunal. I came as soon as I could." As he said these words he could see tears appear in Rose's eyes as her emotions overcame her. "Here, let us sit together," he said sitting down on the bed patting the space beside him.

Rose was almost overwhelmed. His was the only presence that offered her any comfort and his first visit since the tribunal triggered a deep emotional release which she struggled to control as she sat next to him.

"I have just seen your father," he continued in his quiet voice, taking her hand as he could see she needed some physical contact. "And whilst it is hard for him, he says he is praying for you and your mother. He is hopeful the appeals will succeed. Meanwhile we must pray to give him the strength and wisdom to bear this great burden."

"Is Papa really all right?" she managed to say. "I'm so worried about him. It is not right we are treated like this; the appeals have to succeed. Can't you do anything?"

"I have already written a letter pleading for clemency for all of you. But whilst I said I believe the sentences excessively harsh, you must be aware my words alone have little sway. I am sure, however, there will be many other voices added to mine so we must pray and continue to pray."

Although she was so pleased to see him, his call to prayer just brought her anger at God to the surface. God too had come into her firing line over the last few days, for her head was telling her He should have stopped this nightmare; instead He had allowed it to go on and on despite her prayers, in spite of Him knowing they were only in this predicament because of their charity towards the airmen. She could not understand why He had not answered her prayers and exasperated she had told Him so. Now, with the Abbé there she could not hold back.

"Why did God not make them release us? He knows we have done nothing wrong! I prayed hard, very hard, to Him to get us released but nothing has happened. He is supposed to care for us but He hasn't answered my prayers. No one else seems to help us. He must help us or ..." She tailed off partly not wanting to say the words, 'Papa will die', but also because she was reticent to criticise God further in front of the Abbé.

"My child, I share your hurt and pain and that of your father too. The Bible says that God works in ways we cannot always understand. He is all knowing and we have to believe in Him. We pray to Him for many reasons: to praise Him; to thank Him, like at harvest time for the fruits of the earth; or for someone we love who is ill, we pray for them to get better. Or we pray for ourselves: for guidance when we are troubled; or, as you have done, for Him to relieve your own personal suffering.

"Your prayers were heard," said the Abbé in his quiet way, emphasising the words which left Rose in no doubt he believed totally what he was saying. "But sometimes God's plans for us are more important than those we might wish for ourselves. It is difficult to understand and even more difficult to accept when our prayers appear unanswered. We say in the Our Father: 'Thy will be done, on earth, as it is in Heaven.' But we cannot always know what He wants for us which makes it hard when we think our most earnest prayers are not answered immediately. Maybe His answer will come later or we do not have the wisdom to recognise His answer when it is given. But at the time, like now, it is frustrating and hard to bear."

No one had ever spoken to Rose in this way before, personally, addressing her own thoughts and concerns directly, the antithesis of the church sermons she regularly had to listen to but rarely properly understood. For Rose, somehow, the Abbé's presence radiated a light in the cell. She felt spellbound by some quality in him she did not understand. But his words to her were uncomplicated, his messages simple.

"It was difficult too," the Abbé continued, "for Jesus to bear the thought of the agonies he knew he would have to endure on the cross. Just before the crucifixion he prayed to God his Father in the Garden of Gethemane, asking to be relieved of this suffering, which he referred to as 'this cup'. He prayed: 'If it be possible let this cup pass from me: nevertheless not as I wish, but as thou wilt.' Even Jesus in his hour of need knew his wish would only be granted if it was the will of his Father, the will of God."

"I'm sorry, Father," said Rose choking back tears and feeling penitent at her outburst. "I don't want Papa to die. I want us to go home, for all this to end."

"Of course you do, my child. And I will pray for you both, as many others will be doing. You are not alone. Trust in God. He is all wise and all good; He will give you the strength and fortitude you need to bear your ordeal. Read your New Testament, it will ease your troubles."

"I will," said Rose taking a deep breath in an effort to compose herself.

It was remarkable the calming effect Abbé Stock had on Rose and after he left she resolved to continue reading the New Testament and to pray each night with a better understanding of God's will. For the next few days, however, even her changed mood could not overcome the waves of extreme anguish she felt for her father which reduced her quickly to tears. She could not bear the thought of him sitting alone in his cell with the threat of death hanging over him, unable to do anything to help him except pray. She wanted to shut out the thought of him dying, as if by denying the possibility of his death it would mean it could never happen; but however hard she tried these waves of deep sorrow kept coming. It was as if she was already grieving his death yet whatever distractions she contrived visions of her father kept coming back to her. Concerns for herself took a backward step, as did those for her mother. It was her Papa who filled her thoughts.

The key turned in the lock and the cell door opened slowly. The guard stood aside and a female warder ordered Rose to come with them to the chief warder's office without saying why and Rose knew it was useless to ask. But what might it be? Could it be a reprieve? Then an awful thought struck her at which her knees went weak. Was it about Papa? In trepidation she followed her escorts in silence. The chief warder was seated behind her desk and looked up as Rose entered. Rose recognised her as the one who showed some kindness but that did not reduce Rose's high anxiety.

"Sit down," she said, her manner congenial, "I have some news for you. Not the best news but … well, I can tell you your appeal has been allowed to go forward. You will have to stay here, of course, until the outcome of the appeal but at least there is some hope for you." Her voice was gentle and Rose could see in her eyes she was trying to be kind. "I can't tell you how long it will be, some appeals take months so you must be patient although that is difficult I know."

"What about Papa?" Rose interrupted. "What about his appeal?"

"I can't discuss another prisoner," said the woman resorting to her official voice.

"He is my Papa! I must know. Please!"

Normally she would be unbending where rules were concerned but against her better judgement and because of her motherly sympathy for Rose, she replied.

"His appeal too has been allowed."

"Thank you," said Rose thinking a little politeness might help her cause with this official who, although she was in uniform, Rose could not quite come to hate believing she was genuinely trying to be kind. "What happens now, with the appeal?" asked Rose keen to learn more.

"I understand such appeals go to Berlin. That is why it will take some time. In the meantime please behave as I would not wish to have to punish you more."

"Please," said Rose, "can I see Doctor Papin? He said before I should be released because I have a kidney condition. It is getting worse. Look at my arms and legs. He could get me released. I need medicines now or it will get much worse. Please can I see him?"

"I will see," said the wardress writing something on the file. "That is all. You must go back now."

"Can you tell me today's date, please?" asked Rose as she got up from her chair. She had already lost track of time since the tribunal and wanted to mark the days off as she had done before.

"November the twenty-forth," came the answer.

"Thank you," said Rose with a faint smile in appreciation of her special treatment.

As November drifted into December the days grew even colder and the nights colder still. A parcel arrived from her mother containing a most welcome piece of clothing, her winter coat, which had obviously been thoroughly searched as the pockets had been left turned inside out. As usual the parcel was undone; as usual there was no letter. The walls of her cell felt permanently damp as did her clothes and bedding, but at least her coat could act as an extra blanket at night. By day she wore most of her clothes in an effort to keep warm and put on her coat for exercise time if she was not already wearing it, but even then the biting wind that swirled around the yard could not be kept out. Complaints at having to go out in the cold were ignored; and exercise time was only cancelled if it was raining heavily. Before lights out Rose would etch a mark in the plaster on her cell wall to signify the passing of another day, a ritual which became important to her as it meant a day nearer her release whenever that might be. Just knowing the date made her isolation a little easier to bear. A fleeting visit by Abbé Stock lifted her spirits temporarily but he had no news of her father. In her mind she saw Christmas as a sort of target date to be home. She always loved Christmas time with its presents and treats and the carols in church. She desperately wanted to be home, but if not now then by Christmas. Christmas in this place would be unbearable.

Sometimes the routine of the evening was interrupted by air raid warnings. Sirens would wail and the guards would switch off all the prison lights for fear the prison would become a target for the British bombers. Through her small window Rose could see the night sky lit up with searchlights and occasionally she heard aircraft overhead. With no guards patrolling and the building in total darkness some prisoners used the opportunity to sing patriotic songs out of their window as loudly as they could without fear of punishment. Rose joined in at times when she knew the song; singing was defiance and brought a rare sense of togetherness with the other prisoners. Initially she was scared when the sirens went off but as she never heard any explosions such events became an almost welcome distraction.

One day early in December during exercise there was excitement. Word had filtered through from the outside that the German advance in Russia had been halted and the rumour was passed quickly down the line of inmates as they padded round the yard. Gossip of any German setback was always enthusiastically received. And a few days later there was even greater excitement at the news that the United States had joined the war. Rose did not really understand what this meant but she caught the general mood that this was momentous news.

Christmas Day approached without any sign of her release and no visits to relieve the monotony. The days dragged by, one day much like any other with only a change in the routine at weekends. Yet again her request to see Doctor Papin had been ignored. Rose found it helped if she broke down the day into small parcels of time – until the next rations appeared, going down to the exercise yard, the next rations, lights out, sleep – filling each period with a mixture of activities until she ran out of ideas and then she would just sit and think. Whenever she felt it safe to do so she read a passage from her New Testament, or she would make up a game, or pace up and down the cell counting to one hundred steps. Sometimes she would get out all her meagre possessions, spread them out on the bed and check them; a pastime which gave her particular satisfaction as they represented a sort of victory over the authorities to have this secret hoard. Every time she came to the soldier's wedding ring she fingered it wondering who he was, what happened to him, where his wife and family were? A moment's impulse by this poor soldier had left her with this mystery. Could she, perhaps, some time in the future find the soldier's wife and return the ring? She doubted it but the thought appealed to her. It was a strange situation, she mused: the soldier was the enemy and in a way so was his wife, yet the ring seemed to bypass any assumed enmity, representing as it did, just a young woman, possibly only a few years older than she was and probably now a widow whose life had been turned upside down. Who was she? Was she pretty? Did she have a child, perhaps? Rose tried to visualise her and felt a touch of empathy – someone else innocently caught up in this wretched war.

But as the days passed by and Christmas neared Rose became more depressed at the lack of news of their appeals, her sense of abandonment compounded by isolation, cold and loneliness. At times she was startled to find herself in an animated, one-sided conversation, gesturing, muttering to herself usually about the oppression and inequity she was suffering – broodings which started off in her head but somehow, frighteningly, turned themselves into actual speech; usually a verbal tirade at her tormentors. The more she caught herself drifting into this mood the more it worried her. Was she going mad, like that old woman at home who lived alone in a secluded tumble-down cottage along the lane from the farm? She could picture this wizened, little old lady, dressed shabbily in black, bent and shuffling along with the help of a stick often mumbling gibberish to herself or acting very strangely. The older children said she was a mad witch and used to shout at her, calling her names or throwing small stones at her to get a reaction. But they kept at a distance, rather scared of her with her witch-like face and she would shake her walking stick at them and shout after them as they ran away. Rose too had been frightened of her even though her mother said the old woman was harmless. Sometimes Rose watched in amusement when the old lady stopped outside the farm on her way to Sunday Mass. If the weather was not cold or wet the old lady, in her Sunday best but still in black, would walk barefoot as far as the farm then stop and put on her shoes which she had been carrying, muttering away to herself all the time, before heading off into the village, now properly attired for church. Maman said she did it to save wearing out her shoe leather. Was she, Rose, going mad like the old woman? Would she end up like her? The thought scared her and she would try to rouse herself quickly out of her mood.

On Christmas Eve Abbé Stock visited her with presents hidden in his cassock, a tiny individual cake baked by his sister and a small piece of chocolate. His visit alone was present enough for her. He could not stay long, he said, as he had much to do but there was no news of her appeal or of her father as he had yet to visit Cherche Midi. The only news was that he was going back to Germany for a break for a month, back to his family. This upset Rose.

"Oh. That may mean I won't see you again," she said sadly.

"You may be home before I return," he said encouragingly. "Let's hope so. I'll pray that is so."

"You will come back though, won't you?" asked Rose wanting some reassurance.

"Oh yes. Be assured, my ministry is here."

His response was reassuring. She trusted him and knew he would not mislead her, though she was still upset at the prospect of his absence. They offered a brief prayer of hope together and there was just time for Rose to ask him to wish her father Happy Christmas from her.

"Read the Gospel according to Saint Luke, Chapter Two," he said quickly as he turned to leave. And then he was gone. The visit was over all too soon for Rose who wondered whether she would see him again, a bittersweet thought for Christmas Eve.

Before lights out that evening Rose took out her New Testament and found Chapter two of the Gospel according to Saint Luke on page one hundred and nine. She had persisted with her reading of the New Testament, despite the heavy going at times, and had reached nearly two thirds of the way through. So she was curious to go back and see why the Abbé had chosen that text. Very soon she realised it was the nativity story, with shepherds abiding in the fields and the baby lying in a manger, all very familiar to her. But reading it again this Christmas Eve evoked thoughts of home and the excited anticipation of Christmas Eves past. It also reminded her how bleak this Christmas would be for her mother and all of the family, but at least she felt closer to them and had the Abbé to thank for that.

Christmas Day dawned dull and bitterly cold. There was no variation in routine to mark the special day. During exercise there were a few muffled seasonal greetings passed down the line but everyone was so cold there was little enthusiasm in their 'Joyeux Noël'. Back in her cell Rose was surprised when a warder opened the door and offered her some grapes which she refused on principle; but later she regretted her pig-headedness at what was a genuine act of charity. That afternoon, as a treat she allowed herself a bite of the Abbé's cake and a nibble of his chocolate, planning to make both morsels last for several days but, as she savoured the taste, they only served to remind her of what she was missing. When she felt it was safe she again laid out all her secret possessions on the bed. The most precious was of course her father's note and today she looked on it as his special Christmas present to her.

Ever since she could remember Christmas at home was a highlight of the year. Morning Mass was magical and despite being poor, Maman somehow managed to fill the larder so when the whole family gathered they feasted in front of a roaring fire. Everyone would be in festive mood. Papa would hide wonderful little traditional treats around the house which the children would hunt for. In the evening she would sit on her father's knee while he told tales that had everyone laughing. Rose loved giving presents. She made many of the gifts herself or with help from her mother as she had little money to spend. For her mother's and father's present however she tried to save up to buy them a little luxury, a small bar of fragrant soap perhaps for Maman, and a cigar for Papa which Fernand had to buy for her as she was too young, but last Christmas it was difficult to get anything after the fall of France. All the gifts handed out by the family were extremely modest and often very practical but none of that mattered. All the preparations added to the excitement which she had found hard to contain when she was younger but for the last few years she had tried to be more grown up. Now though, she reflected, instead of being at home, safe with her family as she had hoped, she and Papa were still locked up in these horrid places making her sixteenth Christmas the worst imaginable.

On the first of January she carved a longer mark on the wall to signify the New Year. Surely, she said to herself, her release must come any day now. In a few days time she would have been imprisoned for five months, and what for …? Her New Year's resolution was to be brave coupled with the hope to be home for her brother's birthday, the twenty-first of January.

The cold was arctic and relentless and although Rose wore all the clothes she had day and night she could not generate any warmth, especially to her feet and toes which felt like blocks of ice. The walls of her cell were constantly damp with condensation sometimes forming into a little trickle which she would watch run down to the floor. She developed a nagging cough which added to her worries about her health. Heavy snow fell in January and exercise sessions were regularly cancelled. Fortunately most of the time her soup was still quite hot when it reached her and after she had eaten she would cup her hands round the bowl until all the warmth in it had gone. Each day was a struggle and at times she wondered how she could go on. A visit by Abbé Loevenich did little other than confirm her initial thoughts of him that whilst his words may have sounded sincere, the problem was his appearance. Rose could not see beyond his smart military uniform and the highly polished jack boots which for her were a barrier to his otherwise well-meaning pastoral care. She was polite enough to him but her usual unquestioning respect for a priest fell away at the sight of his hated German uniform. What news of Papa, she had asked? But he had not been to see her father yet and the only news he had was that Abbé Stock would be back by the end of the month. If only Abbé Stock could be here now…

Rose was forced to suffer the indignity of visit by a high ranking German officer who had expressed a wish to see the youngest inmate there, this oddity of a girl who only escaped the firing squad because of her young age. He was accompanied by the Austrian warder who reappeared later at Rose's cell door obviously somewhat perturbed. She had only recently returned from leave and was saddened to find Rose still there and was concerned she was still in solitary confinement. Unknown to Rose her status should have changed following the tribunal to that of an ordinary prisoner rather than one under investigation who needed to be held in isolation, and as such she should have been moved to a shared cell but somehow this had not happened. Without telling Rose, the warder had looked to move her to a shared cell but could not find one with a suitable cellmate and so was making arrangements for Rose to be transferred that afternoon to a warmer single cell and to have some privileges. This is what she had come to tell Rose who could not believe the warder would do that for her. Rose thanked her and at the same time asked again to see Doctor Papin about her kidney condition citing additionally her cough which would not go away. As soon as she had gone Rose started to gather her meagre possessions together to take to her new cell. She worried she would be searched thoroughly and punished if they found anything. She wore all her clothes, tucked the New Testament inside her dress and made sure her other treasures were carefully secreted. Then she counted the scratches on the wall representing the days so she did not lose track, counting a second time to be sure.

Later that day Rose was moved to a south facing cell above the kitchens which was indeed a few degrees less icy. She heaved a sigh of relief when no one searched her or her belongings during the transfer. Although her new home was noisier, especially early in the morning as breakfast for the guards was prepared below, after a few days in her new home Rose concluded it was a little better. One benefit was that her soup arrived quite hot as she was closer to the kitchens. Also she found to her delight that on the rare occasions when the sun shone it cast a patch of light which travelled across the far wall marking the passage of the day. One sunny day she imagined what it was like to be warm, remembering that day with Adélina at the beach. Would Adélina be thinking of her, Rose wondered? She hoped so. Perhaps Adélina had written her a letter in the school holidays and taken it to her mother to send on, but as letters never reached her she could not know.

That first day in her new cell, while spreading the thin blanket on the bed she pricked her finger on something which made her jerk her hand away. A drop of blood appeared and she had to suck her finger several times before it stopped bleeding. Carefully she examined the mattress and found the sharp point of something metal sticking out. Gradually she teased out the piece of metal which she was surprised to find was the blade of a small penknife. How curious, she thought! Without doubt a previous prisoner had cleverly hidden it there. What had happened to them? Why hadn't they taken it with them? Had they to leave in a hurry? All sorts of thoughts ran through her mind about the previous owner but now it was another precious possession of hers. It occurred to her the blade would be very useful for scratching the days in the plasterwork and she carved the number of days she had counted from her last cell so she did not forget. As a weapon it was pathetic and she had no idea if she would have the courage to use it as such, nevertheless it gave her reassurance of sorts and was a welcome addition to her little hoard of possessions. After trying a number of hiding places for it she settled on sliding it between the loose heel and the sole of one of her shoes. Shoes, she mused, were good for hiding things.

Rose grew increasingly worried about her health. She felt weak, her cough persisted and her legs were swollen. But despite her latest request there was still no visit to the doctor. Her brother's birthday came and went forcing her to adopt a fresh target date for her release; this time she chose her own birthday, the twenty-third of February. Surely she and Papa would be home by then.

At the imposing Luftwaffe headquarters in Leipziger Strasse, Berlin, the senior military lawyer to Reich Marshal Goering sat in an office on the sixth floor. Around the perimeter of his desk were many thick legal-looking folders with red ties and there were more files stacked in piles of three or four on the floor behind him giving the distinct impression of a man with a very heavy work load who was struggling to manage. His assistant came in with yet more files under his arm.

"Ah. Where had we got to yesterday?" the lawyer asked needing a reminder of the point they had reached before he was called away to yet another urgent meeting.

"The Neau and Gouraud appeals, sir," replied the assistant handing a file over to his superior then sitting down in front of the desk. He crossed his legs and balanced on his knee a piece of paper with some handwritten notes on it. "We didn't get very far with them yesterday but you will remember the office of the Military Commander in France granted a stay of execution pending appeal. Von Stuelpnagel was minded to pardon the men but asked his office to pass the decision on to us as it is a Luftwaffe matter. I reviewed the files later on yesterday and in my opinion the tribunal properly followed Military Law and was fairly conducted in the circumstances. Given the evidence presented I am satisfied the tribunal came to the correct verdicts. In the case of the man Neau it could not have come to any other conclusion – the escaping airmen were found in his bed! In the case of Gouraud, technically the verdict is correct given the strength of the evidence against him. The only element left to consider are the sentences and here there may be mitigating factors which could reduce the death sentences imposed. Perhaps the most powerful of these is that the Gestapo are satisfied these two men were not involved in any subversive activities but merely acted on impulse in this single event during which none of our soldiers were killed or injured and no assets damaged."

"Their infractions were category two, though, were they not?" countered the senior lawyer. "And therefore the death sentence is mandatory."

"That is correct, sir, but certainly at the low end of category two. Submitted with the formal appeal papers are many letters of support, some from local and regional counsellors. One regional councillor expressed the view that a pardon would have a significant beneficial effect in the Vendée where agents of English propaganda are actively working.

"There is also this report on Gouraud to consider. Apparently only the other day he made an attempt to escape prison by filing through the window bars and jumping from the prison wall; hardly the actions of an innocent man. He fell and broke his leg as it happens and is under guard in hospital. The report also quotes his wife is very seriously ill and they have three young children.

"The prison chaplain has also appealed for clemency and on balance I am also inclined to agree. The sentences could reasonably be reduced to imprisonment or deportation."

"We must take a wider view, though," said the lawyer. "Between you and me, Von Stuelpnagel is rather too keen on preserving French co-operation. There is considerable concern among our commanders, particularly of the northern occupied territories, that local resistance is becoming more organised. They expect, quite rightly, the strict application of military law to support them." He paused.

"H'm. What should we do here though?" he asked rhetorically, rubbing his top lip with his left forefinger in thought. "I agree this is a borderline case. But equally I believe we should in the present worsening situation apply the sanctions as set down."

He was about to continue when the phone on the desk rang. The lawyer picked it up and after a brief discussion began to get up. He seemed irritated at the interruption.

"I have to go," he announced. As he gathered his greatcoat and braided cap from the stand by the door he turned and said, "Send the file to the Reich Marshal with my recommendation the appeals fail. But he may well override me if he's in a contrary mood; you know what he's like sometimes."

Just as he was about to go through the door the assistant called across to him.

"What about the Neau girl, sir?"

"Oh, yes." He stopped and considered for a second. "Release her on parole." With that said he hurried off.

It was the twenty-ninth of January when Franz Sock returned to rue Lhomond. Franziska had kept the mission open during his absence and quite naturally was anxious to hear all the family news. He told her their younger brother Heinz, who was a cadet officer on the German destroyer Bruno Heinemann, was already at home on leave when Franz had arrived. He was in good form, but had to return urgently to his ship; 'something big' was about to happen, he had said. Worryingly too there was no news of older brother Ernst who was fighting on the Russian front; but their parents were coping although very anxious about Ernst. He told Franziska too about his trips to his old Archbishop in Cologne, to Strasbourg, to Paderborn to meet with the Archdiocesan authorities there, to a retreat, even to Berlin to raise funds for the Paris mission. To Franziska it all seemed far from the rest he was supposed to be having and she scolded him with a sisterly rebuke. They discussed recent developments. What worried him most, Franz said, was the direction the war was taking, particularly the grim situation on the Russian front and the inevitable escalation of the war across the world with Japan and the United States joining the conflict. But he said he was refreshed by his break and tomorrow he would resume his work here with renewed commitment; there was much to be done.

Whilst he was away he had often thought about his Paris parishioners and prayed for them. He had wondered whether Rose and her father might have been released by the time he returned, but he was doubtful knowing how long appeals could take. He would make it his business to find out as soon as he was back in Paris.

By the time the Abbé's rounds the next day brought him to Rose's cell it was dusk and the light was beginning to fade. He could tell she was so glad to see him but he could also see her condition had considerably worsened during his leave. He explained his visit to her would have to be short this time because there was so much to catch up on since he had been away. He had, however, an idea he hoped she would like, a proposal to bring her spiritually closer to her father. His idea was that she and her father pray for each other every day at this time and that way they would be joined not only in prayer but also in their thoughts for each other. What did she think? He would be visiting her father tomorrow. Rose said it was a lovely idea and readily agreed to his suggestion they begin there and then, even without her father. They knelt side by side and he led them in a simple prayer.

Chapter 17

It was the sound of hurrying steps along the corridor which drew Rose's attention, a sound that sent slight shivers down her spine as usually it meant there was some sort of emergency or someone was going to be in great trouble; and when the footsteps stopped outside her cell Rose held her breath. The key turned in the lock and the door was opened by the kindly Austrian warder who seemed a little flushed.

"Release papers have just arrived for you," she blurted out. "Come. You are free! Hurry up!" The expression on her face showed her obvious pleasure at this unexpected development that finally allowed her to discharge Rose from prison. Rose looked at her stunned and totally nonplussed. "Yes, get your things quickly and come with me!" she urged.

Anyone else and Rose would have been unbelieving but not this warder, the only one to show her any humanity. Rose was already wearing all her clothes as it was so cold in the cell and luckily all her precious, secret belongings were hidden in linings, pockets and shoes. With her heart beating wildly she moved quickly over to the table and swept up her other belongings, a comb and a few toiletries, and stuffed them in her coat pocket, all the time looking earnestly at the warder to ensure there was no doubt this was really happening.

"Yes," the woman reassured her. "The authority came through just a short while ago and I wanted to make sure you do not spend any longer here. Come quickly, I have some papers to issue then you can go." She turned and ushered Rose out onto the corridor. Rose turned for a last look at the empty cell. Was this really the moment she had been waiting for all these months? Somehow the emptiness of the cell said it was. Amazed that this was all happening so quickly, Rose again looked at the warder for reassurance and received a genuine smile as the pair hurried down to the hallway that led to the yard behind the large main gates.

"Sit here for a moment while I make out the papers," said the warder when they were in her office. Rose's head was reeling, so much so she was unable to think clearly, to comprehend the full import of what was taking place. It was all so strange. This was the moment she had thought about, dreamt of, played over and over again in her mind for six long months; but now it was here her mind was scrambled. Suddenly she remembered the knife blade hidden in the heel of her shoe and she went cold with fear. What if she was searched and the blade was found? Would they lock her up again, a fate she was convinced she would not be able to survive? She was sitting there nervously when the phone rang. After a brief exchange the warder told Rose she must wait outside while she took the call, pointing to the door that led directly on to the main prison yard. Her mind was still racing while she stood outside when she became aware of a disturbance across the yard where a number of prisoners were being herded and loaded onto a lorry. One prisoner started struggling and shouting that he did not want to be sent to Germany, his face full of terror. The guards ignored his pleas and manhandled him on to the lorry along with the others most of whom appeared cowed and broken. Rose turned away for a moment not wanting to witness the prisoners' misery when she felt her arm grabbed roughly and suddenly she was being yanked towards the lorry.

"Let me go!" she screamed at the guard whose face was only inches from her own, his expression hateful and determined. He hurt her arm with his grip as he dragged her towards the still open back of the lorry. Struggling she shouted even louder, "Let me go!" but the guard was far too strong for her and he merely shoved her along more roughly almost lifting her off the ground. He made to hoist her on to the lorry.

The Austrian warder opened the door to call Rose back in when her attention was caught by the commotion across the yard and she was horrified to see Rose being manhandled on to the lorry.

"No. Not her!" she shouted above the hubbub, running over to the pair. The startled guard let Rose go, grumbling under his breath, and the woman gently took Rose's arm, claiming possession, and led her back into her office. Rose was badly shaken and the wardress sat her down by the desk.

"Thank goodness I heard you shouting out otherwise you'd be on your way to Germany. But it's all right now. You're going home."

She finished the paperwork while Rose rubbed her throbbing arm, trembling not now from the fear of being searched but from her lucky escape.

"Now then," said the warder eventually putting down her pen. "You have been granted compassionate parole in view of your age. Parole means you are being released but there are conditions which you must obey. Firstly, you must not break any more laws. If you do the part of your sentence you have not served, eighteen months, will be added to any future sentence. The other condition is you must live at your parents' house, nowhere else, for the next eighteen months. If you break this condition you will be put back in prison. Do you understand?"

Rose nodded.

"It's written down here on this official document which you must sign to say you have received a copy. You must keep this safely to show anyone who asks. Now, this card is a temporary identity card. Destroy this when you get home. This last document is a travel warrant to get you home to St. Michel en l'Herm. Show this on a bus or at a railway station and you do not have to pay. It is valid for seven days in case there are delays but I advise you to go straight home. Paris is no place for a young girl alone. Do you know which train station to go to?"

"I think it's the one near here, between here and Cherche Midi prison," said Rose anxious to hurry up proceedings, still concerned she might yet be searched or that something might still go wrong.

"Gare Montparnasse. It's about twenty minutes walk. I walk to Cherche Midi prison sometimes. Turn left out of here, over the cross roads and turn left at the top into a wide tree-lined road. That's Boulevard du Montparnasse where the station is past the big church. There may be a bus along there to save you walking.

"Go home. Keep out of trouble and you will be all right. Sign here and I will let you out." Relieved to find the parole document was in French, Rose read it quickly and signed the copy, and although she did not want any delay she had one pressing question.

"Is Papa being released too?" she asked hopefully. "He's in Cherche Midi. Do you think we can go home together?" It seemed the Austrian woman had anticipated this as she immediately shook her head regretfully.

"I'm sorry; there is no mention of your father in the papers."

"Can you find out?" pressed Rose anxiously.

"I'm sorry; there is nothing I can do. You must go now, quickly. I am off duty in a minute and I want to see you leave myself. I wish I could do more for you but I can't. Here are all your papers; take great care of them. Come."

She led Rose out across the yard that was now quiet, the lorry and its cargo having left. She ordered the guard at the main gate to open up and steered Rose towards the opening. Out of the line of sight of the guard she wished Rose good luck, and then with a smile gave a small wave as Rose headed through the gates.

A hesitant Rose, her heart still thumping, stepped out onto the pavement into the cold morning and she was free. She could hardly believe the moment, this moment that she had waited six months for. She really was free!

It had all happened so quickly and unexpectedly that she felt more disoriented than elated. She stood for a second and looked up to the grey sky, the clouds heavy and low and she shivered. It was almost as though she could not take the first steps away from the hell she had known on the other side of the forbidding gates; away from the four walls of her cell, from the torture and cruelty, the cold, the hunger and the loneliness. She braced herself and tugged her coat more tightly round her, turned left as the warder had said and started to walk, hugging the tall prison wall for shelter. Gradually she picked up her pace, not looking back once, steeling herself for the long journey home, the first leg of which was to get to the station as soon as she could. The pavements were a mirror of the sky, grey and wet and when she reached the tree-lined boulevard, she saw mounds of melting, dirty snow in the gutters, swept there after the recent snowfall. She shivered. The road was straight and appeared very long and like all the streets she had seen in Paris it had tall buildings on either side mostly with shops onto the street. The trees were bare, trapped in winter, and the people were wrapped up and bent against the cold. There was little traffic, only the occasional German military vehicle, car or commercial lorry, and hardy cyclists hunched over their handlebars peddling hard against the chilly wind to get quickly to their destination. At times it was eerily quiet. Rose passed several shops with long queues, mainly of women, but these queues too were silent, the women patiently waiting with their coupons for whatever they could buy. She trudged on, her pace slowing as she tired, her legs feeling heavy. A bus stopped a short way ahead of her and if she had hurried she could have caught it but she dared not as she was too uncertain of where it might take her. One street corner café had big Swastika flags draped on the outside and banners with German lettering strung above the doors signalling it was for German soldiers only. She noticed even a bank had the German flag over its entrance.

Between the distractions of the big city and the anxiety of wondering if she was heading in the right direction, her thoughts turned to her father. She dared to hope he too was free. Surely, she reasoned, since she was released then so would Papa be freed also. The more she thought about her father the more the notion grew in her mind that she must try to find him or at least have news of him before she left Paris. She had been told to go straight home – but how could she go home to Maman and Fernand without news of Papa?

These thoughts were still running round her head when eventually she saw a large church on the other side of the road. She hoped it was the one she had been told about because she was not sure how much further she could walk without resting. At the next junction there was a large sign over the pavement indicating the station was ahead. Encouraged she trudged on and soon came to a large square and there round the corner was the station which she recognised immediately as the one she had arrived at six months ago. She joined a queue for the information kiosk on the main concourse, all the time looking around in the hope Papa was at the station too. It was as much as she could do to stand but she had to. In contrast to the quiet streets outside the place was bustling with people all of whom seemed to know what they were doing and where they were going. People with briefcases walked briskly about their business, others with large suitcases struggled along or sat patiently waiting for their train. She found the noise and bustle somewhat disconcerting after the silence of La Santé. Everyone was wrapped up against the cold with hats and gloves. Rose felt very self-conscious among the smart-looking crowds as by comparison she must appear decidedly unkempt in her shabby clothes, with no hat to cover her unwashed and dirty hair. But thankfully it was not so cold inside the station building. The queue shuffled slowly forward until Rose was next. She had practiced what she wanted to ask.

"Next," the lady kiosk attendant called out rather wearily.

"What train do I need to catch to go to St. Michel-en-l'Herm and when does it leave, please? I have a travel warrant."

The lady did not look up but flicked through a well-thumbed, bulky timetable. She went back and forward a few times before announcing blankly, "There's no SNCF station there. Where is it near?"

"Oh. Luçon is the nearest mainline station," said Rose.

"Tut," clicked the lady tetchily, leafing through the timetable again. "08.20, 19.32 and 22.00 daily; Platform D. Change at Nantes."

"Can you write that down for me please?" asked Rose. "And can you tell me what day it is?" The attendant, who was used to the whole spectrum of the French general public, from cheeky street urchins to haughty Parisians who expected the SNCF to run trains personally just for them, was somewhat taken aback at Rose's second question. She was about to give Rose the sharpness of her tongue when she saw that Rose really was not well.

"Are you all right, dear?" she asked.

"I'm just hungry," said Rose.

"Here," the attendant said pushing her written note of the train times under the glass screen. "It's Tuesday the third of February. There is a café over there where you can buy something to eat," she added trying to be a little more helpful.

Rose panicked at the sudden realisation that she had no money.

"Thank you but I haven't any money," she admitted meekly.

The attendant took pity on her sensing an unusual innocence in the somewhat dishevelled young girl in front of her and leaning forward spoke confidentially.

"There's a soup kitchen round the side of the station. Go there. They will give you something."

"Thank you," said Rose embarrassed and headed off in the direction the lady had indicated.

Just along the covered walkway at the side of the station Rose saw a curious cluster of a dozen or so down-and-outs milling around a small cart on which stood a large metal cooking pot with copious amounts of steam rising from it into the cold air. Although no one took any notice of Rose they appeared rather intimidating; all of them looking old, unwashed and shabbily dressed. One man who was wearing a beret and a filthy jacket was leaning on a crutch spooning some hot soup into his mouth from an old tin can held in a wad of newspaper. His eyes were staring, his face sunken. A crippled old lady, bent almost double, wearing several layers of dirty, ill-fitting and inappropriate clothes was imploringly holding her hand up high for something. Rose hesitated to go nearer. She was spotted by one of the two nuns who were standing behind the cart helping to dish out the soup and rolls. The nun said something to her colleague and approached Rose, casting a caring and knowing eye over her.

"Are you all right?" enquired the nun softly, noticing her unease. "Are you hungry?"

"Yes," was all Rose could say, unsure of the situation.

"Let me get you some soup then," said the nun.

"Thank you," said Rose still standing apart from the group. "But I haven't any money."

"Come with me," the nun invited, "It's warmer by the cart. Sit down here," she said indicating a wooden crate turned on its end. A moment later the nun gave her some soup and a roll.

"Thank you," said Rose still tentative.

She sipped the hot soup from an old tin can, holding it in a wodge of newspaper like the man with the crutch, and tore large chunks out of the soft bread roll. She nearly dropped the roll her fingers were so cold. The soup was thick with pieces of meat in it. It tasted glorious and after a few sips Rose gave the nun a smile which said how good it was.

As Rose ate the nun observed her closely with unusual concern because this poor girl was not the normal soup kitchen patron. She was very young, very pale and a little unsteady on her feet. She was not really dressed for the bitter weather. Above all she looked innocent, lost and bewildered.

"Perhaps you should go home to the warm when you have finished that," the nun suggested as a way of starting a conversation. When she saw tears come to Rose's eyes she asked gently, "What is it, my child?"

"I'm supposed to go home but I want to find out about my Papa. He's been held by the Germans like me. They've just set me free and I can't go home without knowing if Papa is free too. They wouldn't tell me when they let me go. But I don't know what to do." Her eyes welled with tears.

"Where was your father held?" asked the nun.

"Cherche Midi prison. I know it's near here," she said wiping her eyes with the back of her hand.

"You say you were held by the Germans too?"

"Yes, for helping some English airmen. They released me this morning from La Santé." As soon as she had mentioned the airmen she regretted it and just hoped she could trust the nun. "But if Papa has been released he will be looking for me. I didn't see him on the station. We live a long way from Paris. I must find him! I can't go home without finding him."

Gradually by gentle questioning the nun understood more of Rose's plight and of the urgency of finding her father.

"It's nearly two o'clock," said the nun, "and we will be leaving in a moment to return to the convent. We go by the prison. It's not far. Come with us and maybe we can find out about your father before you catch your train home."

Rose readily accepted the invitation, feeling altogether a little stronger not only for having eaten but also because of the nun's sympathy and offer of help. She waited patiently still apart from the thinning group at the soup cart. She watched the nuns dealing with the vagrants, their movements calm and deliberate, and their manner gentle and caring. Rose was fascinated by their headdresses, the likes of which she had never seen before. Their very large white cornets amused her, reminding her of the sails of a schooner.

As the three set off in the direction of the prison Rose learned their names, Sister Agnès and Sister Delphine. They were from The Daughters of Charity convent they said. Walking between the two nuns with their flowing robes and improbable cornets Rose could not really believe the turn of events. Freedom and Paris were bewildering. But as they headed along rue du Cherche Midi her attention was fully on her father. By the time they arrived at the prison's main gate her heart was beating fast in anticipation of seeing her father. Was Papa still here, she wondered? Would she be allowed to see him? Or has he been released? Perhaps he was frantically searching for her? Maybe they had missed each other at the station? But she also felt a dread of entering that place again, a fear she knew she had to overcome in order to get news of her father. She was unsure of what to expect.

Sensing Rose's hesitation Sister Agnès approached and spoke to the guard outside the gate. After an anxious wait they were allowed inside and into a reception room and this time Rose braced herself as they approached the desk and Sister Agnès explained to the guard that Rose wanted to see her father. Again they were told to wait. Rose sat next to Sister Agnès feeling extremely tense and no one spoke. The one comfort was the support of the two Sisters. Without them Rose was not sure she could have faced entering this place again. Eventually the guard returned and tersely told Rose she could not see her father as he had had a visitor already that day.

"He's still here!" she exclaimed, her knees weakening at the devastating news he had not been released. She steadied herself against the counter top. "When can I see him?" she pressed, tears welling in her eyes. "What visitor?"

Maybe tomorrow, the guard told her and turned away in a manner that indicated there was no further discussion.

Rose tried to hold back her tears but the nuns could see her distress and tried to calm her down, saying it was best if she go back to the station to catch the train home. But Rose, unable to contain her bitter disappointment, became more distraught.

"I must see Papa! I cannot go back home without seeing him. I'll come tomorrow."

"But you have nowhere to stay and no money. There is a blackout and a curfew. It is far too dangerous for you to stay out alone. You are weak. You should go home," urged Sister Agnès.

"I'll find somewhere," cried Rose becoming hysterical. "I don't want to go home without seeing Papa." Her words were defiant but belied by her countenance which was crestfallen and tearful.

Sister Delphine gave Sister Agnès a look that said she thought they should do something to help this poor girl who appeared close to a breakdown.

"We can't stay here," said Sister Agnès. "Let's go to the convent. We can talk there. It's just around the corner." Rose dabbed her damp eyes with a handkerchief, wiped her runny nose and nodded her agreement.

From the pavement the only outward sign of the convent was the Madonna and Child statue in an alcove above the large arched, ornate doorway; otherwise the stone-clad building was like many others in the typically narrow Parisian side street. Stepping inside the gate was, however, like stepping into another world, a world of peace and calm, of order and quiet. Rose immediately sensed the atmosphere and calmed down as she was ushered into a warm, spotlessly clean and polished reception room.

"Are you a bit better now?" asked Sister Agnès as they sat down.

"Yes, thank you Sister," answered Rose.

"Before we can see how we can help you we should see what papers you have or else we can get into trouble ourselves which will never do."

Rose handed over her release papers. Sister Agnès checked the identity card and the travel warrant and Sister Delphine examined the parole document.

"Sister Agnès. Look at this!" she exclaimed, showing her the document and pointing at something. Sister Agnès looked up at Rose.

"Rose! It says here you have been in prison for six months. Is that right? You didn't tell us you had been in prison all that time. We had no idea you had been detained for that long."

"I didn't tell you because I thought you would think badly of me. I have only seen Papa once since we were arrested by the Germans. He was condemned to death in November but there was an appeal. You can see why I must see him." Rose looked up pleadingly at the nuns who were shocked that someone so young had been detained for so long. They knew Cherche Midi prison well as they had visited prisoners there before the Germans took it over. They were well aware of conditions there and at La Santé too. And the poor girl had the added burden of the death sentence hanging over her father.

"This changes things," said Sister Agnès. "Wait here Rose, please. Sister Delphine will stay with you." With that she left taking the papers with her to return shortly.

"I have good news. The Mother Superior has said you can stay here tonight. We have a guest room. Soon we nuns must go to afternoon meditation but there is just time for Sister Delphine to take you to the kitchens to see if there is something tasty for you and then she will show you to your room. Tomorrow we can try again to see your father."

Rose was grateful beyond words. Later, having had some tea and a little bread and cheese in the kitchen, she was sitting in the guest room close to a radiator which was just warm enough to take the chill off the room. She surveyed her new surroundings. The room was small, but much larger than her cell, with a tall ceiling and a stained glass window in one wall. It was sparsely furnished, just a bed, a chair and a washstand. There was a crucifix above the bed headboard and a statue of Our Lady on the wall opposite. Sister Delphine suggested Rose might like to read some of the literature on the washstand about the convent and the chapel but as she thawed out and with her stomach full Rose began to feel very, very tired. She took off her coat and shoes, lay on the comfortable, proper mattress and pulled the covers over her. Within minutes she was fast asleep.

It was not until eleven o'clock the following morning that Rose awoke, very gradually at first and then she became aware of someone else in the room.

"Hello, I'm Novice Thérèsa," said the young woman as she got up from the chair. "I've been asked to sit with you. How are you feeling this morning? You've had a big sleep."

Rose still felt washed out but the recognition of where she was produced a warm euphoria knowing she was free. She smiled at Novice Thérèsa who told her she had slept for over eighteen hours. But as Rose tried to get up she came over faint and very wobbly and at Novice Thérèsa's suggestion laid back on the bed for a while. The novice brought her some tea and a biscuit and told her Sister Agnès would come to see her a little later. In the meantime she should rest.

"But I must go and see Papa!" Rose protested.

"Hopefully you will later when you have had some food and feel stronger," said the young novice.

Rose worried that if the prison refused a visit again the nuns would say she had to go home that night and it was not until they were on the way to the Cherche Midi prison that she discovered Sister Agnès had already cleared it with the Mother Superior for her to stay for a few days if needs be.

Disappointment awaited Rose again at the prison. The response was the same as the day before: not today; maybe tomorrow. On the way back to the convent Sister Agnès had a suggestion.

"While we are at afternoon meditation why don't you write a letter to your father and if the news is still not good tomorrow you can leave your letter for him?"

While the nuns were at meditation Rose prayed for her father, after admonishing herself that yesterday she had gone to sleep before remembering. Then, provided with a pen and paper Rose carefully wrote:

Paris 4th February 1942

Dearest Papa

I was freed yesterday and I was hoping you too had been freed and we could go home together. I called at the prison but they would not let me see you. I will keep calling but I have to go home in the next few days. I am well and being looked after by nuns from The Daughters of Charity convent very close by.
I pray for you every afternoon as Abbé Stock said.

From your affectionate daughter

Rose

I can't wait till we are all together.

Novice Thérèsa came to see Rose after meditation and to take her to the refectory where they joined the nuns sharing an evening meal. As they chatted quietly the novice explained some of the routine of the convent and the work the nuns did with the sick and the poor. She was very caring and friendly and Rose took to her. Indeed she thought the two of them looked quite alike. Would it be a good idea if they washed some of Rose's clothes in the morning, the novice suggested? And Rose could have a bath and wash her hair so she could look her best for her father and for her mother when she got home. Gratefully Rose agreed without hesitation. The routine meant the nuns and novices retired to their rooms for the night after their evening meal so Rose was shown to her room. For her it was still early and although tired she decided to read the leaflets on the washstand by the light of a candle. The first leaflet she read was about The Daughters of Charity and their work but the contents of the second one captivated her. She read the story of Sister Catherine Labouré who, in 1830, had two visions of the Virgin Mary in the chapel at the very convent where she was. Initially Rose could hardly believe what she was reading – a vision of the

Virgin Mary right here! Fascinated, she read on, learning how Sister Labouré's second vision gave rise to the Miraculous Medal, a specially minted medallion, which was said to bestow great graces to the wearer. Intrigued Rose determined to ask Novice Thérèsa more about this in the morning. Tired and feeling full after supper, although the meal was very modest, she changed into the fresh nightdress set out for her and with a delicious feeling of comfort she lay down on her bed pulling the covers tight to her chin. In the quiet darkness she sensed this whole place radiated a restful, enveloping atmosphere of sanctuary, a mixture of both refuge and holiness, which calmed and reassured her, suppressing for now some of her anxieties and uncertainties about her father. Soon she drifted into a deep, untroubled sleep.

The following day took much the same pattern as the day before. Her high hopes of seeing her father were cruelly dashed yet again, only this time she had the small satisfaction of handing in her letter which was accepted. The disappointment was added to somewhat as she felt much more presentable for her father having had the luxury of a bath, her hair washed and, astonishingly, finding her clothes washed and ironed even before she woke up. Feeling clean had done wonders for her spirits.

The first evening in the guest room she had seen a hand mirror on the washstand mirror-side down but she could not bring herself to pick it up fearing she would see one of those down-and-outs from the railway station staring back at her. But after coming from the bathroom that morning she could not hold back her curiosity and checked herself in the mirror. Six months had passed since she had seen herself properly and she was not sure what to expect; in the event, neither good nor bad was her verdict. Her face was very pale and her skin puffy, but it was her hair that surprised her most. She knew it had grown well below her shoulders but seeing the full result, how thick it had become and how unmanageable, she was even more desperate for it to be cut to how she liked it.

Novice Thérèsa had been there again when Rose woke up, calmly and quietly helping; acting as nurse and companion to make sure she was properly looked after in her strange new surroundings. Between the midday meal and leaving with Sister

Agnès to go to the prison Rose walked with Novice Thérèsa around the inner cloisters of the convent, partly to pass the time and also to help her regain some strength. The cloisters had a beautifully laid out garden in the middle and there was a magnificent curved stone stairway leading to the first floor, all of which, Rose thought, was the antithesis to the drab exercise yard at La Santé. As if to emphasise the difference Rose could hear singing coming from the chapel, faint and melodious, that simply added to the ambiance of peace and tranquillity. Occasionally one of the nuns or novices hurried by, greeting them silently with a smile and a nod, walking a little faster than usual because of the cold. The two talked intermittently; for Rose the companionship was wonderful beyond words. She did not need or want to talk much and Novice Thérèsa did not push for conversation. She explained at one point that the cloisters were normally a bustling, lively place with lots of visitors but since the invasion many of the nuns lived and worked in the community as most of the convent had been given over as a field hospital. Rose's mind wandered during the silences, not really concentrating on anything in particular but at one point she did remember to ask about Sister Catherine Labouré and the Miraculous Medal, a topic on which the novice had much to tell. If the opportunity arose, she said, maybe she could take Rose into the chapel to see the spot where the visions took place. Rose said she would love that and told her about her own interest through her schoolwork in Joan of Arc. She said she hoped she would be allowed to go back to school to resume her studies even though the terms of her parole required her to be at home. Even though she had been away for over a term now she said she was confident she could catch up because she liked to study.

On the way back after handing in the letter at the prison Sister Agnès planted the idea that Rose should think about when she should go home. It was Thursday now, she said, and Rose's travel warrant expired next Tuesday. Rose should also let her mother know she had been freed the Sister suggested. Rose knew she was right about writing to her mother but kept hoping to arrive home herself before any letter could be delivered. The Sister proposed also that, as she would not be on duty at the soup kitchen the following day, they arrive at the prison at about ten thirty in the morning. That way, she said, there would be time to return later in the day if necessary. Rose agreed, she knew time was running out, and back in her room while the nuns were at meditation she opened her New Testament and read a while. Looking up at the statue of Our Lady she prayed as usual for her father, for him to be freed, this time adding an extra plea that tomorrow she would be allowed to see him. For months now she had wanted nothing more than to go home but since her release that desire had been altogether overtaken by the heartache she felt for her father still held behind bars. She also prayed for her mother and brother saying she was sorry she had not thought of them enough lately. She knew she was feeling stronger and that made her more determined than ever to see her father, to see him free, to feel his arms around her again. She must see him – she must!

Shortly after ten thirty the next morning Rose and Sister Agnès walked the short distance to the prison. Again Rose's heartbeat quickened with anticipation and at the reception counter, a large hatchway in the wall, Rose repeated her request to see her father. Previously her request had been refused after the guard consulted some sort of record which enquirers were obviously not allowed to see. This time though after consulting the record the guard paused a second then moved out of sight. This change raised her hopes that today the answer would be yes. Soon an officer appeared whom Rose recognised from her time there. He addressed Rose impassively in stilted French.

"I have to advise you will not be able to see your father. He is to be deported soon. By the end of this month he will have left for Rheinbach near Bonn where he won't be unhappy as the prisoners will work in teams on the fields and the prisons are warm. You are advised to return home. That is all." He turned and walked off.

Rose was stunned, not knowing what to say. Since her release all her hopes had been geared to her father being pardoned and released; she had not considered he would be deported and for a moment she was unable to take in the news. That the threat of the death sentence had gone hardly registered. But she could not accept that her father was not being released and her instinct was to challenge the officer. Surely his terse statement could not be right. She had been released: why not her father? He must be wrong; there must be some mistake. She was about to say so but the officer had gone by the time she had gathered her thoughts. Tears welled in her eyes. What should she do? She wanted to shout for the officer to come back, to give her answers; but she stopped herself, fearing she would be arrested if she made a fuss and she could not face that. The guard who had stood behind the officer watching impassively was still there.

Sister Agnès was the first to speak. She had been standing beside Rose and addressed the guard politely, "Could you ask the officer again please; it's important."

"Not possible," was his reply.

Rose meekly pleaded with him again but he simply looked past her at Sister Agnès and shook his head.

Rose turned to the Sister, a look of bewilderment on her face, about to ask her what they should do.

Sister Agnès put her arm around Rose's shoulder. "It's best we go back," she said, gently steering Rose towards the door. "We need to decide what to do now we know what is to happen to your father. We thank God his life has been spared," she said trying to comfort Rose in her bitter disappointment. As they returned to the convent though Rose's shock had turned to anger and frustration which would not go away. Why will they not allow me to see Papa, she kept asking herself? There must be a way. I must see him before he is deported. Surely there is a way, she kept saying to herself over and over again.

In a quiet room at the convent Sister Agnès sat with Rose gently trying to convince her she should now make plans to go home. After all, she told Rose, her mother has been worrying all this time. She must be told the news of her father without delay and Rose should go home to comfort and support her. Other imperatives, Sister Agnès pointed out, were the terms of her parole and the expiry of her travel warrant.

"Is there nothing you can do?" Rose implored. "Papa might be years in Germany and he was not strong the last time I saw him at the tribunal."

"Think about what I have said and perhaps we can talk again after lunch. Go to your room and I'll ask Novice Thérèsa to take you to lunch with her," said Sister Agnès hoping Rose would calm down and see reason. She would instruct the novice to persuade Rose to come round to her way of thinking.

It was not long before Novice Thérèsa appeared. She said how upset she was to hear that Rose's father was being deported and sorry that Rose was still unable to see him and that she too thought it was time for Rose to go home. She had, however, a suggestion to fill in the time before going to the refectory.

"We could visit the chapel," she said. "Would you like that? I can show you the place where Sister Catherine had her visions." Rose agreed although she was not exactly in the right mood but was too polite to say so. A few minutes later they entered the chapel.

Immediately Rose's eyes were taken to the end of the polished aisle and up to the wonderful arched altar at the far end of the chapel. Rose could not remember seeing anything so beautiful before; more beautiful even than the cathedral at Luçon. The chapel itself was not large; perhaps a little smaller than her church at home, she thought. In contrast to the plain, unadorned body of the chapel with its high, white domed ceiling, the altar was framed by a magnificent pale blue fresco as high as the ceiling depicting Sister Labouré's first apparition accompanied by a host of angels. The altar itself of marble and gold was set back in its own ornate domed alcove within which was a soaring statue of Our Lady, her head crowned by twelve stars, the centrepiece of the whole chapel. Below the fresco either side of the main altar were two smaller ornate altars surmounted by marble statues set against beautiful mosaics of blue and green. To left and right again were further side altars with more statues and colourful frescos. But it was not just the breathtaking sight that struck Rose but the atmosphere too. They were alone but nevertheless Novice Thérèsa spoke very softly as they walked down the aisle and pointed to the right hand statue saying that was where the vision of the Blessed Virgin appeared to Sister Catherine. They approached the statue and went up the few steps and knelt at the altar rail in front of the tomb of Sister Catherine whose body had been laid there.

"Up there," said Novice Thérèsa, pointing to the words around the main arch, "are the words that Sister Catherine saw forming around the apparition of the Blessed Virgin, 'O Mary Conceived Without Sin Pray For Us Who Have Recourse To You.' It's beautiful, isn't it?" She paused before suggesting, "Shall we pray quietly for a moment for Mary to give you and your family strength at this time?"

Rose was utterly moved by the whole scene and sanctity of the place. She put her hands together, closed her eyes and prayed earnestly.

"Thank you," whispered Rose as they walked back down the aisle, her mood totally transformed. She looked over her shoulder to take in the splendour once more when suddenly the notion came into her head that Abbé Stock must be able to arrange access to her father, probably the only person who could! What inspired this idea she could not be sure unless, … could it have been in answer to her prayers offered just a few moments ago in this extraordinary place? Excitedly she told Novice Thérèsa her idea as soon as they were outside again, explaining who the Abbé was and how good he had been to her, but Novice Thérèsa sounded a note of caution, making the point that Sister Agnès would need convincing.

It was a little while after lunch before Sister Agnès came to Rose's room. They would go now to see the Mother Superior, she announced, to decide what should be done. On the way she explained she was aware of Rose's idea for a last opportunity to see her father which is why they must see the Mother Superior. Rose was apprehensive; it was rather like being taken to see the headmaster at school, she thought.

"Sit down, my child," said the Mother Superior. "Sister Agnès has told me all about you. You have had a terrible ordeal. Tell me how you are feeling now?"

"I am much better, thank you. The Sisters and Novice Thérèsa have been very kind to me."

"I am glad to hear you have been well looked after, but you will be well advised to make immediate plans to go home," said the Mother Superior gently. She was elderly, only small in stature, but her lively, piercing eyes gave Rose the impression she was not only wise but acutely shrewd too; and also that she did not expect her words to be challenged. "Your mother will be anxious and will need your help, Rose. Besides which the terms of your release require you to go home and I must not put our convent at risk of harbouring someone breaking their parole. We usually find hostels or other shelters for the needy but because you are so young and vulnerable we took you under our roof. It is difficult for me to allow you to stay here much longer. I am sure you agree."

"I have been trying to see my father in Cherche Midi prison before he is deported," started Rose. "We were imprisoned because we helped two British airmen who were shot down in July near where we live. I know I must get home but the prison guards keep telling me I cannot see my father. If I don't see him now, I don't know when I will see him again." She felt her emotions rising and wanted to put her case for one last chance. "If only I can see Abbé Stock, he will be able to arrange a visit, I know he will. He's the prison chaplain and visited me and Papa and passed messages between us. He gave me this New Testament, look!" said Rose fetching the little book from her pocket. "He helped me understand God's will and without his help I don't know how I could have survived. I know he will help." With tears beginning to appear, she beseeched, "Please let me stay just long enough to see the Abbé; it's my only chance of seeing Papa!"

The Mother Superior considered Rose's plea. "H'm. I have heard of Abbé Stock and the work of his Mission. Very well then, Sister Agnès will take you to see him tomorrow after morning Mass and she will let me know how you get on. Meanwhile I suggest you write a letter to your mother to let her know your good news, about your father too and that you will be home very soon."

"I will, and thank you," said Rose calming down.

Later that afternoon before she settled to write to her mother she prayed for her father as the Abbé had said and for some reason she felt closer to him than usual; not only because they were praying in unison as she imagined but also because he would happy for her knowing from her letter that she was free.

The following morning Rose sat in her room eagerly awaiting the visit to Abbé Stock whom she was convinced would pull all the strings necessary for a last meeting with her father before he was sent away. She tried not to think about him suffering forced labour in Germany, a fate which she had narrowly escaped. She hated the word 'deportation' with all its connotations but if Papa was to work on the land, she reasoned, he could cope with it and efforts could still continue to secure his release. But she would miss him terribly and could never be happy again until he was home. On her lap was the letter she had written to her mother the evening before at the Mother Superior's suggestion. It was brief, just saying that she was free and being well looked after, that she had been told Papa would be sent to a farm in Germany at the end of the month and that she was trying to see him before she came home which would be very soon. There was no point in worrying her mother too much, she thought. She sat waiting patiently for Sister Agnès.

Later that morning at rue Lhomond, a distracted Abbé Stock sat at his desk putting some papers into his satchel before leaving for Fresnes prison. Twenty-four hours earlier his housekeeper, Elizabeth, had come into his office with a telegram. It was from his father to say his brother Heinz was missing in action at sea, news which shocked and devastated both he and his sister Franziska. Elizabeth, who was almost one of the family, had joined them both in prayers in the little chapel, after which the Abbé said he must leave because there was important work for him. He asked Elizabeth to stay with his sister and comfort her. Franziska had desperately wanted her brother to stay so he could be comforted too, but she knew 'important work' meant there were others in very great need of her brother and that he would answer their call ahead of his own grief; so she did not try to prevent him from leaving, saying only she would write to their parents.

The subdued mood in the household from the day before still hung in the air.

"Good morning Franz. Any more news of Heinz?" Elizabeth asked solemnly when she came into the office to check whether the Abbé had everything before he left for Fresnes.

"Sadly no," said the Abbé. "All we can do is hope he is still alive somewhere. Maybe we'll hear something later."

Elizabeth was about to ask if he had all he needed when she was interrupted by the door bell ringing and she left to answer it. A few moments later she came back.

"It's a Sister from the convent in rue du Bac with a young girl called Mademoiselle Rose Neau who would like you to arrange for her to see her father in Cherche Midi. Shall I just take the message or ask them to come back?" said Elizabeth thinking he might want to avoid casual visitors today. On hearing Rose's name though the Abbé suddenly looked up from fastening the straps of his satchel.

"Rose Neau is here?" he exclaimed, checking his understanding.

"Yes," said Elizabeth somewhat surprised at his reaction. "She is in the reception room with a Sister Agnès."

The Abbé thought for a moment and then, making a conscious effort to set aside his grief for his brother, said calmly, "I must see her. Show her into the chapel and tell her I will be with her in a moment. Ask the Sister to wait in the reception room; I must speak with her first."

Rose sat in anticipation on the front pew, relieved the Abbé was at home and so looking forward to seeing him again. The tiny chapel was simple, almost austere, and chilly but Rose did not mind the cold as she waited expecting any moment to feel the warmth of the Abbé's presence. Hearing footsteps she turned her head as he appeared through the small door at the back of the chapel his head slightly bowed, as though deep in thought. The expression on his face was unusually sombre as he approached which rather dented Rose's eager expectation.

"Rose," he quietly greeted her as he reached the pew.

Something told Rose all was not right. Nevertheless she began her prepared request.

"Father, I am sorry to bother you, but have you seen my father? Is he well? I wanted to ask you …" He held up his hand to stop her as he sat down close to her. He took both her hands in his.

"I know why you have come and I am glad you are free," he started, very quietly as though he was struggling to get his words out. He paused briefly then looked directly at her, his intense blue eyes so full of love and compassion, a look of such caring that Rose was yet again drawn to him. For her his gaze overflowed with tenderness and kindness just as usual – yet did she sense a sadness there too?

"But Rose," he continued, "it's no longer possible to see your father."

He felt her tense.

"I'm sorry but I have to tell you the appeals for your father's life, Rose, did not succeed. He died yesterday." He continued to look into her eyes seeing first disbelief and denial at his words.

Utterly stunned and traumatized Rose started to shake her head, about to say this cannot be true, that she had been told Papa would be sent to Germany and would not be unhappy there; but before the words could reach her lips she knew the Abbé would never lie to her, that what she was hearing was the awful, devastating truth. A sinking hollowness at the shattering news ran right through her. In that single instant of comprehension, grasping the gravity of what she had just heard, in that millisecond of a missed heartbeat she immediately realised the news would change her life for ever. The realisation was almost instantaneous but her reaction was delayed, her head sent into total confusion as she tried to absorb this bolt from the blue, this totally unexpected defining moment with all its implications. Her body stiffened as her mind started to clear and the horror of her father's suffering began to dawn on her.

"I was there to comfort him," said the Abbé seeking words that might offer her some consolation. "I accompanied him all the way and at the end he sought the sacrament of penance for his sins. I granted him absolution and blessed him. He was brave, Rose; very brave."

Tears filled her eyes as she looked at him shocked and bewildered. She started to shake and threw herself on his shoulder weeping uncontrollably as she was swamped with anguish for her father, at what he had faced in those final hours. It was too much for her to bear. The Abbé put his arm around her, gently holding her head to his own chest, her dark hair brushing his cheek as she sobbed. Try as he might to control his own emotions, tears began to roll down his cheeks to mingle with Rose's hair. But the Abbé's tears were mostly for a different grief.

After several minutes the initial waves of emotion subsided. Rose pulled away slightly and gazed up at the Abbé enquiringly. She noticed his tears but would never know they were not all shed for her and her father.

Knowing Rose, the Abbé was sure she would want to know more about how her father had died and he was debating what he should and should not relate; her young age making it a delicate balance for him. Occasionally he met the relatives of those executed and sometimes was obliged to tread a circumspect path when answering their questions out of respect for the dead. Others preferred to ask nothing because they could not bear the thought of their relative's last suffering, in which case the Abbé bore witness to his personal diary only.

He composed himself a little and again took her hands into his.

"Your father told me he prayed for you yesterday; in the afternoon as usual. He gave thanks you were free," the Abbé said.

"I prayed for him then too," Rose sobbed.

"Then you were at one with him in his last moments which will have brought him great comfort; and that knowledge will give you great comfort too. You can tell your mother and your brother he prayed for them also, and you can tell his family he died heroically, refusing a blindfold in order to see till the very end.

"I came to know your father quite well, Rose, and I felt privileged to be with him in the final moments of his earthly life. I wish I could have done more for him. During my visits he talked a lot about you, your mother and your brother. He was especially very proud of you. He felt deeply your suffering in prison and was immensely relieved to know you had been released. But his great sadness yesterday was that he would not see his beloved family again. In his last hours his thoughts were for each of you and he wrote you letters, five in all, which you should collect and take home."

"Where is Papa now, Father?" Rose enquired haltingly through her sniffles. "I must know. Maman will want to know."

"Of course. You can tell your mother I attended his burial yesterday evening in a cemetery at Ivry in the south of Paris. You and your family may visit the grave – I have the details.

"Meanwhile, Rose, I believe your duty is now to your mother. She will have great need of you and you of her. Support her and your brother all you can. Grieve for your father, Rose. You will feel pain and at times you will feel angry and embittered. Remember it's normal to have these feelings but don't let your anger forever burn inside you, don't let bitterness gnaw away at you and change who you are, Rose; that's not what your father would want. Stay true for him. It will not be easy and you will need God's help; seek His help. My heart goes out to you and I will pray for you all." He waited a moment to give Rose the opportunity to talk but when he sensed she was struggling to cope he suggested they say a final prayer for her father.

They knelt at the altar rail as he recited, "For our dearly departed Fernand Neau: Eternal rest, grant unto him, O Lord, and let perpetual light shine upon him. May he rest in peace. Amen." They stayed kneeling for a few moments longer with their own private thoughts. "We should go now to Sister Agnès," he said finally.

Seeing Sister Agnès set off Rose's emotions once again and she could not speak for being so choked with anguish. Sister Agnès too was caught up in the sentiment of it all and could not stop saying, "My poor child." They sat hand in hand while the Abbé suggested to them it would be best if they could collect the letters and her father's belongings as the authorities were very slow to deal with such matters. He left them for a few minutes and returned with a piece of paper on which he had written where to collect the letters and belongings and also the details of the burial plot at Ivry.

“You can stay here a while but I must go now,” he said. “Take care of her, Sister. And Rose, seek solace in the Lord.” As he turned to leave Rose knew somehow she would not see him again. How could she thank him? He had helped her survive by his kindness and compassion, and by keeping her in touch with her father which had been so important to her. What could she say?

A weak, “Thank you,” was all she could manage. It was almost inaudible, hopelessly inadequate but all she could say. His eyes held hers for the briefest of moments.

“God be with you,” he said and was gone.

Battling against the cold Rose and Sister Agnès struggled back to the convent, weighed down with sorrow. During the journey Sister Agnès talked to Rose gently about what they should do next. Rose was too upset to go immediately to Cherche Midi prison to collect her father’s belongings even though it was close by. They decided to go there the following morning after which they would go to the tribunal building in rue du Faubourg Saint-Honoré where the letters were. Rose said she also wanted to go to Ivry to see her father’s grave. Sister Agnès had said they could try but only if the train times allowed because she must go home tomorrow to her mother.

It was a long time before Rose could sleep that night. Wave after wave of grief kept rolling over her, at first for her father and then for her mother. That final sight of her father at the tribunal when he looked so crushed haunted her time and time again and the thought of what he went through in those last hours was unbearable. Her poor, brave Papa …

She had no real idea of how an execution was carried out and although the Abbé had said her father refused a blindfold, her mind thankfully did not try to visualise his very last minutes. But the thought of her mother and how distraught she would be at the news simply added another layer to her torment.

On waking the next morning her first thought was of her father and tears quickly filled her eyes. Novice Thérèsa had been sitting patiently in the room as before waiting for Rose to wake up and when she saw Rose’s tears her eyes too welled up with emotion. Unable to say anything she went over and knelt by Rose's bed and placed her arm over Rose's shoulder and the two sobbed together. Eventually Rose said she didn't know how she was going to manage today, having to go once more to the prison to collect her father's belongings and then to collect his letters. She hoped she could visit his grave, she told Novice Thérèsa, and after that she had the journey home. It all appeared daunting.

"God will give you the strength," said the young Novice with all sincerity. "And Sister Agnès has told me to say she will be with you as long as you need."

Rose and the Sister were at the Cherche Midi reception as soon as it opened asking for her father's belongings. After some delay Rose was required to accompany a guard across the yard to the prisoner discharge office where the belongings could be collected. She steeled herself at the thought of going further into the prison. As she crossed the yard some soldiers sniggered at her, suggesting some obscene purpose for her visit but their officer quickly told them to be quiet. Rose was hardly aware of them as she struggled to keep her composure through this unexpected extra ordeal.

"Sign here," ordered the warden. Next to the sheet of paper he was pointing to was her father's old and battered leather jacket folded with his pair of espadrilles on top. Rose reached out to touch them.

"Is that all?" she said timidly.

"That's all. Sign here."

Outside as she and Sister Agnès waited for a bus to take them across the river to rue du Faubourg Saint-Honoré Rose clutched the jacket and shoes tightly to her, tears rolling down her face, her emotions triggered by what they represented. After her experience at the prison she was not sure how she could face going into the tribunal building but she knew she must. As they entered Rose recognised one of the soldiers on guard from the many times she was taken there. He saw her and obviously recognised her too because he promptly disappeared which made Rose think he must have been one of the firing squad that executed her father. Again they had to wait, this time outside an office. As they waited she was acutely conscious of how much she hated this place and everyone in it. Soon they were called into the office and immediately Rose's eyes were drawn to a small stack of envelopes there on the desk. Written on the top one in her father's distinctive handwriting was her mother's name, Renée. Until that moment Rose had not given any real thought to the letters but suddenly on seeing her mother's name the enormous significance of the letters became apparent to her. They contained her father's farewell words, his very last, there could be no more. That made them very precious. All of a sudden taking delivery of these letters assumed a much greater responsibility than Rose had imagined. Her eyes stayed fixed on them as the civilian administration clerk explained there were five letters to sign for. He was middle-aged, portly and appeared uncomfortable with the nature of his task, wanting it over quickly. Rose put her father's jacket and shoes on the desk and signed the receipt after which the man invited her to pick up the envelopes. She hesitated. Till that moment there was still a small part of her that had not totally accepted her father was dead, that all this was not happening and that at any moment everything would be restored. It was almost as though these letters represented her father's coffin, confirmation there was no fantasy and that her father really was dead. In his honour she picked up the precious letters very gently, reverently. Needing to know if there was a letter for her she thumbed through them. There was; it was the last one and the most precious one! He had addressed it 'Rose' and her heart skipped a beat when she saw he had also written underneath, 'Zézette', a name he had sometimes called her when she was a small child. It would need a special time and place for her to open the envelope and to read her father's final words. The other three letters she noted were for her brother; for her father's brother and sister – Uncle Bernard and Aunt Sophie – and lastly one for her father's elderly parents – Papy and Mamie, who lived with Aunt Sophie and Uncle Bernard.

"We can go now," she said looking up at Sister Agnès, picking up the jacket and shoes. The Sister thanked the clerk as they left the room. Rose could not get out of the building quickly enough and holding the letters securely looked straight ahead until she was outside. When the Sister caught up with her Rose said, “One of the letters is for me but I don’t want to read it yet.” Then she asked pleadingly, “There must still be time to go to the cemetery, surely?”

“Of course,” said Sister Agnès. “We will need to take the Métro though as the buses are difficult to Ivry.”

“Is it expensive? I haven’t any money. I can send you some money when I get home though,” said Rose in desperation, not having thought that money might be needed for fares.

“Don’t worry,” said Sister Agnès confidently. “They usually let us on the Métro for free. They know we are on a mission of mercy; it’s their way of giving. This is when our distinctive cornets come into their own – everyone knows who we are. This way.” They headed to the Madeleine Métro station. Rose had seen a few pictures of the Métro before but this would be her first experience of it. In spite of the nature of her journey she was quite distracted by everything, even the entrance to the station with its cast-iron balustrade decorated in plant-like motifs against which leant dozens of bicycles. Under ground it was a wonder of tunnels and stairs eventually leading to a long platform with brightly coloured advertisements on the curved walls and dark tunnels at either end. The Sister was right; the ticket collector at the gate waved them through with a modest bow. Sister Agnès gave Rose a little satisfied smile, a twinkle in her eye. At first Rose had not really taken to Sister Agnès who, though gently spoken, initially had appeared rather matter of fact, somewhat standoffish. But yesterday and again today Rose saw her in a different light, more friendly and open, motherly even, and Rose realised she could not have coped these last few days without her. They boarded the first train to arrive and Rose was somewhat unnerved at the weird sensation she felt as it left the brightly lit platform and entered the pitch-black tunnel. They had to change at the next station and she marveled at the labyrinth of tunnels and thought that she would surely have got lost on her own amongst the crowds of people who hurried along seemingly knowing where they were going, minding their own business. Eventually they arrived at Porte de Choisy station where they were told the cemetery was about a fifteen minutes walk. It was cold still and trying to snow but Rose was glad to be in the open air. As they walked she braced herself again, this time in growing trepidation of what she was about to see. This was a journey, a pilgrimage, she knew she had to undertake and she was determined to see it through. But it was also a journey she wished with all her heart she did not have to take. Her face was set; she looked straight ahead. She did not want to speak. More than once she felt inside her coat pocket to ensure the letters were safe, holding her father's jacket and shoes to her. They came to a long wall with tall trees behind as they had been told to expect and arrived at a gateway with a flower stall outside and an attendant's hut inside. Rose stood looking through the open green gates as she felt in her pocket for the piece of paper on which the details of the grave were written. Sister Agnès meanwhile approached the flower seller and after a brief exchange came back with two daffodils and an early iris.

"For your father's grave," said Sister Agnès as she passed the flowers to Rose. "The flower lady doesn't want any money; she is happy to give them for someone who died for France."

Rose acknowledged the flower-seller's generosity with a half-smile but as her head was so full of thoughts, the remark that her father had died a hero barely registered. However, the appealing notion did lodge somewhere in the back of her mind.

An elderly attendant greeted them and consulted Rose's piece of paper, showing recognition at the name and number written on it. Respectfully he invited them to follow him as he headed down a long avenue of trees towards the rear of the cemetery. There in a corner were a number of new graves. The attendant pointed to the nearest of them. Sister Agnès put a comforting arm around Rose.

"Fernand Neau," he said solemnly. "I make the little crosses myself and put the names on." Then he added with a touch of disgust in his voice, "They don't mark them at all."

Rose edged forward and knelt at her father's grave on the cold, hard ground, placing the flowers at the foot of the mound of fresh earth.

"I'm here, Papa," she said quietly her eyes swimming with tears. A puff of cold February wind brushed her cheek and rustled the grass beside her. To Rose it felt as though her father had heard her and was saying he knew she was there. Her grief overwhelmed her yet again and she sobbed her heart out. Sister Agnès and the old attendant had difficulty keeping their composure too – Sister Agnès because she had become quite attached to Rose and the attendant, an old soldier, because he knew Rose's father was yet another victim of the Occupation.

For a while the two adults stood behind the kneeling Rose, each with their own thoughts, giving Rose all the time she needed to say farewell to her father. Eventually she stood up and nestled against Sister Agnès who put a consoling arm around her. Rose continued to stare at the grave, hearing contradictory voices in her head; one telling her it really was her father there in the grave: the other coming from the part of her that did not want to accept his death, trying to deny the reality. But she knew it was the truth. She also knew she must turn and leave her father and she looked around trying to take in the place where he was. To one side there were several freshly dug open graves awaiting, Rose thought, other martyrs to join her father. She glanced at the grave on the other side of her father's, at the name written on the small, home-made wooden cross and was shocked to see the name 'Alphonse Gouraud'. She winced as though a sharp pain had caught her. Monsieur Gouraud! Him too! And they had only been trying to help the airmen. Was there no end to this nightmare? His poor family, she pitied, and explained who he was to Sister Agnès. She then leant down and took one of the daffodils from her father's grave and placed it on Alphonse Gouraud's grave.

Sister Agnès spoke for the first time, suggesting they say the Eternal Rest for her father and Monsieur Gouraud and after the prayer she turned to Rose and said softly, "There's nothing more you can do here. It's time to think about getting you home now."

Rose, still choked and biting her bottom lip, nodded her agreement.

Chapter 18

With a slight jerk the train began to pull out of Gare Montparnasse taking Rose away from Paris where she had suffered so much. Now, at long last, she was setting off for home, but to a home that would never be the same again. Even before the terrible events of the past six months, the war and the Occupation had already made the future uncertain and insecure, but the shattering death of her father had now removed the rock on which the Neau family was built.

Rose sat in a corner of the carriage by a window. It was dark outside and even travelling through the suburbs of Paris there was nothing to be seen because of the blackout. Inside the carriage there was only a dim night light, all that was allowed, again because of the blackout, which meant Rose was left with little to divert her from her own thoughts. She was tired and tried to get comfortable, leaning her head against the padded seat, her father's shoes by her side. She had folded her father's jacket on her lap and every now and again she fingered the soft leather seeking closeness to him. There were few other passengers scattered throughout the carriage, the closest being a mother and her daughter, Rose presumed, who got on just after her. The mother had smiled at her as they made their way past and sat on the seat opposite but to the other side of the carriage. She had been nervous of travelling on her own and was glad to have them near. It did not take long for the passengers to settle down for the two and a half hours it would take to the first stop at Le Mans. Fortunately the carriage was warm and with the dim light, the gentle rocking of the train and the rhythmic drumming of the wheels the atmosphere soon became soporific. The little girl opposite snuggled up to her mother and soon their eyes were shut. But Rose, despite her tiredness, could not even doze to start with, unable to shut out the motion of the train, the smell of coal smoke and steam, the clatter of the wheels over the points, all unfamiliar and intruding. Her mind turned over and over the events of the last hours and days and how she would break the dreadful news to her mother. She had been able to send her a telegram from the station to say she was coming home and to expect her at one o'clock in the afternoon the next day but she had not mentioned her father in the brief message.

The telegram had been arranged by Sister Agnès, like everything else over the last few days. When she and Rose had arrived earlier at Gare Montparnasse Sister Agnès had made straight for the concourse manager's office and while Rose sat outside the Sister had spoken to the manager whom she seemed to know. After a few minutes Rose had been invited into the office and Sister Agnès explained that the manager had offered to look after her and make sure she caught the right train. He was a tall, distinguished looking man who looked important in his braided uniform and cap. He cast a fatherly look at Rose while Sister Agnès asked if it was possible to arrange a telegram even though it was explained Rose had no money. He agreed; there would be no charge he had said with a slight, respectful nod at Sister Agnès. Although embarrassed, Rose could not help a little smile at the well practised, unabashed way Sister Agnès asked for charity and always seemed to receive it. The concourse manager had asked for Rose's papers and being satisfied that her travel warrant was in order consulted his timetables and suggested she catch the evening train at ten o'clock, changing at Nantes Orléans for Luçon. Rose remembered she had been told there was a train earlier in the evening and said so. There was, he explained but that would not get her to St. Michel-en-l'Herm any earlier and would mean she would have a very long wait in the dark on her own at Luçon. The later train would be safer, he assured her and Sister Agnès. He wrote it all down on a piece of paper and he said Rose could wait just outside his office; he would come to collect her before her train was due. At that point Sister Agnès said she must return to the convent and had wished Rose God's blessing. They had embraced tightly in an emotional farewell. Thinking back on that moment, Rose regretted she had not found more words to thank her, for Rose could not imagine what she would have done these last few days without Sister Agnès and the others at The Daughters of Charity who had given her, a complete stranger, not only food and shelter but also love and understanding.

It was a long wait till ten o'clock but Rose did not dare to wander from her bench seat outside the manager's office. There was plenty of activity to divert her thoughts: porters with their trolleys piled high with luggage or sacks of mail or boxes of produce, fashionable ladies with their escorts, businessmen in their smart coats and hats. People milled about and then some of them would head for a platform when an announcement was made over the public address system. Conscious she was young, alone and with no luggage, Rose had tried to make herself small and inconspicuous, desperately trying to avoid the attention of the many German soldiers who came and went, some striding uncomfortably close to her. She was convinced that if challenged she would be arrested and taken back to Cherche Midi prison for not being at home as her parole required. She even rehearsed her excuses for having stayed on in Paris. Later the manager invited her back into his office during his break and offered to share his light supper of cold croque monsieur, a slice of thin apple tart and some ersatz coffee for which Rose was very grateful having reconciled herself to going hungry till she reached home. He explained that Sister Agnès had told him about her grief and suffering and he appeared genuinely sympathetic. Rose had been thankful to have been tucked under his wing because she was unused to such a major railway station and worried about missing her train or catching the wrong one. As the evening had drawn on the number of people around grew fewer and Rose had been glad when the manager had said it was time to go. He saw her into a carriage and Rose thanked him for all his kindness. He said that he would telegraph his colleague at Nantes station to look out for her.

As the train rumbled through the blackness Rose sat in the corner of the carriage, her thoughts confused, her mind in emotional turmoil. She was free and on her way home, her most earnest wish for the last six months, yet she felt no elation. It was as though she could not touch her freedom just yet; that she had landed in some sort of no-man's-land which was not prison but neither did it taste of freedom; the physical constraints were left behind but she still felt hemmed in and oppressed by her father's death. Waves of grief wafted over her, some driven by thoughts of her father, others by the desperate anguish she felt for her mother whose world was about to be torn apart. She drew up her father's jacket close to her cheek, rather like a child with a comfort blanket, to feel it on her face and to catch his aroma. By deliberately omitting her father's fate from the telegram Rose knew she would have to face her mother, dreading the moment when she must tell her the truth – that Papa was never coming home. She tried to construct a form of words for that moment but she could not even begin, she just kept thinking about the distress she was about to visit on her Maman.

At one point she took out the letters from her pocket and looked at the one addressed to her mother. She could not begin to imagine what Papa had said. How could he even put pen to paper? He was no letter writer; in fact Rose could not remember the last time he had written a personal letter. Usually it was Maman who wrote if any correspondence was needed. Then she looked at her own letter, running her finger over the name 'Zézette'. Typical of her father, she thought, that despite the enormity of the moment he had to add another touch, an endearment, no doubt remembering when she was his little girl. Still she could not bring herself to open it and together with the others she tucked it back safely in her pocket.

The loss of her father and her mother's impending anguish dominated her thoughts. Whenever her mind wandered to her own suffering it dwelt there only momentarily. The physical and mental abuse she had experienced, the hunger, the cold and the loneliness all receded somehow to the background – it was her father's death and its consequences that took centre stage. She tried to recall Abbé Stock's words about staying true to her father, about supporting her mother and about seeking God's help. She struggled to remember everything he had said but simply going through what she could remember eased the pain. Just thinking of the Abbé gave her comfort, born out of his infinite kindness and humanity towards her in those desperate weeks and months of imprisonment, born too out of his quiet personality and saintly demeanour which drew her to him. For her he was the only light that had entered her cell. Thinking back it was right and proper that it was he who had broken the news of her father's death as it made it very personal, not just because of her relationship with him but also because of his relationship with her father – in his cell, at his death and at his burial. If there was any shred of consolation over her father's death, it was provided by the Abbé. He had been the link between them; he had been there for both of them. It was he who had suggested she and her father pray at the same time each day. And that last time, that last prayer, she had sensed that she and her father were together. She knew it.

The train stopped briefly at Le Mans and Angers before arriving just before four o'clock in the morning at Nantes Orléans station. As the train had slowed on its approach the lady opposite leaned over towards Rose and told her that they were shortly to arrive at Nantes and that she had been asked on the quiet by the stationmaster at Gare Montparnasse to make sure Rose changed trains here. Rose thanked her and remarked how kind everyone was to her. She showed the lady the piece of paper with the times of the trains written on it, just readable in the dim light. We are going the same way, the lady had said with surprise and even her sleepy daughter sat up and took notice. The woman explained she was returning to l'Aiguillon-sur-Mer and said Rose could travel with them for the rest of the journey if she would like. Both the lady and her daughter were smartly dressed and appeared well-to-do. Sensing she was friendly and genuinely concerned Rose agreed to travel with her believing she would be less conspicuous that way. The lady then introduced herself as Madame Veillon and said her daughter was Dominique. The little girl, who was about five or six years old, shyly pressed close to her mother.

It was still pitch black when they got off the train and Rose could only just make out the high canopy roof over the station and the huge archways at either end which she remembered from the brief stop there under escort on her way to Paris. The stationmaster had been on the lookout for a young lady on her own and spotted Rose as the only possible candidate. He approached and led the group to the waiting room but was content to leave Rose in the hands of Madame Veillon. The waiting room was dimly lit and uninviting but there was no real alternative for the long wait for the connecting train to La Rochelle and Bordeaux. They settled in a corner as best they could away from the dozen or so other passengers waiting for connections. Rose thought she must have dozed off fitfully at times on the journey, but the hard seats and echoing waiting room made the idea of further sleep look impossible.

"Do you need any help?" Madame Veillon asked quietly, "You seemed very upset at times on the journey. Is there something wrong?"

The question brought an emotional outpouring as all of Rose's heartache and sorrow surfaced, "I'm not yet seventeen years old and no longer have my father. He was executed on Friday by the Germans and I have to tell this to my mother."

Madame Veillon was totally taken aback by this outburst to her gentle enquiry. Suddenly she found herself having to cope with a totally different and unexpected situation and it took her several moments to gather her thoughts, to react to Rose's stark revelation.

"You poor child," she said feeling quite inadequate and finding the right words difficult. She was to repeat this phase several times as Rose told her story briefly. At first Madame Veillon could hardly believe what she was hearing. She was an astute and intelligent woman, not easily taken in. But Rose's sincerity soon convinced her, added to which she remembered the stationmaster at Gare Montparnasse asking her to look out for Rose – this must be why. Her heart was drawn to this clearly troubled young girl – but for now she could not begin to comprehend fully Rose's suffering. Hesitating to pry and mindful her young daughter was listening she did not enquire further. She was glad though that she had asked Rose to join them for the rest of the journey, now feeling extra protective towards her. She offered some words of comfort, "Stay with us for now. You'll soon be home."

As six o'clock approached Madame said the station café would open soon and they could have some breakfast before their train departed otherwise they would be very hungry. Embarrassed at having no money Rose said she could manage without as she was used to being hungry but Madame Veillon would not hear of it.

"A little treat, on me," she said in such a way that Rose could no longer resist.

Over a breakfast of croissants, jam and a delicious hot chocolate, a luxury for Rose, Madame Veillon explained that she had been visiting her husband in Paris where he worked and where they normally lived but that she and her daughter had moved to a house at l'Aiguillon-sur-Mer to escape the bombing and where it was safer. She regularly made this journey at weekends to see her husband, she said, so was very familiar with it but it was tediously slow because of the war. The next stage to Luçon would take three hours, she bemoaned, as the train stopped at every station. Eventually the announcement came that the train for La Rochelle and Bordeaux was standing at the platform and Rose, Dominique and Madame Veillon made their way to board it, glad the seemingly endless wait was over. Fortified with breakfast and with the morning twilight beginning to show in the east they felt the day was at last beginning to turn for the better. At seven thirty the train rumbled over the bridge across the wide Loire river out of Nantes, the little girl sitting by the window of the carriage, Rose next and then Madame Veillon. The human contact of just sitting between them gave Rose a warm glow. Dominique, who was no longer shy with Rose, chatted away asking all sorts of questions and at one point her mother even mildly rebuked her for being an inquisitive nuisance. But Rose was happy to have the distraction as it put off thoughts of meeting her Maman and how she would break the news of Papa. Madame asked Rose what she would do after she was back at home to which Rose said she wanted to resume her baccalaureate studies but was unsure if she would be allowed because she was supposed to live at home. In any case she would have missed two terms at her school in Luçon and her grant may well have been stopped. She would have to wait and see. It took two hours to reach La Roche-sur-Yon and another hour to arrive at Luçon and all the time as the sun came up on the clear, crisp Monday morning the sights and names became more familiar. At one point Rose likened the station stops along the way to the lines she made on her cell wall to mark off the days to freedom – only this time each stop was one step nearer to home and to seeing her mother – but each one was also a step nearer the moment she was dreading. She was the herald of her father's death. She was the bearer of news that would break her mother's heart.

Having arrived at Luçon there was another long wait. Sitting quietly in the station waiting room Madame Veillon could see Rose was becoming even more anxious and when Dominique went outside to skip along the platform she asked again if she could do anything. Rose confided what was on her mind and Madame Veillon suggested it would be better if Rose first went to a relation, an aunt or uncle, or to a grandparent, who could then accompany her when she went to see her mother. Rose agreed that was a good idea, saying she would go first to her grandparents' house and thanked Madame Veillon for the advice. She felt relieved. Telling her grandparents the news first would be so much easier than facing her mother on her own. A little later Madame Veillon also asked Rose whether she would perhaps like to keep in touch and write to her, and when Rose handed her a piece of paper on which to put her address Madame Veillon noticed what appeared to be the name of a cemetery and grave number written on it.

"Is this where your father is buried? At Ivry?"

"Yes," said Rose. "I must not lose that piece of paper. It is important for Maman."

"Perhaps you could ask your mother if she would like me to put some flowers on your father's grave the next time I am in Paris. Write and let me know. It is easy for me to get to Ivry."

"Thank you. I will," said Rose gratefully. "I'm sure she would like that. You are very kind."

Suddenly Dominique ran back into the waiting room saying there were lots of soldiers arriving. Rose froze.

"What are they doing?" she asked urgently. Madame Veillon, seeing Rose's reaction went to the door to see what was happening.

"They just seem to be gathering on the platform," she reported. "I expect they are going to the military camp at l'Aiguillon," she surmised, trying to calm Rose's nerves.

“I don’t want to go near them,” said Rose warily.

“We’ll get in another carriage,” assured Madame Veillon. “Stay with me.”

Rose leaned forward and could just see some of the soldiers through the waiting room window. They were standing casually, chatting away, apparently in good spirits. They seemed totally unconcerned and as such appeared not to be a threat. Nevertheless Rose pulled back out of their sight, her heart beating hard. Her overwhelming emotion was fear; fear of being re-arrested because she had convinced herself she could not survive another term of imprisonment. She stayed out of sight until it was time to board the little narrow-gauge train to l’Aiguillon-sur-Mer. The soldiers were the first to board, taking over the carriage behind the goods van, the first of the two passenger carriages. Madame Veillon was right about their destination, it seemed. Rose, Madame Veillon and Dominique made for the back of the last carriage and soon the little train with its tall funnel puffing strongly slowly pulled out of the station. On the move, Rose felt a great deal safer and as her fear subsided, hatred took over; hatred of those soldiers who, just by their presence, induced such terror in her to the extent her hands were sweating and her heart was racing. If it had been possible to travel home by any other means she would have fled the station to avoid them. The long journey from Paris had allowed her time to dwell on those she held responsible for her father’s death and she could not help thinking of the soldiers who had pulled the trigger; like the one at the tribunal building who quickly disappeared when he saw her. Why could they not have had the courage to refuse the order like the one who gave her his wedding ring! They were guilty of murder and she hated them, yet it was a hate she was impotent to do anything about. The Abbé’s dictum that she should not let bitterness gnaw away at her was going to be difficult to fulfil. The train trundled on and Rose and Madame Veillon sat absorbed with their own thoughts; even Dominique sensed the tension and just looked out at the passing scenery. Rose checked for the umpteenth time that the precious letters were safely in her pocket and she touched the jacket and shoes by her side. She planned her arrival at St. Michel-en-l’Herm station; she intended to be the first off the train and to run to the exit and to continue running all the way to her grandparents' house if she still had the strength. At all costs she vowed to avoid the soldiers and she did not want to talk to anyone she might meet on the way. As the train slowed on its approach to St. Michel-en-l'Herm she readied herself. She embraced Madame Veillon and thanked her for all her help, and embraced Dominique. The train came to a halt in the station with a judder. As Rose quickly alighted onto the platform the little girl gave a wave of her tiny hand but Rose did not look back. She was about to make her dash for the exit when all of a sudden she heard her name called and, turning, she saw her mother standing further down the platform.

Startled, Rose stopped immediately. It had not occurred to her that her mother would meet her off the train; she had always been waiting at home before. This was not what she planned. She had often imagined the reunion, running into the kitchen at home and into her arms. But suddenly, taken aback by the sight of her mother, she froze; her initial instinct was to rush to her and to feel her arms around her but the dreadful news of her father weighed her down, anchoring her to the spot.

Renée had been waiting anxiously at the station with mixed emotions. She was desperate to see her daughter home safe at last after all this time, worried what state she would be in physically, wanting to hold her again, to protect her from further harm, to help her overcome her ordeal. But in the telegram Rose did not mention her father. Why not? Was there no news of him? Had she not seen her father? Why the silence? She stood on the windswept station platform, holding her coat tightly around her against the biting wind, the wait just adding to her pent-up anxiety. The tension became almost unbearable as the little engine pulled to a noisy, hissing stop just past her. Then suddenly there was Rose jumping onto the platform from the rear of the train.

Having called out Rose's name, Renée began to rush forward; but then, as Rose stopped and turned at the sound of her name, she caught the look on her daughter's face that told her something was wrong. It was then she caught sight of the familiar leather jacket folded over Rose's arm. In an instant she recognised it as Fernand's, the jacket her husband always wore, and the jacket he would need in Rheinbach. Rose returning with her father's jacket could only mean one thing – Fernand was dead.

"No!" she cried in anguish, stopping by the carriage full of the German soldiers and clasping her hands to her head. Unaware of the events outside the soldiers in the carriage were carrying on with their noisy banter, some laughing loudly only a yard from where Renée stood. Somehow their laughter seemed to penetrate those first moments of Renée's desolation sparking an uncharacteristically heated reaction. Angrily she turned to the soldiers and started shouting at them.

"Assassins! Murderers!" she spat venomously at the faces along the carriage. "Murderers; all of you!"

Rose, seeing what was happening and fearing she would be re-arrested and sent back to prison, raced up to her mother and threw her arms round her neck, trying to turn her away from the soldiers.

"Don't! Maman, I can't go back there!" she pleaded. "Leave them! Please!"

Hearing the commotion the stationmaster, who knew the Neau family well, came running down the platform. All the time Rose feared the soldiers would come after them and to her the whole scene seemed to take place in slow motion. The stationmaster took Renée's arm gently and steered them into his office and closed the door quickly. But it still seemed ages before the train gradually moved off and Rose's panic subsided.

"Stay here. Sit with your mother, Rose, and look after her," said the stationmaster. "I'll send my assistant to see if Monsieur Bon can take you home in his taxi." Seeing Rose had returned alone and with Madame Neau so distraught, he had guessed what had happened.

"Oh, Rose. Rose," Renée bewailed, the realisation of her worst fears simply swamping the joy of seeing her daughter. Here was the moment she had been waiting so long for, her cherished daughter home from an unbearable suffering, yet her maternal emotions were being overshadowed by the sudden anguish she herself was suffering for her lost husband.

All Rose could say was, "Oh, Maman," over and over again as they hugged each other and wept until Monsieur Bon arrived. No one spoke while he drove them the short journey from the station to rue de la Fontaine.

The farmhouse drew into view. Although Rose was very nearly home, a scene she had longingly dreamt of so many times over the past months, her spirits as they approached did not match those dreams. The building had not altered but she knew the home she had yearned for was changed for ever. In prison she had prayed earnestly that when she returned everything would revert to normal once more; but that hope would never be realised now. They thanked Monsieur Bon as he dropped them at the gate. He too was caught up in their grief, refused any payment and made a polite withdrawal to drive straight home to tell his wife the news.

Once inside the house Rose sat her mother in the tall-backed chair by the warm range and knelt at her feet, holding her hands and unconsciously stroking them gently. For a little while they remained as they were; Rose completely caught up in her mother's utter distress yet realising she must be strong for her. Gradually Rose began to unfold the events of the last few days, beginning with her release and how she had been taken in by the nuns and looked after. She explained how she had been lied to about the deportation and that she could not believe it when Abbé Stock told her of Papa's death. Her mother just sat slumped in total shock, leaning her head against the chair back staring vacantly into the distance, unresponsive as though all her strength had ebbed away. On her lap lay her husband's jacket; a stark manifestation of her loss. Rose was trying her best to tell her mother quietly and slowly but to see her mother in this state frightened her.

It was only a few minutes after she had talked of the meeting with Abbé Stock that she heard a noise at the door. She turned to see her brother standing in the doorway.

"Rose! ...," he began, but then paused. It took him only an instant to grasp the situation, that the news was the worst. "... It's Papa, isn't it?" he said slowly, almost rhetorically. Rose nodded in confirmation.

"Papa died on Friday. They lied to me he would be deported," said Rose.

"Bastards! The bastards! They'll pay for this, I swear! They'll pay. You see!" he shouted in a rage, still standing in the doorway.

At the news, news he had feared for some time, the only emotion he could express was anger. Ever since his release he had been increasingly troubled by a confusing mixture of thoughts and feelings; but he had kept them to himself, not wanting to add to his mother's already heavy burden. He could not reconcile on the one hand that he had saved the lives of the two airmen: yet on the other his actions in doing so had seen the whole family threatened with terrible consequences, the worst of which had now happened. He had ignored the warnings of his fellow workmen against getting involved; but what else could he have done? Should he have stopped his father going to see the airmen; insisted his father handed them over to the authorities? He had desperately wanted to make amends over the theft of the beans, but all of this had just made matters worse. These questions and others besides had swirled around in his head, seemingly irreconcilable. He had, however, one shred of comfort in all this; it was the knowledge that despite the efforts of his interrogators he had not denounced his father or anyone else. But an acute sense of guilt had played constantly on his mind since the tribunal, guilt that he was free yet his father and sister continued to suffer. Although his sister was now free; his father was dead, executed.

He held back, racked by the sudden news of his father's death, tormented by his own persecution which, for just that moment, masked his own grief and prevented him from sharing in the grief of his mother and sister. So he hid behind his anger towards the Germans. "They'll pay. You see," he repeated; then said, "I'll go and get Grandpapa and Grandmaman." He turned and made off before Rose could say anything, fleeing because he could not deal with his confused emotions.

Rose jumped up. "Fernand!" she called after him but either he did not hear or he ignored her because he did not come back. She was upset by his reactions which she could not understand. "He didn't even greet me or ask how I am," she said looking at the empty doorway, perplexed and hurt at her brother's apparent lack of feelings towards her and their mother. But she was relieved that her grandparents would soon be coming.

"I worry about Fernand," her mother said weakly, her first words for a while. "He's all tied up inside and moody; but he won't talk about it. I'm sure he thinks he's responsible somehow."

"Oh, Maman," said Rose. "He shouldn't think like that."

"He has the farm now but something has been eating away inside him. I'm worried it will be worse now. I don't know what he'll do."

At this point, Rose remembered the letters from her father. She took them out of her pocket and placed them carefully in her mother's lap, her mother's letter on top, explaining what they were. Her mother stared at them, hesitant even to touch them, as though they were her husband's ashes. There were five letters, Rose explained, and spread them out so her mother could see who they were for. Her mother leant forward slowly to look at them more closely, her expression a mixture of incredulity and awe. She then looked up at Rose and then back at the envelopes, touching very lightly the one addressed to her.

"I haven't opened mine," said Rose. "Look, Papa has even written Zézette on it."

"So he has," said her mother slowly, casting an eye over Rose's envelope before staring at each of the others in turn for far longer than it would take to read the name written on it. Rose could not imagine what was going through her mother's mind as she stared at the writing on the five envelopes but her mother's ponderous, hesitant movements began to concern her. Her mother had always been sharp and controlled, but now she appeared bewildered, in some sort of a daze and acting like an old lady who did not quite have the full use of all her faculties.

"Oh, Maman," Rose sighed.

"You'd better have yours," her mother said quietly, nudging the letter towards Rose with her forefinger.

As Rose picked it up noises from the yard heralded the arrival of her grandparents who came straight in, Renée's mother with her arms outstretched and tears streaming down her face.

"Poor Renée. My poor Renée," was all she could manage to comfort her daughter, struggling to find words of consolation. "And my poor Rose, freed at last."

In turn they embraced Rose and her mother; Grandpapa's eyes revealing his great sadness.

They stayed very close together for some while as Rose gradually repeated for her grandparents what she had told her mother, handing over to Grandmaman the piece of paper with the details of the grave and the address of Madame Veillon. The one person missing from the grieving family group was young Fernand. He had accompanied his grandparents back to the farmhouse but he had not followed them in and had gone off on his own somewhere. Eventually Rose said she wanted to go to her room for a little while and made her way up the stairs clutching her letter. Her room was as she had left it and the sensation she felt entering it was the same as she used to feel when coming home from school at Luçon. She sat on her bed and looked around at all the familiar items that filled her room – the mirror on the wall with the small crucifix above it, her little box of trinkets; all still there, all in their place. For a moment it felt a little strange, but the moment did not last. She was free, she was home, but home could never be the same again without Papa.

She had placed her father's letter on the bed beside her while she re-acclimatised herself but then her eyes came back to it and she sat there staring at it, wondering what her father had said, wanting to know. But there was another part of her that stopped her opening the envelope, the part that could not bear the thought of what it contained. How her Papa could put pen to paper in the circumstances was beyond her. She had never known him write anything other than fill in forms or something simple to do with the farm. When praising her schoolwork he had often said that he had never learnt to write properly like her, so writing these five personal letters must have been a monumental effort for him.

Previously she had resolved she would only read her letter when the time was right, but when would that be? Was it now? It seemed at that moment she could not even raise the strength to reach out for the letter, her hands felt like lead in her lap. Yet as she looked at the envelope the names on it stared back at her,

'Rose', 'Zézette'; it was almost as if her father was speaking to her, telling her to read his words. She summoned the strength to reach out and in slow motion picked up the envelope, turned it over and bit by bit opened the flap. She held back the flap and hesitantly began to withdraw the folded letter but as soon as her father's writing appeared her resolve faded and she set it down, looking away with tears again welling in her eyes. She sat like this for a while, swallowing every now and again as her emotions caught at her throat. Finally she breathed in slowly, picked up the envelope once more, fully withdrew the letter and unfolded it. She focussed her eyes at the top of the page at her father's large and distinctive handwriting. She read:

Paris 6th February 1942
My darling little Rosette,
I've just received your letter, I know you've been set free, that can't be said for me, I've only got another four hours to live. My poor daughter, be very brave, make sure your dear mother finds happiness again after I've gone. Be a friend to her.

Throw yourself into your studies, and give your dear mother lots of kisses from me, don't let her be lonely and unhappy, poor Renée. Embrace everyone who's dear to me, keep an eye on your dear brother. I kiss you all before I die. It's not long until. Go on being a good daughter to your mother, don't forget your father, and do what you can to help your mother find happiness again later.

I embrace you and say goodbye forever, farewell, darling girl who I adore like your mother and your brother.

From the father you won't see again.
Fernand
Goodbye dear little Zézette, be brave, I am, there are no tears in my eyes.

With tears streaming down her cheeks, Rose stared at the letter, at her father's last precious words to her, at his final biddings and said very quietly, "Oh, Papa! I will try. I will try."